ATTACHMENT

Bury Me Standing: The Gypsies and Their Journey

Attachment

Isabel Fonseca

Chatto & Windus
LONDON

Published by Chatto & Windus 2008
First published in the United States of America by Alfred A. Knopf in 2008

2 4 6 8 10 9 7 5 3 1

Copyright © Isabel Fonseca 2008

Isabel Fonseca has asserted her right under the Copyright, Designs
and Patents Act 1988 to be identified as the author of this work

Grateful acknowledgment is made to Faber and Faber Ltd, for permission to
reprint excerpts from "An Arundel Tomb" and "High Windows" from *Collected Poems* by
Philip Larkin, copyright © 1998, 2003 by the Estate of Philip Larkin. Reprinted by
permission of Faber and Faber Ltd.

. First published in Great Britain in 2008 by
Chatto & Windus
Random House, 20 Vauxhall Bridge Road,
London SW1V 2SA

www.rbooks.co.uk

Addresses for companies within The Random House Group Limited
can be found at: www.randomhouse.co.uk/offices.htm

The Random House Group Limited Reg. No. 954009

A CIP catalogue record for this book
is available from the British Library

ISBN 9780701181741

The Random House Group Limited supports The Forest Stewardship Council (FSC), the leading
international forest certification organisation. All our titles that are printed on Greenpeace approved
FSC certified paper carry the FSC logo. Our paper procurement policy can be found at
www.rbooks.co.uk/environment

Mixed Sources
Product group from well-managed
forests and other controlled sources
www.fsc.org Cert no. TT-COC-2139
© 1996 Forest Stewardship Council
FSC

Printed and bound in Great Britain by
CPI Mackays, Chatham, ME5 8TD

To Martin

THE CITY OF EDINBURGH COUNCIL	
COO26059355	
Bertrams	01.06.08
DONT USE	£15.99
GL	GEN

St. Jacques

A sudden sinking of the spirits—life sadness, Aminata called it—was explained among the Liberians on the island as a problem of open *moleh*.

"*Moleh*," she'd said, pouring cold shampoo onto the crown of Jean's head, "you know, the fontanel"—the spot on the skull that remains unsealed for the first weeks of life, soft essentials pulsing under silky new skin. Aminata Dia, proud proprietress of St. Jacques' only beauty parlor, traced slow circles around Jean's scalp. She worked her way outward, big shoulders raised, and then back in, elbows down, her strong hands lost in lather stiff and thick as beaten egg whites.

"Problem be *moleh* when she open again and you are grown—through the *moleh* trouble pour in straight down. You let it out, you tell Aminata, and the *moleh* she closes shut again."

Jean had gotten a column out of this conversation her first week on the island. She'd found it harder to file than to write— the humid phone lines fizzed and crackled and sometimes cut out altogether. But when she finally succeeded in e-mailing the piece to the editor of *Mrs* magazine from an Internet café in town, her satisfaction was only increased by these difficulties. She loved everything about the island: patchy connections were a liberation from the phone, while the Internet café, with its sandy floor and sleeping dogs blocking the entrance, offered a seductive relief from her natural solitude, allowing her to be in a group yet remain alone.

Working on the island was a breeze; Mark had been right about that. "A hot and sultry breeze," he'd said, "with material for your column falling from the palms like coconuts." Certainly enough of them littered their place on the hill, the abandoned office of an old tin mine above Grand Baie. Mark always needed a project, and St. Jacques had been his. "What's the point," as he'd put it, "of owning your own firm if it enslaves you?" He ran one of the most innovative ad agencies in London, and his hunt for the subversive was so broad and so remorseless that he called himself Interpol. The move would automatically lead to discoveries, he believed, indeed to whole spheres of discovery. Jean, too, was relatively freewheeling: she wrote a syndicated health column and, so long as she filed her 1,150 words every other Wednesday, she could live on Mars.

Much better, though, to have landed on tiny St. Jacques, a speck in the Indian Ocean. The small scale greatly appealed to Jean: the miniature rain forest and the lone big town of Toussaint, the string of demi-hamlets connected by a single red-dirt ring road, the jammed markets, the friendly, nondesperate people, the bright and thrillingly imperiled birdlife. . . . Over three months, she'd been luxuriating in this prolonged junket with sunshine and copy, all of it as manageable as a diorama. Until now.

The slow wooden fan did little to dispel the heat in the waiting room of the women's health clinic. Jean looked at the alien form she'd been given to fill out; she found it hard to focus. Instead she thought about the open *moleh* and pretended not to stare at the lady sitting opposite her—a big, solid woman like Aminata, in tribal dress. She must have five yards of fabric wrapped around her head, Jean thought, resisting a desire to reach across and touch it—test the construction of a headpiece more osprey's nest than turban.

To avoid her own churning thoughts, Jean tried to guess where the woman had come from—West Africa for sure, but Senegal, like Aminata? Not Liberia or Sierra Leone? Jean was becoming a refined cataloger of islanders—the small community of exiled West Africans, the scattered enclaves of East Africans, Indians from the subcontinent, Christians and Muslims and Hindus. Most people were a mix, though there was a segregated group of Chinese, descendants of indentured laborers, and, at the northernmost tip of the island, a settlement of "Frenchmen"—whites of distant European origin. Jean herself was a deep, angry-baby pink, and not only because of the unusual heat that day; her cheeks blazed with the shock of the morning, when she'd blundered into heavy knowledge.

Jean had found the letter buried in a new shipment of old mail—the magazines and travel-worn invitations for cocktail parties, charity dos, and client lunches, all long past by the time they traveled six thousand miles to reach the Hubbards.

Every month, Christian, the stoned mailman, chugged up the road on his gold home-painted moped. He carried the bag diagonally across his back just as the women of St. Jacques tied on their babies. Christian's baby was his hair: the twenty-inch loaf like an overgrown sea sponge, lovingly swaddled in a rainbow sock.

She'd spotted him from the kitchen window where she stood

slicing papaya. Wiping her hands on her apron, she went out the front door and stood there, her open smile and hands on hips, framed by two pink hibiscus bushes in full bloom.

"Bonjour, Madame Oobahd," Christian shouted from the driveway. "How does our perfect day find the lady of the house?"

"Never better," she answered. He pulled right up to the front door and grinned to show his gold tooth. Jean had reviewed that morning a hundred times: How Christian had risen ceremoniously from his gilt chariot and leaned toward her, stroking his goatee and supporting himself with one arm on the wall of the house. She knew he would not have stood so close if Mark was at the door beside her—six foot four in bare feet and striking with his grayed hair swept back, wind-eroded dune grass above the expanding beach of his still boyish face.

No, Christian would not have lingered, spreading that smile of the busy seducer she had no reason to doubt he was. Never mind the fat joint tucked behind his ear; Jean remembered thinking that his pressed shirt saved him from coming across as seedy.

The fresh breeze, the hibiscus, the sun warming her bare shoulders; it was April Fool's Day, and what a glorious hallucination this was, Jean thought, watching as Christian—and, one beat behind, his crocheted hair cocoon—bumped back down the track and out of sight. She wondered if smoking pot would be a good idea and if she could ask him for some. Hugging the bag, she turned into the house.

"Ah. Disposable rubbish, conveniently packaged in its own bin liner," Mark had said, cheerful as the salesman he was, taking the plastic sack off Jean and leading her out to the terrace at the back of the house. From there you could see the best of the long, sloping, coconut-strewn garden and beyond—past the gated wall at the property's edge, down to the red-dirt road and all the way out to the blue hills, rising in the west. The ocean, which you couldn't see from the house, was just beyond those smoky hills. Most foreigners came for St. Jacques' white beaches, but Jean and Mark agreed, the more time you spent here, the more you liked the look of the interior: verdant, wild, unvisited. For now, all eyes were on the bag, which Mark lowered onto the table as if he was presenting a magnificent roast. Still standing, he sliced into it with the serrated knife. Jean glanced over the spoils, enjoying the performance, and went back inside to get coffee.

"Milk's off!" she called through the kitchen window. "Lemon tea? Or have it black?"

"Black's fine," Mark replied, taking a large bite of bread overloaded with blueberry jam and starting to sift through the magazines. Here was everything that couldn't be dispatched by e-mail, couriered to them by Mark's not-very-discriminating secretary, Noleen, along with the mail from Albert Street. Still, when all you could get on St. Jacques were soggy copies of last season's—no, last *year's*—*Paris Match*, this delivery radiated the festive anticipation of a piñata, and neither Jean nor Mark was indifferent to its spell.

Waiting for the coffee to filter, Jean watched through the window as Mark sorted the magazines. He didn't have his glasses on, but they both knew what they'd find: the *Atlantic Monthly* and the *New Yorker* (hers), the *Spectator* (his and, for the crossword, hers), *Private Eye* (his), the *New Statesman* (hers, for the weekly competitions), and a stack of *The Week* (theirs). She knew he'd go straight to *The Week* and, in particular, to the UK weather report—hoping for rain. "The raison d'être," he'd said, "of every Englishman abroad." Leaving untouched her copies of *American Health* and *Modern Maturity,* the geriatric journals she combed for column ideas, he returned to the house on the daily hunt for his reading glasses.

Jean had dressed carefully—that morning she had an appointment down at the women's clinic. Later she'd wonder about the instinct—best foot forward in a crisis. The checked dirndl with the shiny curved belt, the crisp-collared sleeveless shirt. If you didn't make an effort around here, you were soon living in a tablecloth. As Mark said, the sarong was the tropical tracksuit.

"Mmmm. And where are you off to this morning, Lois Lane?" he said, amused, pausing at the French windows to let her pass. Jean slid carefully by, balancing the coffee tray. As she brushed past she winked at him. He was unshaven, she noticed, and barely belted into his blue cotton robe. A glob of black jam stuck to the corner of his mouth. He was often daubed by the end of breakfast, she thought with affection, though never at dinner, as if eating had to be learned from scratch, each day.

"Date," she replied, deadpan, glad he'd forgotten this routine mammogram. Bad enough to have your breasts intentionally crushed without also having everyone else imagining it happen.

She was immediately drawn to the tape-sealed envelope with Mark's name on it. She hadn't opened it surreptitiously, or in error, or even out of any special curiosity about the contents; this was a simple and greedy urge to open the one real letter in the bag. But having opened it, Jean was put on immediate alert, for the sheet of paper inside was not addressed to Mark, or not, anyway, to a Mark she recognized. Hopeless handwriting, she had time to think, as she cast an eye over the unschooled jumble of cursive and caps at a left-handed slant.

Dear Thing 1,

GREETINGS FROM DOWN UNDER! Missing you already, Sexy Beast. You looked older. Tan covering more of your face! But I'm older too. 26 this week! Still, more proposals than ever, if possible. Did you find me older and wiser? Aged to perfection, ripe for eating? Or just older and DIRTIER?

I'm going to send you a reminder to drool over, you unbelievably filthy old man, if your not too senile to open the attachment. But these sweet thighs be 4 YOUR EYES ONLY and so I have created a beautiful new account for you. (I don't think the office one is a good idea) Your pleasure address is: Naughtyboy1@hotmail.com. Naughtyboy already taken, of course . . . but I promise, not by me! The subject will be 69. How could I resist? You gorgeous gargantuan, remember to wash hands before returning to work. Ciao bello!

XXX Thing 2

Ps the password is M———. A test: to see if you can guess. A suck-u-lent plant whose seeds are used for food, remember? MM-mmmm.

Jean looked up from the letter and met the black eye of a chameleon frozen on the wall of the house. The long tail was a loose spiral, the same pattern as the lizard tattoo their daughter, Victoria, recently had punctured into the dip of her pelvis (so the lizard would look like it was peeping out of her underpants?). On the wall, the dull green creature was utterly still, a brooch to match the tattoo, no more lifelike. But as Jean continued to stare, wanting to be able to report all its features to her daughter, she saw that it was panting—rapid, shallow breaths.

Then, with surprising and revolting suddenness and speed, it shot away into a crack. So much that's surprising and revolting, she thought, and it was only breakfast time.

Trying to keep calm, she revisited her day so far. The elaborate outfit, the mail drop, the rotten milk. She felt depressed, foolish, and hot in her city clothes. Pathetic, how she'd basked in Christian's attentions. Now, finally, she realized—he'd been waiting for a tip. Of course! Mark had wildly overtipped him the last time he came. And why had she *winked*? If there was one gesture she hated it was this, the knowing cuteness of it. Jean knew she was delaying any true reckoning with what the letter might mean, but she could chart an immediate adjustment in her outlook. Already Mark, still inside the house, was transfigured; for example, that blob of jam: suddenly it was the opposite of endearing.

Sitting on the terrace, listening to the parrots shrieking in the eucalyptus trees, Jean thought of the other Mrs. Hubbard, Mark's mother. The woman who worshipped her son, permitted him everything, and had probably wiped his mouth so often he'd never gotten the hang of it. There was a certain helplessness in him, and an indifference to other people—such as leaving his boxers on the bathroom floor, inches from the laundry hamper—that always made Jean think, Mrs. H. The old snob with her groundless sense of superiority. . . . She'd never truly acknowledged her American daughter-in-law and sneered, Jean knew, at the idea that Mark might pick up his own clothes—evidence of his wife's laziness, as far as Mrs. H. was concerned, or, worse, her pretentious feminism.

So she found herself blaming Mrs. H. for this letter as well. Though of course she knew—underpants, hampers, and sticky mouths aside—Mark's ancient mother, however limited, wasn't responsible for any feature of their marriage. And as she groped around for an explanation, she grasped within herself a change

that was basic, mineral, beyond the realm of mere disappointment. The day was only hours old and already she was cur-
dling inside, helpless to stop the contamination from
spreading. She needed to get out of these ridiculous clothes, to
get away from the table, from Mark, to be alone.

She ran into the house as he was coming back out. "What
the—*dar*ling?" he said, frowning as she pushed past. Ten minutes later, freshly composed in a white linen sundress and ready
to walk over to the table and toss the letter onto his plate, she
stood at the window and saw that Mark, midyawn, was rising to
leave. Jean registered that he'd moved past his flicker of concern, and she hesitated. He gathered himself up, idly twirling a
few chest hairs in his fingers, reading as he walked, and, still
reading, disappeared through the side door with at least two
further copies of *The Week* underarm. Her plan, and possibly
all her courage, had been derailed by his morning shit.

Jean wasn't a stranger to sudden disaster, but no earlier deso-
lation could help here. What she'd read was unmistakably a
lover's letter, and she felt winded, as if punched in the gut. She
would confront Mark right away and take what came. That had
been the extent of her strategy. She believed, and so it would
prove, that the period of advantage, of nerve, was very short.

Still waiting, with Mark barricaded in the bathroom, Jean
laid out a solitaire of old invitations—though no longer as if
fingering a bruise, testing for homesickness. This time it was a
genuine game of patience.

Until now, the ritual of the mail had been a comfort. It
absolved her, briefly, of her failure in the field of domestic
administration: her lifelong allergy to dealing with any kind of
request. It could hardly be her fault, out here in the Indian
Ocean, if letters went unanswered. Ever since her daughter's
early years, Jean had been oppressed by this kind of nonessen-
tial communication, and how *innocent* that all seemed now: the

library-volunteer sign-up, the spring fair, charity day, the bright birthday invitations with their clip'n'send reply blanks (did *anyone* clip'n'send?), the uniform order slip that Victoria, by age eleven, was filling out for herself.

And now Victoria, who had stayed behind in Camden Town, minding the house in Albert Street, was still dealing with the mail. Though unlike in St. Jacques, they never greeted the mailman in London—in fact, they dodged him, the cheerless Korean who *drove* from house to house and still managed to get the post wet.

What exactly was being asked of Jean with this affair, and, moreover, how would Victoria cope with this, her mother's ultimate failure in domestic administration? She must never know. Jean forcibly returned her attention to the spread on the blue tablecloth: the latest batch of expired announcements and last-chance offers seemed to prove that, if you waited long enough, nothing mattered. You wouldn't have to deal with any of it. Very soon the most ASAP item would cease to exert the remotest tug. The same might be true of a lover's letter.

Things losing their force—like this envelope that had lost its stickum and needed tape, Jean thought. Like *any* envelope on this humid island. Jean had taken to tracking fade-out in many fields. She was a health writer; decay was her turf. But not until now had she considered the field of her marriage.

Ten more minutes passed, and still Mark did not return. Jean's fiddling was becoming clipped, agitated. She rose, covered the fruit with a mesh dome, rinsed the breakfast dishes, crumpled and cleared the junk mail. It would take her a good hour to get to the clinic, and she was running out of time.

"Mark?" she called, fully aware that this was the least opportune moment to consult her husband, let alone confront him. (He was the type who believed the entire square mile around his toilet should be discreetly evacuated every morning, until

he was done.) She coughed. "I'm going to have to set off now."
No reply. Fine, she'd go down to Toussaint on her own—space
and time to think. She swooped through the house, collecting
her purse, her hat, and, on impulse, her gym bag, and went out
to the car.

The uniformed nurse at the front desk said her name twice
before Jean recognized it.

"Jhanh OO-bahd?" the nurse said again, and Jean jumped
up, catapulting onto the floor the straw shoulder bag she'd
wedged beside her on the seat. Mark called these gaping nose-
bags of hers "beggars' lucky dip." Had he meant all along that
she was the beggar? Jean wondered, squatting and raking in
handfuls at a time of ink-stained lists, ink-stained pens, wads of
nearly worthless ink-stained banknotes—basically garbage.

She was now on her knees, reaching after a rolling ink-
stained lip sunblock and wondering how spoiled it would look
to ignore the lottery of loose coins that had already bounced
and wheeled so far out she'd have to crawl to the four corners
to recover it all.

A glance at the nurse-receptionist told her to forget the
coins—how childish the sacklike cut of her white dress suddenly seemed—and concentrate on the additional medical forms
she'd been handed. With increasing speed and irritation Jean
filled in the facts of her life: Jean Warner Hubbard, forty-five
years old, born New York City, August 1957, daughter of . . .
She skimmed over the questions: father, mother, education,
driver's license, nationality, insurance, marital status, first men-
struation, number of pregnancies, number of children, age at
first pregnancy, age at birth of first child, name(s) of child(ren),
name(s) of child(ren)'s father(s). . . . How impertinent, she

thought, to ask the names of "father(s)," about pregnancies and children in separate questions, as if expecting them not to match up, as if it was any of their goddamn business.

She wondered what Thing 2's real name was. Was this her business? Maybe she should just open the e-mail herself. Why not—she'd already opened the letter. Surely she had the right, whether or not she had the stomach for what she might find there. It was clear they'd just seen each other, presumably on Mark's recent trip to London, and Thing 2 was trying to keep it going. Still working on the form, Jean imagined a male version in which there was one question about the number of ejaculations and another about the number of children produced. But they didn't have these for men, and there was no men's clinic on St. Jacques—though she supposed the island's one hospital had mostly geezers racked up in rows of steel-tube beds, inmates looking down from high windows at the old buffers still upright enough to bowl in the sand under the lavender-feathered jacaranda trees.

Jean had noticed that, unlike the men, St. Jacques' women didn't linger in the square. As their reproductive function ended, they grew to resemble their husbands—thickening and flattening and even sprouting whiskers—but they didn't have time for bowling, and when they hurried past, expertly balancing shopping on their hips and heads, the square must have looked to them like nothing so much as the hospital's waiting room. On any other day, Jean would've used this time to stitch such thoughts into a column; but sitting here now, stunned and unprepared, all she could conjure up was an endless procession of old women, bent under heavy bundles, shuffling along single file. . . .

She handed back the form and tried, in an effort to tame her panic, to think chronologically, to remember their purpose here. For Mark, time on the island offered a practice retirement. He was only fifty-three, but it was a phase he'd planned as assiduously as his many business trips. In fact, his retirement might be a business venture: he was talking again about the advertising-world board game he was going to devise, what he called, and thought he might just name, "my pension." Cocktails on the terrace were ever earlier; he'd at least set up his easel on the back terrace. She'd been pleased to think he'd be around more. But now she wondered. Was all this exaggerated retiree behavior overcompensation for a frenetic, belated oat-sowing when he went away without her?

Jean had never even considered not working. On the contrary, as they both got older, things would pick up. Advanced age, the older the better, would be a boon for a health writer—all the new ailments to cover, and so many keen readers, readers with time. This was one thing she'd never doubted they had—time. She'd always assumed, naïve though it seemed to her now, that separation would come only with death.

The clinic was virtually empty—just the lady in the turban and Jean. What was taking so long? She rested her head against the wall and watched the geriatric fan. The looming terrors—infidelity, denials and recriminations, the sundering—made her long, almost physically, for the respite of a more innocent time. Closing her eyes, she placed herself thirty-five years before, in the Adirondacks. Those end-of-summer dances with all the chairs pushed back against the walls of the high-ceilinged Quonset hut, girls on one side in calico and gingham, helplessly gripping their seats, and the boys opposite, wetted-down hair cleanly parted and no eye contact whatsoever. Everyone listens to the caller, the buzz-cut head of camp, and Jean tries not to think about being left unpicked when the next line of boys crosses over. *Do-si-do! Swing your partner round and round! Duck for the oyster, dig for the clam!* She *needs* to be picked. This is the best night of the summer and it's half over. *And it's on to*

*the next in the valley, and you circle to your left and to your right . . .
and you swing with the girl who loves you maybe, and you swing
with your Red River gal.*

Again someone called her name. She was led down a
long echoing hall, shown into a small examining room, and
abandoned.

Affairs don't just happen, Jean told herself, not sure if she
should undress or just wait. There had to be a reason; if only
she could think hard enough, she probably already knew what
it was. So she tried, and found nothing. She was aware women
liked Mark, felt lucky if they were seated next to him. Of course
they did—everybody did. He was handsome and witty but not
too challenging. He was at ease with most people and a frank
appreciator of womankind. Jean felt clear about that, and also
that he didn't like to be cornered by other men's wives. She
assumed he had his chances—successful males always have,
since long before man separated from monkey—but was also
confident he played it straight, did his work, paid his taxes, and
slept well at night.

And she knew, however much she didn't like to admit it, that
he'd *had* his sexual obsession, more than a decade before
they'd even met, one summer in Brittany. Now, by extension,
he loved all things French: French clients, which meant more
time in France; French wine, French islands, French actresses,
French butter—tasteless logs, in Jean's opinion, unsalted fat.
Like Thing 2's "sweet thighs"? What kind of person called her
own thighs "sweet"? But she didn't mind Mark's French
bug, even if it was a trip to Paris that had made him miss the
birth of their daughter. Energetic enthusiasms, *comprehensive*
enthusiasms—these were his kind of charm.

"Put this on," said a surprise nurse, leaving Jean alone with
her folded green smock. There was a large cutout for the head,
and open sides, so it hung over the torso like a saddlebag. Thus

draped, she crossed her naked arms, looked around the cramped examining room, and waited.

This dead time spent waiting, especially in poor countries . . . it converted everybody going about his daily business into a disaster victim, queuing for relief. Mass paralysis—a phenomenon, she thought, to compete with mass migration, meriting international treaties, conventions, philanthropic interest. And for Jean? She somehow knew, having failed to confront Mark at *once,* she'd entered the waiting game of her life.

The room contained a padded table, another lethargic fan, and, in the corner by a high window, an old-fashioned wicker hat rack where Jean had hung her clothes, bra discreetly tucked under the childish sundress, and the letter folded into childish sundress pocket. Another standing object filled the center of the room, stainless steel and glass, loaded with dials and levers— yesteryear's futuristic. After a decade of annual mammograms, Jean knew the machine and the drill. Here she was again, stripped, bored, and coursing with dread. She tried to distance herself by considering alternative uses for the Senograph, with its motorized compression device: patty maker, phone booth, mechanical valet, time machine.

But distraction was not encouraged here. On the wall, above the examining table, hung a framed poster of a vagina and a womb—in the family of the butcher's chart, sectioned, colored, and neatly labeled in teachers' script. Jean wondered what sort of image awaited Mark at the Internet café. Photographs of Thing 2's privates would be a lot harder to ignore than this diagram. As if being ignored might come into a Thing's plan.

In England, she thought, hearing footsteps and checking her gown, such a room would have a picture of wild ponies on Exmoor, Brighton Pavilion, or an Alma-Tadema muse draped in billowing gauze. In the States you might get fall foliage or

Capitol Hill. And in either country—she now saw a hairy arm opening the door from the corridor—the radiologist would not have been a man. This one was wearing short sleeves and a hospital V-neck, as if to feature his pelt. And a paper hat.

Jean didn't want to look at this man, so like an entertainer escaped from a children's party. She didn't want to look at the vagina and womb. She didn't want to say anything, with her hopeless French and miserable state of mind. He wasn't even a doctor. More like a mechanic, brought in to mind the precious robot. Someone else would interpret the pictures he took, hunting for messages among the lucent smudges and ghost tracks, the familiar crescents rendered deathly in monochrome. So she studied the ceiling fan and imagined herself levitating to just the right height whereby the rotating blades could serve as a guillotine for her obviously imperfect breasts.

Meanwhile the radiologist busied himself. His soap-scented arms extended one of hers around the time machine. Dignity demanded that she be as involved as a mannequin being dressed in a store window, and she, shy flower, could only submit as he fussed with the display—frowning, squinting, making several seemingly insignificant changes to her position. The pose she struck was elaborately casual, like in the first photograph she'd sent her parents of herself with Mark, her arm reaching awkwardly up around his shoulder. Too tall by half, was her mother's verdict following that first experimental airing of his existence, not knowing that Jean had already decided. His height was the first thing she loved about him, her personal lightning rod. Feeling safe with Mark: before she felt it, she had not been aware of any special vulnerability or want. Much of what he brought her came in this form of unanticipated necessity.

With her upper body strained into the leaning position, Jean's breast had naturally swung out from the sideless smock onto the machine's glass tray—the coolness of the glass not unwelcome in this close heat—and the technician positioned it with his hairy hands, as focused as a potter centering a lump of clay. This, Jean thought, was the real reason younger women didn't get mammograms: their breasts couldn't yet *swing out* onto the tray. And then she thought of Thing 2, "26 this week."

She knew what came next and that it didn't serve to watch: the central shaft of the machine would be lowered like a dumb-waiter, pinning her to the glass, sandwiching her breast in a painful wedge, as if the whole extrusion was designed not to take a photograph that could save her life but to hasten nature's decline. Why else did they clamp so hard, as if squeezing the last drops from a lemon? Why crank the vise when no other tissue impeded the view? They'd explain it was to allow the lowest possible dose of radiation, but Jean would be more convinced if they said it was to deter second-thoughters. And what a sisterhood of silent fury, as each annual twenty-second examination undid the faithful bra wearing of the preceding year. . . .

It was best to look away, not just from the radiation but because it wasn't a good sight. The clamp was released and the dumbwaiter sent upstairs, but the pale breast lay there, spread and settled on the tray like an uncooked Danish. With her arm still thrown in a pally hug around the X-ray machine, Jean was sure Thing 2's breasts never looked like pastry dough.

"You can remove yourself." The radiologist startled her, looking her in the eye for the first time before leaving the room.

Jean wasn't so sure. She thought her breast might stick when she tried to unpeel it from the glass, and possibly rip, like a rug's rubber underlay.

As she slowly pieced herself back together, looking at the diagram on the wall, she remembered the sheep's heart she'd been given to dissect in a high school biology class, and how dense it was—rubbery, solid, slime-coated, and intermittently spongy, anything but breakable. Where had that come from, the broken heart? Jean had loved dissecting, and as she left the clinic she realized it had been the graphic precursor to her job as a columnist: that sheep's heart, one time a whole frog, even the lowly pods and leaves. Then, suddenly, she knew exactly what the secret password was—why hadn't it struck her before? Munyeroo, a fleshy Australian plant, whose leaves and seeds, as Thing 2 helpfully pointed out, could be eaten. Mark had told her about it just the other day, after his trip home, and even suggested Munyeroo—bashfully, in fact—as a name for the stray cat who'd come along but abandoned them as soon as Mark returned. Clearly it hadn't appreciated being named after his crude mistress. Jean knew now just what she was going to do. She was going down to the Internet café to open e-mail 69.

Back in the waiting room, the stately woman in her turban was still sitting patiently. What would she be thinking as she watched a dazed Jean walk past, making for the door? *How did people with such raw-looking skin get the idea that they could rule the world? What made you believe you were entitled to happiness?* As Jean stepped outside, her idle hand feeling the top of her own head, she couldn't help imagining that the lady's crown of fabric wasn't for cushioning freight, and not for fashion either. Maybe it was an elaborate bandage that covered a gaping hole.

Jean was practically quivering with adrenaline as she drove to the Internet café, her diesel engine roaring. And then she instinctively pulled over: for the willed caution of delay, the gym. Under the glinting gilt cupola at the top of Le Royaume, the only smart hotel not on the coast, Jean, changed into old canvas tennis shoes and faded sweats, took her place alongside two unimprovably trim and toned women on a row of step machines. Most people came here to develop their bodies. What she wanted to develop was an attitude. Did she dare find out any more about this Thing 2? Could she—or they—survive an affair? And if not, was she remotely prepared to paddle off in her own canoe? Had Mark already done just that? Maybe the whole business of choice had already been settled. He was the one who had acted, and decisively.

She started to climb. Soon she was hanging on, hunch-backed, as if riding a motorcycle into strong wind, sinking as she gripped the bars, putting as much weight as possible on her arms. The women beside her, both wearing bright Lycra out-fits, didn't seem to notice they were exerting themselves at all; they chatted effortlessly, their rounded backsides pushed up and out like the rumps of show ponies. Watching the ceiling-mounted television hurt Jean's neck. Head down, she was forced to eavesdrop—which was, she couldn't help thinking, exactly what she planned to do at the Internet café.

"Well, every time we meet, he say me 'You have a beautiful ass, I love di *tex*ture' "—Jean heard "*taste*tour"—"always di ass you know. Latinos day love di ass. And den, one day, no more texture. Now he say me, 'I can teach you song good essersizes for you ass.' Das how I starting in di tango feet."

"Tango feet?" The other climber whipped around, frowning with interest.

"Yes, tango wit di beat, you know, tango for di feetness."

"Oh, tango *fit*. Cool. Can I have a listen?"

The other one was Australian, Jean guessed, mesmerized by the sight of the woman's bouncing chest, as extravagantly upholstered as Tangofeet's, only Jean thought hers might be real.

"Chore." The Argentine, if that's what she was, passed the earphones to her friend.

Attachment

What, Jean wondered, did Thing 2 look like? What sort of "texture" was she? That was an advanced sort of concern, wasn't it? Jean would settle for shape. She thought of her boyish straight line from pits to hips and moved away to try an arm machine. Settling her bottom on the seat pad, she imagined a man's body being lowered onto hers, his sneakered feet in the air: 69, the yin-yang of sex positions. A pose for show-offs, Jean thought: fundamentally unserious. You could hardly meditate on your own pleasure doing *that*. Anyway, Mark was too tall to be the 9 to any woman's 6—unless Thing 2 was an Amazon. Or would that be Jean, she thought mirthlessly, remembering how the Amazons' breasts were lopped off to facilitate the use of a bow. Jean never wanted to pick up her mammogram results, let alone a weapon. But the thought of those warrior women emboldened her: she would at least take a look.

The cyber café was unusually crowded. Jean got the corner computer, beside a black teenager whose forehead glistened like a polished plum. He was typing one-sentence replies to one-sentence questions: instant messaging. She knew what this was—one new skill she didn't feel called on to acquire. She checked her work e-mail first, and then the joint account set up by and mainly for Victoria. The boy beside her didn't look up as she finally typed in the new account name, naughtyboy1, and the password, munyeroo. And there was 69, a lonely pair of inverted spermatozoa, each chasing the other's tail. The sender slot was discreetly blanked. Steeling herself to click and open, she looked again at the letter in the white envelope. Munyeroo. Jean immediately thought of the Australian at the gym, the blond woman with the spectacular natural frontage. But there was Italian here as well—that *ciao bello*. An Australian of Italian descent, that's it, Jean thought. She remembered Mark joking, many years ago, that the primary appeal of Australian girls in London was their departure the following morning for New South Wales, *forever*. But the letter had originated in London. Thing 2 didn't play by the rules.

Jean opened the attachment. It took a long time to download. Luckily the boy next to her left before the full-screen image appeared.

Jesus! Australia didn't waste time. She wondered how much a chest like that might weigh. At almost life-size, it was a not-so-good pair, she thought—big nippled and uniformly bronzed. Jean believed in the essential sexiness of untanned triangles—the idea, at least, that not just anyone enjoyed this view—not that her skin ever turned anything but redder, or that she ever wore a bikini. But these were undeniably young and undeniably large. And what was that black thing? The edge of a tattoo? A whole generation of young people—including Victoria with her lizard—in painful pursuit of decoration and emphasis, just what they didn't need. Their inkings should warn off persons from their parents' era, Jean thought. In fact, that might be just the sort of boundary tattoos were there to demarcate—noli me tangere.

There were a couple of other photographs, all with elaborate captions. "Giovana" promised Mark *L.O.V.E.—long overdue experience,* even fucking that up; but then Giovana with one *n* couldn't even spell her own name. Which was probably Joan anyway. Or Jean—who just now remembered that, when she was about fifteen and yearning for instant glamour, she'd briefly insisted on being called Gina.

Giovana thanked him for the "replacement" underpants, which she gamely modeled on her round bottom—*fat,* Victoria would've said, taking her mother's side. A red ribbon was threaded through chubby cheeks—buried, actually—reappearing at the top to bloom into a triangular swatch of white trimmed with red, like a yield sign. What happened to the first pair? Were they the same, or cut to resemble a different traffic warning: a red octagon of phony protest (STOP!), or maybe a slinky something in yellow and black (SLIPPERY WHEN WET)? Helpless against the tide of imagining, Jean stolidly went on, in punishing detail. So, underpants #1, given, and kept, as a souvenir? Ripped by his teeth in the heat of the moment? Tossed from a moving taxi? Ridiculous. Right?

Another photo—headless like the first two—gave a side view of the same body, this time pantyless and bending at the waist, wearing a frilly white apron that served as a sling for heavy breasts, with a giant birthday-present bow tied at the back. An unfamiliar hand trained the nozzle of a vacuum cleaner on the crescent seam of her buttocks. What was Jean supposed to make of that? Had Mark put in a request in the housewife department? The crassness of these offerings stunned Jean, though she couldn't say if she'd be any less stunned by *tasteful* nude shots of Mark's lover. Her ability to think clearly about any of this was hampered by the much more upsetting thought that, after twenty-three years together, she didn't really know her husband.

Plainly, this was a spoof of some kind. She could see you weren't supposed to take it seriously. But affairs were always corny, always an imitation of other affairs. What would be the point of a highly original affair? Repetition was the whole idea, with thrilling (and repetitive) limits on time and place. Nothing like a marriage, with all its unrelieved specificity unfurling over the years, in a variety of landscapes, public and private, rural and urban, in the long roll from innocence to . . . loss of innocence. (Jean wasn't sure anymore about knowledge: what did she know?) But being corny didn't make it harmless, even if that's what he'd told himself.

Before she knew it, she was typing her reply.

Thing 2: Is it really you? (I'd forgotten how wonderful you look: was that—rather, were those—really you? More! Never 2 soon. PLEASE.)

Write back. Telling detail, please, so I can be sure its you.

T1

Darling Munyeroo, bella stella giovanela, you slut! I adore you!

She didn't pause. And when she was done she read over her reply: not bad, she thought. Mark could be whimsical, uncertain about punctuation; his favorite word was "wonderful," and "adore" his second favorite. Jean didn't resist matching Giovana's stray numeral—"4 your eyes only"—a rotting fish tossed to a trained seal. She *had* wavered between "slag" and "slut," worried that the latter was too American, but finally decided it was somehow jollier, and above all she could hear him saying it. Finally, she trusted the recipient's vanity to weaken her sleuthing skills.

Jean sat upright and looked blankly through the window. Outside, the blinding day. She was acting almost robotically, but she couldn't stop. The moral high ground held no appeal— and no *information*. She would continue even though, before she sent a single line, she knew that soon she would be like the boy who'd just left—foolishly awaiting replies she would then foolishly return, in a gripping, humiliating dunces' volley. She checked her reply once more and pressed the send button. And she was, however briefly, euphoric.

Driving home around the outskirts of Toussaint, Jean thought how much of her day so far had been about the body—a particular strain considering she'd always felt most herself with the smallest amount of movement: reading, thinking, writing; and watching, absolutely frozen, birds through binoculars. Very early on she'd discovered you could learn a great deal if you just stayed still and more or less left your body out of it. Suddenly it was all bodies—and breasts were in the air! Blown up and plastered on posters and billboards, or plumply rolling by on the sides of public buses, perfect pairs assailed her, incongruous and looming in this lapsed, rust-encrusted, weed-infested, sugarcaning community.

The ads, featuring skin tones not seen here except on tourists, weren't much noticed by locals, who passed them by in threes on mopeds and bicycles, or on foot, balancing barrels on their heads or bent under back loads of kindling. Jean passed a flock of schoolchildren in checked uniforms, skipping alongside leaching salt beds; she tracked broken-down farms and roadside food stands and *tabagies* and, in and among all this, stationed at regular intervals, the local prostitutes, their breasts spilling from front-tied halter-neck tops. Gift wrapped, she thought, helplessly slowing down to look.

Out on the coastal road, the bay flashing beside her like a vast mirror, she was blocked by a delivery truck attempting to turn. She stopped right under a breast-festooned billboard. "There you go," she said, as if it was proof of a general conspiracy, this one an ad for fizzy orange drink, in the photograph falling from some height, like a waterfall, into the mouth of an ecstatic bosomy teenager.

The side of the long truck was blazoned with a hand-painted globe, denoting worldwide scope in the local style. Jean stared at the homely planet as the truck inched through its dangerous maneuvers, shielding her face from the wall of sunlight beaming from the west. And she felt, sitting under a womanly chest the size of her car, that she herself was stuck, and not just in this wedge of narrow road, with the wild ocean storming below. It seemed to Jean there were no facts; that rules might give way to exceptions and that everything was open to interpretation, the play of the light, the smacking waves of further revelation. The trapped feeling reminded her of a terrifying childhood episode: out of her depth, caught in the tides, she'd been thrashed between two volcanic boulders, scraped, sick and gasping for air, gulping salt water from a lurching horizon. That time, Dad plucked her out and brought her in, carrying her tight against his huge chest back to shore. And this time?

Over the next two and a half months, Jean exchanged dozens of juicy e-mails with Thing 2, with Munyeroo, with My Own Mountain Goat, with Ginger, who didn't have red hair, or with just plain Giovana. She watched for reactions from Mark. She worried when he went to London—and surely met his mistress—that her interference would be revealed. But in her compulsion to follow the trail, she persuaded herself that, even if Mark could do such a thing, he'd never, ever *talk* about it—and his characteristic cheer on his return seemed to confirm her hope. She explained her frequent trips to town (and the Internet café) as a newfound passion for fitness—the gym. She did feel energized, as if she'd run a mile.

Anticipation, in particular, was better than any treadmilled endorphins. Yes! There was something in her in-box. Every time she opened the account she felt the flush of excitement, like a child spying the glint of colored foil across a garden, a chocolate egg "hidden" by a parent directly in her line of sight. Her pleasure in the moment was embarrassing, or it would have been if she'd been less engrossed, and less anonymous. She could forget that she wasn't supposed to see these letters, and Giovana abetted her illusion by never using Mark's name. Though Jean often cringed at the names she got, she never retreated from the feeling that she *was* Thing 1, Lover, Big, Huge, Gigantor, Master, Manster, Bun, Boss, Rod (Rodney, Rod Stewart), or, and in the end best of all, just Sir. Giovana's e-mails were almost exclusively about sex, and each included at least one photograph—a contraband brownie smuggled into her lunch box.

In one message, which Jean then particularly feared would give her identity away, she forgot her impersonation of Mark and tried, with all her native and professional usefulness, to neutralize her rival with advice.

You're not bad looking, Gio, she found herself typing. *You have lovely hair. You should be more self-confident. Really, you needn't try so hard. . . .*

In addition to recommending two esteem-building manuals and a hairdo that didn't cover half the face, she'd thought it worth pointing out, gently, that extruding your breasts through the slash holes of a tightly laced PVC bodice was a plausible definition of trying too hard. But maybe Mark disagreed. (Giovana, anyway, was exasperatingly humbled: under a picture of herself in a puff-sleeved dress and licking a lollipop, she had apologized. *I did bad. XXX Tell me how I am to be punished.*) Jean wondered what kind of experience PVC bustiers promised—if, just possibly, all this theatrical strut and know-how went beyond sex toward a counterintuitive, postfeminist liberation. Would she, in her own future happiness, dress like this? The word "negligée" could mean "neglected," Jean thought while examining Giovana in a filmy transparent babydoll of tan-enhancing blue, but it might also mean "to give little thought to"—to be cool.

She skated over the notion that she was having her own affair with Giovana—flirting and fantasizing like deluded typers all over the world. (Did it matter, really, about her hidden quest or the murderous nature of her fantasies?) Far from busting Mark, maybe she was actually backing him up. She *was* Mark; she was Thing 1; of course she knew how he felt. Sometimes, her interest drew mainly from her own side of the conversation—a challenging diversification for any columnist, who was, inevitably, something of a persona. And her Thing 1 was, if she said it herself, debonair. As Mark could be—an amalgamation of Christopher Plummer, Roger Moore just past his prime, with a pinch of revamped, upper-class Terence Stamp, whom Mark, with his bright pale eyes and wide brow, inescapably did resemble. This was more or less where she pitched it—she had a perverse wish for Mark to be *worth* having an affair with—and she was justly proud of her creation.

Mark didn't seem to notice her obsession, but her work was suffering. One column about healthy minibreaks hardly lifted above the industry standard, recommending, under a banner of "ecotourism," short hikes and the reuse of hotel towels, while the next one promoted a seaweed cure-all of absolutely no use to her readers, none of whom lived within a thousand miles of a source of magic algae. And strangely, though no more strangely than a lot of other things these days, she missed Mark.

What would he say if she let him in? Imagine getting beyond denials and the tawdry local phenomena of whens and wheres. He'd probably tell her that, if only she'd left things alone, been less proactive ("less American," he would surely have said), he'd have been onto a leggy Swede before the original letter arrived in Christian's sack, and finished with her, too.

She wondered if he ever wrote to Giovana himself, from the St. Jerome Hotel where he went to play tennis and check his office e-mail. Certainly there'd been a few unexplained endearments: *Bubischnudel* was one that stuck in her mind, along with other Teutonic notes—*bis bald*—see you later—and *tschüss!* Maybe this was just the residue of his German projects, but it was new. Jean had heard the lovers on the phone—she'd walked in on them mid-conversation. She specifically heard him whisper "darling"—softly, as if he was talking to a child, one he was trying to jolly back from a tantrum. Thinking it must be a distressed Victoria calling for comfort, she'd waited, and was surprised when he abruptly hung up with a bizarre yet perfunctory "Got to run, Dan"—obviously some preestablished code. Mark called lots of people darling, men and women, including everyone whose name he couldn't remember. But he didn't *whisper* it.

A feeling too good to last: Jean had been right about that. In the days and weeks following the discovery, she found herself soberly trawling through the past—hers, Mark's, and theirs, plus the parents'—combing for any warning of impending calamity and, less hopefully, for any solution. In addition, Jean took on the hard work of cold-shouldering her panic. She weeded her garden and she yawned a lot, just couldn't stop yawning.

And though she didn't know why, earlier desolations—newly revealed as practice panics—bubbled up to consciousness with seismic force: as when Jean was packing to go up to Oxford and her Anglophile mother, hot at the prospect of vicarious pleasures, presented her with a taffeta ball gown—immense, and yellow.

Now, clad in her usual grubby gardening gear, Jean could hardly countenance the existence of such an item, let alone its place among her possessions.

But this parting gift was exactly Phyllis's idea of fun or, rather, fun in an ancient European setting. In her worldview, it was axiomatic that if you had the clothes, the experience would surely follow. At that moment, Jean, holding the bunched yards of dully shining silk with both hands, came to know a couple of things she had not yet even suspected. The first was that her mother—pretty, neat, and short, though Phyllis preferred "petite"—had married too early to get in her fair share of fun. Jean's father, William Warner, attorney-at-law, was shrewd, thoughtful, droll, and arguably dapper, but not the kind of fast-talking high-spirited fun her mother seemed to want. It was Jean who'd taken his advice to go to Oxford and follow him in the study of the law, even though she'd already completed a perfectly good American degree in English literature; it was Jean who admired and shared his crackling brand of humor, so dry you might miss it, this wit that made Mark's punsome ways seem like slapstick. The other thing Jean understood on the presentation of the dress was that she wouldn't be going to the ball. Not ever.

Nevertheless, she'd kept the spinster gown, old but unworn, rolled in mothballs and stowed now for decades in a box marked MAY. Jean never considered offering it to nineteen-year-old Victoria, already launched in her own weightless selection of slinky, shimmery dresses worn as tight as Ace bandages—and not just because it was yellow and dated, out of the dance at Twelve Oaks in *Gone with the Wind*. Jean passionately wished not to press any freighted idea of allure on Victoria, particularly not one she herself had rejected.

But the unflattering dress, with its explosion of fabric just at the hip, had done its work, and perhaps this is what saved it from Oxfam. For it was while *not* attending her own year's May Ball that Jean had met Mark, deep in Crime and Thriller at the back of Iffley Road Video.

"I grew up in this town, but I don't go to the university," he'd told her, answering the evidently obvious question on her face. "I make collages, you see. In London." Jean hadn't known what to say. He seemed so much older than her fellow students and even her tutors. He'd been to Camberwell art school in South London and, that May, he was on a rare visit home, for his first solo exhibition at a new gallery in Jericho. As they waited for their videos at the cash register, he held out an invitation to the opening.

"You *must* come," he said, refusing to dilute his command with an ingratiating smile, both of their hands on the card. "Just exactly as you are: don't change a single thing." She remembered how she'd looked down at her bumpy brown hand-knit sweater and jeans. And that, from the beginning, was Mark: he'd had a vivid and unshakable idea of her qualities and, even better, his compliments gave pleasure long after they'd been paid. She wasn't just beautiful; to Mark, hers was a *"refreshing* beauty." He didn't just adore her; she "filled the sky." His clarity of purpose, and the apposite phrase, were talents he shared with her father, perhaps the only things they had in common, and for Jean that was enough, the nonnegotiable minimum.

For the first time in decades, Jean wondered what her father had said that caught her mother's attention the first time they met.

"Worse ski accident I ever had," he joked after the divorce, twenty-eight years later. He'd met Phyllis Jean Amery by chance, in Aspen, Colorado, in February 1955, in a lift queue. So what had Bill said to her mother as they rose through the cold mountain air, suspended between slope and sky? Jean thought he'd probably begun by trying to impress her with some interesting fact about the natural world—too absorbed to notice, as he should have, that conversations with no people in them made Phyllis fidgety. Once, also on a chairlift, he'd told Jean that it took a snowflake eight minutes to complete its fall to earth, the same amount of time it took the image of the setting sun to reach the human eye. And, like Mark in the video store, her father had only had about that long to make his pitch, to make Phyllis want to get *back* in line with him. Jean's brother, Billy, was born in November the same year, on Thanksgiving Day; still, she had the idea that whatever her father had come up with on that chairlift also contained the seed of her parents' separation: the fact of it encoded in that first encounter, imprinted, unalterable.

When she thought about it now, the Warner children's personal creation myth, with its clean sound track of sleigh bells wafting up from the old mining town at the bottom of the mountain, Jean was once again searching for some explanation of their individual destinies. And, once again, any hint of the real shape of things remained blurred. Back on the shelf, then, that random meeting she kept in a small glass dome, nostalgia enhanced by poor visibility in this pocket-size blizzard of love.

Mark was due for another trip "ashore"—their word for home, as if St. Jacques was not an island but a raft. She knew she had to pull back from his affair, whatever else she decided to do about it, but had she learned enough yet? What mission had been accomplished that could allow her to lay off? Looking out the kitchen window over her sinkful of dirty, misshapen vegetables, Jean saw the hummingbird she called Emerald flickering in the bushes: busy, always so busy. A bird of work. And she thought about Mark's work. "I cut up magazines," he'd told her that first day in the video shop and though she thought he'd been joking that's exactly what he did. He cut and reassembled and reanimated images clipped from advertisements, and the results were judged to be "political." In fact, Mark had no politics and was instead guided by his feel for shape and color, for the lovely lines of old products, for unusual typefaces, and by a distinctive, fairly childish sense of humor.

That first Oxford show received solemn praise and sold out, Jean's lumpy sweater swelling with pride when she heard the news. Like Mark himself, the collages were a compelling mix of the elegant and the slightly goofy, and sometimes they were touching, even if, as with all good art, it was hard to say quite why they should've been, these homemade gardens of ultra-earthly delights: consumer galaxies of known brands, household products gaining in beauty and strangeness as they were wrenched from humdrum uses and set on a planetary course that revolved, in one way or another, around him.

The first piece she saw at the exhibition in Jericho had at its center a photograph of the artist at eight, blue eyed and blond, a perfect dimpled cupcake of a face, with thick mother-combed hair. He was irresistible: his nose sprinkled with freckles, his bright eyes peering out with the look of slight hesitancy he wore even now. Was it the work she'd fallen for—and the idea of untouched innocence at the still heart of this mundane swirl—or just this dear, unsure English boy, his clever eyes both daring and held in check? Jean simply could not imagine what someone like Giovana would see in him, and her failure to conjure up a connection only increased her solitude.

Maybe something in her own character invited betrayal. If this sounded like the mind-set of a victim, the opposite was true: a lawyer by training and inheritance, Jean could not accept a fate devoid of responsibility, and she knew that in her marriage she'd been, as her daughter might put it, actively passive. Until that evening in the video shop, she'd wished she could be the kind of girl who not only went to the May Ball but who twirled like a weather vane atop a dawn-lit fountain in a soaked and possibly shredded yellow gown. But Mark had changed all that. He was an artist with a sold-out one-man show. And she no longer worried about graduating with a law degree that wouldn't be recognized in her own country. That wasn't going to matter, because Jean wasn't going to live in America.

She hadn't bargained, though, on his abandoning his work.

They were married late in the fall after her Finals, and gradually Mark stopped making his collages. Against her protestations, he'd even pulled out of a group show at Oxford's Museum of Modern Art. "An artist should be judged by the exhibitions he declines" was how he put it, even as he declined to be an artist. A commission from a family friend—a company logo, then a publicity campaign—grew, like any one of his previous works, into a dizzying commercial cosmos. Soon the jobs were pouring in. Jean thought his success was due to his childlike outlook, his chief purpose being to amuse himself. He logged long hours but always gave the impression of a man at play. When he gave up art for good, he did so without hesitation; his life would be his biggest and best collage, he said, and he put Jean's freckled nose at the center of his universe—and Victoria's, too, when she appeared, a dainty six-pound parcel, in the spring of 1983.

So what had gone wrong? Both of them had been restless, and they'd traveled, taking baby Vic along. He loved the markets and the alien signage; Jean liked being on the road with him, and here they were, still on the road. She'd given up her law career before it even began. She was newly twenty-three when she gave up her name and her country. It now struck her with painful force that she'd been crazily precipitate and, as a result, her isolation without Mark would be total. All those years, she'd believed their delicious *shared* isolation, their sense of twinship, arose from intense and intimate sufficiency. Now she saw that he might, just possibly, have been keeping her in a compartment, a nice base from which he could wander. To sustain her complicity, he'd even found her a job. At that point she still wrote the occasional legal column, an extension of what she'd written for *Cherwell*, the Oxford student paper. But it was Mark who'd come up with the health column, something to keep her busy during her confinement. She seized on this antique term, of course without realizing just how extensive a confinement it was to become.

For the final four months before Victoria's birth, pre-eclampsia kept Jean horizontal. Mark would mix them cocktails—a festive virgin punch for her—while she read out the latest installment of the diary that was the kernel of her column, these idiosyncratic, and addictive, musings through the prism of the body: high blood pressure, alarming fluid retention, strange pee. . . . Mark, in his enthusiasm, foisted some of her pages on a client, the owner of *Mrs* magazine, and his instinct was soon vindicated by thousands of paying read-ers. Who could have predicted such a vast unabashed voyeur-ism, which generated more mail from readers than the magazine had ever received?

The column, "Inside Out with Jean Hubbard," had been syndicated on its fifth anniversary—toasted by proud Mark with his ready champagne and by Victoria, not yet five her-self, with a finger-painted card—and now also appeared in a Scottish weekly, a free subsidized newspaper in Ireland, and a new Russian women's magazine whose meager fee Jean waived for the chance to reach across the blighted steppes to need-ier women, many—as they wrote to tell her—with a half-dozen kitchen abortions behind them. Her brand-new agent got her into the Australian magazine *HO—Her Own*—and the "younger" American *Splash*, where her column had been mis-leadingly retitled "In Your Shoes," accompanied this time not by a stamp-size author photo but by a fashion sketch in purple of a stiletto-heel pump. The years brought further magazines, an ever-increasing flow of letters, and also social invitations. But on the whole Jean and Mark continued, for ever longer periods of time, to stay in.

Now she tried to determine if there'd been a pattern to their spasms of seclusion—a coincident abstinence from sex, say, or any other hint of infidelity. Nothing. Their frequent trips—whether together or apart, Jean to the grandparents in New York with Vic, and Mark to the Continent in pursuit of new clients—made friends unsure of their reliability as dinner guests and enabled them to dodge what invitations they did get.

They'd loved to imagine living in another country and traveled whenever they could—but work or school had conspired to keep them mainly in Camden. So, with Vic settled at university, Mark promoted himself to a nonadministrative role. ("How about 'nonresident genius'?" he'd polled his wife, in search of a title.) When he identified St. Jacques, glamorously distant, undiscovered, and not on the way to anywhere, Jean immediately called Mackay, her editor, to discuss a slight change of emphasis in her column: the time had come to bring the world to the wonderful readers of *Mrs.*

Just to herself, Jean thought: on the island they'd be *étrangers*, foreigners, but also strangers; their strangeness gone legit—not quirk, just fact. There they wouldn't be snobs but stoics, in a tropical, Frenchified setting. What more could you possibly want?

No one had worked harder at shutting down their London life than Victoria. She sprinkled mothballs with the theatrical zeal of a television cook. Her boxing and labeling and sealing and stacking might have been filmed as an exercise video: burn fat while you pack. As the departure day neared and the frenzy to be ready mounted, Vic also answered readers' letters as "Jean Hubbard"; she was faithful to her mother's straight style, only once or twice, out of boredom, slipping in a note of ingratiation or hauteur. For her father she assembled from her beloved vintage shops a complete tropical uniform (successfully complying with his strict instruction: no turquoise and no palm trees), aware that it would have to stand in for his bold collection of city suits, the grasshopper-green gabardine, the red pinstripe, the navy silk Nehru collar, and not forgetting the triple-breasted gray flannel suit he'd designed himself with a middle lane of buttons: a joke and, like the others, exquisitely tailored.

Vic would stay on in the little house in Albert Street, the envy of her friends, who called it the Mum's Away Café. She would feed the cat, begin her second term at University College, and stick with her Saturday job at Vinyl Solution, alphabetizing the secondhand records. She'd asked Mark and Jean—as she'd taken to calling them—if she should clear out all their old albums, now that they didn't even own a turntable. And, though they hadn't offered, Jean had a pretty good idea she'd move into their bedroom. She saw all this one day, still making piles on the floor—toss, store, pack—while Vic stood with her friend Maya in the doorway. Maya, who had a stream of boyfriends and was living in an austere college room, looked at the Hubbards' great barge of a bed and sighed. What Jean didn't see till later was how much Victoria wished she'd been consulted about their leaving. How much she hadn't wanted them to go.

People need social interaction, Jean concluded during this period of agonized review, struggling to ground the flying debris of her life—and shut out the unsummoned images of a gyrating Giovana that swiveled through her mind. Slamming the door on such unsolicited stripograms, she'd tell herself that Mark had plenty of interaction at the office. There was Noleen, gentle, reliable, good for laughing at his jokes—with her smoker's baritone and unrevised side-parted sixties hairstyle held in place by a lone, low-slid bobby pin. Sure, there were also the revolving interns who filled any successful agency—not such a consoling prospect as Noleen—but weren't they Dan's department? Dan, who'd turned up at Mark's office one Monday, taking the stairs three at a time, letting himself in, and asking about a job as if responding to an advertisement. He'd admired some of Mark's ads, particularly his campaign for a secretarial course: a photo of a curvy girl's fingers spread provocatively over a keyboard, above the line *Isn't it time you learned your place?* This insinuating secretary tapped on people's peripheral vision across the city—and certainly on Dan's, who then took the initiative to track down the creator.

Mark liked that about him. Dan hadn't gone to university, or even to art school, but he clearly had no doubt about his rightful place in the world. Twenty-seven and boasting a blank CV, he was a broad, big-voiced, strong-jawed northerner with pink cheeks and narrow rectangular glasses that had looked dated when they were new—a detail that endeared him to Jean, an old hand at, even a believer in, failed fashion. Within six months he was Mark's heir apparent at the firm—and "hair replacement," as Victoria joked to her mother, referring to his mane, as black, rich, and shiny as crude oil. But he was, perhaps above all, Mark's link to a male world and a male future, one of willed camaraderie and surrogate sexual adventuring, artfully packaged in the service of commerce.

In the Internet café one morning, toward the end of her unusual infatuation, Jean gazed at the latest Giovana: wearing only a dog collar, on all fours and a leash, tongue out as if panting. How could Mark go for this stuff? she wondered. How could *Jean*? Pretending to be your husband's libido was no parlor game. And of course every exchange with Thing 2 led her to a punishing image of Mark and Giovana fucking—with its free reminder of her own enforced celibacy.

Writing as Mark, she had to consider Giovana from his point of view. The person who granted such extensive permission had to be, Jean thought, beloved. He would at least be very grateful. Giovana must be a love object, not merely a collection of warm, suctioning chambers—mouth, cunt, ass, hands, the deep engulfing crevice of cleavage, she could see him fucking that, and also, with nostalgia for the intercrural solution of his long years away at school, her powerful-looking thighs.

She imagined Mark making new sounds with Giovana. When she and Mark made love it was like a silent movie, with some happy and winded joint sighing at the end if it all worked out, as if they'd just made it indoors from an unforeseen hailstorm. But with Giovana, she was convinced, Mark had entered a brighter, louder world. He would believe he was at last giving proper expression to the quintessential sacrament, and that he was doing it in the name of all men. His primal score—which in Jean's private listening room ranged from Gregorian chant to the howl of an unanesthetized amputee— was also wonderfully validating for Giovana, and this she let him know with her rhythmic panting and meandering moans as he tirelessly pounded the air out of her. It was a yodeling duet fueled by self-praise, a paean to fabulous athleticism and abandon. But they had nothing else to say to each other; Jean felt pretty sure of that. All the e-mails, her own included, were written versions of those moans and slurps, noises that had to stand in for more evolved endearments, for expressions of love between equals.

Once, Giovana apologized for having begged him to stop whatever unspecified but infinitely trying thing he'd been doing to her. Pinned, cornered, trapped, gasping and gagging, Giovana would've raised a surprisingly delicate hand, pleading for a time-out, and how masterful Mark would've felt, condescending— or not—to let her breathe. Having his way: it was something he "needed" to do, Jean thought, because it had no place in their marriage, where the flow was naturally companionable, proactively considerate. *Her* Mark would pull the car over during her sneeze attacks in hay-fever season, just to pat her back. This Mark "headboarded" Giovana, pumping indifferently past her frantically flapping hands until—how had she put it?— *my eyes pop and roll out of my head on the stream of yr satin come.* Going too far, that was their pact. For Giovana, Jean thought, reading and rereading this latest scene, submission was a source of power. It kept Mark there because it made him believe the opposite of the truth: that he was in charge. But the further Jean went the less likely it seemed she would ever again put herself in that position. And what position was that anyway? On her knees, on all fours?

Attachment

Thanks for the nice description, Jean wrote back the following day, in comically understated reply to this tranche of highly worked porno, sent by the star herself. Jean intended to limit herself to simple, gurgling appreciation. Wasn't that what everybody wanted? Not Giovana.

Nice? was all she wrote back, uncharacteristically terse, and in punishment sent no new images.

Jean did indeed feel chastised, and deprived, but increasingly she also sensed that whatever she wrote and whatever Mark did to her, both Hubbards giving it their all, for Giovana it wasn't nearly enough. And it never would be. What she wanted—no, demanded—was *more.* Escalation had been steep from their first contact. Jean could easily see how for Mark things had quickly gotten out of control.

The next morning she again found herself in the Internet café, installed, as usual, before the last, and most private, cubby. She was staring at Giovana straddling a shocking-pink air mattress, adrift in a pool of eye-smarting blue. Her head was thrown back, and Jean wondered if all that thick, perfectly undulating black hair could possibly be natural. Her sun-browned breasts sparkled with sweat or suntan oil, and she squeezed them together between her down-stretched arms so they swelled like loaves of glazed bread, her mouth slightly open, and her eyes half closed in familiar rapture.

Jean stared at the screen and consciously erased Mark from her mind. She had discovered, in the past few weeks, the satisfaction of imagining Giovana's body being used, and not gently, by other men altogether, and there was a host of them to choose from, including Aminata's son Amadou, *all* the boys from the taxi rank in Toussaint, and the dreadlocked Christian, but beginning, of course, with the customs inspectors, just doing their job in a small soundproofed room at the airport.

Today, for reasons she couldn't have explained or maybe for no reason at all, she settled on Mark's deputy.

She slotted him into the poolside view she had before her, and there was Dan taking Giovana from behind, thumbs planted in her soft hips, slapping noisily against her wobbly brown haunches and pushing her half off her float, which had been dragged out of the pool, her long nails digging for purchase between the tiles. Giovana was looking very worried; she could hardly take it but she *was* taking it. The noises she made in Jean's head moved from apprehensive animal utterance to frightened animal utterance to clenched silence—one indistinguishable from the many kinds of silence: concentration, meditation, fear, or indeed speechless ecstasy.

Though Jean had never before drummed up Dan and didn't consider him remotely sexy, she did find him perfect for Giovana—sufficiently ruthless and brutal—and without realizing it, she found herself awkwardly perched on the hard edge of her chair, helplessly frozen in a moment of unplanned release, like when she was a girl in the playground before she knew what an orgasm was, paralyzed on the climbing rope. Thinking about this later, Jean was mortified, and depressed—not so much at having been aroused by Giovana, who was, after all, made (and managed and decorated) for pleasure, but at her excitement in the *violence* of it.

Mark went to London and Jean stayed away from town, even though the fact that there'd be nothing new while he was with his lover hardly made a virtue of this abstinence. Too late for virtue. Everything was sullied, and she was rotting from within. She felt crabbed, soiled, tired, and old. Finally she felt so ill she went to one of St. Jacques' spa hotels to see a fabled nutritionist, who diagnosed her as suffering from "adrenal exhaustion." Expensive new term for infidelity, Jean thought as she grimly wrote out her check—noting, with additional chagrin, that there wasn't even a word for the female cuckold.

Although she could give up wheat as instructed, and avoid the Internet café, she couldn't stop following, obsessively in her mind, this thread that seemed to be leading her deeper into and not out of the labyrinth. It was only an enforced interruption that broke the spell, and that interruption was Phyllis.

Jean's mother had invited herself to stay—and Jean, generous at a distance of nine thousand miles, had encouraged her. Maybe it was her new loneliness, but she wanted to see Phyllis; surely she could refrain from childish flare-ups—generally provoked, after all, by Phyllis's criticism of *Mark*.

With Mark away she began to make plans for the visit. She imagined long walks on the beach. And then what? She'd take her mother to the old rum distillery that was now a museum. They'd go to the famous botanical garden, which Jean had yet to visit, and to the Beausoleil Captive Breeding Center, where there was that kestrel project she'd read about in *Le Quotidien*. A delegation of British and American bird lovers was attempting to boost a depleted population of kestrels— they were down to four pairs when the center opened. They finger-fed them prekilled mice; they incubated their eggs, and, in time, they would reintroduce them into their ancestral habitat in the St. Jacques jungle, itself shrinking and in urgent need of conservation.

The Beausoleil Captive Breeding Center: like the Beausoleil Hotel, only more literal, Jean thought. (She'd been trying to shape a column about the well-known if hard-to-prove link between foreign holidays and fertility.) She drove around to see if she could get Phyllis day passes to the big hotels, where she would be pampered and entertained. She could see why tourists didn't want to leave the expensively irrigated grounds, where they spent a week or two nearly naked, adding only a ribbon around the hips for meals, and where even the swimming pools were saronglike, wrapped around semisubmerged pool bars.

Then there were all those coupons to get through: the step classes and the spinning sessions, the beach buffet and poolside cocktails, the moonlit ride on the banana boat and the dawn freestyle kite surf, the all-island steel-band competition and the Kiddy Klub Karaoke Kontest, the limbo, the bingo, the rumba, the rummy, and of course the room service—the in-house Cecils and Cedrics, the Rangoolams and Rishabs, the towel boys and waiters, the lifeguards and fitness coaches and, first among men, the deep-sea-diving instructors, including Aminata's hunky son Amadou. This, anyway, was the picture Jean got from Aminata, with her many eyes and ears on the island, each with the perspective of a different uniform. And even if Jean sometimes bristled, it was a view that tallied with her emerging expectation of universal depravity. If Mark was in on it, why not everyone else?

She had to ask Amadou if it was safe for older people to dive; Phyllis would love the carnival colors of the coral reef, the fetal weightlessness of the aquanaut, the reassuring presence of a broad-shouldered guide like Amadou, part-time Poseidon, blue-lit sea husband. She laughed to think of her mother in a tiny wetsuit and a cat's-eyes mask, her flippers with kitten heels. When she finally tracked Amadou down between diving trips out to the reef, he reassured her that the only clients warned off were those who were pregnant or who suspected they might be. Women guests apparently came into the category of baggage everyone was always having to account for.

And suddenly, Jean thought, the hitherto mind-numbing airport query "Did you pack this bag yourself?" gained fresh
poetry and meaning. Abass, another of Aminata's sons, worked
at customs, and Jean had heard how the best-looking girls were
whisked straight through immigration. Taxi drivers had two
decisive advantages over rival predators: they were boys with
cars and, like the crew on a cruise liner, they got first dibs. If
Aminata's family covered the full arc of experience on St.
Jacques, her daughter Aissatou, a nurse at the hospital, stood at
the dead end of the rainbow and witnessed the rising incidence
of venereal disease: old-fashioned ailment, new kind of holiday
souvenir.

Driving back from Amadou's hotel, Jean wondered if it
was possible to write about the health hazards of sexual liberation without sounding 102. Wedding and honeymoon packages were standard offerings at all the big hotels, but some
catered to singles—the young and not-so-young Western
women on the party trail. Frantically carefree, they crammed
it in before they got down to worrying about their own wed-
dings. On the way home, she stopped in at the salon.

Aminata—who trimmed Jean's hair as her part of the Phyllis preparations—told her all about the wild Brits and mostly
Australians. Salon gossip had always been a source of uncomplicated fascination for Jean, but now, with her head uncom-
fortably tilted back and worrying about damage to the nerve
roots leading from the spinal cord (she'd once written a column about this, salon-sink radiculopathy), she found she no
longer wanted to know about sexual misadventure. She certainly didn't want to hear Aminata's equally airy excuses for
female genital cutting or polygamy; she'd grown intolerant of
her relentless disdain for tourists, which, at times, was hard
to distinguish from plain racism. She had to stop herself from
telling Aminata to rein in her rampaging sons instead of slan-

dering the girls they screwed—the same girls she overcharged, sometimes the same day.

But she regretted this new rigidity in herself. She wanted to keep her lively friend and contact, and she wanted to be able to bring Phyllis to the salon; she'd be charmed by her. She'd remind her, as she had Jean, of their beloved housekeeper from the sixties and seventies, Gladys Williams from South Carolina, whose own hairstyle was a shiny black helmet of a wig. And Phyllis would love the little salon itself, with its flower-stenciled pink walls and matching rose sink sets.

About the office-house Jean had no doubt: her mother would hate it. She'd look around and think they'd moved here to save money. In fact, Jean had been so enchanted by the former mining office, with the filigree portico of a Victorian railroad station and its rows of rattan benches, she'd immediately decided to buy it. But now she saw it with her mother's eyes: potholes running the length of the drive; broken paving stones; cracked plaster walls green with mildew; a net of creepers engulfing most of the building; the tin roof giving a standing ovation whenever the rain rattled down.

For Jean that sound—the amplified downpour—was forever charged with afternoon lovemaking, occasioned solely by the luck, their first day in the house, of being caught inside rather than out during a thunderstorm, knowing that no one would bother them for as long as it lasted. This uproarious greeting had cheered them just as they'd finished dragging in all the boxes and duffels—it made them feel both actively dry and safely *home*. In obeisance to these promising new household gods, they'd immediately sought the still-sheetless four-poster moored in an alcove deep in the Bureau du Directeur.

Afterward, Mark had run out into the soft and steady rain to pick a mango they'd been amazed to spot through the window. They couldn't find a knife and so had bitten into the extravagantly scented flesh, its "skin like a sunset," as he put it. Then they held their faces out the window, straight into the rain, to wash away the juice. And they felt more than cleansed. It was just then, Jean thought heavily, that they'd first called the office, and by extension the entire island, the good place.

But Phyllis would see at once that it wasn't a house at all and wouldn't be amused by the idea of not having to go to the office because you'd woken up there. She would think how, through the years, Mark and Jean had chosen to drag their little daughter all over the third world, boiling water as they went, luggage heavy with diarrhea blockers and fruit-flavored ion-packed powders, and *then* he'd *voluntarily* taken a pay cut in order to live here, in this *office*. What was the point of being in advertising if it wasn't to make money?

Her mother hadn't told her why she was coming, and Jean, not wanting to admit she thought there might be a dreadful reason, didn't ask. Instead, she cleaned. She knew Phyllis would find something to be disappointed about. Still, for three days she scrubbed—emptying the dead bugs from light fittings, sponging down the woodwork, beating the rag rugs, washing the pale blue slipcovers. She gave the guest bed the only unpatched mosquito net, wrenching her back with the hanging, and wondered if Phyllis would be seduced by the fairy cloud of white gauze or worried by what the net foretold. She must make Mark promise not to mention the scorpions.

And then, in the last hour of her manic making ready, she gave herself some fine stigmata: standing on a wobbly stool, attempting to rehang a cupboard door that had come unhinged, she knocked herself in the eye and it immediately pooled with blood. She made things much worse by daubing it with that "magic" seaweed that Aminata had pressed on her, filmy green strips used on the island for everything from wound cleaner to omelette filler (thank goodness her readers couldn't get hold of any). The eye became so goopy and inflamed that she had to wear a makeshift patch—a cosmetic pad under a rakishly angled bandanna that kept slipping like a badly tied blindfold.

Yet with all her cleaning, she couldn't scrape away the bad feeling that she carried inside her and that became more acutely disagreeable as Phyllis's visit approached. She got up early and immediately sought the shower, soaping and scrubbing herself in the hottest water she could stand. In the past, morning had been the Hubbards' time for sex. The ingrained impulse alone accounted for her unease as she woke, even when Mark wasn't there, and for her unclean feeling, if only because it led her each day, before she'd even washed her face, to thoughts of Giovana. And the day after he returned, only four before Phyllis was due, the same difficulty followed her to the next trial—of breakfast.

Regarding Mark across the table, all she could see was his decline, and travel fatigue didn't account for it. He looked gray, pouchy along the jawline. His jokes were reflexive, also old. As he fiddled with the tea strainer, his bottom lip slid out a fraction—once sexy, suddenly irritating, elderly. His habit of constantly fingercombing his hair seemed vain and faggy, and of course the egg and jam at the corner of his mouth were positively enraging. (She felt sure they wouldn't be there with Giovana across the table.) She could manage this surfeit of hostility only by avoiding him, walking outside when he came in, pretending to be asleep when he ambled into the bedroom, drunk, more often than not. But it wasn't just Mark. Even the birds—perhaps the thing she loved most on St. Jacques—looked tainted.

Gangs of parrots ruled the tall eucalyptus trees behind the house, their piercing screech echoing through the valley. At first she'd been thrilled to see them, with their paint-box colors. Now she felt there was something delinquent about them, like

The interior road to the airport was shorter and therefore favored by Mark, but it was unpaved and deserted. Jean imagined herself tracked by vultures and dumbfounded goats, kneeling beside the new hatchback and wrestling with the rust-jammed jack, her airport skirt coated with red dirt. So instead she took the coast road, lined all along with reassuring life. Hands firm at ten and two, she was relieved to discover that the thought of Phyllis no longer irritated her. This was auspicious; surely most irritation started in the expectation of it, and the trick was to avoid the dread, not the encounter. Her mood was lightened by the breeze coming through the window, by the open road, and for the rest of the drive she sang.

Phyllis was the last off the twelve-seater plane, picking her way down the aluminum steps with precision and delicacy, sidesaddle: the picture, to her health-expert daughter, of a woman intimate with her bone-density reading. Windswept on the tarmac, with a geometric scarf tied under her chin, enormous sunglasses, and fuchsia lipstick, she looked even smaller than Jean remembered. Or did her head seem disproportionately large, as if there was a hat under her scarf? This head, on this skinny body, gave Phyllis the appearance of an alien; and she hardly grew bigger as she got closer. But neither did she look as though she'd been on an airplane for two days—or rather three airplanes for two days, first toiling over to London before catching the eastbound jumbo, then the hop from Mauritius, the Big Island, as the locals called it. No, it was Jean who looked disheveled, with her wind-ruined hair and rumpled linen, then the bandage on her eye that seesawed her sunglasses.

"This place is a *riot*. Fabulous," Phyllis said, taking in at a glance the tiny airport, making Jean feel instantly defensive. "Your eye! Your *skin!*" Phyllis was peering closely at Jean, still gripping her arms from their hug. "I'll give you my hat when I leave," she announced with resolute generosity, unwrapping herself to show she indeed had one under the scarf, a narrow-rimmed raffia, part boater, part cloche, neatly placed on her immaculate chin-length hair, which was still tucked girlishly behind her ears.

Well, that didn't take long, Jean thought, wondering if Mark would call this headgear a bloche or a cloater, and deciding that she absolutely, categorically, hated the word "fabulous." Jean was irrationally enraged by the large quantity of Phyllis's luggage—and they were waiting for a *third* bag.

"Darn," said Phyllis. "It's my shoe bag. I bet someone's stolen it." She squinted at the uniformed and armed security guard, then at the barefoot kids hanging around the entrance scanning the new arrivals, sizing up tips.

"Mom, I really don't think anybody's stolen your shoe bag," Jean said. The relationship to shoes, as everyone knew, was a kind of litmus test for female equilibrium. Hadn't Phyllis been a neat little packer in the old days, ever scornful of wheelies and garment bags, chic with just her carry-on? That was what Jean remembered from her mother's visits to Oxford, watching through the rain-streaked window of the Randolph Hotel tea-room as Phyllis stepped out of a black London taxi, a complex fugue in brown, layers fashioned from the hides and hairs of at least four kinds of mountain dweller—alpaca, vicuña, llama, fox. No shoe bag in those days. "What happened to your packer's principle, Mom: 'Halve the clothes and double the money'?"

"Well, how do you know I've abandoned it?" Phyllis replied, gamely enough. Jean, already worried about driving home in the dark, began casting about for someone to complain to. She had to wonder if more and bigger luggage signaled bloat elsewhere with her mother—amplified anxiety, panicky indecision, forgetfulness—and she felt a heavy presentiment of near and future trials. Never mind, she told herself. It was imperative that she manage the visit well: she was forty-five years old, nearly forty-six for Christ's sake, even if for nearly half that time, for nearly half her *life,* she'd had Mark to share the load. In fact, she suddenly realized, over the years Phyllis had become *his* department.

The shoe bag was finally found outside on the tarmac, where it had been off-loaded and forgotten; Jean added it to the already precarious cart and pushed it out to the parking lot and the lone car.

"So, is Mark working terribly hard?"

Wrestling the bags into the back, Jean understood just what she was getting at—Why the hell didn't he come to meet me at the airport? She agreed that wedging bags into a small trunk was very much the sort of challenge Mark liked, though she wasn't about to say so. "Yes, actually, he is. He's working on a big account for kitchen appliances."

Phyllis, who'd left her hometown of Salt Lake City far behind, was an event planner at the New York Public Library, responsible for luncheons and fund-raisers and lavish dinners in the Great Hall. She didn't choose the readings or entertainments but saw to the caterers, the extra coatracks, the massive floral displays. Jean didn't have the energy to ask what her work was like now and was mindful, too, of holding a few safe topics like this in reserve. Phyllis, small as a child in the passenger seat, puckered and peered into a compact, reapplying her bougainvillea lipstick. Jean tried to remember why when she was little Phyllis's public daubing had struck her as nothing less than indecent. She'd felt similarly scandalized whenever she'd seen a square of blotter tissue floating unflushed in her mother's toilet with a ghostly lipstick-on-your-collar mouth print, like a kiss blown up from the sewer to tell her there was more to this woman than she'd ever know.

"*Gosh* I'm glad to be here," Phyllis said. "You have no idea how I've looked forward to getting some rest." On the drive home she dozed, and when she intermittently jerked awake she told Jean again how tired she was, how desperate for early nights and quiet days, how advancing age had made drinking alcohol nearly impossible, how she'd given up her evening martini altogether, indeed how sobriety was the secret of human happiness.

Six hours later, on the Hubbards' terrace in the moonlight, Phyllis was going strong. She'd switched from champagne to the local firewater—demented cane, as Mark called it—served in thimble-size glasses he'd brought out sometime after twelve.

"She would've stayed up talking all night if I'd let her," Jean complained in the bathroom the next morning, testing with a finger the watery pouches under her eyes—eyes as red as if she'd spent the night in the ocean, her tongue pale, dry, and scallop edged like St. Jacques' beaches. "If I could keep *up* with her," she said in revision, whispering even though there was no chance her mother could hear. "What was all that about needing a *rest*?" No point chastising Mark for hauling out the shot glasses; nobody had made her drink. A world-class pourer, he didn't believe in saving people from themselves.

Jean didn't complain about Phyllis's frump remark and wasn't about to remind him. What her mother had said, at 12:40, was "I really *admire* the way you completely ignore your appearance, Jeannie. You are so *cool*. And you're absolutely right: hair, makeup, clothes, they're *totally* unimportant, so why *not* just go for comfort?" And she certainly didn't tell him about Phyllis's unsolicited update on Larry Mond, the meteoric lawyer Jean had worked for in New York all those summers ago: the one who got away—or so her mother saw it. But in fact it was Jean who'd gotten away, run away, back to England, just as soon as things started to heat up with Larry, in truth the more likely candidate. At that age "likely" was no different from her mother's approval: it was an active demerit.

Phyllis had pronounced the house "adorable," which Jean chose to be satisfied with. She popped two painkillers—one thousand milligrams of the common anti-inflammatory that had replaced the automatic aspirin of her college hangovers, and this did seem a better fit: a shrinking was just what she needed, of her capacity for emotion, by any means necessary, drugs, caffeine, and the resolve these ritual preparations hailed.

Before going out to breakfast, she scanned the bedroom shelves for guidebooks and maps. Jean was going to plan her way to an early night. Forget the rum museum, which might offer free tastings. In the coming week they'd visit the picturesque port and the kestrel project, spend a day at a spa hotel, hit the covered market. Phyllis, the professional organizer, was commensurately responsive to any show of forethought. She'd be really impressed if there was both structure and choice, an expedition arranged like a multichambered candy dish set out for guests, and no place fit this bill better than the botanical gardens at Terre Haute.

The vast gardens, near a ragtag village, radiated outward from the patch on which the island's first governor had laid his vegetable plot. But according to Jean's guidebook the botanical garden had been the dream of a Belgian, two Frenchmen, and then a Scot, each of whom had brought some new dimension to the enterprise. After that, under the authority of the newly created Department of Agriculture, nothing more had been added; or, Jean understood, the spirit of invention turned as murky and stagnant as the lily ponds.

She stopped reading to look around her. Of course a garden had to be the projection of a single mind, or at least a succession of single minds. Unlike a marriage, she thought, even if marriage was often likened to a garden—a private district. What the Belgian and the Frenchmen and the Scot had in common was this: they'd dared to shape paradise on an island that could easily have won the bid for Eden just as they found it. "For these men," she ventured out loud, auditioning a sentence for use in print, "nothing they *found* could compare with what they could *make*." Phyllis was squinting at a hand-painted map of the gardens.

"What did you find, honey?"

Jean was just warming up and didn't really want, just yet, to explain her free associations, these thoughts that ran from plants to persons and other imports. Ideas percolating, voiced aloud—this was a familiar, delicate process signaling the start of a column, just a nibble, nothing more, usually accompanied by a disproportionate surge of euphoria: the glow of being useful. Since Giovana, Jean was overcome with a desire to do good, like her lawyer-dad, in fact like both her parents, as if only this could turn everything around.

Anyway, the next week's column was now solved. Forget the properties of individual plants; it was digging in the dirt that rejuvenated (and that explained the rarity of the teenage gardener). A commonplace? Or was weeding salutary only in contrast to her recent life of stunting imposture and filth?

"Well, what a perfect place for a party," Phyllis said, inspecting a hothouse of ferns, orchids, begonias, and anthuriums. They came through juniper and Indian walnut trees, past a great banyan with exposed roots hanging like hair, to a massive mahogany and, irresistibly placed before it, a bench. "You know what I wish?" Phyllis said, plonking herself down.

"What do you wish, Mom?" Jean sat beside her.

"That instead of scattering the ashes we'd buried them under a big, beautiful tree. So we could sit with him. I hate to think of him swilling around out there in that freezing ocean."

Jean was accustomed to her mother starting this conversation in the middle, the thought never far from any of their minds. Billy, her older—and now much younger—brother, was killed at fifteen by a drunk driver in the winter of 1970. They'd scattered his ashes at sea; in fact, in New York Harbor, below a snow-cloaked Statue of Liberty.

"Hmm," Jean said. In a way her mother was right—he was still out there. Matter remained, forever. "Maybe we should bury something else of Billy's under a big beautiful tree. Like that yellow ski hat. Whatever happened to that thing anyway?"

Phyllis laughed. "Oh, I have it." For a whole year, his last year, Billy had worn his stupid ski hat, during the day when he could get away with it and every single night, in an effort to mat down his wild wiry hair.

"Do you ever worry that you're forgetting him?" Jean asked.

"Never. I think about him all the time." One more way, Jean thought, grief was different for the mother, who was accustomed from the start to tracking her child's constantly changing form. Maybe, for her, Billy's deathly shape was only a "phase"; his being dead now, swilling around out there in the dark deep, this was just the next thing and not any kind of end to his story. Jean *had* worried that he was fading—his laugh was less distinct, though not, for some reason, his croaky, still-unresolved voice. But it wasn't he who had faded; she'd finally figured that out. It was everyone else, including her. After his death Jean had withdrawn a little, hanging back, perhaps to stay or get nearer to Billy. Who knows if she wouldn't have been wildly outgoing if he'd been around? The dead of course were undiminished, Jean thought, and the ghosts were all still alive, wandering along their garden paths. Certainly, on account of Billy, she simply couldn't take any more: *no more death.*

That's it, she realized. That explained her dread of Phyllis's visit: the possibility, now ever present, that her mother would come bringing the very worst news. Just as she had that snowy Saturday morning, after her night of hospital vigil beside her artificially breathing son, to tell Jean, at the breakfast table eating her cereal—Life cereal, in fact—that he was gone.

"Come on, Mom." Jean helped her up from the bench. "We've got miles more to go." They turned and by wordless consent headed toward the famed lily ponds. They hadn't gone far before Phyllis stopped again, before a towering tree—an Indian Albizia, sturdy, smooth, its trunk the warm gray of a Weimaraner. But it wasn't the color that had arrested her mother. The tall tree was, in fact, two tall trees. A twisted vine, a vigorous Australian vine, had grown upward from the Albizia's center, splitting the trunk to nest within it, entwining itself in the upper branches. "Symbiosis? Or parasitism?" Jean asked her mother, but Phyllis was completely captivated by this impossibly slow dance. The vision of eternal embrace made Jean think of "An Arundel Tomb," the Larkin poem about a noble couple carved in marble, one she'd written about her senior year. She ran the end of it, or at least what she could remember, silently past her ear:

> *Above their scrap of history,*
> *Only an attitude remains:*
> *Time has transfigured them into*
> *Untruth. The stone fidelity*
> *They hardly meant has come to be*
> *Their final blazon, and to prove*
> *Our almost-instinct almost true:*
> *What will survive of us is love.*

It was "the stone fidelity they hardly meant" that pierced Jean now, forced as she was to think of Mark, entwined with his own Australian creeper; but to her mother she quoted only the famous last line. And she told Phyllis that the marble couple was holding hands. Her mother responded by squeezing her wrist, as if she didn't want to presume to hold hands. Keen to dispel the solemnity of the moment, Jean reported something she'd read in Larkin's biography, what he'd scribbled on a draft of the poem: *Love isn't stronger than death just because statues hold hands for six hundred years.* She didn't tell her mother another tidbit from the life, one that hadn't struck her when she read it: that the poet liked his pornography. He would circle specialist outlets on his trips to London, usually "funking" actual ingress, losing his nerve. Schoolgirls and spanking, that's what did it for Larkin, and a magazine called *Swish*.

They stood there a while longer not talking, and then Phyllis said, "Have you been in touch with your father?"

So here it comes. "Yes. I spoke to him, let's see, about a week ago. Why? Any special news?" It was odd that Phyllis had said "your father," not just "Dad." She heard the wistful note in her mother's voice—and it wasn't the talk of Billy: on the contrary, communing with him was a refusal to consign him to death.

Was Dad ill? But she'd have called, not flown for eighteen hours to tell her so.

It was twenty years since their divorce. Could there possibly be someone new in her mother's life? No, she'd have known. In Dad's? Childish, of course, but the thought filled her with revulsion. No, no, and no. The parents were going to stay just as they were: plain divorced. So what was on her mother's mind? Again she had the uneasy feeling of a preview, this one suggesting that time and age could unmake any agreement—if not her own marriage, then her parents' divorce.

When Phyllis spoke again she was looking at the tree, not at her daughter.

"For nearly thirty years, I thought we'd never part. And then, for what was perhaps a mere . . . peccadillo—Bill was extremely handsome in those days—well, part we did. I was right. But I was also wrong. I don't know how to explain it to you. Not so easy to disentangle, you know. However much you have right on your side."

Okay, this was not a death notice. But the word "peccadillo"—it was almost jaunty, the Great Peccadillo on his flying trapeze. Where was the virtue in downgrading emotion? Behind this question was her impatience with Mark's mustn't-grumble British upbringing—the prime cause, she felt, of his missing candor now. She wished everyone would quit trying to shield her, if that's what they imagined they were doing. Jean remembered how she'd had to insist on being allowed to go to the hospital and see Billy one last time, to say good-bye before they unplugged his breathing machine. "Are you saying you and Dad split up because he was having an affair?"

"Yes. In a word. I am."

"Mom, I was twenty-six years old then. Why wait to tell me now?"

"It wasn't the moment. And your father, he isn't well, Jean. *This* is what I wanted to tell you. He's had—I don't know how much you know—several what they call ministrokes, no one even knows how many. Some of them symptomatically the same as a stroke stroke but not supposed to do any lasting damage. So they say this week. You know Dad. He's not going to make an announcement. And he's going to ignore it as long as possible. Practically deaf and he won't *consider* a hearing aid. But to answer your question, I didn't tell you at the time because, well, you had your own difficulties. Your pregnancy— with the prewhatchamacallit."

"Preeclampsia."

"Right. I just didn't think you needed that information. I know how close you are to your father."

There was a long pause during which Phyllis combed through her bag, looking for her eyedrops. Jean continued to let the silence between them weigh as she watched her mother finger each eye in turn and deposit her tears.

"You mean you felt humiliated," Jean said at last.

"Well, it wasn't a barrel of laughs, you're not wrong there."

Another longish silence. Phyllis wiped her eyes with the back of a spotted hand. Peccadillo, ministroke, all quite harmless and unlikely to lead to minideath, Jean thought—and then she remembered that this was, according to Mark, the French term for orgasm: *le petit mort*. But she'd turn away from his mental universe—how was Dad really? How was Phyllis? Jean wondered if she had, maybe unconsciously, used eyedrops to cover any natural tears she didn't want her to see.

"I guess I should thank you. I know you were trying to be protective."

"Well, yes. But truth be told, we were just getting through. And frankly it was before the age—or before *my* age—when *talking* about something seemed like any kind of help. I hardly knew what hit me, and then, suddenly, it was all decided and there was no . . . recourse. Almost like I wasn't even there."

Jean thought this might be an invitation to speak out about her own marriage, though she wasn't ready for that either. "I don't mean this as a complaint, Mom, but you know, for Marianne and me, it might actually have been better to think there was a *reason*."

"There's always a reason, Jeannie."

They crossed wooden bridges and cobbled walkways, and before long they met a large tortoise, uncaged and untethered, its wrinkly neck the only indication of its vast age. The rounded shell was like a toy car big enough to sit in, not so much standing still as parked.

"They live to be something like a hundred and twenty years old," Jean said, unconsciously putting her hand to her own throat, touching the fold in the loosening skin where, she often thought, standing in front of the mirror, the frown line between her eyes had now reached—a facial bifurcation gradually extending like some new section of highway. When she'd first spotted this groove, she considered how next it would supply her first marked cleavage, and eventually she'd be fully traced down the middle and easy to snap in half, like a dried-out wishbone.

"The trick is to not move at all, is that it?" Phyllis said.

"Maybe you should recommend that in one of your columns, Jeannie: Don't move, and live forever."

Phyllis was suddenly in high spirits, perhaps relieved to be unburdened at last of her secret. She was wearing an Easter-bright twinset, obviously bought for the trip. Even her skin looked different—some new self-tanning product? Surely she'd have known about a face-lift, Jean thought, absently stroking her old brown skirt, one Mark particularly disliked, made from a fabric like milled granola—more proof that clothes don't matter.

New clothes, special creams, possible face-lift: Jean wondered if all this worried effort had begun with Bill's affair. That's what it did to people, forced them to unpick and unravel themselves year by year until they got back to where they started in the marriage, and then begin again as they found themselves now, all squiggled and jangly and unsure. After the divorce Phyllis had taken her first job ever, as a docent at the American Folk Art Museum, where she was like one of those brave ladies on a naïve weather vane, arm extended, finger pointing to the horizon, tin skirt permanently rippling in the wind. Jean now saw what was expected of her: she'd not only have to endure Mark's affair but be *improved* by it.

At least Phyllis's cheerful mood made their silence companionable, though Jean sensed her mother was tiring, and she steered her toward a pair of empty benches in the shade.

Phyllis stretched fully out on one, arranged her bag for a pillow, and laid an arm across her eyes. "Just the smallest of naps. . . . You won't sneak off and leave me if I doze awhile, will you?" Her mother was out before Jean could think of a reply. She claimed the companion bench, spreading her stuff along it so no one else could sit down. And then, as if in celebration of their having completed the full loop around the garden, a brilliant cloud of butterflies unfurled over them, white as the wake of a speedboat. A breathtaking sight, it reminded Jean of a different kind of day trip, more than twenty years ago, to Bayonne, New Jersey, with Larry Mond: there, too, they'd been surprised by a great lather of butterflies churning over a field of yellow flowers.

She hadn't mentioned, during Phyllis's update on Larry the night before, that she'd bumped into him not so long ago—about two weeks before they decamped for St. Jacques. That last chunk of London time had been filled with unremitting errands, back-to-back chores of the deadliest kind, jobs that Vic undertook but also Jean, head down, as a fair price for her great escape. It was on one such day, a rainy December afternoon, burdened by still more of Mark's exotic suits, that she'd been astonished to find Larry at the Paradise dry cleaner in Parkway.

Two identical dark blue jackets over his arm, that's what she noticed first—because they were so much more sober than Mark's—and on the other arm a brown trench coat, limp and heavy as roadkill. Unnerved, even considering a quick escape, she glanced out the storefront window at the busy street, people jogging and darting, holding newspapers and plastic bags up for shelter from a sudden downpour. Damn, no umbrella. Larry wasn't looking at her load, but staring straight at her, waiting for her to pay attention.

"*Jean.*"

"Larry!"

"I can't believe I'm seeing you here—today. It's absolutely incredible."

"Really? I wish it were. I seem to spend all my time in here. Back and forth, up and down Parkway, in and out of the Paradise, every day." Jean wondered, as she did every time she saw him, about the color of those eyes. Sapphire blue? Maine-lake blue? No, a color represented nowhere else in nature.

"Really. You see, just this morning, well, I was thinking about you when I woke up."

"You were?"

"Yeah. . . . And then, when I went out to get the papers, I remembered I had a dream about you last night."

"You did?"

"Uh-huh. You were wearing a kind of nightgown and holding a funny little posy of wildflowers, and you had a daisy chain or some buttercups in a wreath around your head, and—forgive me, you must think I'm completely nuts—you were walking toward me like Persephone recovered from the depths, with that sweet nearsighted look of yours, growing accustomed to the glare. Across a meadow, with lots of butterflies dancing around, do you remember?"

"*Remember?* I wasn't actually there. I don't think. I would've remembered that. Definitely. But, yes, I do remember the butterflies. . . . Anyway, how on earth are you? What are you doing here? Why aren't you in Princeton?"

"I can't believe I'm seeing you."

"Well . . . here I am. Much the same—from the inside, anyway. Only blinder. A lot blinder. Are you teaching?"

"Yes, here you are. . . . And, yes, I'm teaching—or giving some talks. At UCL—the Bentham Lectures. They gave me digs not far from here. . . . I'd forgotten this was your patch."

Jean had worked as a paralegal in New York after her last year at St. Hilda's, having promised her mother a summer at home: a cooling-off period, Jean understood, prescribed to treat her growing attachment to Mark. "You never know," was all Phyllis said, even if Jean thought she did know. Primarily out of love for her father—whose initials, WWW, long before they'd become a byword for easy access to the entire known, unknown, and unknowable world, had looked to her like the private airwaves connecting them—she'd gone to work in his law office. There she'd been assigned to Larry Mond: thirty years old and already a partner. But she'd seen him before. Her first term at Oxford had been his last and as a visiting lecturer he'd given such a compelling series of talks ("Taking Liberties") that she'd done her Special Paper in his field, ethics.

So it had been somewhat surprising, in the summer of 1980, to find him in New York hunched over one particular third-party litigation. A group of shipyard workers was suing a cigarette manufacturer for the dramatically amplified effects of workplace asbestos when combined with smoke inhalation, a lethal mix not only known but also concealed, their lawyers argued, by both the cigarette manufacturer and the tobacco company that owned it. Bill Warner's firm, and specifically Larry, represented the tobacco company. On the thirty-third floor of Rockefeller Center, in the wood-paneled, air-conditioned offices of Dexter, Warner and Whipple, the plaintiffs were known as the Dirtbags—Larry's own joke about his role as the workers' determined foe.

He had weekly lunches with the tobacco crew, southerners come up to the big city to see this mess through and keep an eye on the young attorney. They were good old boys with bear hugs and beer guts, midlevel managers on expenses who liked their Jack Daniel's and didn't care who knew it. Every Friday, they'd take Larry to the Autopub, a grotto on Fifth Avenue and Fifty-eighth with booths designed to look like classic cars.

When he returned to the office, Larry would perch on the corner of Jean's desk and tell her which car they'd sat in that week. He'd be a little drunk—it was Friday, after all, and this was definitely *work*—and his imitations delighted her: the childish collapse of a big-chinned smile, the perplexed bunching of a forehead, how they raised their upper lips to signal incomprehension and bared tobacco-stained teeth when he had to explain, once again, why he couldn't use the dirt they'd dug up on the Dirtbags' wives. . . .

And though she was laughing when she said it, one afternoon she told him that he couldn't have all the fun, and the next week she went with him. Soon they were both looking forward to Fridays, when at the end of lunch one of the managers would open the car door at the end of the table for Jean and ask, as she slid across: "What's a pretty little lady like you doing in a nasty business like lawyerin'?" She had privately asked herself the same question, but what she always said was that they should let her know if there were any openings in tobacco.

In this romantic and parentally blessed setting, one afternoon Jeannie Warner had gone undercover with Larry to document with a foot-long lens and without her father's knowledge the asbestos situation in the long-shut boatyard over in New Jersey. Through holes in the ceiling they had seen a mattress-thick insulation of solid asbestos: sufficiently toxic, as Larry would argue in court, to make a nicotine habit irrelevant. For the recce to the old shipyard, Jean had a fake name. Though she could remember hers (Debbie Ackerman), she'd never had to use it, this name he'd protectively given her, in case they were caught trespassing.

He was uneasy about being at the yard, and even more so about representing tobacco interests, but as a lawyer he'd do his best to win. Jean had thought her father might be testing his strength of mind, like the king in a fairy tale who sets obstacles for the suitor seeking his daughter's hand. He couldn't *assume* that Larry's crushing the Dirtbags would guarantee her love, but he was completely confident of at least one outcome, and so it would prove: the Dirtbags lost their case.

After the evidence was duly photographed, Larry had torn his shirt climbing over a chain-link fence. He'd pulled the shirt off over his head to examine the damage and, Jean supposed, to show her his chest. He thinks he's plain so he works on his body, that's what she thought when she saw it, touched by the surprise insecurity and duly impressed. He put it back on and they walked silently to the car, Larry's ripped shirttails billowing out behind him like raggedy wings, glowing in the late-afternoon sun. It was then that the butterflies appeared: white froth over the field of flowering rye, just beyond where they'd parked. A lifetime later, Jean stood before him under a load of her husband's suits and remembered the excitement of that summer afternoon in New Jersey, also the day she somehow and incontrovertibly knew she could never be a lawyer.

"Whatever happened to the Dirtbags?" she blurted, forgetting to ask after his wife.

Though she couldn't be entirely sure, she thought that before answering he'd let out a little yelp. "Oh, they're good. They're great!" Still maneuvering the suits, Larry crossed his arms and widened his stance, rolling onto the outsides of his feet.

The Dirtbags are good? They're *great*? But Jean was already too distracted to seize on his unexpected reply. American men stand like that, even our intellectuals, she thought, legs far apart to make themselves approachably shorter and to show they're not about to rush off. Mark, tall as he was, neither spread his legs nor stooped. He didn't have a listener's stance. He kept his hands like tent pegs plunged deep in his pockets, and bounced on the balls of his feet while he was talking, as if in danger of springing up and away at any moment. "Never apologize, never explain" was his motto, the opposite of her own.

Jean tried to listen, watching Larry's lips move, afraid she wouldn't catch what he was saying; but she loved that American accommodation Mark had to mock; in fact, was suddenly high with love as if she'd been inhaling it along with these cleaning chemicals, even though she recognized it might only be something *like* love—a loose patriotism, maybe, or homesickness. Her mind was sprinting, trying to rein in a childishly skipping heart before it bounced into dangerous traffic, while Larry kept talking, still rolling onto the fillets of his outer soles.

"Joe's at Wesleyan; Rebecca, the other twin, she's taking a year off, volunteering for Doctors Without Borders. Looks like she may be sent to Monrovia—worrying. Now Jenny, if you can believe it, Jen'll graduate from Concord Academy in the spring. . . ."

Apparently—no, unmistakably—he thought she'd been asking about his children. Jean realized that he'd told his wife about the Dirtbags and that, in affectionate insult, the name had become family code for their kids. After all, hadn't she and Mark called Vic the Rat, the Grub, the Nit, and (when it became clear she was going to be tall) the Runt, and not just Petal, or Flower, and Pie? And when Larry told Mrs. Larry— Jean couldn't remember her name, the girl who'd replaced her at the firm—about the original Dirtbags and his heroic role in discovering, right over where the Dirtbags labored, more than enough asbestos to exonerate the tobacco companies, did he also, she wondered, tell her about Jean? Had he told her about teaching Jean to dance the *vallenato* in the conference room— the nine weeks of close but tensely technical instruction in the tricky wrong-footing of this dance that he'd picked up during his American Field Service year in Colombia, and the confusing distraction in that long room of his clean citrusy smell while everyone else took their lunch down to the plaza and sat, dangling their legs over the ice rink that was, just for the summer, a café?

She'd last seen Larry ten years ago, at her father's retirement dinner in New York. And just as she had when she sat next to him at that dinner, Jean found herself wondering what might've happened if she'd lived all these years where Larry lived instead of where Mark lived. With what seemed to her a Herculean effort, shielded by the steamed-up storefront of the dry cleaner, they managed to exchange some news. Before the Bentham Lectures he'd given a seminar at Oxford, though he was still notionally attached to the firm and went back and forth to New York.

"I thought you were at Princeton," Jean ventured again.

"I moved to Columbia a few years ago, though the house is there, of course, and Melanie—" Now Jean remembered: his wife worked at the university press. He was keener to talk about his new book. He'd wanted to send it to her but didn't know where to mail it. *A Theory of Equality;* she'd buy a copy. No, he'd mail her one, what was her address? He was the first person she knew who'd heard of St. Jacques. In fact he was better informed about it than she was.

Larry knew she was married to Mark Hubbard, pronouncing this as if it was a widely admired brand name, which it wasn't, not quite. So she understood that with nothing else to build on, he was approving her choice, and this flummoxed her. Larry asked and she answered; he talked and she listened. She wanted to ask him twenty other things, but also, and urgently, she wanted to get away. He didn't try to stop her when she backed out of the Paradise into the rain, nearly stumbling onto the pavement, Mark's suits sliding on her arm.

Down the block, she ducked into the other dry cleaner, Blenheim and Blouson—which Mark called Stain 'Em and Lose 'Em—and she started hating herself. Why had she run out like that? Why couldn't she go back and say how about a coffee? She hadn't noticed that young woman when she came in—she was staring at Jean. Plumping her rain-flattened hair, Jean guessed she must look especially, even alarmingly, bedraggled.

Attachment

The woman, who had long stringy hair not unlike Victoria's and the lowest blink rate Jean had ever consciously registered, looked as if she was about to speak, or sneeze, or burst into tears.

"You do not know me," she said to Jean, who immediately gave the only possible reply. "Of *course* I do." Her pupils were dilated, glassy, as if she was on medication.

"I am Sophie," she said.

"Of course you are," Jean answered, having completely and obviously failed, despite the heavy French accent, to recognize Sophie de Vilmorin, the daughter of Mark's famous first love.

Christ, she thought, it's dangerous getting your clothes cleaned in Camden Town. There was still another dry cleaner around the corner, Jeeves, the expensive one. And which maximally taxing acquaintance would she find in there? Mrs. H., up from Oxford for the day? Or her editor, Edwin fishlips Mackay, baldly spying on her, away from her desk?

"How *are* you, my dear?" she asked, squeezing Sophie's thin shoulder, trying to make her feel better, almost moved that she seemed so hurt not to be recognized. Good God, she looked awful, nervous and waxy, her skin like plasticene. Probably a vegan, Jean thought, incredulously calculating that she must be in her thirties already. Jean remembered a charming, gamine girl of around eighteen. And here was this staring creature with hair that looked as if it had never been cut. Something generally unstable about her. It was the middle of December and she wasn't wearing a coat.

They talked as the day outside darkened with the promise of still more rain and the man behind the counter searched for Sophie's lost shirt, stabbing blindly like a fruit picker with his forked pole into the high branches of hanging clothes. Or rather Jean talked and the young woman listened, occasionally rubbing her eyes. She told the iron-starved Sophie about their imminent move to St. Jacques, situating it for her on the map while taking in her bony frame, the reddened nose and chewed fingers, positive she hadn't had a period in *years*, scattering a few facts about the island economy she'd just learned from Larry.

The rain showed no sign of easing as Sophie, shivering and empty-handed (her shirt unrecovered), headed for the door. Jean reached out to touch her and made Sophie promise, without offering a specific date, "absolutely and without fail" to come by for a drink before they left.

"You are so kind." A look of alarm crossed her wan little face. "If you're sure Mark will not be sorry?"

"Sorry! I'm sure he'll be delighted to see you again, as will I." Poor Sophie, she thought, as awkward and fragile as a fallen hatchling. Relieved to be alone, she at last pushed her damp load across the counter, knowing she might as well dump it right into an incinerator. She was unsettled by Sophie de Vilmorin. If something was seriously wrong, maybe it wasn't such a great idea to invite her over. What if she was crazy? No coat, and no shirt either, as the dry cleaner insisted. Had she followed Jean inside just to talk to her, the lost laundry ticket a fabrication? Every now and then she made this kind of mistake, getting drawn into intimate correspondence with a troubled reader. . . . She wanted to rewind now, and take shelter in the earlier, nicer surprise of the afternoon: Larry, with his grace of movement and that steady blue gaze that beamed his entire, focused intelligence straight into you. She could be persuaded she'd only dreamed him, wearing—what was it? A nightgown and crown of weeds.

How could you leave her alone in London at this vulnerable age?" Phyllis asked, standing erect, fists on hips, clearly refreshed. Her question, possibly prompted by the sight of a couple kissing right on the same bench as her dozing daughter, jolted Jean out of her reverie, and for a moment she thought she was asking about Sophie de Vilmorin. But instead Phyllis was "concerned"—that is, accusatory—about Victoria. "Who's looking after her?" Jean knew it was useless to say Vic didn't need looking after, that Victoria had always looked after *them*. She only rallied with the next concern. "How on earth did Victoria become so interested in communism? Do you think maybe it's a reaction to the kind of work Mark does—contriving to sell people a whole lot of stuff they don't need?"

"Marxism, not communism," Jean said, ignoring the attack on Mark, and not bothering to ask how long Phyllis would last without her refrigerator. She'd made the mistake earlier in the day of mentioning a Marxism seminar Vic had been particularly stimulated by, which belatedly set Phyllis off. This was new, the way she could be *launched* at any time by a detail she then would not let go of. Jean knew exactly what her mother was worried about—the scruffy sort of boys Victoria would meet in such courses. Just like Phyllis to have it all ways: Mark's capitalism was filthy and unworthy; Vic's "communism" a desperate fate.

"Victoria is wonderfully attuned to every kind of social injustice, exactly as one should be at nineteen," Jean said. "She's switched to anthropology and sociology—she's really found her subject. Or subjects. I couldn't be more pleased. And what, may I ask, is wrong with Marxism?"

She couldn't believe she'd started down this road. She might as well push her mother into the lily pond, if they could ever find it. But there was no stopping now. "The Marxists are great theorists. The analysis is right. It's just the solution that's always wrong. . . ." She thought of her searching conversations on the subject with Victoria who, as it happened, had trouble with the same distinctions. "Oh, forget it," Jean said, petulant. She immediately regretted losing her cool, though her mother's downcast eyes and compressed lips suggested she thought she'd lost that some time ago. Possibly when she gave up law. All that education and then—nothing. Phyllis couldn't understand it. Imagine telling her mother she'd just been daydreaming, at extraordinarily detailed length, about her favorite lawyer. Marry Larry—Phyllis's silent command that long-ago summer. Jean walked and her mother followed, leaving behind the indifferent couple still conjoined at the lips, until they found the lily pond.

Enormous round leaves with raised edges like trays dotted the green surface. Mother and daughter watched bubbles rising to the surface, a frog or a fish, or, Jean liked to think, underwater waiters—and on their trays, proudly delivered up, the glory of the tropics, the great water lily of the Amazon. Jean bent and squinted, to read: VICTORIA AMAZONICA.

"Hey!" they said in unison, exchanging a rare look of complicity, and headed for the exit.

That evening, Mark took Phyllis and Jean out for dinner at

the Royal Palm, the best hotel on the island, but not, therefore, one devoid of a steel band. Their table was near the moonlit dance floor, and so the three of them sat and watched, Phyllis air-tapping a tiny foot—no question of Mark dancing with either of them. But he'd danced with Giovana, Jean knew (recklessly, gaily), hence the "Ginger." On many St. Jacques nights the betrayal of *dancing* burned most bitterly of all as she lay rigid with sleeplessness on the cliff edge of her side of the bed, listening to whole congregations of frogs in the puddles outside, chiming and pinging through the dark hours just like a steel band. Why was the dancing such an affront? Because he didn't dance, and therefore, all these many years, neither had she. Ginger even boasted about sambas and tangos. Come *on*.

Jean leapt up from the table—the ladies' room, she pleaded. In the dim hotel garden she passed a kissing couple, one she'd seen earlier on the dance floor, a beautiful young woman in an asymmetrical blue dress and a much older man. Of course, the Royal Palm was a very expensive place, catering to old French couples who had to get through their money and to pairs like this one pressed up against a palm tree—hardly a consoling sight for Jean. She turned back to the dining terrace. Did Mark take Giovana to fancy hotels? Did he then pretend in the elevator that he didn't know her? Did he buy her overpriced presents from the lobby shops and tell the salesgirls they were for his wife? Or didn't people bother with that anymore? Nowadays it seemed more likely that, for a mere lunch break in the Presidential Suite, the salesgirls might themselves become recipients of these shiny trinkets. Anyone could, anyone but a wife.

As a matter of survival, Jean started each day of Phyllis's visit with a run along the road. She avoided the gym in Toussaint:

too close to the Internet café. But one week into this routine, Jean found herself driving into town. Not trusting her daughter to have the basics, Phyllis had packed a nontravel hairdryer along with a five-pound transformer, but to no avail. She fretted for days under a halo of humidity-generated frizz before Jean took pity on her and brought her in to see Aminata. Later, Mark would pick Phyllis up and take her out on the boat belonging to the American who ran the Bamboo Bar. Jean, desperate for a day off, hadn't wanted to point out that her hair would of course be reruined.

She headed straight for the Internet café and settled in to look at her readers' letters and to check the joint account. There was a business e-mail from France for Mark (*À l'attention de M. Hubbard*), a notice from Amazon and another from e-Bay, no word from Victoria. With nothing worth opening, she signed out.

And then, absolutely determined not to open Naughtyboy1, Jean reached for the next best thing: real pornography—the world behind Thing 2. *Research,* Jean told herself, the most reassuring word in the dictionary. She logged on purposefully, beginning at the only site she could come up with, Playboy.com.

Settling in for a good look, Jean was impressed, above all, by the hard work that went into being wanted. It reminded her of sixth-grade preening and posturing and parading in the cafeteria, often by girls who were pretty and already popular but still had this unaccountable *drive,* though she suspected it was the formerly not-so-popular girls who were putting in the real man-hours.

She gravitated to the amateur sites where she supposed she had to place Giovana, among the other would-be actresses and models—along with housewives and students and travel agents and caterers, swimming instructors, accountants, productsafety inspectors, as well, she had no doubt, as lawyers, posing in bad lighting on half-made beds, squeezing breasts together as directed, peeking up from lowered heads or down through hooded eyes, generally looking evil or sedated. Occasionally there was a hairy arm at the edge of the picture, presumably the husband or boyfriend, positioning this woman, his prize pig at the county fair, her flesh oozing like melted cheese over too-tight mail-order bodices. Cheesy piglets. In fact, these images gave her just the uncomfortable feeling she had whenever she saw pictures of animals dressed in clothes or performing in a circus.

None of us has any idea how we look, she thought, and particularly not, for obvious reasons, from behind. The one other thing you could safely say about the amateurs was that they were all optimists. Giovana's pictures looked more professional than these, Jean noted, confirming her hunch that her correspondent was a working model, probably doing catalogs for "full-size" ladies—with the distant dream of Page Three. Mark met these girls all the time during auditions for new campaigns. She wasn't even a runner-up, but he'd taken her number, "just in case." He often worked closely on an ad, in quiet conference with a bevy of stylists and whichever ponytailed ego they were using as a photographer. Sitting here examining the images people put on the Internet all by themselves, for the first time she appreciated those stylists.

Jean ordered a ham sandwich before the owner—he was also the cashier, cook, and cleaner—stepped out, leaving her alone in her corner. And she went on looking, either for the variety she herself now craved, or because she still hadn't cracked why anyone—Mark, say—should really need a constant supply of fresh material. Hadn't people done just fine with one battered magazine passed like the town slut from hand to hand? But now they had to contend with a gallery of new girls, a roster, a harem, a yearbook of new faces, *every day*. And with this relentless variety, why the samey feel? Real difference—along with noninadvertent humor—was elusive. While you can marvel at the supposedly endless range and specialization of human need and human want, Jean thought, in the end the physical possibilities are pretty limited.

Maybe pornography was like the bullfight. The first stage might be mesmerizing, upsetting, with scattered moments of surprising grace, each in turn or all at once. Yet by stage three you're looking at your watch and wondering if you should stay just because your seats are so good. Jean knew she didn't have much to go on, but she thought that however predictable or disappointing the experience might be, no one in real life yawned like a hippo halfway through. Why *was* it so boring, and how in the world could it be boring and arousing at the same time? Perhaps because porno couldn't be tender? Actually, she thought it could, if, like her, you constantly wondered how these girls got themselves into this mess in the first place—a generic sympathy she rarely extended to Giovana.

Still, and these viewings confirmed it, Giovana remained for her a porn star apart. Jean was like a parent at a school play, exclusively interested in this one performer. And not because she had more to offer than a lot of other exhibitionists. No, she thought, only Giovana could shock because she wasn't an actress. Her faking was for real—and it was all for Mark, a fact that not only continued to hurt Jean, but that also now confused her as she found, disagreeably, unmistakably, neglectedly, that she was *jealous,* and not of Giovana.

Soon she would sign out; first, a last little tour, skipping the gruesome S-and-M stuff, which—and this was at least something—she felt sure wouldn't have anything to tell her about Mark. So: there *were* specialist sites featuring women who'd retained their pubic hair. And there was a more widespread fetish, Jean was glad to see, for "mature" women. But she soon discovered that this didn't mean older women or experienced women but, rather, desperate women. (She imagined the geriatric journal she subscribed to changing its name accordingly: *Modern Desperation*.) Then she found the MILFs, Moms-I'd-Like-to-Fuck, and though at least these weren't the producers' own moms, she was still disappointed that the moms in question were barely out of training bras.

Jean was just thinking that they never accounted for cold in pornography when, with delicious serendipity, she stumbled on a Norwegian product, set in a winter wonderland that hung suggestively with opalescent icicles. A giant blonde dressed only in fur boots was draped over the balcony of a snowcapped chalet, poised to lick an icicle, transported not by hypothermia but rapture, apparently unconcerned that her tongue might get stuck to it. In need of the lifeline of comedy, Jean wondered how she herself might feature. Working at her desk in her birthday suit? Or spinning lettuce at the kitchen sink wearing nothing except flip-flops—thongs for the feet. But she realized she'd merely look like an outtake from some documentary about a German nudist colony: a cure for sex.

She found nothing here to help her with Mark; there was no fit. How could that be, since Giovana was so unmistakably rooted in all this? What did Giovana do that wasn't done better at Superboobs.com, at Asstastic.com, Farmgirls.com, Golden shower.com, or by the indentured youth at www.lilteens? The answer, Jean realized, was this: Mark's Giovana-featuring productions were, like all his other work, funny—childish, prankish, but somehow witty, and *light*. Whereas with this stuff, it seemed to Jean, the thread was hatred—always humorless—whatever else it pretended to be about: men determined to con and dupe, to corral and harness. Head 'em up and move 'em out. The format was as reliable as any Western—the cowboys using not only the good-hearted whores and sultry señoritas but also the Indians, the horses, the cattle, and sometimes even the faithful little dog.

Jean signed out. She didn't believe that turning away could restore her to a state of innocence or, for that matter, get rid of Giovana, with whom she had so incongruously and enthusiastically grappled. But at least she'd learned something—that she'd had enough.

She was looking for her car keys and called out to check on how ready Phyllis was. Totally ready; it was Jean who was searching for her sunglasses now, and where was the good map? These two weeks felt like a month. Time to go to the airport.

To her amazement, her mother seemed to count the visit a perfect success and in the car was brimming with praise for all things Jean—her house, her island, even her *hair*. As Phyllis herself might say, Who'd a thunk it? They tooled along the red road, ticking off the highlights: the botanical garden for sure, the Baie des Anges, but best of all, the Beausoleil Captive Breeding Center, where Jean had made a date to go back and interview the director, Bruce McGhee, about his plans to release all the kestrels into the wild. She'd never forget feeding that runty bird—what was his name, Bud?—and was determined to write about it, but not for Mackay. *Mrs* readers wouldn't take an interest in extinction unless it was unfolding on Exmoor.

She'd held out a dead white mouse on her flattened palm, like an apple offered to a horse. And as with her first up-close pony at age six, she'd been nervous, had wanted to toss or at least *dangle* the bait. A tail, a stem—who's to say that's not what they're for? The horse with his smoker's teeth had rewarded her stillness with a gummy tickle that had given her a first idea of what kissing a boy might be like. And here, forty years on, with the same palm outstretched as if for fortune-telling, she'd again stood still. The bird swooped: the brown wings, speckled white body and bright black eye, and a ripple of air no greater than from a baby yawning—then the almost imperceptible caress of talons on her hand as the kestrel took the mouse, bore it off, lifting up and out of sight.

While Phyllis looked out the car window, committing the island to memory, Jean imagined how she'd soon hug her and then wave at her in the window of the small plane, how she'd stand on the runway still waving as the wind of the propeller flattened and then raised and then flattened her hair, giving the lie, and comically, to Phyllis's praise. When the little plane was finally out of sight Jean would walk, no, she would stride over to the rental car, the late sun on her shoulders, and treat herself by not returning it today, or even tomorrow. On the way home her spirits instead of sinking would continue to rise.

In the event, it wasn't quite like this. Driving back, she saw the women's clinic ahead and remembered that she'd never picked up her mammogram results. Surely they'd have called her if there was anything wrong, but it was too infantile not to go in and collect them. As she crossed the waiting room, jangling her keys to dispel the silence, the formerly cool nurse rose and came around from behind the reception desk to greet her. It seemed they'd been trying to contact her—hadn't she gotten the letter? Jean registered a brief surge of nausea.

Handing over the wobbly manila envelope containing her X-rays, the nurse explained that the mammogram was unsatisfactory—or did she mean inconclusive? They recommended *une échographie*. Jean had difficulty taking in this information and not only because of her French. I'm being handled, she thought. Smiling pastoral care. They know something they're not telling me. Though she wasn't quite clear what an *échographie* was, like a docile heifer to the slaughterhouse she booked an appointment, and left.

Jean wasn't entirely surprised—why else hadn't she stopped in for her results? And she could now admit to herself the conviction she'd suppressed, that there *was* something there, on her right side. Not a lump, exactly, but a change in texture, as if deep therein lodged a scrap of . . . cheap mattress foam. Back on the ring road, she wondered if by her inaction she'd already decided this was a stray shred of foam, a lost bit of packing peanut that she could live with, or around. Maybe it would dissolve with exercise, or worry. Or grief.

Jean's hands ached from her grip on the steering wheel. Dread settled in her stomach like a brick that no army of enzymes could dent, going at it with their worst acids, every digestive pickax and drill. And it told her she was, apparently, being evicted. Not from the house, or even from her marriage, but from the island.

The harsh light hurt her eyes, and sunglasses only seemed to introduce a burning contrast at the edges. Every bloom looked garish: the orange flamboya tree, the purple jacaranda, the fuchsia bougainvillea, red-orifice hibiscus, the gardenia stink bomb, the obscene anthurium. Even her favorite, the pale blue plumbago, seemed to overreach itself, crawling in everywhere it wasn't wanted. She pined for a plain pot of hardy geraniums, suburban blue hydrangea, a tidy vase of odorless tulips. Instead, all around her, the full, indifferent jungle pressed in. Everything smelled either putrid or chokingly sweet.

She may as well turn right around and motor straight back to the airport, she thought, because all of a sudden she couldn't stop things from looking ugly—like the garbage all along the road. And as she knew from her walks with Phyllis, the more beautiful the place, the more trash people tossed there. The Black River Gorges had great heaps of it, specially carted in. She'd taken Phyllis down the trail, and soon she'd been pointing up at fictional birds, anything to distract her mother not only from the garbage, but from the carpet of used condoms covering the path like confetti on a church walk.

Jean swerved to avoid hitting a dog. Death-wish dogs near death already, they littered the island. It was a common sight, the mutt hit and then left on the road to die, rolled out like cookie dough as drivers flattened it in two directions, until it wore away altogether. Nobody valued anything here. Families tramped out into the woods and chopped down a tree for firewood—so that the big rains that came every year brought floods and mud slides, every year. Images of whole settlements whisked off their toothpick moorings occasionally caught the attention of a foreign television crew or a foreign aid agency, but nobody planted more trees.

She passed through a cluster of food stands and patchwork shacks. If St. Jacques was rejecting her, she thought—experimentally, defensively—she'd do the same. Look at these people, just sitting on the curb scratching their heads and pulling on their earlobes, dumbly turning to watch her drive past, people with luck so bad it must be deserved. But it didn't work. Jean was miserable; she thought all she could ever want was to be allowed to stay on as before, unsingled-out.

How could she forgive Mark *this,* the unfixable lost love affair with paradise itself, her island no longer a haven and a home but a quarantine—hadn't it actually been a leper colony at one time?—and so far from *home* home, far from Victoria, and her own doctor. Mark had so comprehensively uprooted their lives, with Jean idiotically following—never mind the broken connection she was experiencing now, loosened but not severed, no luxury of drama here, no mud slide, no television crew; just a regular, entirely foreseeable mistake. But going back and undoing the damage, this wasn't going to be a simple detour with a clear price, like returning the rental car a week late.

Forty minutes of fast driving and Jean came to the market spread across a large clearing by the road. On an impulse she pulled over, just for a moment. She stepped out of the car and breathed deeply, surveying the scene: swarms of shoppers and vendors, with their fortifications of rolled rugs and tilted coffers of ground spices, pulverized remedies for everything from *echauffage*, overheating, to "oppression." Women steamed stuffed leaves, their gums bloodred from betel nut; boys pushed cartfuls of sliced jelly and blue coconut cakes; men roasted entrails over low fires in the middle of the street. Jean knew why she was drawn to this riot of sensations—for the bodies other than her own.

Beside her stood the only covered section of the market, on stilts, above this teeming life. And it was teeming death. Whole animals swung from iron hooks in the meat market, thick with sensuality and rot. Every corner of this longhouse had an entrance, at the top of a rickety wooden staircase, each door marked by a sign for illiterates that showed a single painted image: goat, cow, fish, fowl. So, she thought, utterly desolate, here, as everywhere, you had to follow the correct flow—go out of the building and down the steps and then up again to reenter by the proper door if it was some other creature you were after. Before you could begin, you had to know how you'd end. You had to know what you wanted. Head-down buying: humorlessly pointing, *bargaining*. This was a tug-of-war—the very thing she couldn't bring herself to do.

That's what was wrong with her, she realized—apart, of course, from her riddled corpus. There beside the longhouse it struck her, trying not to inhale the stench of rotting flesh. It wasn't just her own decay. Or her shyness. It was not knowing what she wanted. Wanting not to know: this, it turned out, was not enough. You couldn't treat a disease, you couldn't make someone love you, you couldn't get around the Internet and its infinity of filth, you couldn't be useful to your child, you couldn't even buy dinner, not without knowing what you wanted. What happened to feeling your way? What happened to things just as they were, to not going to the gym and *not* rearranging the furniture, which had worked for everyone's ancestors for centuries, until now? This was all gone.

She hurried back to the car, pursued by an old woman selling prawns from a bucket. Just to get rid of her, Jean bought the lot, and back on the road she thought once more, This is what's wrong with you—and what, she guessed, was right with Giovana. The clarity of purpose. She wondered how much time she had left. She'd read about it—she'd even written about it—how suddenly it could strike you, a matter of weeks. Forget the *échographie*, whatever the hell stopgap measure that was. She was desperate to get rid of her breasts, not that she expected excision or mastectomy to work. You could chop down the tree, but the roots remained below, with their ever-extending reach; a destiny courtesy of the St. Jacques Ministry of Health—the antique X-ray and the inexperienced eye—as you had only to expect on an outpost island in an outpost ocean.

Three months: she couldn't bear to think what kind of difference to her life span it might have made if she'd collected her results straightaway. There was no more time to waste. She had to become more like her rival, and more like Mark. He, too, had always known what he wanted. He was already specialized when she met him. There he was in Crime and Thriller, while she gazed over the long rows of General Release—Drama, Period, Romantic Comedy.

That night Jean passed out in the bath and had to be helped to bed, wrapped by Mark in the shroud of his blue robe. When she woke, twelve hours later, he was standing beside her holding a mug of milky tea.

"Tragic nap?" he asked sweetly (in his habits of speech Mark enjoyed compression even more than exaggeration: the twelve-hour "nap"). She could only nod assent and obediently sip, nursing the cup in two hands, and when he left her to go back to work, she looked down at her partially exposed breasts—still there, showing nothing . . . they were all such good little liars now. Farther down, she saw that her body was imprinted with a diamond pattern from the waffle weave of the fabric, like a fishnet catsuit.

In the bathroom, Jean judged that sleep, or dehydration, was working in her favor: she looked firmer than she would later in the day, as if she'd spent the night in a big woman-shaped Jell-O mold and her form had settled and temporarily solidified. Gravity would bag it out again and, hours later, the fishnet would still be there, but it would hold nothing in. No more holding in and no more springing back. And even as she had this thought—just the kind of cold-eyed, womanly observation that made her the mass-read health writer she was—she realized it, too, would have to be revised, through the prism of gratitude that was contingent on major illness.

Mark, belted into what he called his dressy dressing gown of patterned vintage rayon—a gift from Victoria—had spent the entire morning in the small study, working on the campaign for that line of nostalgic appliances: rotund ovens and fridges. He was stumped. In St. Jacques *all* appliances looked like this, but they were painstakingly maintained antiques, not winking retro. Sitting with coffee, Jean watched him go in and out of the fridge three times for beer, and it wasn't yet lunchtime.

"What are you doing now?" she asked, as if she couldn't see. Dan would be calling to go over the pitch in less than an hour.

"Making a proper drink," he said, defiant. "Dark rum, a splash of our favored cane, a squeeze of lime, a spriglet of mint, and two heaping tablespoons of vanilla sugar—nectar of the gods."

But Jean could see he was distracted by a bigger worry— and she hadn't even told him about the clinic. For the first time she thought it entirely possible Giovana would dump him first. Or maybe it was that he couldn't work here. Advertising was about tuning in to local mood, trends, perversions, aspirations, even weather. In fact mainly weather. People shopped to make up for weather. Of course it didn't matter what kind of fridge you had in St. Jacques, so long as it got cold enough. (So, here too, it was about weather.) He couldn't connect at a distance; he couldn't *care* enough about the shape of a refrigerator. That's what Jean saw in the upped booze consumption, Mark trying to give a shit, with consequences. His deadlines always triggered an increase. Because he didn't acknowledge stress, thinking it newfangled and possibly American, he convinced himself that pressure stirred his creative juices. But increasingly, his elaborate cocktails *were* his creative juices.

How long could they last if he couldn't work? Jean was also

having problems with her column. She couldn't write about betel nut, the local stimulant and digestive aid, because it wasn't yet available in Tesco or CVS. But what kind of health story *could* she do while she was facing down cancer? She really didn't want to write about that—like those obituaries filed years in advance. And she didn't want to talk to him about it before she decided what to do. Maybe *neither* of them could work here, she thought, spinning lettuce at the sink, spinning, spinning, spinning. Oh my God, there he was again, back in that fridge, still muttering about "these fat fucking fridges."

Jean didn't respond, just kept about her task, assembling lunch, and through the window, she spotted Christian chugging along the track. Well, at least she'd already had the horrible news from the clinic—what other surprises might he have in his bag of tricks? She followed his progress, his bob and his weave, climbing toward the house. Up here at her high command station by the kitchen window she felt like a lighthouse keeper. Jean plunged the prawns into the boiling water and watched as they turned, almost instantly, from gray to pink. That must be what it's like, she thought. Having an affair.

She was prepared to meet Christian, but Mark—clearly desperate for any interruption—beat her to it. A few minutes later he wandered back inside carrying a couple of small parcels, a large envelope—probably from the clinic. Over his head he was waving a letter. "From Vic," he said, depositing the packages on the shelf, out of the way of her lunch making. She glanced up at the first one. The minuscule handwriting was vaguely familiar but not readily identifiable. Mark frisked himself for his glasses; Jean peeled the prawns and waited. She might not tell him about the clinic at all, she thought. What perspicacity and foresight he showed, having someone lined up to comfort him and, one fine day in the not-too-distant future, to replace her. Before he got the letter out of the envelope, the phone rang.

"Shit. Dan!? Hi. Theo, that you? Connie? Is Connie on? Hang on a mo'." He covered the mouthpiece and said to Jean, "Don't wait for me. This'll take about half an hour. Unless we get cut off."

He took his beer from the counter and disappeared with the cordless phone, and the letter, into his study. Now Jean had to wait to hear Vic's news. She stood at the sink, eating a giant prawn, and thought that would be one good thing about living on her own: no more *meals*. When she took down the two packages, her equanimity, such as it was, vanished. The small handwriting would have to wait; she *knew* who'd sent the second one and it made her scalp itch. A book bag that didn't have a book in it, addressed to Mark. She studied the big block capitals, slanted backward—Giovana's unschooled hand. London postmark, no return address.

A natural nosiness in Jean had, over these stealthy months, hardened into skill, and in a glance she saw that the packet had not been taped or glued, just stapled: these could easily be reinserted. Holding it out of sight in the depths of the sink, she unpicked the light aluminum staples and placed them in a saucer on the shelf, then she reached into the bag and pulled out something hard and bubble-wrapped.

She removed the plastic and looked at the naked item that rolled into her palm, mystified. Hard purple rubber, it could be some sort of pacifier, or designer kitchen utensil. A bottle stopper, or maybe something for mixing cocktails? No doubt Mark and Giovana enjoyed their cocktails. But this was more like a teething ring, the kind you put in the freezer first. She held it up to the light to look for markings. Well, there was a ring, but too small for even a baby's hand. And protruding from one end was a thick, flattish tab, made of the same molded rubber but ribbed. An instrument of torture? Jean looked again in the bag and saw a folded sheet of instructions: *Fig. 1, pull ring down onto erect penis.* It wasn't a pacifier; it was a stimulator, for Giovana's pleasure. No, for *Jean's* pleasure. Why else had she sent it here? Just showing off, pushing the limits, as everybody knew you could with a man in thrall. A souvenir, like those underpants with the road signs? Was it *used*? She had the gizmo rewrapped and restapled and back on the shelf in under a minute. It took her longer to wash her hands, scrubbing and staring blindly through the window. When she was finished, she took the package down off the shelf and tossed it in the garbage under the sink.

She washed her hands again, still staring out the open window. Jean saw a bird of traffic-cone orange, sitting on the fence that marked the edge of the property. He was one of her regulars, and she called him Highlighter, for his fluorescent feathers. Poor creature, camouflaged nowhere, except in the bird book where she'd been unable to find a likeness. She leaned forward, holding some crumbs out through the window, urging him closer, trying to forget what she'd seen.

Jean hadn't heard Mark leave the house, but there he was now, walking toward the road. She put on her glasses for detailed viewing and saw that as he walked he held his dressing gown together with his hands, letting the belt trail behind in the dust. He'd gone to close the gate. She knew it annoyed him that Christian left it open, and that it was Christian himself who grated. She watched as he struggled to hook the wire loop over the post with one hand, still holding his robe closed. She couldn't help smiling as he tried to hold the robe closed with his elbow, to free up the other hand, now using *both* elbows. The wind had come up and lifted his hair, probably pulling at his dressing gown, too. He must be swearing his head off, she thought as he stepped back but held his robe tightly closed with his arms crossed, waiting and watching for the gate to spring open by itself, which it sometimes did. Just, he believed, to thwart him.

When Mark returned, his belt tied not in a bow but in a double knot, Jean was already sitting outside, sipping coffee. A pot on the table, a cup for him.

"We got cut off," he said. "I'm going to have to go down to the St. Jerome in an hour."

"Can we have Vic's letter first?"

"I was just coming to that," he said, pulling the envelope from his robe pocket and rummaging in the other for his rimless reading glasses. ("So much easier to lose," he'd said, "designed especially, to get it over with.") He sat down and read aloud. *"Dear Mum and Dad."* Mark immediately interrupted himself. "Thank *God* we're Mum and Dad again—I really loathed that Jean and Mark business. She probably read somewhere it makes your parents respect you more, never mind how you behave. . . ."

"Read!" said Jean.

"Dear Mum and Dad, everything here is copacetic, bodacious, and superfabulicious! Usual appalling weather not that you care! Finished my essay on Engels, the gloomy bahst. I do love that Vic has given the short for *bastard* a proper permanent spelling, don't you? Specially conceived to avoid an American pronunciation, you'll note. Now where was I? *Did you know he used to live in Primrose Hill—little known facts about gloomy bahsts. I've begun in on Max Weber. Durkheim and his anomie were good but* . . . Hmm, let's see."

"Don't skip!"

"Excellent 21st for Fiona who got at least three iPods. . . . hint, hint. *I wore my green bead dress and some really good silver shoes I*

got in the market almost new for £5. I still haven't got anything for Fi. Have you noticed how hard it is to shop ie spend money for a prezzie <u>after</u> the party?"

Mark paused to exchange a look of pleasure with Jean. *"The do was at Tramps, sad posh club in South Ken for your age crowd—Oy!—lots of lovely free drink all laid on by her dad who kept groping girls and saying sad things like 'You're as young as the woman you feel!' Poor Fiona. Yes, I have forwarded all the post to Noleen . . . Maya broke up with Gavin and has been staying at the house, which has been really good, her staying I mean. Send money ha ha. PS Mum, have you already forgotten how to e-mail?? How's life in paradise? Ex ex ex, Vic.* Well," he said, refolding the letter, "she sounds good. Really upbeat."

"Definitely something new in her tone."

"Yes, no arrows of guilt, no slings of complaint."

Jean let this pass. "Can I see it now, please?"

"Hang on. Doesn't it say, here at the end?" He unfolded the letter again, pushed his glasses up the bridge of his nose and turned it over, looking for whatever it was he'd left out. "She says she met someone. *Remember I went to the Hobsbawm lecture? Well Vikram was there and we met in the queue for the free glass of wine. I hope when you visit you'll meet him. When are you coming? El oh el. Exclamation mark.*"

"Hey, you didn't read that. Let me see it." Jean tried to snatch the letter but he held it tight to his chest. She began to complain, then stopped to watch his face change. She saw him hating the idea of Victoria with a boyfriend. He hadn't even wanted to convert it to fact by reading it out loud.

"Come on. Let's wait and see," she said. "You've been wondering all year why she hasn't got a boyfriend."

Mark looked troubled, as if he hadn't heard her. He didn't reply: he really *did* mind.

Victoria's letter was unrecognizable, not her usual tally of private grievances and public complaint (demanding friends, injustices committed against the rate payers of the great borough of Camden), nothing at all, in fact, about her feelings. And then this surprise, tacked-on ending. Jean thought she knew what the change in her was, the source of her new lightness, the awkward chattiness in the letter. She'd had sex.

Jean didn't imagine Vic was a virgin; in fact she was pretty sure she wasn't. But anything before this would count as a technicality. And so, to distract Mark, or maybe to give him something worth brooding over, she told him about her stop at the clinic.

"And I have to go back. They want to do another test—*une échographie*. That means something's wrong."

"You don't know that."

"What else can it mean?"

"They want to be sure. It's their job; that's just a sonogram. Maybe things are unclear, that's all."

"That's what I said. Something's wrong. God, I'm exhausted. I'm going to lie down for an hour." She brushed past him. Despite her huge sleep the night before, she was suddenly hit by a fatigue of gale force—the final proof, she thought, of her symptoms. She didn't want comfort, and she'd had enough of comforting *him*.

Jean sat on the bed, taking off her earrings—fat silver stars, a present from Vic. She took off her Moroccan silver beads, the only jewelry of hers Victoria coveted, and as she rolled them in her fingers like a rosary she thought about her daughter's letter. It wasn't sex. Victoria was in love. Typical of Jean's mental squalor that she'd fixed on the first—purple teething cock ring, indeed. What would Giovana be sending next? Turquoise butt plugs? Three months ago, I didn't know what a butt plug *was*, Jean thought, too downcast to renew her fury against Mark. She dropped the necklace onto the night table and put her hands over her breasts and pressed. Then she lay down. And her breasts lay down, too—unleavened, spread, sliding to the edges of the flat earth. Hardly there anyway, she thought, trying not to cry.

She heard a bird cooing outside the window, beyond the closed curtain, and wondered who it was. *Echo-shay, echo-shay*—that's what it sounded like. *Écorché:* the word came into her mind before she could remember what it meant. A painting of the body with the skin removed. To show what lies beneath. The French for "flayed"—now how do I even know that word? Already dozing off into a deep and dreamless sleep, she remembered the book bag on the shelf and realized who it was from—the small, neat handwriting. Larry Mond. It was Larry's book.

By early evening Jean had decided she'd go to London. She'd cancel her *échographie*—ultrasound, just like Mark said. Perhaps he was right, they were just being sure, but she wanted to see her own doctor, and she wanted to see Victoria. Mark was again sequestered in the study and talking on the phone: the fridge campaign, this time with the client. He'd offered to prepare a meal when he was done, a welcome gesture. Her pleasure in "getting dinner" (shopping, cooking, and then clearing up afterward), never high, had also been canceled by Giovana; apparently she and Mark spent almost as much time eating as fucking. It was all one thing: *appetite*. Something she not only didn't have but couldn't imagine ever having again.

When she went to get a drink, she saw the corner of Vic's letter sticking out from a high shelf where Mark had left it— deliberately putting it out of the way, or merely inconsiderate (and *tall*)? She poured a glass of cold white wine and stood on a chair to get Vic's letter, grabbing, on the way down, the remaining package: Larry's book. She found a yellow legal pad (the only trace of her wasted education) and went out to the terrace. And as she read the letter she thought she'd been right: it was love. Maybe sex, too, but that was the wrong emphasis;

of this she must find a way to convince Mark—though possibly the diverting of Victoria's love away from him, as he seemed prepared to view it, would upset him even more.

She glanced over the other side of the letter. After the postscript about Vikram she saw there was another: *You'll never guess who stopped by. Sophie de Vilmorin—nice!* So, she finally did go around, the coatless waif from the dry cleaner, daughter of Mark's famous ex. Typical that he hadn't read that out—once again shielding her, or not wanting to "bore" her. So what if Sophie was weird? Thousands of women regularly looked to Jean for guidance, and her own husband treated her like a child.

Jean picked up *A Theory of Equality* and held it out to inspect: a pair of red scales on the cover, the university press imprint, no author photograph, a serious book. She opened it as wide as she could without cracking the spine, deeply inhaling at the seam, and as she did so a sealed envelope dropped into her lap. She didn't open it yet. First, she made a list.

Scully, Vic (Maya move <u>out</u>), travel agent

Then she wrote *G.* She wanted to write to Giovana without delay. The stop at the clinic, and then that *package,* had made Giovana's continuing presence seem utterly frivolous, like the White House affair with the intern: folly in a time of ease and plenty. In this new world of peril, there was no place for such fripperies. It was not enough that she hadn't checked the Naughtyboy1 account. She knew that if she signed in the next day and there was a message blinking in her in-box, a message dense with time and place, with detail morbid and high—well, she might not have had enough after all. Jean badly wanted to believe in willpower. But willpower was a restraining order, not a change of heart. Her measured, and weakening, resistance was itself an engagement she wanted rid of. She'd go to the Internet café in the morning, after the travel agent and before the gym, and break it off.

Listen to you! she thought, resolving to "break it off," as if Giovana was her own lover, not a complete stranger. She'd leave it for tomorrow, but still she thought about how she'd do it.

Dear Giovana, For these past months, without knowing it, you have been corresponding with me, Jean Hubbard.

Yeah, me, Mrs. Hubbard to you—capeesh?

Hi, this is Jean here.

Well, *that* didn't work. What was she going to say?

Dear Giovana, For the past two and a half months I've been impersonating my husband. Yours truly this time, Jean Hubbard

She tried again.

Dearest Gio. No.
Dear Gio. No!

Dear Giovana, The time has come to call it a day. And here I must thank you. All your patient, indeed painstaking, ministrations have made me the lover my wife has always desired and goodness knows she deserves. . . .

Oh, sure. Still, it was in the right direction. She'd cut Giovana off with the one thing she had and that girl would never have: the marriage. The bedrock of twenty-three mostly happy—no, twenty-three plain happy years. Or how about,

Dear Slut, I adore you, but I have a new slut to call my own!

"You wouldn't be talking about me, now wouldja?" Jean asked herself aloud, in the Bugs Bunny voice she and Vic used to denote comic lack of self-knowledge, together with indignant frowns, feet pointing out, hands on hips.

Or, how about . . . nothing. The best, the coolest, would be just to stop. And say nothing.

The sun had gone down behind the distant blue hills, and the air was suddenly cool. All the detail was gone, the earth a solid shape, the silhouette of a sleeping animal. Even the parrots in the tall eucalyptus trees were quiet. The sky was a deep yellow streaked with black, as if scrawled over, two fisted, by a toddler wielding charcoal. Jean could hear Mark running a bath—so much for getting dinner. To think they used to share baths, two alligators in a tiny swamp.

Jean lit the potted citronella candles on the table and took out Larry's envelope. Inside was a postcard, part of a painting by Boucher, *Cupid a Captive,* 1754. The detail was of a flowing fountain, adorned with two gray stone putti, one poised to administer to the other mouth-to-mouth resuscitation. She turned it over to see the familiar small, clear handwriting.

> *Whence thou return'st, and whither went'st, I know;*
> *For God is also in sleep, and dreams advise . . .*
> *In me is no delay; with thee to go,*
> *Is to stay here; without thee here to stay,*
> *Is to go hence unwilling . . .*

Jean looked up—hang on, that was a bit much, wasn't it? What was he saying? She knew it was Milton; Larry loved Milton. But why now? She recognized the lines, from *Paradise Lost.* He'd written them out for her once before, the part when Adam and Eve must leave paradise and become fully human.

She'd found these same lines written in this same hand, in her paralegal's desk as she was clearing out, getting ready to leave New York. She read it again now and blushed to remember (as if she could forget) the line that followed those closing ellipses, "thou to me Art all things under heaven, all places thou." Instead, he'd written, *And the dry cleaner lost all my suits— maybe they should change their name?*

She looked up again. It was nearly dark. So, he wasn't declaring his undying love. Well, thank goodness for that, she told herself, embarrassed by her eagerness. He *wasn't* saying he was still waiting for her; he was making a crappy joke about the Paradise dry cleaner, now rechristened Paradise Lost. A mosquito seethed close to her ear. Again she looked down, trying hard to swallow. There was more.

Are you ever coming back? Please give a call if and when.

L.

Jean looked over at the distant hills just as they disappeared into night. Maybe he meant *she* was lost, here in paradise. She felt her throat constrict. How could he know that? Into the envelope he'd also put his business card, with a cell number handwritten and underlined, twice. She put the two cards back in the envelope and stuck it deep inside her legal pad. A bit flirtatious, she thought, even if it was also a heavy-handed joke. And the *L* was more intimate than Larry. *L,* the letter for love, like Vic's *LOL:* lots of love. Or, for Vic's generation, did that always mean "laugh out loud"—suggesting there might be another way to laugh. Then Mark, clean shaven and handsome with his wet hair slicked straight back from the forehead, reappeared.

"They *adored* the pitch," he said, grinning, as if he'd just gotten away with something. Which she supposed he had. "*Mad* for it."

She slapped her leg. The mosquitoes were drinking their fill. "Fantastic. *Really*—well done." She slapped her arm, hard. "Goddamn! These candles *never* work. They make absolutely no difference."

"Shall we go out and celebrate? A festive cocktail at the Bamboo Bar and then the Beausoleil, the Royal Palm? Your pick, Gorgeous. You name it."

Jean smiled, thinking of how her nonsarong clothes were all flecked with mold, which you wouldn't really see at night—but the *smell*. She certainly wasn't going to wear the checked dirndl, last seen on the day Giovana's letter arrived. But what then? There was a sense for Jean now in which trepidation made dress important, as if she was preparing each day for the battle of unknown eventuality, and what did you wear for that? Everything cotton gave off the acrid blast you'd get by sticking your head in a bag of wild mushrooms; everything wool reeked of damp dog.

Twenty minutes later, in an old blue crepe dress, Jean was sitting beside an elated Mark as he steered the creaking truck down the drive, talking with an unexpected lightness about Victoria and her newfound love, and she thought again of Adam and Eve taking "their solitary way." She crossed her arms and looked out into the blackness, resting her middle finger on the worry zone under her bra—calcification? Or mere microcalcification? Fibrosis or just neurosis? How amazing that she remembered the Milton. But then she'd read those lines hundreds of times on the plane back to England, and every once in a long while, she'd read them again.

Mark stopped at the gate and put the car in neutral, yanking up the hand brake. "You drive through," he said, then opened the door to get out. Jean slithered and limboed across the gear-box into the driver's seat as she watched him approach the gate in the yellow beam of the headlights. He was looking at the ground and smiling. She was relieved he seemed to be retreat-ing from his agonies over Victoria and Vikram, even as she doubted he could. For who is the father of a daughter, after all, but the man who has loved her more than any other? Not just longer, in Mark's case, but *more*. As he began his struggle with the homemade loop, his hair and jacket flaps whipping in the wind, Jean tried it out loud.

> *In either hand the hastening angel caught*
> *Our lingering parents, and to the eastern gate*
> *Led them direct, and down the cliff as fast*
> *To the subjected plain; then disappeared.*
> *They looking back, all the eastern side beheld*
> *Of Paradise, so late their happy seat . . .*

Something here she couldn't recapture, seeing Mark struggle with the twanging catch and no longer smiling, and then the end came back to her—the natural tears.

> *Some natural tears they dropped, but wiped them soon;*
> *The world was all before them, where to choose*
> *Their place of rest, and providence their guide:*
> *They hand in hand with wandering steps and slow,*
> *Through Eden took their solitary way.*

Mark stood by holding the gate open, flattening his hair against his head with his free hand, as Jean shot past him and through to the other side.

London

Thursday morning, Gatwick Airport. Jean had been hoping for a powerful intuition, a clear apprehension of her future here in her adopted country. If she was to return—and in her mind she'd already begun folding her T-shirts and rolling her sarongs—she wanted to feel the Kingdom was fighting to have her back, not merely that she'd been "given leave to remain," as the smudged stamp in her passport said. She knew that desperate thousands would be overjoyed with "given leave," but she, in her turn, had given England her twenties and her thirties; she'd studied here; she'd married here, had a child here, and raised a British daughter. She'd toiled, paid her taxes, and over two decades of writing contributed to the health of the nation, and now she wanted to be sought after, not *given leave*. This was no time for assumptions or ambiguities. What if this island shunned her as St. Jacques recently had?

Inside the terminal the Hubbards walked the long walk, heavy hand luggage becoming heavy shoulder and heavy back luggage. Only an airport golf cart gave the idea of forward motion, the pompously beeping buggy speeding through the stream of travelers, its spike-haired young driver avoiding the eyes of weary old people in need of a lift. Keeping up the pace, Jean glanced outside at skim-milk clouds spilling across the sky, thinly covering all the blue. She remembered this: by noon in England, the best part of the day was past. Did that count as an intuition about her place here? No. She'd fallen out with the hectoring, unrelenting sun.

It wasn't until they were on the shuttle connecting the north and the south terminals that Mark said anything at all. "Vic and Mark backwards. Do you think that's significant? I mean even subconsciously?"

"I don't know what you're talking about," Jean said, too mesmerized to look up from the rows of summer-bright trees below the flying train.

" 'Vic'—and 'Mark' backwards," he repeated, still puzzling, "makes 'Vikram.' "

"Oh, I *see*," Jean said. "I don't think so. Not even subconsciously. But why don't you ask them tonight?"

Mark stuck with his frown of stolid, committed perplexity as they boarded the Gatwick Express.

"Victoria Station," Jean said, looking at her ticket as if she'd never noticed the link between the station and her own daughter. She was experiencing the fresh-ear, fresh-eye sensation that lasts only a short while on return. Mark, who unlike Jean had made the journey back several times, was more engaged by the miracle of a working cell phone.

She couldn't remember cappuccino on the train before. Was England joining Europe after all? Mark stuck with tea, as if reaffirming his national allegiance, a process that would normally reach its peak with *Match of the Day* on Saturday night—how gaily the three Hubbards used to hum and whistle the theme tune—but not this weekend, she registered, the festive jingle petering out as she remembered why not.

Mark was going to Germany for a two-day retreat with his biggest client. He'd listen to the Bavarian managing director's lousy ideas for the new campaign, then hunt wild boar with the core team of Germans and Brits. He'd been complaining about the trip for weeks, but never very convincingly—only enough to put her off joining him or, as he stressed, joining the wives. She thought he was in fact looking forward to it—a little male company, a little death, a lot of drinking. Or just a lot of hotel time with Giovana? Were all "client retreats" dirty weekends?

Jean resisted reaching over to help Mark peel the lid off a plastic thimble of milk. He was frowning more than ever, head angled back because he was too lazy to rummage for his glasses, stabbing at the foil edge with a blunt finger. It was a piteous sight, but she knew he'd be annoyed if she intervened. His tea was cold by now, Jean thought, unable to watch any longer.

She turned to the rows of houses whizzing past, terraces of identical brown brick, neat and grimy and tall. Individuality was expressed by the recently added decks, one with an ornate newel post, another with diagonally laid blond planks. Then, at Croydon, back to uniformity, this time in a pebble-dash finish, the cream surface with its infinity of pits and ridges attracting and retaining soot. Brown train breath scorched the paintwork from the bottom up, staining it, Jean thought, like her coffee seeping in along the edges of white foam.

At Thornton Heath, some relief from the chestnut trees: a red hawthorn, a yellow Indian laburnum. Balham was buried under scaffolding and FOR SALE signs. Jean fixed on a school yard, a secondary, the boys and girls in black blazers; a group of them sneaking a smoke behind a bike shed. She saw each figure clearly defined, the entire life of the playground in a single glimpse, like a Brueghel. Beyond the smokers, the emerald sward of the sports field, and even from here, even at this speed, you could see it was too soggy for play.

"Maybe we need to set out a few more rules about who can and cannot stay in Albert Street, what do you think?" Jean said, gearing up for her return to mothering. "Maya Stayanovich,

Sophie de Vilmorin, these *orphans*—I mean, we're not running a shelter, and if Vic can't say no. . . ." Looking out the window, feeling a little queasy for facing in the wrong direction, she thought for a moment of the waif and stray Sophie de Vilmorin and of how Mark had ignored repeated questions about her contact with Victoria, possibly out of boredom with the line of inquiry. Instead he'd talked so enthusiastically about a new contract, "in St. Malo, of all places," to design the literary festival there. Was the evasion deliberate? *Jean* was bored, by the mistrust that engulfed her.

Mark didn't reply now, either, too busy trying to read the stamp-size screen of his cell phone. Clapham Junction, and Jean's unease grew—she was unnerved, countrified. All around her, passengers were gabbing loudly on their phones. Mark with his tiny folding device was among them—no attempt at a whisper as he checked in with the office, licking the milk off his finger. In the end he'd succeeded in puncturing the foil with his nail, displacing all but a few drops.

Battersea, scattered with satellite dishes and self-storage warehouses. Another train going in the opposite direction shot past, making her jump in her seat, and when it was gone what was left behind was the grand, wheeling geometry of a raised and elaborately riveted Victorian gasworks. Next, the inverted worktable of the old Battersea power station, and at last the Thames, brown and low this morning, but swift. Nothing outmoded there.

Jean didn't comment when, finally in Albert Street, Mark paid the cabdriver a month's wages on St. Jacques. She was distracted by their house: weirdly still there but looking much smaller, behind its shiny spears of black railing and the narrow black front door. The ornamental purple cabbages in the window boxes were all gone. Dead heads carefully disposed of by the person who forgot to water them? Or gleefully decapitated by one of Camden Town's roving Kings of Swing? Moving to help Mark free a suitcase wheel that had wedged itself between concrete paving slabs, Jean decided she wasn't going to mind about *anything*—and certainly not missing cabbages.

Victoria had suggested dinner at the tapas place in Parkway; afterward they walked her and Vikram to the tube station, a peninsula in a sea of violent northbound traffic, and returned for coffee in their old, semisubterranean kitchen.

"So, not worried anymore about Vic and Mark backwards?" Jean asked, cupping her brown mug in both hands, teasing him only because he clearly was relieved. They were sitting at the kitchen table, just the two of them plus Elizabeth the cat, relaxing into the night exactly as they had thousands of times before, and it was possible to imagine they'd never gone away.

"I think he's *terrific*. Bright, pretty, clever, and clearly in love with Vic. Didn't understand a word he said about eccentric ellipses and crazy orbits and, and, expoplanentiary exploration. But so long as it's astromony and not astrology, I'm sure it's all brilliant marvelous stuff. In fact, I can't see anything *not* terrific about him. *Mildly* touchy, hm?"

"That's ex*o*planetary exploration."

"Yes, and *astronomy* and none of that horoscope shit, with all due . . . you're seeing that sad-sack editor of yours tomorrow, aren't you?" It was true, Edwin Mackay wrote the magazine's star chart, under the byline of Mrs. Moonlight.

"Mm, for lunch, after Scully. The gyno and the editor— a gay morning program. But what might Vikram feel even mildly touchy about? From what I gathered he comes from a rather posh Bombay family. What can he think of *us*, more like." Jean glanced around at all the dingy stripped pine and vowed to whitewash the entire place. As soon as she could be bothered.

"Mumbai, please." Mark was referring to Vikram's correction over dinner. "Let's wipe out all trace of the evil British Empire, shall we? Never mind, say, the parliamentary system or an independent judiciary. Perhaps he'd prefer to hail from Zaire, or should I say the Democratic Republic of the Congo? I guess we should be grateful we're not dining with Burkina Faso or Xianggang."

"I think you were right the first time: he's terrific," Jean said, steering Mark back around. "A bit pedantic, I grant you." She picked at some food caught in the tabletop. In fact, she thought Vikram had been strikingly pompous. But Victoria was so full of hope and, here again, their absence made them unnaturally restrained in their judgments. As, she imagined, did Vikram's appearance: he was pretty and clever—and brown; any criticism was unsayable, and for Victoria completely unthinkable.

"You have to make allowances," Jean said, as much to herself as to Mark. "He was, after all, meeting the parents."

"Not that he seemed remotely intimidated by either one of *us*."

"*Good.*" She laughed. "You can see how *that* would appeal to Vic: someone who can more than hold his own." Rugby? Radley? She'd already forgotten which middling public school he'd been to—and then she realized, that's what Mark, himself an old Etonian, meant by Vikram's touchiness. The narcissism of minor difference, as far as Jean was concerned. "She certainly seems to like him. I can't remember her so . . . *curious* about what someone else has to say. It's a compliment to you, really, that our darling socialist has ended up with a public-school boy, don't you think?"

"How do you mean, 'ended up'?"

"I don't mean anything, just that I agree: he's extremely

nice. I still can't seem to get used to how grown-up she is, though. It never bothers me to think of it, but to *see* her going off, down into the tube hand in hand to sleep who knows where. . . ."

"I can't believe this is *you*. Imagine if she'd gone off who knows where, as you say, with that singer if you can call him that—remember that scrawny bass player? His black drainpipes so tight they might've been tattoos. Rick or Mick, what was his name? A true Camden hero. The Ex-husbands, we saw them play at the Dublin Castle, remember? Now that's what I call love. You complained for weeks that your hair smelled of beer. Not a problem for Dad, that, with hardly a hair left to speak of. Did you know that beer is incredibly nutritious for the scalp? Of course you do—I read it in your column. No, no, no—it could be *far* worse. Far, far worse." He saw that Jean still wore a worried face. "How would you like it if she was in the sweaty embrace of some hulking rugger bugger? He *knows* things, about the *universe* for fuck's sake, he doesn't just spout ill-informed opinions like most people their age. Or any age, for that matter. He's got real, what is it, *quiddidity*."

"Are you drunk?" She got up and cleared their cups, leaving them unrinsed in the sink. "And it's 'quiddity.' "

Jean thought of Vikram trying to explain cosmic weather to this most earthbound family, how he'd spread his long, delicate fingers on the table and concentrated, seeming to stare at the dust on the inside of his glasses, and of his habit of clearing his throat or stuttering when anyone else tried to speak, fending off interruption—pretty much the only form of talk the Hubbards knew.

Outside the kitchen window, four legs were clacking by on the sidewalk, two in fishnets and stilettos, two in pointy black boots with the tips curling up like gondolas. A cigarette bounced off the glass and down into the light well.

"Charming!" Jean called after them through the foot-high gap of open window, suddenly exhausted. Mark was at the bar end of the counter, unscrewing a bottle of duty-free scotch. "Is that wise?" she asked.

"Certainly not," he replied, hunched but elated, liberally pouring.

Early the next morning Jean would see Scully and, even earlier, Mark would fly to Munich. She was troubled by what awaited him at the *Gasthof*, but she was eager to see Vic properly and to be alone in her own house. "I'm *finished*," she said, yawning, beginning her lap around the room to turn out the lights.

"Me too," said Mark, banging down his empty glass and beating her to the bathroom.

When Jean opened her eyes at dawn on Friday, Mark was already dressed. She hadn't slept well—her appointment, his trip—but also it was so noisy, with not only muted traffic sounds but every conversation, every laugh, every footfall funneling up from the sidewalk straight into their bedroom. She sat up. Mark was not only dressed, he was in his coat, the long green loden they'd bought together in Vienna. His hair was slicked back.

"Well, you certainly look the part, Herr Hubbard." Jean yawned. "Very handsome. Maybe your Barbour would be more like it, though."

"Gathering mold in St. Jacques. Don't worry. I feel sure Fleischauer will lay on the full kit—including lederhosen, I shouldn't wonder. Good-bye, darling, I'll call tonight. I want to hear exactly what Scully has to say, so take notes, will you? And please don't forget to take my sketches to Dan. Bye, darling."

The quick peck between his good-byes showed some eagerness to be off. But what was that *goo* he had on his hair? It smelled old, faintly medicinal. And, wait a minute, was that a pompadour? Yes, it was, a very small pompadour—not a Memphis wave, more like an English escarpment, one inch high. Still, she thought, patting his shoulder and not commenting, he had to be horribly hungover.

Mark's long strides took him outside in twenty seconds, the door slamming behind him. From one floor up, Jean could hear his rap with the knocker, as if to say sorry, or just to say goodbye again, like someone driving away and tooting his horn, pleased to have made a clean escape.

5:55. Always these tidy numbers: the little men who lived in the clock were fanatical neatniks. She looked out at densely metallic clouds—lead admixed with antimony and copper. Friday already—impossible to go back to sleep now, even if the sky wore its own blackout curtain. Somewhere up there was a sun, but London was under wraps.

Jean arrived on time in Harley Street, refreshed by a windy, surprisingly sun-dappled walk across Regent's Park. Mounting through the core of this ornate Adam town house, wary as the one-person birdcage elevator lurched upward, she remembered earlier visits—annual checkups but particularly when she was pregnant and the cage was even tighter, before she was condemned to bed rest with the preeclampsia.

Scully specialized in this mysterious condition not known to occur in any other species, he'd explained, just as only human babies amassed thick layers of fat—nutrients successfully diverted from the mother. In fact, he'd chosen to focus on the disease because it seemed to support his hunch that pregnancy represented a maternal-fetal conflict—an intensely fraught competition for nutrients and even for survival—rather than the spontaneous harmony the rest of the culture insisted on, biologists included. At the time, Jean had been greatly relieved there might be a medical basis for her anxiety, a kind of pre-natal depression she'd at first put down to the imminent breakup of her exclusive intimacy with Mark, though her shame, and her dread, were instantly dispelled when Vic herself appeared.

Scully, fit and young looking with a full head of dark hair, was waiting on the landing when she stepped out of the elevator. Special treatment: he must have known she was worried. He took her lightly by the shoulders, kissed her cheek, and stepped back with the pursed smile that didn't want to show its teeth.

Jean was, as she expected to be, immensely relieved to see him. He was a great man. Despite a labor made more difficult by the continuing threat from preeclampsia—to her liver, her heart, her brain—he'd safely delivered Victoria. Jean thought it must be wonderful to be Mr. Scully (despite the inevitable intimacies she'd never been able to call him Francis, and no one in England called the top guys "Dr."), with his power not only to bring forth new life but to calm and soothe life all too firmly established. He clearly relished it, the God role in countless nativity plays—and here, as in the more famous version, the father had been relegated (or anyway stuck, grounded in Paris by a baggage handlers' strike). Scully was a smash hit, as the densely scrawled-over wall calendar in his reception room confirmed; he was sold out for the next three years.

He dressed accordingly—bright shirts and brocade waist-coats, gold signet pinkie ring, the collection of bold ties. The style could support a watch fob and a reassuring paunch, but Mr. Scully was taut and springy as a cheetah. She appreciated the dressing up, not necessarily the clothes themselves—today a sunflower-yellow shirt and a wide tie swirling with red and gold fleurs-de-lis. No, it was that the gesture showed sensitivity, a sense of decorum, an understanding of the physics of the relationship: if someone had to be undressed, the other should be dressed enough for two.

"So, where do we start?" he asked, smiling, his forearms flat on his burl veneer desk.

She leaned back in the leather club chair, legs and arms crossed, momentarily speechless. She'd told him on the phone about the spot—she was touching it now, as if to cover its ears. "Well," she ventured, "I had a mammogram a few months ago, the results are there in the envelope, and then they suggested the *échographie*." Now he'd think she was being coy, but she'd forgotten; what the hell was it called in English?

"Okay," he replied finally. "Do you want to hop up on the table."

As he rose to wash his hands in the little corner sink, she unzipped her brown suede boots—an embarrassingly loud and suggestive sound—and wondered, briefly alarmed, if this hand washing meant he'd given up using gloves. Hanging from the back of the door was a choice of fat terry-cloth bathrobes, blue or yellow. Every movement in this room was so self-conscious that she could almost see the "study" in the *Journal of Gynecology and Obstetrics:* "seventy percent of women over forty-five choose the blue robe." She duly unhooked the blue and slipped behind the folding screen that separated the examining table from all the leather and polished wood.

Letting her boots clunk to the floor, wriggling out of snug jeans, she imagined slinging a stocking over the zigzagged screen—wasn't that what they were for? Then she remembered she was wearing socks: thick, opaque, "skin-colored" knee-highs, putty hued and smooth, like prosthetic limbs. Somehow she felt sure that Giovana didn't touch knee-highs. Unpeeling the dun socks she saw the top bands had left reddish crenellated marks in her airplane-swollen calves. Mmm, she thought, scrunching up the nylon to wipe the boot grime from between her sweaty toes: sexy.

Mr. Scully was gloveless as he began by palpating her breasts, the two hands working together like a piano tuner. He homed right in on the dense nodule, tapping repeatedly, a note that was giving him particular trouble, his head cocked as if he was *listening* to her bosom.

"Lumpy," he pronounced neutrally as he turned away from her, stepping over to his workstation beyond her feet. Short for "lumpectomy"? she wanted to ask. She watched him through the V of her feet as he squeezed an upright forearm into a rubber glove. His hand opened and closed like someone in charades miming the beam of a lighthouse, his fingers working their way into their individual condoms. "Now slide right down, put your knees up, and just let your legs *fall* open," Mr. Scully said, squarely facing her. She tensed as he slipped a hand inside her, and kept her eyes fixed on the busy much-painted plasterwork of distant cornices. One finger, she thought the middle finger, poked and prodded up toward the surface of her lower abdomen at the bikini line, where his other hand pressed down from outside.

This probably was not the moment to ask him if the G-spot really existed—but wasn't it supposed to be around there somewhere? And when would that moment be, she asked herself, trying to lighten her spirits so she could breathe. Again his head was turned to the wall, as if not looking helped him to feel. (Mark, she thought unhelpfully, did this during sex, like someone on a rollicking, squall-tossed boat focuses on a cleat, trying not to be sick.) Scully poked around some more, covering the bases. "Feels absolutely fine," he said, turning to look at her and bringing his hand mostly out, leaving in just a couple of fingers. "Now squeeze for me."

She obediently squeezed.

"*Very* good. How often do you do your exercises?" he asked, looking straight at her and nodding and smiling encouragement. His hand was still inside her while he waited for her to answer, and she continued to grip.

"I don't know," Jean said, inhaling, her eyes wheeling around the room, still hanging on, quickly exhaling and inhaling again. "Whenever I remember." The true answer, of course, was "never."

Had he ever fucked anyone on this bench? Just let your legs *fall* open. When the idea of doctor-patient coupling first occurred to her, during her pregnancy, Jean thought: He couldn't. He *wouldn't*. Now—many years after her cocooning in the purity of impending motherhood and convinced as she was of a universal corruption—she wasn't so sure. Wouldn't she do it herself, in return for not having breast cancer? She was already making deals with the reaper.

On balance, she still guessed he didn't or, at least, not very often. Of course Jean was joking to herself—how else did you get through these sessions? Still, she thought one thing was for sure: every odalisque who'd graced the padded slab had wondered the same thing.

"I'll take a smear," he said, turning to the sterilizer to get his speculum, a steel instrument shaped like an eyelash curler, with its wide-set pliers grip. The part she truly dreaded. And I'll take a Diet Coke, she thought, desperately clinging to her humor like a life belt. He slipped it in. Not very cold but not very warm either. *When* would a female gynecologist introduce heated instruments, Jean wondered, not for the first time, already sketching the campaign in her column.

He followed with another tool, and then the muted *clip*. Nothing hurt, more as if someone had snipped off the callus on her heel. Finally he unparked the second instrument and turned back to his sink, perhaps to arrange the lab sample on a slide, *leaving the speculum inside her.* How could she explain the outrage of this?

But she trusted Mr. Scully. Preeclampsia was a serious condition, and the only cure was delivery. How pathetic, she reminded herself, to whine about a routine pelvic exam. He removed the offending tool, and her knees snapped shut.

"You can get dressed now."

Back at the desk Scully examined the St. Jacques mammogram pictures she'd brought with her. "Mm-hm," he murmured, holding them up against his lightbox, taking, she thought, an excessively long time. "Nothing necessarily unusual here. Cloudy. Fibrous. Quite normal for your age, particularly if you've had children late."

She'd been twenty-six. But biologically, of course, she could be a grandmother—even a great-grandmother, she thought, not really wanting to ponder what he meant by nothing *necessarily* unusual, or *quite* normal. Maybe that's how Scully really saw her: a great-grandmotherly womb in side-zip boots. She hoped he wasn't going to start talking to her about menopause.

"The good news is, your mammogram looks fine. There is this fibrous matter that we may want to aspirate, but I would feel better, and I'm sure you would too, if instead we settled the matter definitively, which means a biopsy."

"Do I have to go to the hospital?" she said, babyish.

"No, we can do it here. In fact, if we can get a sample to the lab by eleven"—he looked at his thin gold watch—"we'll know where we are on Monday. How does that sound?"

"Sounds good."

"Okay. Why don't you get back on the table, take off your blouse, and I'll give you an anesthetic."

By the time she was numb, Jean was no longer distracted by thoughts of Mr. Scully as a man. The doctor had returned by popular demand for another performance as God. This time she didn't look and, as he cut away a tissue sample from the underside of her right breast, she didn't feel a thing.

"I'll call you soon as I get the results, around this time Monday. Certainly before noon," he said, returning his hands to her shoulders, as they'd begun this meeting. "Try to have a decent weekend."

The sun had gone in but the air was fresh. Jean had a free hour before she was due to meet her editor for lunch in Piccadilly and then head up to the office to hand in Mark's reworked sketches for the fridge campaign (he didn't trust couriers). She walked south toward Oxford Street, intending to shop for clothes, only to find when she got there too much reality for her first day in London for six months—and stripping off again in the middle of the day? Only for a doctor or a lover. She saw a naked Giovana, brainless Eve skipping and bouncing through a black forest, her pale Adam in gay pursuit. She thought of Mark this morning with his revised hairstyle and unfamiliar scent: too handsome, and too much effort, for a dawn business trip. Jean urgently needed to ignore the body and recover the spirit. She retreated north for a block and turned to the west: the Wallace Collection.

It was proximity alone that drew her in. She didn't particularly like eighteenth-century French painting—those rheumy portraits of milkmaids and duchesses and striding cavaliers— or the spindly-legged gilt furniture and blue Sèvres porcelain cluttering those well-proportioned rooms. So it was no great loss that she got only as far as the gift shop, paralyzed there by the unexpected sight of Larry's postcard, *Cupid a Captive,* on a rack near the entrance. This—and the pale, weirdly familiar duchess disdainfully observing her from an adjacent postcard—sent Jean straight back into the daylight.

A moment of bright sunshine gave way to fast-moving clouds and even the threat of rain in the short time it took her to cross Manchester Square, and Jean found it exhilarating. Maybe this island was more promising after all, she thought, walking down Bond Street, past the auction houses and galleries, the fancy linen and leather goods, the jewelry and the gowns. . . . At least in England you still had the seasons intact, even if all four sometimes turned up in a single day. She wondered if the rhythm didn't somehow give you a better shot at living each season of your life.

So which season had she gotten up to? She figured spring was Oxford, when she first arrived in England, where she met Mark at the very end of her schooling, on the night of the May Ball. Jean imagined her family as in a Victorian calendar, little fairies, costumed in flowers of the season. Summer was all their life together—Victoria a petal-capped budding baby, sprouting from the center of a hand-painted rose—until St. Jacques, oddly. Not of course St. Jacques' fault, but Giovana's, who had banished Jean to still another island, from whose shores she could only wave and hope for rescue. And so, she supposed, without warning she'd begun the autumn of her life—Jean floating down, zigzagging to the ground on yellow leaves, as in the Yeats poem about first love ending, yellow leaves falling "like faint meteors in the gloom."

The advent of Giovana had also brought a change of season for Mark—only he of course had gone the other way. Through her, he'd returned to spring, wasn't that the idea? Rejuvenation—Mark's long legs sketched as daffodil stems—through his elective realignment with a natural world in bloom.

Why couldn't he have tried gardening? The sky had turned a dense gunpowder gray—rain coming and, as usual, Jean had no umbrella. She glanced at her watch: plenty of time for a pit stop.

She pressed through Hatchards' heavy brass-handled doors just as it began to come down in earnest. After half a year on print-scarce St. Jacques, her hands helplessly grazed the teetering fiction towers, the solid ramparts of history and biography, the table groaning with glossy cookbooks. Poor St. Jacques, where the finest print was a woodcut. She dropped her bag on the floor and picked up a heavy loaf of a recipe book, contented as if she was in a warm cake-scented kitchen, turning the thick satin pages of browns and creams and raspberry reds, until she was called away from the feast by a familiar voice.

"Well *hello,* Mrs. Hubbard. . . ."

It was her college friend Iona Mackenzie, the other St. Hilda's First in Law. More than two years had passed since they'd last met, also briefly and by chance. Iona looked the same: tall, erect, and narrow hipped, wavy black hair scraped back from a middle part. She was wearing a faded jean jacket lined with fur and carrying a big, dark brown leather bag— a thing so luscious it might have been poured from the pages of this cookbook. Jean eyed the bag and beheld in it all the temptations of the great city, and she nudged her own sorry sack under the display table with her boot.

"*Iona.* How great to see you—completely unchanged." Mrs. Hubbard: was that for Old Mother Hubbard or just a dig at her having taken Mark's name, unlike Iona, so insanely proud of her roots? Even if she'd only ever been to Scotland once a year, for "Hogmanay." She leaned across the large book to kiss Iona's cheek and saw behind her a little boy of about nine, with his mother's wavy dark hair and blue eyes, climbing up and jumping off from the third step of the staircase she was never going to get to now. "That must be Robert," she said, pleased she'd remembered a name.

"Torean, actually. Number four. Cry for help, right?"

Four? When had that happened? Jean felt the current of jealousy pass through her like an electric shock, sickening, but over in an instant. Cry for help, oh what a winsome remark, she thought irritably, pretty sure Iona Mackenzie had plenty of help. She was annoyed, too, by the nutria-lined jean jacket—"luxurious casual": laborious cool. But she'd been close to Iona, especially that final year.

"Torean. *Torean.* Come and meet Mummy's *old friend.*"

So, Old Mother Hubbard. Iona was clever but, Jean long ago decided, just too competitive for friendship. Which made no sense: she was the one who'd had the serious career. She'd been a successful solicitor in the City before she finally quit, with child number three, to devote herself to the school run. "Is it a crime to waste your talents?"—this was the question from their Moral Philosophy Final they'd rushed to affirm all those years ago. How would they answer it now?

"Robert's headed for Edinburgh—a *golfing* scholarship of all things, it's almost embarrassing. Though of course Dom is thrilled to bits, and, let's see, Caitrionagh *says* she aced her prelims, modern history—Christ Church."

"No surprise there—she always was the brightest of the bright," Jean said, not wanting to volley with an update on Vic. Instead she asked after another Hildean, their friend Ellie Antonucci, now a costume designer in New York. "Speaking of Oxford, have you heard from Ellie?"

"Not only heard from but *saw:* with her gorgeous little boy. Yes—she's got a baby, didn't you know? A baby at our age, can you imagine? No man in the picture, of course." Iona raised her eyebrows.

Jean knew Ellie was expecting but hadn't heard the result. And now Iona's smug expression made her furious. Looking away for a moment, she tried to get ahold of herself: why was she so petty and ungenerous, why was she *overcome* this way? Iona had been a good friend, and a rare friend—a peer but also an equal. She recalled their long afternoons in Oxford's covered market, arguing passionately over toasted sandwiches about Rawls versus Dworkin, Nagel, and Dennett, about *Language, Truth and Logic* and *Anarchy, State, and Utopia*. . . .

Suddenly Torean, jumping from five steps up, gave her a feeling she hadn't had in years, one that used to nag at her like a hangnail: Where's my handsome giant, where's my *son*? Even semiemployed Ellie Antonucci, who famously didn't have enduring relationships with men, had a son. When Vic was still little and Jean was questioned about further children, she'd reply that "Real estate is destiny," and there was no room at the inn. In fact, her other pregnancies, and there'd been a few, had ended when the embryo failed to attach to the uterine wall. Victoria, it turned out, was a kind of miracle.

Torean was now leaping from the sixth step and causing consternation among the staff.

"Torie! *Torean*. Come here at *once*," Iona called. The boy bounded over, hopping from foot to foot in huge steps, as if he was bravely crisscrossing an invisible live wire. Iona grabbed his shirt collar as he issued a karate kick in Jean's direction. "Do you want to go home and straight to bed?" She practically lifted him off the ground from the neck. "Torean is off ill today. We *were* on our way to Fortnum's for an ice-cream sundae."

"How old are you, Torean, nine?" Jean asked, leaning toward him, admiring the gap where his front teeth should have been, and the dividing ridge on the gum like a seam pinched from Play-Doh. Torean slouched theatrically and sighed, letting his head roll back.

"Seven this week!" his mother answered for him, overlaying her weariness with something bouncy as the boy disappeared under the table.

"My goodness!" Jean said, knowing she sounded like someone who had never spoken to and possibly had never seen a child before.

"Yes, he's enormous. They're all monsters," Iona said, leaning pointedly over the open book in Jean's hands and snorting, theatrical like Torean, as if she'd caught her old pal with *The Joy of Sex*. "Mmmm," Iona murmured, looking at a rococo violet syllabub. "Entertaining a lot?"

Jean couldn't imagine ordering let alone making this velvety, occasion-streaked dessert. "Too heavy to carry back to Albert Street, never mind St. Jacques," she said, setting the book down on the table. A curly dark head popped up between them, making Jean start.

"Look, Mummy!" he shouted, holding up Jean's purse like a sack full of gold. "I found a funny old bag. Can I keep it?"

"That would be mine, that funny old bag," Jean admitted, "or that would be *me*," she said, glancing at Iona, wishing she wouldn't unpeel his fingers quite so forcefully. Turning away from this mother-child tussle, she picked up the cookbook, opening at random to a recipe for pasta sauce made from leftovers—*borsa della nonna,* grandmother's handbag. She imagined rough-crushed laxatives and floating tubes of Dentugrip with a sprinkling of biscuit crumbs. What would her own grubby sack yield, a blue coulis of sunblock and exploded-pen ink? Jean was instinctively working up a joke to lighten the mood, but the spectacle of Iona manhandling her son made her just want to crawl back under the table with him. Poor Torean, with his gapped mouth like a sandwich someone had taken a bite out of.

Even though she knew there was more to her old friend than

what she was seeing now, she hated her. And she hated herself. She was bare bones: so reduced, she'd become a person who hated perhaps the best friend she could ever have. Then she saw Larry's book in a stack near the cash register. She made for the pile, slightly overeager, and Iona followed her movements.

"Oh yes, your old swain. I hear it's wonderful."

"Yes, it is," Jean said proprietorially, though she'd barely cracked open her own copy. "Let me buy it for you." She remembered their moral philosophy tutor. "In honor of Dr. Ernst Niestokel."

"Kneestroker!" Iona shrieked. "He *must* be dead by now."

Jean went to pay. "I've got to run," she said. "Lunch with my editor." She guessed Iona would be impressed by this, while she herself was merely downcast as she faced the second grim task on her list. Mackay was an old egotist and lech, but her unease went beyond the boredom of that to a niggling sense of her own false position. How could she once again sit though lunch, stirring up enthusiasm for her column, "Inside Out with Jean Hubbard"?

She was twenty minutes late to her date with Edwin Mackay, and she didn't care. The moment she emerged from the revolving door into the restaurant she spotted him sipping peach juice at the bar: fatter, balder, but the unmistakable protuberant pucker—"Mrs. Moonlight with his D-cup lips," according to Mark.

"Bellini?" he asked her, frog eyes popping. And D-cup *eyeballs,* she thought, with his prominent lower lids like a terrible balconette bra.

Two more Bellinis later—they were very small—Jean, who in Mackay's presence was usually stripped of all ideas, found herself proposing a series of columns on gynecology. "My readers are all women, and this is the information they *need*. Men will read it for reasons of their own," she added, just trying to bulk up her numbers.

Mackay was definitely leering at her now. Jean solemnly vowed she was never going to have lunch with him again. It was a mistake even to say the word "gynecology." Made men like Mackay think of pussy, or would that be "minge"—her least favorite word for it. Every term was bad in its way, but this was the worst, with its suggestion of mean and dingy. For a moment she thought of Giovana, and how amazing it was that she didn't know the sound of her voice but she knew her pubic coiffure: a trim little square, as dark and dense as an After Eight Mint.

She looked away from Mackay—scanning for help among her immediate neighbors. Pussy, she thought again, as she absorbed the group of curvy women at the next table—all young and provocatively dressed—arranged around a hideous man in dark glasses. Professionals, Jean assumed, since power alone couldn't deliver those bodies to that face. This tableau gave her an idea for a different series altogether, on the seven deadly sins, several of which she'd researched already: lust, anger, envy, pride.

Mackay, stupidly chewing, briefly flickered with life at this suggestion. "Great idea," he said. "I like a bit of sin." Which was just as well, because Jean thought the series might be her last.

For recently, following her meeting with Bruce McGhee at the Captive Breeding Center, she'd offered a serious British newspaper an article about the vanishing kestrel population on St. Jacques. The editor was keen, and over lunch with Mackay this boost gave her a steady charge of inner power. Like the frisson of adultery, she couldn't help thinking: having something up your sleeve, something you didn't share, helped you to endure the daily grind. If the paper published the piece, she could move on from *Mrs* and from Mackay, who over nearly twenty years had been her principal sponsor—the guardian, however implausibly, of her independence. But she wasn't quite ready to quit. Before they'd gone to St. Jacques she'd overheard Mark's deputy at the Christmas party, dispensing sound advice to a young employee who wanted to try her luck as a dancer: "Don't quit the day job." He was probably right. But how, in your spare time, were you ever going to find out if you were a dancer? *Was* it a crime, or maybe a sin, to waste your talents?

"One sin a month. From the health point of view," she added helpfully, thinking she could do both: the column and the kestrels, a little moonlighting from Mrs. Moonlight. Mackay probably never even looked at a paper that wasn't a tabloid. She would use her own name, Warner, never mind if her own agent said she was "Jean Hubbard or nobody."

Although *borsa della nonna* was sadly not on the menu, Jean was pleased to see that her *penne e formaggio al forno*—basically macaroni and cheese, or what Phyllis used to call Kraft dinner—cost £22.50. She couldn't leave before coffee, so she was going, instead, to order a serious dessert: the chocolate cappuccino mousse (£16.50). When it arrived, she remembered Iona's marvelous bag. Awash with fresh regret over her missed chance in the bookstore, she longed to get beyond the force field of mousse-smooth goods and even of old friends. She couldn't wait to be back with her daughter, at home in Camden Town, where pink hair was still cool and a feedbag might do for funky.

Outside it was raining hard, but nothing could make her linger. Mackay had just failed to tip the coat-check girl and was now blinking and working his arms into a too-small trench coat; he looked like a seagull trying to lift up out of an oil spill.

Jean, stepping into the revolving door, could almost feel the willpower it cost him not to press in behind her, and when she turned to say good-bye, holding her coat over her head against the rain, she saw in his bulging eyes the commensurate will to reward his self-control—with a fat wet kiss smack on her lips. A fat wet kiss followed by fat wet tongue. It was over before she could protest, and she ran down Albemarle Street screaming and waving at the wonder of a free black cab, vowing that she wouldn't allow herself to think about it again, ever.

And she vowed that if the newspaper published her kestrel piece she would quit her job, whatever came next. She'd finally grasped this dangerous fact: *Mrs* wasn't just a dull, successful formula magazine with a pervy, pea-brained editor; it was the perfect expression of the calcified mind-set of its prize columnist. She had to stop *being* this *Mrs.* She knew Iona and Ellie would wonder why she didn't just confront Mark. But they didn't love him. It was easy to be righteous; what was hard was loving people, even when they were *so* unlovable. Wouldn't she go on loving Victoria if she forged her mother's checks, or ran a brothel out of Albert Street, or secretly converted to Hinduism and married her boyfriend in Mumbai? Wouldn't she herself hope to be forgiven, and still loved?

But maybe Mark yearned less for return than for liberation. Maybe you could love someone and yet wish for that—freedom. Or maybe she'd forgive him, to their mutual great relief, only to find, unhappily, that the ghost of Giovana was as robust and toxic as her rumor had been. . . . Basically, my friends, Jean said to her imaginary critics, there's nothing here you can eagerly assent to. With uncharacteristic clarity she understood that—one way or another—when she did confront him, and breathe life into the phantasmagoria of Giovana, their marriage would be over. Of course she resisted final confirmation of Mark's betrayal; of *course* she preferred her shred of doubt, real and instinctive as loving him, and she clung to it, smoothed it with her flattened palm, wrapped herself in it each night, and each night, as she didn't need her friends to tell her, it covered her a little less.

The cab rolled through the rain, and Jean, desperate for air and a good sluicing, pulled the window down and leaned her face out, helplessly recalling that long-ago christening of the office-house with Mark, the roof's standing ovation in a downpour.

Jean was so spent and bedraggled by the time she got to Mark's office, an entire building in a lane behind Clerkenwell Green, she couldn't believe she agreed to go with Dan "down the pub." But he greeted her as she stepped out of the cab, opening an enormous orange umbrella over their heads like a sun—how did you say no to that? He took the updated drawings from her, tossed them onto the polyp-shaped reception desk, and locked the office door behind him. He threw his heavy key chain up into the air, and then backhandedly caught it, ringing in the weekend.

All those keys, Jean thought, taking the arm he offered as they set off down the street. Dan was, she knew, much trusted. She thought she might talk to him about Giovana. Not *talk* exactly, and not confide—just somehow air the subject. He could tell her the weight a thing like this had for Mark: the male point of view. But then she remembered, her body temperature precipitously rising, she'd already given Dan the male view of Giovana, that day in the Internet café . . . and silently she fell into step.

"I've never understood why pubs insist on squelchy beer-soaked carpets instead of washable boards, like in American bars," Jean said, unpeeling her sodden mac. "But it sure is snug in here." With its patterned, deep red wall-to-wall and the afternoon fire casting a glow over the room that they had, for just a while longer, to themselves, the Hope and Anchor was indeed enchanted.

Dan just smiled. "What can I get you?"

Already collapsed into a high-backed sofa near the fire, Jean surprised herself by ordering a half-pint of shandy. It was what she used to drink with Mark at the country pubs around Oxford, the Perch, and the Trout, in those carefree weeks after Finals, before she was banished to New York. They'd cycle out of town for lazy lunches, then spend the afternoons reading in the long grass at Port Meadow, sprung forever from the library.

She stretched her arms and legs while Dan went to get the drinks. She'd checked two feared appointments off her list: Scully, who if he was alarmed didn't show it, and Mackay, whose revolting performance was a blessing because she was now determined to free herself from him. And she had at least parted from Iona without revealing the miasma of her soul. She'd crossed London in the rain to deliver Mark's work for him, and soon there would be dinner, just her and Vic. Tomorrow was Saturday—finally, she could relax.

"We're moving away from crisps and cleaning products and that sort of thing." Dan was keen to tell Jean about the new accounts. "Mark's given everyone so much freedom in the office—you can really see the new talent taking off. So, for example, you've got Theo and Blake working more or less independently on the National Gallery and the Arts Council. And most of the time, well, I'm pitching new stuff—new clients but also new gear: high-speed trains, electric cars, improved pedestrian signage; cool fluorescent self-locking bicycles for the urban rider. . . ."

"You're such a boy—very focused on modes of transportation." Jean liked to listen to him talk. She realized Mark never really told her anything about work; as he would say, he "spared her." She was thinking she didn't want to be spared. "And what's this I hear about a Clio?" she asked, knowing that Dan had picked up a prize for the firm at the ad industry's awards ceremony: for best public advertisement, poster category. Mark told her that Dan had worked on it in his spare time, pro bono, and it had been selected for the new Women's Aid campaign.

"Have you seen it?" He looked at her sidelong, blowing smoke away from her out of the corner of his mouth.

"No, not yet," she said apologetically, wondering how old he was. "But I'm sure I will."

"Only marginally less depressing than the old one," he said. "You know, the one with a blurry, sepia-tinted bint holding a steak over her eye with one hand while dialing the emergency services with the other. Mine has a mobile, no bruises, and the girl's texting. You're supposed to be reminded of the old advert—and the same old problem. But my girl, she's a looker, in addition to being in color and in razor-sharp focus—yep, that's what clinched it. You can actually see the girl." He laughed, suppressing a cough.

"Well, it's accurate, I'm sure. And that's useful," she said with effort. The ad didn't *sound* very remarkable—every ad she'd seen in London today seemed to feature a pretty girl texting. "Most domestic abuse probably is fairly hidden, right? No welt doesn't mean no abuse."

"Exactly right, Mrs. Hubbard. Could be that lass right there," he said nodding his head toward a busty redhead pressing coins into the cigarette machine.

"Mrs. Hubbard" again. Maybe it was just that everyone agreed with her: Jean was about the ugliest name in the language. One short of Mildred—or Phyllis, for that matter. She looked over at the redhead, impressed that a girl with such a rack had the nerve to wear a sweater so tight and so fluffy, and pink for a redhead—there practically used to be a law against it. Too confident, anyway, for a victim of abuse, Jean thought, still staring. The chubby girl looked up as if she sensed they were talking about her and broke into a gummy big-toothed smile. She waved childishly at Dan, who winked back and turned to Jean.

"Another half?"

Jean glanced at her watch—quarter to five. "Okay," she said. "You know her?"

"Yes ma'am. Shirley. Our latest intern, just three months in the saddle. Shall I introduce you?"

But the girl in pink had vanished, as if she'd fallen through the floor. Dan shrugged as if this was no more than you could expect from interns these days and headed back to the bar. The place was filling with young office workers, their arms spiking the air as in a classroom, trying to get the bartender's attention.

Lots of people leaving work early, she thought, wanting to be off herself, regretting the beer on the way. But Dan was good company. She realized that, for the first time all day, she was *not* annoyed by anything.

Okay, he was a little cocky, but she liked this certainty that seemed not so much earned as a part of him, like his shortened vowels and his wide, athletic stance, like his inky hair and the jut of his big jaw, the sharp break in his long, thin nose. Dan sounded like Ted Hughes, *that's* who he sounded like. In fact he looked a little like the great northern bard—Ted Hughes before life turned his hair gray. Jean, momentarily embarrassed to be caught studying him, looked down at the rain-soaked suede boots she hoped would revive with some vigorous brushing. Dan, she saw, had very wide feet and sturdy inelegant shoes that didn't mind the rain and didn't mind how they looked.

"There's something different about you," she said. "When did we last see each other? At the Christmas party?" He looked straight at her as she studied his face. "I know what it is: your glasses. You're not wearing glasses."

"Yeah, I finally got contacts," he said, pleased she noticed. Jean held it against him only a little, this small vanity that didn't go with the rest of his rugged self. Hard to imagine him getting the invisible sequins into his eyes with those thick, stiff-looking laborer's fingers; and she thought of Mark's long tapering hands, stabbing ineffectually at the tublet of milk on the train. Jean guessed that she and Dan didn't have much more to say to each other, but also that the silence was fine. You could say nothing, or you could talk to him about anything at all: a discovery that made her feel lucky, as if she'd just found a twenty-pound note in the pocket of an old jacket.

Jean drained her second shandy, not as delicious as the first. "Remember that intern—Natalie, I think her name was? The one who wanted to be a dancer."

"Sure do. She was great."

"*Was* great? You mean she left? So she didn't take your advice. Don't quit the day job."

"You remember that?" Dan turned to look at her, intrigued, and a little surprised. "Well, she wasn't as good a listener as you. I don't know why I bother. No one ever takes my advice."

"What about Giovana? Is she a good listener?" It just popped out. She offered him a cool, corrective little smile, as if she was not only unruffled but maybe even amused by the whole business.

He stared at her, and his characteristically mobile face went still. He didn't exhale the smoke in his mouth as he waited for another word, not yet sure what she knew. Then he grinned—or was that a smirk? So he did know about Giovana. Of course he did. Maybe *everybody* knew. And why was he giving her that loony look, or was it supposed to be "meaningful"? But no, this was just intense embarrassment on her behalf. She immediately set to framing the disaster, telling herself she should *not* be humiliated, that it was *good* that Dan knew she knew. And if he chose to pass it on, well, maybe this was the only way she would ever communicate with Mark who over all these months she had utterly failed to confront.

Some new arrivals in the pub stopped by their sofa, and Dan leapt up to talk to them. Jean didn't care that he didn't introduce her; she just wanted to go home. And now she could stop pretending, as she occasionally had, that it was all an elaborate hoax. Giovana was no joke, and what's more, she was clearly still around. When Jean rose to go she saw the room was jammed and the clock above the bar said six o'clock.

"*Shit*. Vic will be home any minute."

Dan touched her arm, sensing she was about to sneak away. "Wait," he said, and broke off his other conversation. "Let me get you a cab."

Outside, the rain had broken and left behind a gray and yellow sky so bright at the bottom it looked manufactured, like the glow from a distant stadium. She violently inhaled the clean air and wobbled on her boots. Dan put up a steadying hand and squeezed her elbow.

"What are your plans for the weekend?" he asked, keeping an eye out for a taxi.

"Vic has a big do in Cambridge tomorrow night. A flurry of twenty-firsts, a *hail* of twenty-firsts. *Sooo,* I will probably do as Mark has urged me to, and see a double double feature of Bulgarian documentaries."

They both laughed, knowing Mark's preference in movies for what he himself called the billion-dollar bloodbath.

"Actually," Dan said, pulling up the collar of his leather jacket and plunging his hands into his jeans pockets, "there's a brilliant *Chinese* film festival on at the NFT. Would that do?"

"It might, so long as it's all double features, no intervals, and preferably no subtitles. And please, black and white only."

"I'm dying to see the uncut version of He Lu Hui's *Shroud of Dew*, but I have to admit, I can't find a sinner in Christendom who'll go with me. Tomorrow's the last night. You mad enough to come with me? *Please* say yes."

"Hmmm, *Shroud of Dew*, huh?" Then she saw that he was serious, looking at her as if something depended on it. "All right. I will," Jean said, looking up from a level head, gamely and quietly as the question demanded, feeling that she was in a movie herself, not having given it even a minute's thought, as if this conversation had no bearing on what she might do tomorrow night or any other night of her life.

"You won't chuck, will you?" Dan asked.

Jean liked the way he said "chook," along with "look" for "luck." "No, I won't chuck," she promised. "Now may I go home?"

Dan stuck two fingers in his mouth and let out an almighty whistle, bringing a passing cab to a halt right in front of them.

"That was good," Jean said, still facing him and folding herself into the cab while he held the door open. She pushed the window down and said "Thanks," which she meant, resting her paws on the glass like an upright rabbit.

Vic was leaning on the railing when she arrived. Jean, shelling out her third twenty-pound note of the day, was stricken.

"Oh darling, I am so sorry," she said. Dan with his orange umbrella and black leather jacket receded like a Halloween dream. "Where's your key, sweetheart?" When she kissed her she smelled smoke on her breath. So, she smokes. No point asking her.

"Vikram has it. I thought you'd be here. Don't worry about it, Mum."

"Do you mind if we stay home?" She was blindly sifting through the rubble at the bottom of her damp bag. "We can order in. I am so sick of being out. The jet lag is really beginning to hit me." And that second shandy, she thought as the door swung open and banged into the wall. Elizabeth was whining, her cat's cry almost human. Definitely *not* going to any *Cloud of Mist* at the NFT, she thought, remembering her ridiculous promise. She imagined Mark's amusement at the image of her setting off south of the river, for a *Chinese documentary,* and wondered if he'd called. Just then, she saw his mobile phone, left behind on the hall table.

"I don't mind at all. Ramen, or are you depressed by a noodle dinner? I've given up meat."

"You have? Wow. Impressive, I guess. Your pick, darling," Jean said, kicking off her boots and shaking out her hair like a dog. "I just want a crack at that bath. *God,* I'm glad to be home. Do you mind if I go first? How's your day been?"

"Good," Vic said, already at the bend in the stairs going down to the kitchen. "I'm going to feed Elizabeth. I have things to tell you when you come down."

What things? Smoking vegetarianism was enough news for one day. Jean ran a bath. Naked, waiting for the tub to fill, she caught herself in the mirror. The right breast was bruised, a blush irradiating out from the biopsy spot; she thought for a moment of Dan and his campaign against domestic violence.

The white marble bath surround was lined with unfamiliar products—pink-luster bath-oil beads, discount cream shampoo and iridescent cream rinse in two-gallon jugs. Even Vic wouldn't buy this stuff, Jean thought. Traces of the heart-broken Maya Stayanovich. Traces she saw, looking around, she was going to have to borrow.

Wait, there was a tube of something maybe a little nicer. Jean unscrewed it and sniffed—that faintly medicinal gel Mark had on his hair this morning. She held out her arm as far as it would reach and read the label through the steam rising from the tub: Ortho-Gynol jelly. She smiled. Mark had gotten the wet look with Maya's contraceptive cream. Vic will love this, she thought, so pleased to be home, not for a moment considering that the tube might belong to her daughter. Stepping into the bath she stretched right out, keen to wash off the Hope and Anchor, and sank below the waterline.

Jean had no idea how long she'd been in the bath when she heard Vic hollering. It used to drive her crazy, the preference of her family for yelling over walking ten feet into the next room. Now it filled her with happiness.

"Mum!"

"Yeah?!" She wasn't above yelling back—not ready to abandon her soak.

"It's Dad!"

"I'm in the bath! Get a number!" Silence. Mark's call seemed to make the water go cold. She wrapped herself in a flower-power Barbie beach towel—more Maya. She did like the look of that cosmetics console, though—a dozen shades of pink and purple eye shadow arranged in the drawers of a chromed bureau for a doll. Jean dressed quickly. Checking the mirror, she raised her eyebrows to reverse the frown that had become her neutral gear and went downstairs.

"Dad sounded good," said Vic, sitting on the counter, fiddling with her empty wineglass. It didn't seem *very* long ago that she and her friends were standing right here on crates, rolling out cookies.

"And?" said Jean. "Did you get a number?" Jean was sure the answer would be no; for all she knew, he'd called from a hotel in Mayfair.

"He said they were about to go in to dinner but he'd call back and that he hadn't killed anything or anyone. And, oh yeah, that everyone including him is drinking 'lakefuls' of Riesling."

She could feel her daughter eyeing her as she got out the plates and cutlery, padding around in a pair of loose yoga pants that hadn't made the island cut and Maya's giant Garfield slippers.

"Hey Mum, you look really good in those."

"These flattering pantaloons?" Jean held them out at their greatest, clownish width. "What do you think? Ideal pants for a pantisocracy, everybody gets a pair."

"No thanks," said Vic, "not even for the greater good. But *those,* on the other hand, now you're talking." Vic was smiling down at Jean's feet.

"Oh yes, I know," Jean said, frowning. "Aren't they *gorgeous.* I must get my own pair, some black ones. Sort of panthery, you know, for evening." She pointed one bulbed orange toe. "Do you think Elizabeth might be jealous?" Jean picked up the cat and stroked her silky gray coat. Then she told Vic about Maya's other contribution to family fashion, the unorthodox quiff.

"I can't *believe* Dad put that stuff in his hair," Vic said, refilling her glass.

Jean, who hoped this story wouldn't be wheeled out too often, doubted she could have this kind of fun with a boy child. At such moments, she positively envied single mothers. *This* was the basic relationship; even biologically they were on the same side. "Take it easy," she said. "You haven't eaten anything." And then, not wanting to go that way, she said, "Poor Dad. We are *not* telling him. He'll be miserable."

"Of *course* we're telling him. In fact, I think we should call right now and make an announcement over the PA system at the *Biergarten*."

Biergarten. Jean smiled. She herself had pictured a long, dark dining hall festooned with link sausages and lined with mounted boars' heads and, for servers, Fräuleins with yellow braids and heaving bosoms, packed into scoop-necked peasant blouses. And where was the Fräulein Giovana in this festive scene? Upstairs, she supposed, kneeling by the bed and praying.

The doorbell was so loud that after more than twenty years it still made Jean jump.

The two women sat opposite each other across the scrubbed pine table, the low enamel lamp casting a circle of yellow light, and sipped their noodle soup in silence. Jean thought Victoria looked too thin. She'd never been fat, but now, sucking broth off her porcelain spoon, she had that sunken, haunted Hubbard look where you could easily make out the shape of the skull. But that was all you could make out.

Her generation was so secretive, Jean thought. "Do you see much of the old gang?"

"Some," said Vic, laughing at her mother's archaic slang. "Maya, obviously. And Fi. It's Charlotte's party tomorrow night, though I hardly ever see her now that she's at Cambridge."

Quite a few of her friends were a little older, but then Vic had grown up alone with her parents. Or with her parents, alone. "What, the gang plus Vikram? It must be a *little* different."

"Yeah, course it is."

Jean sighed, giving up. "What is that *pink* on your eyes?" she asked, changing tack. Eye shadow, obviously, but evenly spread over both lids, deepening in hue at the brow bone, like stage makeup spread not to cover but to illustrate a bruise. Worried about her Phyllis-like tone, she added, "I like it."

"You *do?*" Vic said, tapping her eyelids as if to check that the swelling had gone down. "My friend Sophie gave it to me." She said, glancing up, "I mean your friend Sophie."

"*My* friend Sophie? Do I have a friend called Sophie?" Jean asked, rising to clear the bowls.

"I told you about her in my letter. I wanted to ask you . . . well, I think she's Dad's friend really. I guess. Or her mother was or something."

"You mean Sophie de Vilmorin."

"You *do* know her!"

Why Vic was so delighted Jean couldn't imagine. She remembered the postcard in the Wallace Collection: the pale duchess. "Funny you should mention her because just today I saw a portrait that looked like her. I couldn't think who it reminded me of and that's who. Serendipity. Salad?" She didn't like Vic's blazing eyes, looking at her as she would have, at least a few years ago, if Jean had confessed to a casual acquaintance with Kylie Minogue. "What was she doing here, anyway? You said in your letter that she'd come round."

"I invited her. But then she said *you'd* invited her too, when you saw her in the dry cleaners, was it? I kept seeing her around—I thought maybe she was some weird Camden lesbian. She was always smiling at me—and then one day, me and Vikram and Maya were having breakfast at the caff and she like came right up to me and said 'You are Victoria Hubbard?' " Vic said her name with a good French accent, opening her eyes wide to show alarm. "So we got talking and she said she used to *live* here. Here in Albert Street—in this house."

"*Tu exagères, ma fille.* She stayed here once—for maybe three weeks. A month, max. When you were about eighteen months old, or less." Jesus, Jean thought, *was* Sophie de Vilmorin a predatory lesbian? There was definitely something creepy about her that day in the dry cleaners. If she was nursing a crush on Vic, that would explain it.

"Anyway, she asked if she could see the house again and how it was like the happiest time of her life here, and that she babysat me, and she was like *there*, in the room, when I said my first word—'minibar.' So I knew it was true."

"Babysat? She's making herself sound like our au pair. Which she wasn't—no one was. You never had any kind of nanny, a fact of which I'm rather proud. Though you may see it differently. And your first word, I'm sorry to inform you, was 'doh'—for 'dog.' You used to point a little bent finger at every dog in Primrose Hill and say 'Doh!' True, 'minibar' was not far behind, when we stayed at the Carlyle on that glory trip to New York, to show you off to Gran and Noddy. Sophie wasn't there."

Jean felt uneasy contradicting the compelling account of an acquaintance-cum-intruder. But as she'd tell herself later, sleepless at dawn in her empty bed, this threatened feeling, this insane suspicion, was simply the product of her own moral degeneration—something she really couldn't allow to infect her every judgment and feeling.

"So you brought her to the house?"

"Yes, I did. It was a great evening. We looked at all the old albums for hours and it was amazing. She remembered everything, like the glow-in-the-dark stars on my ceiling and the cracked blue glass on the landing loo door. The broken loo chain."

"Lucky her."

"We were going to call you, but then I don't know what happened."

"What happened is that you didn't call me."

"Oh Mum, I hope you don't mind, but she stayed for a few days. This is what I wanted to tell you. I thought it was all right. As she'd stayed here before and everything. Maya had just moved out and so, well, I gave her your room."

Jean shuddered, dissembling through extreme attention to salad tossing. "Look, darling, you have basically very good judgment, but the truth is, well, you can't just have people to stay. Not because we don't trust *you*. . . . The responsibility is just overwhelming, for *anyone*—and these things do have a way of spiraling out of control. . . ." Here she could speak with authority. "When was that anyway? What's she up to?"

"It was a few weeks ago. That's the thing. I don't really know. I think she lives in Paris, but she didn't give me her number or anything. She was around Camden 'cause I saw her on and off for ages. And then she was gone. Maybe this is weird, but I kind of miss her. She was really nice and wanted to know all about you and Dad and St. Jacques and stuff—I gave her your e-mail address, though I guess she didn't write."

Jean suddenly remembered the French e-mail for Mark she'd seen in their in-box before leaving St. Jacques; she'd completely forgotten to tell him about it. Perhaps it wasn't a business e-mail at all. Perhaps Sophie *had* written, just not to her. "I'd be a bit careful if she turns up again, darling. She doesn't seem to be a very stable person. Understandably enough."

"How do you mean 'understandably,' Mum?" Vic looked so worried that Jean saw she was going to have to give her something.

"She had a pretty rough start, to say the least. You know that Sophie is the daughter of an old girlfriend of your father's. Sandrine, a French girl he was nuts about a hundred years ago. Nineteen sixty-seven, I guess it was, because Dad was seventeen. He spent the summer with her family, in Brittany. St. Malo." Vic clearly was waiting for more.

"You really have to ask Daddy, but the thing was, Sandrine then went off with someone else. And she got pregnant. It's a very sad story," Jean pressed on, mopping spilled vinegar from the table. "Maybe Sophie told you. Her father died on the day she was born. Some horrific car accident, actually on his way to the hospital to see her for the first time. Terrible. Poor little thing."

"Wow. She didn't tell me that." Vic looked puzzled, maybe a little hurt, to think her big new friend hadn't trusted her with this pivotal fact.

"Yes, there was flooding all across Europe that spring—you must've heard Dad talk about it—Easter, I think it was. Well, we saw her a couple of times when you were little, but then we lost touch. I'm sure Mark used to have some contact with the mother, Sandrine. Though I seem to remember she moved away to . . . Canada? I don't know. It really was very sad. Want some ice cream, sweetie? Mango sorbet from Manzi's. Or mint—tastes so much like toothpaste, you could even skip brushing."

"No thanks, Mum. Vikram and I don't eat sugar."

That, to Jean's relief, was the end of the conversation. They'd thought about going to see a movie—a romantic comedy, of course, without Mark in tow—but instead, after dinner, they settled in the living room with refilled wineglasses. Jean closed the shutters while Victoria flicked through *Time Out*.

"Cool," she said, reaching for the remote. "*When a Man Loves a Woman*. That's the one with Meg Ryan as a drunk. Just started."

"Oh, good. I never saw that. Who's the man, Dennis Quaid?" Jean tucked her knees under her and took Elizabeth onto her lap, nestling down into the big squashy blue sofa. Which, she noticed, was a whole shade dirtier. "He's her real husband, you know. Or was." Probably had an affair with a younger, curvier actress, Jean thought. And then Meg had her lips done, as if that was going to help.

"No wonder she's a drunk," Vic offered.

"She isn't *really* an alcoholic. And I think Dennis Quaid's a hunk. That *smile*. Of course he's only about three feet tall. They're all midgets. I wonder why they split up. She is kind of annoying—so cute-as-a-button."

"Not in this one. What they call a 'brave role' round Oscar time."

"No, brave was that orgasm in *When Harry Met Sally*."

"Brave or desperate. Yoo-hoo, Oscar! By the way, I know she isn't really an alcoholic, Mum. Andy Garcia, it says here."

"Ooh. Even better," Jean said, happy but nearly ready for bed. "Vikram looks a little like Andy Garcia, does anyone ever say that? Hey, Dad never called back."

"Too busy draining all that sweet wine?" Vic said, taking another sip.

Jean must've fallen asleep because the movie was almost over when Vic said, "I really wish Meg would fall off the wagon. She's *so* much better drunk." The phone was ringing in the kitchen.

"Where's the *phone*?" Jean asked, annoyed it was no longer in its cradle on the side table and that Vic didn't even seem to hear it.

"It broke."

Typical of a much younger Vic, Jean thought, racing to the kitchen phone: "It broke," "It fell"—never "I dropped it."

"Hi!" Jean said, straining to hear. It was Mark. "Sounds like you're calling from a nightclub—where *are* you?" She tried to ignore an image of Giovana facedown in his lap at the darkened back of an after-hours club, Mark stroking her hair while he talked to home, her head like a silky little spaniel. When she hung up, she patted Elizabeth, who was purring at her ankles. Then she pulled a bottle of water from the fridge and headed for the stairs.

"Good night, darling," she called from the living room

level, still climbing. "I'm hitting the sack—won't make it if I stop. Mwa."

"Night, Mum. Wake me up, okay? We have to get the train at one forty-five."

"I will." She paused, smiling to think Vic needed to be shaken awake for an afternoon send-off, until she saw her daughter was crying, the light dancing over her face in frantic blue geometries. "Oh, no," she said, "what is it?"

"It's so sad," Vic said, laughing now, and so pretty with her big, brown, tear-shined eyes. "She just isn't falling off the wagon. I keep willing her to, but she won't. It's a *tragedy*, Mum. Sleep tight."

The coffee was snoring through the electric drip, and Jean was replaying Mark's message—listening, she had to admit, for non-German background noises—when the phone rang. She pushed the stop button on the answering machine, and when she slid the glass coffeepot from its burner to pour herself a cup, the black stream kept coming. Now Jean had a ringing phone and hot coffee bleeding across the counter. She tossed a hastily wrung shred of a sponge at the mess just as the answering machine kicked back in.

"Hello, Mrs. Hubbard. This is your escort for the evening. The last showing of *Shroud of Dew*—and, mind you, it *is* three hours long—begins at seven o'clock. I hope you won't think me a total shit if we meet there, as I have to go to Sussex now, for the day. Lunch!"

She winced at his "loonch" and "Soosix," listening with both hands on her throat, like a person feeling for swollen glands. Dan was still talking. "What was it you said about being judged by the lunches you chuck? Well no chucking the film, or supper for that matter, which is on me if we survive to eat it. So see you there, at the box office, six forty-five? I've booked the tickets in your name. Bye, now." Click.

Jean had been standing watching the phone in her robe and Maya's Garfield slippers, still holding her neck as if only her hands were keeping her head from falling off—too horrified to pick up, too horrified to sip the coffee that made such a mess. She was more horrified still when she realized Dan hadn't left a cell number. She quickly dialed 1471 and was told "Number withheld." She'd call him at home—just say Vic decided not to go to her party after all. His number *had* to be here among the two decades' worth scribbled by different hands in many pens on the wall around the kitchen phone. "*Yes,*" she said when she spotted it, *Dan Manning—H,* for home. She stabbed at the buttons as if there was smoke everywhere and she was calling the fire department.

"This is Dan."

"Dan! It's Jean!" she shrieked.

But he kept on talking. "I don't seem to be here at the moment . . ." With a jammed ballpoint, the only pen in sight, Jean carved the number into the side of the cereal box. Only when she'd finished and he signed off did she realize it was the office number.

"Shit," she said. "Shit, shit, *shit.*"

"Good morning to you too," Victoria said, wandering in, midyawn, coming to a stop in front of the fridge. Both arms rose and trembled as if they were hefting invisible weights. She rolled onto the outsides of her feet. For once Jean was too distracted to worry about her daughter's instep. The big yawn lifted Vic's big T-shirt, grazing her slim bowed thighs and showing, at full stretch, her underpants. God she's tall, Jean thought. And Jesus, she's wearing a thong.

"It was Dan Manning leaving a message I couldn't intercept

because someone not mentioning any names didn't clean the coffee machine." Jean's indignation suffocated her shock at Vic's underwear—too many syllables for so small a garment.

"What'd he want that freaked you out so much?"

"You don't like Dan, do you."

"He's all right," Vic said dismissively. "Just that he slept with Maya about thirty seconds after she split up with Gavin."

"Really?"

"He's a total predator."

"Well, she *had* broken up. Did he cheer her up at least?"

Vic flashed her mother a look of exaggerated disgust and pity, an expression that might have been borrowed from a sitcom, and then she softened into an authentic smirk. "Actually, she said he was *brilliant* in bed. 'Genius,' to use her exact word. She got all worked up about him, but he didn't want to know. What did he want, anyway?"

Given Vic's obvious contempt for Dan, Jean was embarrassed to tell her about the film—anyway, she planned to get out of going. "Oh, I forgot to give him the revised drawings for Dad's fridge campaign and he needs them today. I'll have to run them round later."

"Maybe I could drop them off if he can't be . . . bothered to come get them," Victoria offered, uncharacteristically helpful. "We're leaving from King's Cross."

"No, don't worry, darling, I can do it later. I'll walk and get some fresh air." She hadn't told Vic about the biopsy, and though she almost wished she had, she still couldn't imagine bringing it up.

"It'll take you till Tuesday to walk to Clerkenwell, Mum. And it looks like more rain," Vic said, peering out the window up to the street, adding her own *"Shit."*

"Tell you what," Jean said, inspired, shifting the hissing coffee machine to get at the trapped spillage. "I'll drop you

at King's Cross and go on to the office. That way you don't
have to lug your bag on the tube. We'll cab it. I've got to get
through the rest of my twenty-pound notes at some point this
weekend."

She'd lied, but at least she'd spared Victoria a tube journey.

Saturday evening. Jean was quick to Waterloo. When she emerged from the Underground, she saw that the rain had stopped. Or paused. She gave her magazines to a young woman sitting cross-legged by the entrance, begging with a puppy in her lap, and in the pink early evening she approached the theater with time to spare. She wandered around the leaking concrete complex, feeling shame for the decade of her childhood—the ugly sixties—and in no rush to meet the "total predator." At five to seven she arrived at the National Film Theatre. No Dan.

She stood with her arms crossed and her knees locked together, wishing she'd worn something warmer. She had on her brown suede boots, black tights patterned with holes like chair caning, a thin brown dress, and her mac, still puckered from yesterday's downpour.

The last film lovers were moving into the cinema when Dan appeared, running, his olive-drab T-shirt faintly pricked with sweat, leather jacket flapping behind him. "I'm so sorry," he panted, combing his fingers through wind-bent hair, guiding her into the semidarkness with a flat palm on her back. "Appalling traffic."

Was there any other kind, she thought, furious she'd let herself in for this but maintaining a dignified silence—at least until she saw the near-empty theater. "Good thing we prebooked," she said. Dan's chest was heaving as the lights dimmed to black. With her eyes not yet adjusted, she leaned toward him and asked, "Did you *run* all the way from Sussex?" Still too winded to reply, he squeezed her forearm instead.

Apparently he'd been playing rugby all day. "My fortnightly Old Fucks' game," he explained when he caught his breath. "And then tea with the godchild."

"What position do you play? And just how old are you?"

"Wing. Thirty-one. Anything else you'd like to know, Mrs. H.?"

Yeah, she thought, what exactly did Maya Stayanovich mean by "genius"? Instead she smiled her serene boss's wife smile, silently doubting the discernment of the breathless, eternally embroiled Maya Stayanovich. Finally, the film was about to begin—no reminders to turn off cell phones, no jingles or trailers, just the scratched countdown of numbers. Jean glanced around. Adult education, she thought gloomily, her stomach rumbling.

She leaned and whispered to Dan, "They only sell drinks out there, right?"

"'Fraid so. Can I get you one?"

"Sure, g and t if they've got it." And then, in a scarcely audible whisper as Dan ducked back down the aisle, she tried out "rugger bugger." It was her own fault, of course. She'd been counting on some popcorn to keep her going. But all hunger and irritation was soon crowded out by incredulity. The film was in black and white. Three hours long, he'd said, and the first four minutes felt like fifteen: a long panning shot of Chinese trees in colorless blossom. . . . Unzipping her boots, she prepared to nap.

. . .

Jean had to say it—she wanted to tell everybody—*Shroud of Dew*, this misty *Othello* set in China at the time of the last emperor, was fantastic. When Dan offered to leave at the intermission, she insisted on staying. And she couldn't stop crying—all the cross-purposes and tragic misapprehensions. The fresh gin and tonic in the squeezy plastic cup helped, but still the tears kept leaking out. Jet lag, she murmured, exhausted, and glad for the dark because she knew she must look terrible.

When she turned toward Dan, his leather jacket on his lap like a pet, she could see his neat, slightly wolfish teeth in the dark. He was watching the screen but smiling; and as they settled into the second half, he produced a handkerchief, one which in the dark he had carefully folded for her. "You can check," he whispered, loud enough to provoke a hiss from a woman sitting in front of them, "no strawberries."

So he'd read *Othello*, Jean thought, and carefully: how many people would even remember the strawberries embroidered on Desdemona's handkerchief? As she handed it back, she wondered why he'd folded it for her anyway; not because it was snot-encrusted on the other side. No, he'd done it as you might partially unwrap a chocolate bar for a small child, lending a hand. The white cotton square gave off a good strong aroma, just like him: clean laundry cut with unclean leather jacket.

"Mark would love that movie," Jean said, pink eyed, blinking with discovery in the sharp night air. "Too bad he'd never see it. Not in a million."

Another discovery: the pleasure, after the movie, of talking about it. Mark hated talking about movies. He thought they were like books, an entirely private experience. And Jean thought the loneliest walks of her life were not along some wind-lashed beach in Ireland but the two blocks home from the Odeon in Parkway. Jean told Dan about Mark's perverse post-movie rules—emphatically, as if fervor would justify the mild disloyalty. She wanted to know if he agreed—that with all the ads and all the reviewing of all the ads, as Mark had told her a hundred times, reviewing the movie was too much like work.

Consensus withheld: Dan not only loved the postmortem, he seemed to like all the same movies she did, even if she had instinctively edited out the worst. But then, Dan seemed so amenable, he couldn't hold *Bridget Jones* against her. Never mind that he'd parked a mile away and the rain had started again; he understood that what she needed right now, this weekend, was the sunny and uncomplicated. She wasn't about to muddy that gift with any speculation over whether he was in fact hoping to seduce her or just going through the motions. Who cared, anyway? She was just going to the movies.

"Fuck!" As she stepped down from the curb to get into his car, she'd landed her left foot up to the ankle in a puddle. It was soaked, and this time the boots were truly ruined. Trying to ignore her squidgy toes, now inside the little car—a black VW Beetle which, as Mrs. Mark Hubbard, she knew was not just some old banger but a "design classic"—she was still talking when he started over the bridge, wiping out an earlier suggestion of finding dinner on the South Bank.

"I'm taking you home," he said.

Jean, finally quiet, hanging on to misty twenties China, was looking out the window at the glittering lava of the Thames below. She wasn't sure whether she was disappointed or alarmed—did he mean dropping her off at her place or taking her back to his?

"Are you now," she said neutrally, waiting to see what he meant, waiting to see how she felt. Don't be an idiot, she told herself. Maya Stayanovich probably threw herself at him. Must happen all the time. In her own case, he was politely chaperoning the boss's wife; it was his *job*. For an unhappy moment she wondered if Mark had asked him to look after her, because of Scully, and his being away.

"Yes, ma'am. I've got a gorgeous dinner all ready in the boot. A perfect picnic provided by the mother of my godchild and dear friend, Sarah Mustoe. God bless Sally."

Mustang Sally. An old girlfriend, Jean supposed, not saying anything yet. At least he stayed friends with them. She thought for a second of the chubby redhead waving inanely at the pub.

"You do seem well looked after."

"Ay, that I am. Now, we can go to your place, which is a bit nearer, or we can go to mine, which I marginally prefer only because I have the perfect bottle of wine to drink with the perfect picnic. A 1988 Puligny-Montrachet. And a microwave, which I'll bet money doesn't deface the Hubbard household decor."

"Well, you're right on the wine front—I don't think I have *any* after my night in with Vic." In honor of Meg Ryan's performance, Jean didn't mind sounding like a lush, but she wasn't at all sure about his tone—was "decor" ever not a term of insult?—or for that matter about going to his place. When she spoke to Mark she hadn't mentioned her date with Dan; she thought she'd still get out of it. The remote possibility that he'd arranged her date made that an awkward omission. But once again she was being paranoid. Why shouldn't she go to a movie no one apart from Dan would dream of seeing—or, indeed, grab a bite afterward? Anyway, if Mark *had* arranged it, he'd have found a way to boast of his thoughtfulness.

Dan was a very skillful and reassuring driver, she noticed, enjoying her accelerated view of the slick London night. Suddenly it was entirely clear. She was hungry and she wanted her dinner. If Dan came over she might never get him out. Going to his place meant she could leave.

"It's late," she said. "Do you really think it's a good idea? I mean, it's been great, but maybe I'll just go home."

Dan shot past the turn for Camden Town. "Don't worry. I'll run you back," he said, his eyes fixed on the road. "It's a very good idea."

Jean had no intention of helping him lay the table or warm the picnic and she wasn't sure she could wait for it. Cold and famished, she looked in the industrial fridge where she found vitamins, film, juice, pickled onions, a jar of almond-stuffed green olives, a half-eaten can of sardines. She attacked the only possibility—the olives—and nearly finished them off before he reached over her shoulder against her laughing but genuine protests and stuck a couple fingers in the jar, nabbing the last one for himself.

A whole fish pie and two bottles of Montrachet later, Jean was wandering barefoot through Dan's thoroughly modern third-floor flat. Loft, she supposed, for its open plan and exposed brickwork, but redeemed in her opinion by the row of double-arched windows admitting slanted Ms of moonlight.

He'd taken off her boots and with a big white towel pat-dried through her tights the puddle-soaked foot. Then she took her tights off because he was right, she'd "never get warm in those wet things," and his manner remained capable—the matchside paramedic addressing a sports injury.

With her feet finally dry and her eyes closed—she was supposed to guess the ingredients—she ate warm, vanilla-scented plums poached in honey and wine, spoon-fed to her by Dan across a long black lacquered table, and what she had to say then, rising to take the plates to the sink, was "I must go." This she said a second time, quietly to the wall, bent away from him to look at a framed, almost invisible pencil drawing of a nude hung opposite the arched windows. When she straightened and turned to say so again Dan was standing very near. He didn't step toward her, just lifted his hands to find her waist. His tongue when he kissed her entered with the forcible promise that he was going to fuck her and soon, and Jean more than anything was relieved that it was settled.

But then again, maybe it wasn't, she thought. Seemed a long time they'd been standing there kissing, her hands holding his shoulders like the sides of a big ladder she was considering climbing. She'd forgotten about kisses like this. The more she got the more she wanted, as if there was something she needed at the back of his mouth and he was not letting her pass. Why couldn't she just *do* it—why did she also have to picture it (their lips like four fingers making taffy, two mouths after the same piece of gum) and add to that a running caption. The last time I kissed like this, Jean thought unhelpfully, Dan was eight. And what about the dressing under her right breast? Why had she told Dan about the biopsy? Subconsciously, to prepare him?

They stopped and looked at each other with no message exchanged, no corny smolder, and for this Jean was grateful. She closed her eyes like pulling down the blinds and Dan picked her up, her legs instantly lifting to wrap around him, and carried her not to his bed but to the long lacquered table.

He placed her carefully like a large terra-cotta urn and skillfully set about his work, as concentrated as a specialist restorer focused on her intricate finish, as if she wasn't even there. A tug here and the top of her dress fell to her waist. He tilted her head back to get under her chin, and his thumbs on her jaw and her throat and her chest moved swiftly, smoothing the skin as if it was quick-drying clay. He pushed the straps of her bra easily off her shoulders and then, for Jean, the first awkward moment. Perhaps it was the still-undiscovered Band-Aid that made her tense or an instinctive flinch for the biopsy spot itself—and none of this helped by the reminder, as he reached a couple exploratory fingers inside the bra, of his greedy grab for the last olive.

But reassuringly, he held her head again and kissed her about her ears. She didn't know about having her ears kissed—how it pulled like a drawstring threaded right through you, teasing, tightening, bringing you in. With each nuzzling kiss the line extended over other parts of her body, gathering into a new constellation of improbable shapeliness—Archer, Boar, Mermaid—another point from among her scatter of solitary stars. His wide hands now completely covered her breasts and with that wolfish smile, he yanked her bra down, forgetting the fiddly hooks—such attractive, hungry, butterfingered frustration.

Dan held her hair back with both hands, he kissed and nibbled her throat and licked her torso, first like a cat—working his way cleanly over a small area, tasting her skin—and then like a dog, with broad-stroked abandon, bunching her breasts together to meet his flattened tongue. She forgot the bandage, if it was even there anymore, her hunger sidelining local soreness, his own vivid appetite returning her breasts to their atavistic nonmedical, nonmaternal purpose. If she had first thought of herself as a pot or a clay nude, she wasn't as passive as that; more like an artist's model, a hard-won stillness as her body shivered through tiny arcs of pleasure and gratitude.

What, she wondered, was her best feature in the past? Her long neck, or her slender ankles? The slim waist maybe, or her breasts, smallish but pretty and unthreatening. However improbable, for some it would always be these freckles that deepened in color with heat or emotion, a Milky Way of discrete blushes. Now, she couldn't help thinking, her best feature was gratitude. Irresistible to certain men. There were tit men, leg men, ass men, and gratitude men. . . . Dan was certainly working hard to earn hers. It took her ages to stop noticing, assessing, and relax, but it seemed he could wait. She didn't know how long it had been—but at last her critical machinery was unplugged. And then, just as she was finally above the foothills, in step for the slow climb then long slide, he picked her up again, leaving her dress behind, a dark island on the glossy table.

Jean would think back on the things that surprised her through the night. She was surprised by her ease, how it flowed—once, that is, he'd silenced her helpless running commentary, those footnotes to every twitch of her cerebral cortex. And she was surprised (no, *stunned*) by Mr. Manning's answer to that question she'd been too embarrassed to ask Mr. Scully: yes, readers of *Mrs,* the spot does exist—although the pleasure of it, as with his kiss, was sheathed in insatiability. And how did you figure those Egyptian cotton sheets—the twelve hundred thread count once again confounding her idea of their chunky-soled rugby-playing owner. But what she kept returning to (sentimental, childish) was how he tucked her in, taking care to cover her evenly and completely, just as earlier he'd folded his handkerchief, and it smelled the same, the big edition, like fresh laundry and damp leather, like Dan.

When Jean awoke she was alone. For just a moment, one glorious moment, she thought she was in St. Jacques. She was disoriented by unfamiliar traffic noises and by the strange light, the morning sun filtering in through thin orange curtains like a tangerine dream. And then she sat up. She hadn't really taken in the upholstered wall behind the bed—was that hessian? A bit seventies, but no doubt that was its point: another design classic. She looked at the time, 8:18. Beside the clock radio, the blue glass ashtray with two butts in it, upright like the legs of a diving duck. One of them was hers. Along with all the rest, that cigarette, which she could still taste, seemed so perfect at the time, *was* perfect at the time, her last bright idea of the evening. And the huge whiskey, a nightcap—or kneecapper, as they called them at home.

Jean stood, gathering the sheet around her, and listened. Not a sound: no one in the bathroom or the kitchen alcove. She was relieved Dan wasn't there—but where'd he gone? Was that a TV? Something was glowing on the long table, facing her. Jean, winding the loose sheet around her, leaned forward. What *was* that? She stepped off the low bed platform (reminded as she moved of each part of her body entrained during the night) and crossed the polished concrete floor to the table. It was a computer monitor, as thin in its class as Mr. Scully's gold watch, the black-and-white screen beaming a message in red letters across the bottom: BACK SOON WITH PANETONE, COFFEE IN KITCHEN.

The image was a photograph, a picture of a sleeping figure, turned away. The artistically arranged sheet reached just below the high hip. Fanned fingertips peeked over the rib cage; a dune rose to the shoulder from the crevice of the waist, head and hair swirled and blurry, like the satellite image of a storm. There were no shadows behind the figure—dozing on a cloud. It looked like an old photograph, but it wasn't. It was Jean.

She covered her mouth, letting drop part of the sheet. Fully awake now, she wanted urgently to be gone. She gathered her things—dress, tights, bra, and underpants (belated shame as she found *them*, buried deep in her bedsheet toga). No coffee: burdened Jean shuffled into the bathroom and got dressed. She squeezed her eyes shut, not ready for contact with the surprisingly fancy mirror, a movable triptych over the sink, and splashed her face. Listening for Dan through the gentle trickle from the tap, she had an idea.

Quick—she'd find the camera and delete the pictures; then maybe she could figure out how to remove the picture from his computer. Jean returned to the glowing screen, stagily placed in empty space, like an advertisement. But she saw instantly she'd never figure it out—this was a new kind of machine, with no buttons or any kind of keyboard. She couldn't even see how to turn it on, or rather *off*. Like the bathroom mirror with its wings—like him, Saturday winger, speeding up from out of nowhere through your blind spot—there were Jeans ad infinitum in that computer. Even if she managed to delete this one another would appear in its place, and another and another, reproducing instead of dying, like chopping up an earthworm, all you could do was make more.

Attachment

She looked over at the bed—the set: that wall fabric, the ideal backdrop for photographs, eating light like velvet. Apart from the fact of it, and the illiterate caption, the picture on the screen wasn't by any means gross—in fact, it was lovely. There was no point in saying, Oh, what a time for vanity, does your shame know no depths? There it already was, lovely and dangerous—and, like the would-be model Giovana, just waiting to be discovered.

Her eyes swept the room. Hardly any clutter, few objects and fewer books on the cantilevered shelf that floated the length of the room—the camera should be easy to find. At last she spotted it on the floor by the bed, next to an asymmetrical plastic bottle of lubricant, the Astroglide. *Not* a design classic, not now, not ever, Jean thought, unable to believe she was here. A foot above the floor there was a bank of electrical outlets. Jean, downcast, remembered she'd had a good long close-up view of this spot last night; she knew just how the cement met the wall, how the chrome plates over the outlets had uneven gaps between them, how the shiny metal distorted her face like a carnival mirror. : . . .

At the time, upended and eyeballing those plug holes, she'd experienced an acute moment of recognition because she was arranged exactly as she'd once seen Giovana, and this familiarity had just made it seem doable, utterly natural and exciting, nothing like a dubious submission her disembodied brain would have to reject. Last night she'd learned such play wasn't peculiar to the desperate man-toy Giovana as she'd piously, *naïvely* thought; it was the thing people did called sex—almost unrelated to the solemn, face-to-face sacrament of her youthful courtship. So she'd also learned that the unexamined feminism of her generation had in fact enforced bans on a number of things that were pleasurable and therefore basically good, and wasn't that—in addition to the momentary fun of it—a thrill?

But—oh, God—the license didn't hold. Jean was ready for shame now; she could feel the floodgates opening. First, however, the memory card. She slid open the camera and unclicked the sliver of plastic. Wouldn't it be wonderful if she could do the same with her own memory, just click it out of its slot, gone. Now where was her bag? Hurry, by the front door. Her mac was there too, right where she'd left it, a sorry heap on the floor. With a glance around for any further traces of herself, she opened the door, softly shutting it behind her.

"You're *not* leaving." His initial smile (did he think she'd run down to greet him?) turning to childish dismay, the two masks eliding, comedy and tragedy. She met Dan right on his doorstep. He had his key out, and all the other keys on the ring jingled with the promise of doors still unopened. Jean thought for a split second: girls' doors. Under his arm he had a shopping bag—she saw a milk bottle (another design classic—yes, she got that) and something boxed, the panettone.

"Actually, I am. Sorry, but I really must get going."

"Not even coffee and a bun? Come on."

"Not even coffee and a bun."

"All right. Let me get these inside—I'll run you home."

Jean was about to protest—but it was clear from the Sunday-morning stillness that it was Dan or hoofing it, and she remembered what Vic said about the walk to Clerkenwell. Imagine how long it would take her to get home from—where was she?—*Hoxton*. Mark had told her he'd be home for lunch. When was lunch?

"Okay," she said softly, trying to smile. She was utterly parched—her throat, her skin, her stinging eyes. Where was the rain *now*?

Dan took the stairs four at a time. Standing in the street, she gulped the cool air and, arms crossed, looked down at her boots, ruined and then ruined again, as she deserved. The left foot was many shades darker than the right, the tarry color of unhealthy feces, with ugly scalloped white stains seeping up from the sole. Maybe, she thought, she could save them by stepping into another puddle, this time with the right foot. Or would it have to be the same puddle—with its particular south-of-the-river salt-streaked grime? Quididdity, she thought, a wave of grief hitting her now. She could hear Dan on the stairs—good. But his descent was much slower, outrageously slow, she thought, preparing to bolt, and when he appeared she saw why: he was carrying a giant white mug of hot coffee.

"I hate that I don't even know if you take sugar," he said, handing her the cup.

"I'm sure it's fine, that's great," Jean said, not telling him, taking the vase-size cylinder in both hands.

Settled in the car, she took a few sips, and realized she should share. Was that what he meant by not bringing a cup for himself? She passed it, sloshing a little into the gearbox, but he refused, occupied as he was with violent downshifting (Jean sensed an ego impeding legitimate use of the brakes). He was strikingly fresh faced, but the driving was definitely tired.

London looked evacuated. Seemed unnecessary, this back route Dan had chosen, snaking through narrow streets. Habit, she supposed, and a desire to show the knowledge. As if she hadn't seen enough of that, Dan's knowledge. Jean looked resolutely out the window. The knowledge: she thought as they bumped along a cobbled mews she hadn't known existed, dribbling coffee onto her conveniently brown dress, Dan could certainly pass an exam covering the A to Z of her body, the roundabouts and closes, the bridges and embankments, the lay-bys and flyovers, the canals and culs-de-sac, no quarter unmapped. Come to think of it, there was a kind of practiced feel to his itinerary, as if he was moving, in considered sequence, through an entire repertoire. A great performance, Jean would give him that. A great *service*.

They weren't talking and that seemed all right. Throughout the drive, he'd been smiling. Save the satisfaction, she thought. Just look at him reviewing his latest coup. Jean was not going to do any more reviewing in this car. And possibly nowhere else either.

"You are wonderful," he said into the silence, keeping his eyes on the road. "And a great beauty."

"Dan," she said, emboldened, thinking it concession enough that she'd used his name. "That picture. You can't keep it on your screen."

"Can't I?" He glanced at her, stung looking, disappointed, she supposed, that this was all she had to say about his wee surprise, his continuing praise. "Didn't you like it? You look so lovely. I was going to make you a proper print, on good acid-free rag. Forty-six by sixty—matte, I thought. Gorgeous."

"It's not that I don't like it. Or that I wouldn't like a print: I don't want there to *be* a print. I want you to wipe it." Jean was speaking slowly and deliberately, as if she was talking someone down from a roof.

"I didn't shoot your face."

Jean blushed deeply. She was going to bathe in her shame; she *wanted* to, forever. "That was thoughtful of you, yes."

"You could be anyone."

"Yes, I know."

"I mean the photograph—it could be anyone, from any time, that's what's so good. It could be anyone. Everywoman. Dreamwoman."

"I know what you mean, Dan." Jean was patient—she hadn't praised him and she understood he wanted praise, just as he praised her. "It is pretty. And yes, it could be anyone. Only it's not anyone. It's me, Dan. It's *me*." She managed a dry little smile. He wasn't smiling anymore. Don't insist. "Look, um," She started, no idea where she was headed. She wanted to be clear: that was *it*. Her tone was serious. "It was great—amazing. *Thank* you. Really." Did that sound final at all? "I need to get some milk. Why don't you drop me there, at the news-agents."

They were just two blocks from the house. Dan obediently and smoothly pulled over. He turned to her and put his hand on her knee. He was going to let her do the talking.

"I guess this is good-bye," she said. "Oh and uh, I didn't mention the movie to Mark. Just so you know."

"Don't worry. I understand," he said, making full eye contact, smiling again, confident, wanting to inspire confidence. Just like he must have looked when he first appeared in the office, asking about a job. She could see why Mark hired him, that healthy black hair gushing from his brow. He didn't have a moment's trouble looking himself in the eye this morning, she thought. She handed him back the huge cup, smiling more eas-ily now that she was almost free. Dan leaned over and gave her a bright daytime kiss on the corner of her mouth, but not insultingly, as if they hadn't done what they did. Good. He got the message.

She slipped out and shut the door behind her. When she bent down, he was leaning toward her, his arm hooked around the passenger headrest as if he'd already found a new date. Frown-ing and smiling at the same time, she gave him the briefest of waves and stepped onto the sidewalk, backing away before he could say anything more. As she walked down the street, she glanced behind her, but he was already gone.

· · ·

Albert Street, 10:01. Jean, exhausted, hungover, and aching everywhere, headed upstairs to run the bath, and then straight back down again to put the milk away. She saw the machine blinking red: eight messages. Probably all Mark, thinking: Where the hell is she? Or maybe the police, asking her to look in at the station and help with their inquiries. Maybe Vic—no nap yet. Jean filled the coffee machine, right up to the six-cup level, not even bothering to take off her mac. She felt in the pocket for the memory card.

Mark's digital camera—it was by the front door where he'd been recharging it and then, along with his phone, he'd forgotten to take it with him. He was in a rush, all right, she thought. Was that really only the day before yesterday? Jean could hardly credit it, mounting the stairs slower this time, pulling herself up along the banister. She shut off the bath and returned to the kitchen with the camera. The slot for the memory card was empty: proof enough to Jean that he was hiding it. First, she poured herself a cup of coffee and hit the play button on the message machine.

Message one. 6:22 pee-em! Vikram. For a sweat-inducing moment she remembered that he had a key to this house. Next she heard the chaotic Maya, who'd missed the train. Then Mark, checking in: "Hello, darling! I can hardly believe I'm still here. Who are these people? Who am I? I'll try you later. Bye! Bye."

But it was her father's voice that dealt her the slap of reality. "Hello, dear. It's Dad, and it's pretty late. I hope if you're not answering you're out on the town. Listen, sweetheart, give the old man a call, will you? I've got some news. Nothing to worry about. Love from Dad."

She replayed the message, listening for crisis. She looked at the wall clock: much too early to call New York. She felt panic rising to her throat. I've been unfaithful and killed my father. The next call was Vic's. Good girl. And then, not to be left out,

Phyllis. "Hi, hon. Listen, could you call me back? Something I want to discuss. Not to worry. Love to Mark and my Vicky. Bye, honey. This is Phyllis."

This is Phyllis. As if Jean might not know that. What was going on? She thought about those ministrokes her mother had told her about in St. Jacques and wondered if it had been strictly necessary to tell Dan about the biopsy—well, there was nothing strictly necessary about last night, but for some reason she regretted this intimacy as much as all the rest. She had not yet experimented with *not* regretting anything. Saving that for the bath. Another call, a hang up, and then Mark again, Saturday 11:48 p.m.

"Darling, where the devil are you? Bulgarian documentary after all? You're probably asleep, you lucky pup. I am absolutely shattered. These sods are very much worse than anticipated, truly appalling. Loads of desperate drinking—drowning my sorrows. I feel absolutely *awful*. All right, darling. See you tomorrow. *Bonne nuit. Schlaffen-sie gut, ja?* Lots of love. G'night, my bride. Night."

Jean pulled Dan's memory card from her pocket and slipped it into Mark's camera. First came the picture that was on Dan's sleek laptop in the flat. She thumbed to the next one, technically the preceding, moving back in time, praying for a Tuscan landscape. He wasn't lying, he didn't get her face, but he got pretty well all the rest of her. Hard to see in this tiny window, but it was Jean all right, on her back, a bent arm across her eyes and the sheet down by her knees. Oh no, oh no, oh *no*. She felt the prickles moving up her neck and across her scalp.

He must have been standing on the bed with his legs either side of her to get this one—her body smack in the center, closer up. She was headless, as if she was a decapitated Greek bust, her arms outstretched off-screen, cruciform. *When?* Was that how she slept, or had he arranged her? How could she be so asleep? Was she drugged? Though why would he drug her *after* . . . and how, for this next one, did he manage to roll her over without waking her? Come to think of it, and these shots confirmed it, he did seem particularly enamored of her backside. Live and learn—a whole new idea of herself she'd have to get around to thinking about.

An earlier photograph showed just the back of her head, shot from above, her hair twisted in a coil down her back like a tornado viewed from a great distance, but, turned around, it looked like a struggling vine, inching upward. Her head was at the bottom, then her shoulders, forming the base of a triangle cropped near the top at the waistline. It looked as if she might be praying. Only she wasn't. The next one, with her again on all fours, framed the open butterfly of her bottom and waist and shoulders. The music! He'd gotten up to put it on, stirring Brazilian music, and just as he'd instructed she hadn't moved. Head down like a swayback nag at the trough, her position resigned. Drunk. She was studying the details of each shot, one at a time, attempting to hold at bay the bigger picture: the consequences of these images, now on this camera, but also in Dan's computer and therefore, if he chose, out in the world.

The next picture of Jean filled the screen: shot from above but also from *behind*—the contemplative one-eyed point of view, as Dan might say (she'd been amused by his comradely relationship with his cock, whom he'd portrayed as a deluded philosopher-king). Jean contemplated her own raised ass. Well, now she knew how she looked from behind.

At last, it was someone else's turn. Unable for the moment to think about what she'd seen, she kept looking at the next and the one after, mechanically moving her thumb.

Ah, here was the landscape. So the great northern Mapplethorpe could also do holiday snaps. A ski trip evidently, the classic white peak rising off darkly melting lower slopes, scenic alpine shot, could be the Matterhorn. That black oval in the middle, maybe it was a cable car. She clicked on. The next shot was of a pale girl in profile, sticking her tongue out. Oh dear, sweetheart or chalet girl? At least it wasn't Maya, whom Jean had vaguely been expecting. Her skin was fluorescent, her red pigtails glowed. On the end of her tongue was a big white blob—more snow. She was sheathed in a figure-hugging dark strapless dress, and her hands were also dark, black or brown, as if in long evening gloves. Jean was getting impatient. She clicked on.

In the next one, the same girl was laughing with her eyes closed and her shoulders raised—oh my God, it was Shirley from the pub, from the *office*. The ends of her pigtails were now dark. Jean looked closely, but it was hard to see, her arms and hands and shoulders were all brown, like she'd been dipped. The next one was just plain Shirley, white as a star, fully frontal, inanely smiling. Her breasts looked even bigger without the fluffy pink sweater, without the brown dress. And there was something off about them—not just that one was marginally more enormous than the other. Seemed he'd done something with the color setting and given her bright red nipples, or maybe they'd been messily colored over with lipstick. She was afraid the next picture would be of a mouth with that lipstick on it, and she was miserable, right back where she'd been with Giovana. It hadn't *felt* like that with Dan.

But the next shot was Shirley again, marshmallow white, overexposed, and bending her head, hair part like a line of chalk. There was something between her breasts. A *banana?* Oh, *Christ.* This was the making, or the unmaking, of an ice-cream sundae, whipped cream, chocolate sauce, and Maraschino nipples. What was she going to *do?*

Jean thought of the moment when she read the first letter from Giovana and of her resolve to tell Mark, of how that resolve vanished before she got the chance. While he was locked in the can. She forced herself to think of the months lost in her "researches," a torturous exercise whatever spin you wanted to put on it, and so *aging,* as if she had voluntarily assumed his extra years. And the entire unfinished episode— the long, infecting soak in his dirty water—might have been avoided if she'd just called him on it right then, that morning on the terrace.

No bath, no breakfast, no nap—she was going to call Dan, *now.*

His machine began answering before a breathless voice interrupted. "'Lo?"

Jean couldn't help imagining he was with someone else, what else would wind him on a Sunday morning? The thought gave her fury a boost. "I should call the police," she said, not quite sure where that came from.

"Whoa! Why would you want to go and do that? Didn't you have a good time, Mrs. Hubbard?"

"I had a good time, Dan. I had a very good time. Just out of curiosity, was that your idea, or did my husband suggest it? Sponsoring a little cheer—spreading the wealth. Where is he this weekend anyway, do you want to tell me that? Come on, Dan, surely no secrets between us *now.*"

"Whoa again—what's all this?" It was his turn to talk some-one down off a roof. "I spoke to him from his *Schloss* not an hour ago—seriously bad weather, apparently—hasn't he called you? And as for last night, I thought it was *your* idea actually— and what a very good one it was, too. Come on now, Jean, you're not really cheesed off about my little wake-up card, are you? A *thank-you* card. I didn't mean any harm. You look . . . mesmerizing. You are, you know."

She couldn't stop herself asking, "Why are you so out of breath?"

"Believe it or not, I just dashed across the flat to answer the phone—some nutter calling me just as I was beginning a lovely kip. Not so fit, you see. False advertising."

This wasn't going as she'd planned. He had to be stopped. "How could you *do* that?"

"Aw, Jean. If you want to come back and shoot some different ones, why, hmm, checking my diary here, it seems I am available, yes, puzzlingly so."

"How could you do that to *Shirley?*"

"Ah, Shirley. Bit greedy, our Shirl. But we aim to please."

"You're an animal," Jean said humorlessly, pressing her lips together when she'd spat out the words, her throat constricting.

"So they tell me. Hubbard—Mr. Hubbard, that is—he especially likes to say that, though I have to admit, until now I always took it as a compliment."

"I want those pictures off your computer."

"Sounds as though you've already got them off my computer, Mrs. H. Come on, Jean, it was all in good fun. And Shirley, she's a big lass. And I don't just mean—"

"That's e*nough.* Don't you ever take a break?"

"Actually, I was trying to, but this mad lady from the islands called me wanting my head. As it were."

She clenched her teeth. "Look Dan, I'm sorry I got a little upset. I'm sure you meant no harm. But you can't *do* that. Really, I'm asking you. Pretty please. Do you promise to delete them all?"

"You're the boss."

His wife, actually. Would he ever give it up? She was searching for a lighter tone, but what was the point? Dan would do what Dan would do.

"Look," she said. "I enjoyed last night more than you know. Well, I think you do know. All this other stuff just spoils it for me—it really freaks me out."

"Don't *worry*, Jean. I am not out to get you. It was heaven, and I think you're great. In fact, I was going to have a kip and then call you and ask you out for lunch. . . ."

"Are you listening to me? That's *it*. Let it go. If you're any kind of friend, just let it go."

"Such a waste, that's all I can say to *that*. Listen, you are not to worry. Yes, I will wipe the pictures. Regretfully but fully. I promise."

Jean didn't know why, but she believed him. "So, I guess we won't need to speak about this again," she said with overkill. "Anyway I'm going back to St. Jacques next week. Soon as I get my results."

Desperate last shot: cancer. Please comply with my dying wish. There was a thoughtful silence from Dan. Had he already forgotten? Or was he derailed by aesthetic, even professional, contemplation of her titless torso? Maybe this was supposed to be a *grave* silence? If that's what you're after, Jean thought, you can forget it. You're not made for solemnity, Dan. Just to nail it, she added, "Mark is so fond of you. Like a son—or a naughty little brother I guess."

"Well, I'm fond of *him*," Dan said without a hint of irony. "Though not quite so fond as I am of you."

Jean, in the bath with her hair piled high and pinned by a toothbrush, looked down at her body, all of it submerged except the two islands floating in this clear green sea, a lone survivor at the center of each. At least they had each other for company—for now. The biopsy spot was sore, sorer than the other sore spots. But sore was okay with Jean.

Closing her eyes she thought of Dan's tongue power-coating his handful of female flesh, nipples not so solitary then, and a shiver ran through her—not like last night's exquisite tremors and quivers, but the shakes of a rapidly advancing disease, one mocked by her oblivion-seeking, late-night self. She wanted to test for other, nonbodily bruises—a moral or spiritual biopsy—but how did you do that?

Isolation: this seemed the most likely immediate outcome of her having crossed the border with Dan, barring anything truly horrible from him. She supposed she'd know just how isolated she was as soon as she saw Mark, if there was a new veil between them. Even more than pictures of herself on the office laptops, this was the consequence she most feared: her own revulsion for her world, for all that she had. Auto-eviction. But fear was a poison. Jean thought of those hugging machines they use on cows before they're led off to slaughter. Nothing to do with animal welfare—fear is toxic, makes the meat taste foul.

She watched the concentric ripples on the water's surface made by a toe that looked out like a periscope and then changed its mind. Had Dan made her feel any better about Mark's excursion, compared, say, with all her busybodying around the Internet? Yes, he had. The impulse to strike out on *any* independent path had to be strengthening, if not exactly cheering. But why feel better about jumping onto a sinking ship? She thought of a small, hard, embroidered pillow, one of those decorative fortune cookies Phyllis collected, which said IF YOU EVER LEAVE ME I'M GOING WITH YOU.

Still, last night hadn't felt related to Mark and her marriage. And not even to Mark and Giovana. Maybe this was just Jean on the brink of forty-six and it didn't *mean* anything. Or maybe this was her true personality coming through, the way alcoholism showed in some people around thirty-five. Jean the philobat, on the pattern of acrobat, the type that prefers to cope alone with difficult, uncertain situations. Though of course she hadn't been alone.

She had to expect that nothing would ever be the same again. But to her intermittent great sadness, nothing ever was. In fact, the whole night was a kind of exercise in nostalgia. Hungry kisses—remember those? Well, they were still there—even more amazing, they were available to her and she'd remembered how it all went. As if she'd stepped straight back into a beloved entertainment from an earlier time, like square dancing.

Of course she was afraid, with good reason. Because along with mortification there had been the shock of pleasure. Even now, with everything else this aching afternoon, she felt a clear and luminous happiness, as if she'd just swum in the ocean and walked out into the hot sunshine.

The phone rang twice while she was in the bath. It had to be Mark, with news of a delay. In a thin cotton nightgown and her white robe, she padded down the jute-covered steps, calm, resigned, ready for whatever came next.

Message one. 11:10 ay-em! Victoria. She was going to sleep off the party, catch the evening train, and get back around midnight. "Don't worry, Mum, we'll be in a big gang."

Message two. 11:25 ay-em! "Darling pup, how is it that I absolutely never find you in? Listen, ghastly news, I'm afraid, divine retribution for all the remarks about my evil German hosts and woe betide me, sweetheart! The weather is seriously awful, a lead blanket of summer fog—quite common apparently, and one more reason to love Germany. But there's no flying out of here, not for love or euros. Believe me, they've been trying. The entire fleet is powered by their engines, and they only own the fucking airport, but no joy! I'll ring you later when I know more, but seems I'm grounded. Supposed to blow over by the morning, and with luck the first flight goes out of Munich into Heathrow, let's see, gaining an hour—what, around oneish? Anyway, the contract looks secure. I should bloody well hope so. Bye, darling. Love to the Viclet. I'll ring again later. Bye."

She felt lower than ever as she played the message again. *Darling pup.* Two decades of canine endearments, Jean always pup or a variation of: puplet, puppling, the pupster, she supposed for her impulsiveness, her laughable early eagerness. Mark upheld the other end: floppy, shaggy, flop, and shaggers, for his hair, but also his general aspect of sniffing old dog, head out on his long neck—way out in front of his long body, doleful, worried. Oh God, what had she *done.* And above all, was it fixable? The toaster sprang loudly and the toast jumped, like Jean whenever the doorbell rang.

Hot buttered toast: this is goodness, Jean thought, making for the stairs. In fact this is ecstasy, seeing as we're on the subject—hot buttered toast in bed, the main event to which anything else in bed was so much overwrought foreplay. Yet it was always forbidden, as if the annoyance of a few crumbs could compare with such pure and simple gratification. Mark used to bring it up on the tea tray, plus the mail—post and toast. When had he stopped doing that? About twenty-two years ago.

She reached her room too tired to feel more than grateful to be alive and alone in her own bed and, quick glance at the clock (12:12), she fell asleep immediately.

Jean awoke feeling that nothing could upset her, not even these sleep lines: carved so deep she looked in the mirror and saw a St. Jacques woodcut. She was splashing her face when the phone rang. It had to be Mark. She lunged, belly-flopping across to her side of the bed.

"Well, hello you! You're sounding chipper." It was Dan. "Listen, do you think I could stop by? I'm in the neighborhood."

Jean sat rigidly erect, as if yanked upright by an invisible rope at the top of her head. He must know that Mark's flight had been delayed—shit, he was coming back for *more*. What should she say? "No" seemed not only rude but dangerous when the man had an entire digital archive. She glanced at her watch: 4 o'clock. "Um," she began, tiptoeing across the room and looking down through the window to see if he was standing outside.

"Just for a minute," he said. "I have something for you."

"Well, I was just about to have some tea," she said. "Do you want to stop by for a couple of minutes?"

"Yes ma'am."

She pulled on a pair of Levi's, added a belt to feel more dressed, the tooled Western one with the worn silver buckle, and gave her hair a good brush. Perhaps to shut out any kind of reconsideration, Jean sang as she headed down the stairs barefoot—the theme from *Rawhide*. "Keep movin', movin', movin'—though they're disapprovin' . . ." She didn't make it to the kitchen before the bell got her out of her skin, so she opened the door almost as soon as he buzzed, giving him a little fright of his own.

"What a nice welcome."

He grinned as he handed her a bunch of pale pink peonies. In his other hand he carried a punnet of ripe strawberries. Dan looked perfectly worn in, like his leather jacket. Jean noted this almost clinically and realized that she was seriously over-relaxed; but she could feel herself tensing down to her bare toes.

"Dan," she said, a touch matronly, as full acknowledgment of the fruit and flowers, wondering if he'd heard her singing. "I have to call New York, but come in for a minute. I'll make some tea. Or maybe strong coffee." She held out a hand for the leather jacket he was unpeeling. As she tossed it over the sofa in the front living room, she caught a whiff of his scent—leather and laundry and what else?

"Coffee's perfect. I never did get that kip."

"Moving in?" she said, aiming for cheerful, eyeing his bulky gym bag and wondering how she was going to get him out of here. He smiled but didn't reply as he followed her down to the kitchen, the bag over his shoulder.

She put the peonies into the blue-and-white Spanish pitcher and took the berries, tipping them into the green bowl. He set his bag on the counter and opened it up and began to unpack his laptop—what was this? Jean did not want any more computer screen; she should say so.

"Listen, I have to call my father—family crisis."

"I just thought you might want to have a quick last look, be sure there isn't one you want a print of before we delete them for good."

Such vanity! He said he'd brought something for her—was this it? The chance to order a *print*? And did he imagine she understood nothing about copies, as if by pressing the delete button with her very own finger it would be real to her as well as ceremonial, like cutting a red ribbon?

Dan took in her doubtful look, which was the best she could manage. A flash of anger crossed his tired face. "Look. I made them for *you*. For your pleasure. I don't wank to pictures, you know. I don't have to. What do I want them for? So I can blackmail your husband into giving me a pay rise—*radically* overdue, I might add. You have to trust me, Jean. I think you can do that. You trusted me last night."

So, on day two, Dan was going to dispense with charm. Jean's head ached; her hangover seemed to swell with the renewed tension. Definite mistake, letting him come over, though of course she knew it was by then a mistake well advanced, a mistake with plenty of momentum. She looked at the clock: nearly noon in New York.

"Just give me five minutes." He ran a slide show of the pictures with a portentous sound track: Albinoni in Venice. She wanted to scream—Dan thinks he's an *artist*. He paused on an image of her long curved spine. "Baby pinecones under snow," he said, pointing to the light track of her vertebrae.

How could she explain to this egomaniac that she didn't want baby pinecones, or poetry of any kind? He was so childish, waiting for praise. But she sensed his volatility. She couldn't just throw him out. She crossed her arms, settling on a kitchen stool, and turned away from the screen. The strawberries in that bowl, she thought, they're perfectly complementary, the red and the green. And as he no doubt intended, she remembered his ready handkerchief in the cinema, his courtly gesture as well as his unexpected reference to Desdemona. And then it occurred to her that he'd never read *Othello*. He'd seen the ad with the strawberry-patterned handkerchief, an ad for a perfume called Jalousie—she'd just seen it herself, at the airport.

"Do you mind talking a minute about Shirley," Jean said, thinking she'd still get on top of this. "Tell me if you mind."

"Fire away," he said, but stopped the slide show. He looked straight at her, as if open-faced meant open-minded, sitting down on the stool beside her.

"Do you really not see the imbalance in your relationship?" she started, unnerved by his candidly unrepentant gaze. "She's not free. You're her *boss*." And now something strange happened. She looked for that part of herself—the part that disapproved—and it wasn't there. "Like students and teachers," she went on tinnily. "Like hookers and their clients. You *pay* her. Don't kid yourself about consenting adults. It's not a level field."

"Actually, we hardly pay our interns anything at all. Hubbard's orders. Does that help?"

Jean smiled but said, "No, actually it doesn't. It's the balance of power and you know what I mean." But *she* didn't know what she meant either, not anymore.

"Well, the balance of power is always a story in these things, isn't it, how it changes. Keeps us all interested, right? Shirley has her power. And so do you. On the page and elsewhere."

Dan ate a handful of strawberries. Then, looking around for something more satisfying, reached for a banana and ate that, and then a hunk ripped from a baguette. "I'm famished. Do you mind?" he asked, his methodical circular grinding like the vortex of a waste disposal. Jean shook her head and just waited, sensing he was midsentence as well as midbite. He was still swallowing when he spoke.

"Why can you not accept that Shirley *likes* it? Surely you're not going to be offended by bad *taste*. I mean, are we communicating? You will rush to tell me about the love deficit in her childhood, but I will tell *you* that this is a girl who's got to have something in her mouth at all times. And where's the harm in that? Makes the world go round. Surely you're not totally mystified, Mrs. H." His tongue was gliding across his teeth, a prominent bulge moving under his lip. She blushed and continued to blush. But she battled on.

"It's not the same between you and me. I mean, I'm older than you. You work for my husband. I make my own living. Sure, you're freer. In every way. But I'm richer." And smarter, she thought to herself. "Parity, that's the thing." She was not sure she wanted to invite such comparisons—and if she was so smart, what was Dan Manning doing in her kitchen? She shifted the focus. "And all the other interns?"

"None. Not a one. Or not lately. Believe me, most of them have much more promising boyfriends. Hedge-funders with summer cars. . . . Can you please explain to me, since you are mistress and supreme diviner of the female psyche—not to mention the *male* psyche, though no extra points for that— why a convertible is *the* undying aphrodisiac for women?"

"Actually, women hate convertibles. They fuck up their hair." But he wasn't even listening.

"Now, let me see, interns. . . . Apart from Shirley, we have Sareen, who sadly is married, and Leslie. Who's a bloke, I think."

"So not resisting on principle, then."

"My principle is one of happiness, if that can be a principle. And regular health checks. Yes, making people happy, including, occasionally, old Bert here. Bert?" he said loudly, talking to his bunched crotch. "You're good people! Actually, until recently even *I* had a real girlfriend. As you will have gathered." He sighed at her memory.

"So what happened to her anyway?" While she thought: What happened to me? Why did he think she *gathered* anything about his love life, apart from the segment that featured herself? She had to get him out of here.

"Thought you'd never ask. She moved back to Brazil. We had a laugh, you know? But in the end she didn't really travel, if you get what I mean. From a poor village near Ouro Preto. You can take the girl out of the village . . . but *you*, you're a mystery. Innocent, truly. Yet so wonderfully playful, so *daring*—a very compelling combination, if I may say so."

Had she been so daring? She could feel her throat coloring and looked at the clock: time's up. She rose, hoping he'd get the point. And he stood up, too.

"*This* is what you saw them on?" he said, inspecting Mark's digital camera, and shaking his head. "Pitiful." He switched it on to see where she'd gotten to. "I see you made it to dessert. Did you realize this is a little film?"

She did not.

"Perhaps you'd like to see it, before I show you the flawless masterpiece I spent the morning editing."

"Not really."

"Oh, come on. It doesn't last a minute." He laughed, turning to the computer, searching through his files. "It's embarrassingly quick. Let's see what you think."

Dan looked at the screen, unmoved, as if he was showing his staff a mock-up for an ad when what they had before them, with full sound, was Shirley noisily sucking his cock. At least she assumed it was Dan's. Jean was appalled, and impressed—the steady application, the forthright energy, made her think, ridiculously, of the refrain from that old book of Vic's, *We're Going on a Bear Hunt:* We can't go over it. We can't go under it. Oh no! We've got to go through it! Yes, she'd done this, and in the course of her researches she'd seen it being done. But never before had she watched something like this with someone else, let alone someone she'd done God knows what with the night before. Was that how *she* looked, like a dope-eyed farm animal bobbing before the farmer? Every now and again there was a fist in the frame, Dan holding the girl's hair, controlling the rhythm—but this was not remotely how she pictured herself: as something ethereal and elegant and goddessy.

Yes, that was Dan. And this, she thought, was Jean: watching pornography with Dan, watching pornography with Dan in it with Dan . . . she could even feel a twinge of mechanical lust. But what kind of man would show a woman such a scene, so utterly confident of her appreciation? This was going to be much harder than she anticipated, managing the new Dan—hideously entitled.

"Same thing for lunch every single day," he said, shaking his head again. "And unlike your own, this is a conscience not bothered. Healthy girl. What *Shirley* worries about is the calorie content of all that jizz. Hey, you're the health writer." He looked over at her companionably. "Is it true that one load of spunk's got twice as many calories as an ice-cream sundae?"

Jean looked at him—was he expecting her to smile fondly? Surely this wasn't a question that demanded an answer.

"And she's been skipping lunch for *weeks*. Only problem with that is I have to skip lunch every day too, hence the sleek form you have before you."

How could she get him out of here? Why did she feel so dazed, inert? She couldn't look at anything but the screen—she certainly couldn't look at him, and wished he wouldn't stand so menacingly close. He leaned against the counter and their arms touched; she leaned forward so they didn't. The clip finally ended—with much gagging and choking and blurring, moaning becoming a roar as the hand holding the camera jerked and the screen went black.

"But wait. I have something much better for you." Before she could protest, he clicked onto a different file.

She could hardly breathe, fearing the worst, and then there it was—the prime of Mrs. Jean Hubbard, not photographs this time, but a sepia-tinted film, accompanied by a strange sound track tapping on her headache; she thought she could detect the sound of a dripping faucet, then something like a box of nails being repeatedly scattered over a hard surface. . . . Well, she hadn't been far wrong: here was goddessy Jean, ethereal and elegant Jean—a gracefully suffering sea nymph in a painful portrait of submission and release.

Of course Dan had to film it: How else would it properly become pornography? How else would it even exist? How would he? Despite her miserably violated feeling, she knew that she could connect again to the person in these images, right here and now, and she absolutely had to get him out of here. She stepped away, and he stepped toward her. Again that chokingly woody, underground scent, and she gasped for air. *Help*—Jean thought, and she pleaded in a thin whisper, gripping the counter behind her, "Go!" He raised his hands toward her. Louder, in an ugly rasping voice she'd never heard before, her fists by her sides, she said, "Didn't you hear me? I said GO—get *out!*"

"Not that way," he said quietly. Unsmiling and jaw clenched (very porno, Jean registered), Dan pulled her close with both hands and she slumped against his chest, freely inhaling. There was no humoring him to wipe those pictures. He was going to make her beg and she was ready to do it. "I came here because I wanted to give something back to you," he told her solemnly. "Something you own as much as I do, something we *created*. But you shouldn't have stolen my memory card."

He grabbed her hand and pressed it against his gut, just above the belt—waiting, she guessed, for her to move her hand voluntarily; he thought she couldn't resist. She could see all this, so why did she feel herself weakening as if drugged? That's just it: Dan was a drug—one you snort. Sensation, she told herself, that's all this was, all they could possibly be feeling—not even pleasure, just *sensation*. And power—his. She closed her eyes, inhaled deeply. Then he squeezed her hand, painful where her ring was, making her open her eyes and pay attention.

"I suppose I should punish you—not, as you think and fear, with the pictures, and not as you want me to do right now."

As *she* wanted? Jean was infuriated, all the more so because it was true. Something they'd created: she hadn't thought of it that way—she'd just been going along with anything and everything on this weird weekend of suspended time. She'd thought she'd smooth things over, that they had a deal. And now she was out of her depth. He was pressing in on her and she couldn't speak.

He kissed her around the ears, forcing her back over the counter, supported by her elbows, her chest pushed up below him, and he whispered, "You're not going to be drunk this time, or playing a part. And I'm not going to punish you even when you beg me to. I know it makes it easier for you if it hurts, as if it's not your fault, if you're overpowered or out of it. You don't *need* to be punished, Jean. And your conscience is not my problem." He turned her around so she was bent over the counter, her back to him, and showed her the delete key. "You go ahead," he breathed into her hair, grappling with her belt buckle, "and don't mind me."

Jean erased first the film and then the photographs, clicking through them, one by one. He struggled with her Levi's as she wiped the images; she knew that she wouldn't stop him and that she wouldn't forget any of it. She was sober, soiled, and horrified; *this* was the punishment, no special force needed. Then, for just a moment, she thought of Vic, age about six, peering up against the sun at the big O over the Odeon cinema in Parkway. *What are you doing?* Jean had asked her, wanting to get home; *Wait,* Vic said. *I'm making a memory.* Dan was yanking her jeans down on one side and then the other, his hand reaching inside her underpants. But something—perhaps Victoria's early clarity and determination—freed her, and she turned and pushed him away.

"*No,* Dan. Not now and not ever. Not again," she said, putting herself back together. "You need to go."

He stepped back, defiantly rearranging himself—and for a couple of seconds she was frightened by the stony look on his face: cresting exasperation. "I thought that's what you wanted. Isn't that what you asked for, Mrs. H.?"

Jean looked hard at him, her arms crossed tight over her chest. "I didn't ask you for anything," she said. "Not a goddamn thing." Upstairs the front door opened and slammed shut.

"*Vic?*"

"Hi, Mum! We're back! Rupert gave me a lift."

She looked wildly at Dan who raised a hand, patting the air in front of his shoulder, as if everything was under control. Jean smoothed her hair; he shut the laptop, took back his memory card, tucked in his T-shirt.

"Come down!" she shouted. "Dan's here!"

"Glad I could show you those mock-ups," he said loudly. "I *like* your idea of a picnic—good food from the same vintage, juicy homemade pies, and rounded, golden loaves of bread, the reddest, ripest berries. . . ." She looked at him sharply, but that didn't stop him. "What's a fridge without food? You're right. They did look very sterile, very showroom. And you know they've done the market research, and it's true, hungry people spend."

The front door slammed again, and in a minute Vic was lumbering downstairs barefoot.

"Oh," said Jean, aiming for disappointment, "did Rupert leave?" She leaned forward to kiss Victoria and smelled smoke—which she welcomed if it overlaid any ambient scent of Dan. Or was she the only one who caught that?

"Yeah. He had to get the car back. Hey, Dan."

"Hello, Victoria." He gave her a stellar smile and, wattage unreturned, moved in anyway to kiss her cheek. "Good bash?"

"Decent." She went to get a mug from the cupboard.

"Darling, remember those fridge things I took to the office after dropping you off yesterday?" Jean said, filling them both in. "Well, Dan's brought them back, to show Mark what he's done with them. And now he's leaving. Dad's stuck in Germany. Fog. Major fog, apparently."

"Really?" Vic perked up. "When's he getting back?"

"Well, tomorrow around one, with luck."

"My phone's completely dead." She moved to plug her cell phone into the charger, glanced at the computer, and said, "I'm going to have a bath."

"All right, darling. Are you hungry?"

"Um, not really. We stopped at a Little Chef. Thoroughly revolting it was too. Anyway, Vikram's coming round with pizza. See you, Dan."

"Yeah, cheers. Lovely to see you. I'd better be off myself," he said as Victoria started back upstairs.

"Okay, well, I'm sure Mark will be in touch. What a pity. Got all your stuff?" she asked as she led him up the stairs, unbelievably even now able to wonder how her blue-jeaned ass looked not only from behind but from *below*. Victoria had barely managed a smile—did she sense something? Maybe she was just very hungover.

How *close* she'd come to succumbing again, and how fine she'd cut it. And how far she'd already fallen, how effortlessly, headlong into her disgrace. Of course Vic was absolutely right about Dan; it must be obvious to anyone. And what would she think if she had any idea who her mother really was?

Victoria's overnight bag was on the mat blocking the door, and her fleece covered Dan's leather jacket on the sofa. Jean pulled it out for him, wondering who to call first, Phyllis or Dad.

"Bye, Jean. Take care."

"Yeah" was all she could say, following him out the door in her bare feet, crossing her arms against the chill and any further bodily contact. Dan planted a kiss on her cheek, mercifully unlingering, and skipped down the two front steps, momentarily unbalanced by the heavy bag. When he recovered, he gave her a terrific smile, intimate, wolfish, but not so much blaze that it would matter if Vic caught it from an upstairs window. He turned toward Parkway, his wide athlete's stance easily bearing the weight, and he didn't look back.

As soon as she shut the front door, Jean went to the phone. She tried her father's apartment on Seventy-second Street, then her sister Marianne in Westport, where he sometimes went on a Sunday. No answer.

Of course, she thought, putting on the kettle. It was July Fourth weekend; they'd all be at Marianne and Doug's beach house. Looking in her overstuffed red book for the number, she prepared herself for a chat with her sister, always so theatrically burdened. Jean was fond of her brother-in-law, a trial lawyer, but the connection hadn't eased relations with Marianne, who picked up on the first ring.

"He*llo?*" You'd think from her tone she single-handedly ran a handicapped circus, not just three young sons. Nothing wrong with their voices, anyway, Jean thought, holding the receiver and their boy screams away from her ear.

"Hi," she said, "it's Jean."

"*There* you are."

"Did you call?"

"*Every*body's been trying to get ahold of you."

"Funny, I didn't get any messages from you."

"Didn't Mom call you? *And* Dad?"

"How is he?"

"Here, why don't you ask him. Dad! It's Jean! John Avery, get down off of there this instant! Dylan! Outside. *Now.*"

So much time passed that Jean wondered if Marianne had just decided to do something else, and she tried to think wholesome, charitable, life-lengthening thoughts. (She knew that her self-disgust deepened her irritation with her sister, a woman about as unlikely as any on earth to fall prey to someone like Dan.) But she lapsed immediately: it wasn't as if Bill was standing right there; she could've filled Jean in, but oh no, too martyred. Finally, she heard the phone change hands and the deep voice she loved. She'd always thought that if Bill Warner was a singer, he'd be Johnny Cash.

"Hello, darling." He sounded tired, winded.

"*Dad*. How *are* you?"

"I'm fine, dear. Just wanted to let you know that I'm going into the hospital tomorrow—no, wait a minute, Tuesday, after the long weekend, for a little procedure. Entirely elective, nothing serious. Maybe I told you about the aneurysm. Going to get it before it gets me. I'll be out Friday, latest."

Not like Dad, that euphemism, to say "procedure" instead of "operation." He had mentioned it, and so had Phyllis, but it seemed such a long shot, an exploding artery, no more vivid to Jean than cosmic impact.

"That does sound quick. Where're you doing it?"

"Columbia-Presbyterian. The best. They do these things every day, a dozen a day, thousands of them every year. Practically like going to the dentist."

"So you decided to do it now."

"You know your old man—once I've got the information, can't not act. Best to get it out of the way. The little bugger's bound to blow at some point—could be six months, could be five years. I'll sleep a whole lot better not thinking about it. And I've got the top guy all signed up."

"Oh Dad, I'd like to come over."

"Well, Jeannie, you know there's no face I'd rather see, but to be honest, it's really not necessary. I'll be out before you get here. How's Victoria? Mark there with you, too?"

"Fine, fine. We're all great." What would her dear, honorable dad say if he knew how great she really was: Jean the eager adulteress and porno queen. "Dad, I'm halfway to New York. I could hop right over. I *want* to."

"Darling, I know I can level with you. I'd just as soon get through this, really nothing serious, and have a good visit when I'm not all out of it and buzzing on drugs."

"Well, then, a little later maybe. I'll be done with my birds in a week or two." From her first visit to the center with Phyllis, Jean had been giving Bill progress reports on the Beausoleil project—she'd had an instinct he'd be gripped and he was.

"Oh my. Are they all set to go?"

"Just about—although there's some doubt about my little Bud, who may have to hold on a bit longer. The runt—remember him?"

"Sure, I do. Well, good. Old Bud and I'll be kept in for observation. And one fine day, we too shall overcome, and be restored. Into the wild."

Jean didn't like the sound of this at all. Into the wild. She saw in her mind's eye a swirling thin-spun cosmos, sickeningly uninhabitable, through which she was catapulting at inhuman speed. Like her poor brother, swilling around in the cold, dark sea. "I'm counting on you, Dad. Let me know. I'll just jump on a plane." I'm counting on you not to die, she meant, and she hoped it didn't come through in her voice.

"Don't worry, dear, I'll be waiting for you. We'll be in close touch. Bye, darling."

He always left the phone abruptly and Jean could never get used to it, or the twinge of undispelled loneliness—the job of the drawn-out good-bye. Still, a child of the Depression, Bill couldn't *not* worry about the phone bill. This time he wandered off without hanging up, and Jean wasn't sure he knew you had to press the button—bound to be a cordless—or if she was supposed to hang on for Marianne.

She heard footsteps getting louder, as if they were marching down some school corridor straight to the principal's office, a scolding on the way. Jean tensed—and for the first time she wondered how the little boys felt when Marianne approached. Then Marianne pressed the button, without checking to see if Jean was still there, and the line went dead.

Jean called her mother, keen to make a plan, but when Phyllis said there was "absolutely no need to come over," she understood it as criticism that she wasn't there already. "Marianne's with him now."

"I know, Mom. I just spoke to him. Dad says this is a straightforward procedure."

"That's right, dear. Though I suppose nothing is ever completely straightforward at eighty."

"Seventy-nine," Jean corrected. When she hung up, having promised she'd coordinate with her sister, she told herself she was going to have to get much better at all this, and fast. She needed some air. Jean grabbed her bag and went up to the living room. Victoria and Vikram were lounging on the sofa watching TV, guidebooks on the floor, their cardboard pizza boxes open on the sofa arms like laptops.

They were planning a summer trip around Indonesia, with a stopover in St. Jacques. Mark and Jean officially approved. Only nine months after the Bali bombings, they dissimulated their worry about terrorism on political and superstitious grounds (the lightning principle) and instead counted themselves lucky they'd been spared the big gap-year excursion, all aimlessness, danger, and expense. They'd contributed frequent-flier miles, budgeted for hotels and, she was sure, Mark would top this up with cash: the "planned economy" Vic advocated.

Vic and Vikram were loosely holding hands and transfixed, gazing at the screen. "Animal magnetism" is not a metaphor, Jean thought, pausing to look at them. They didn't even realize it, but these two had to be touching, making contact at some point, even if it was no more than the tip of a finger on a knee. What were they so solemnly watching? A liposuction operation.

"Back soon," she said, lingering in the doorway as if debating where to go next—St. Jacques or straight to New York? But she could hear the fat-suctioning machine that so riveted Vikram and Victoria and, unacknowledged, slipped outside.

Her next move would depend on the news from Scully. Walking down Albert Street, she thought she'd managed giving birth alone because, well, she wasn't alone. Scully had been there. And Victoria had been there. Now here was just Jean, the same dread, the same doctor, the same competition for Mark's time. Familiar wait, familiar worry. But no baby at the end of it. So *what*, then, at the end of it? She could hardly bear to imagine such an attack on her person, something from Dante's lower circles, the one packed, if she remembered right, with adulterous women.

And as she turned into Parkway, joining the Sunday stream of families coming from the zoo, she was overcome, coursing with fresh recognition of her folly—one she'd justified by Mark's own. There was Dad, about to go into the hospital while she'd elected to romp in pornoland with that worthless pleasure addict. Like liposuction, she thought—disgusting, maybe dangerous, self-indulgent, and totally unnecessary. In fact, it was worse than liposuction, which at least wasn't also disloyal. Jean paused to exchange sorrowful looks with a lone little pug in the pet shop window—or not a pug: a Chinese shar-pei, the sign said. His caramel coat looked about four sizes too big, the fur concertinaed just as if all his puppy fat had been hoovered out. Such worried brown eyes, buried in those folds—imagine a creature particularly valued for its wrinkles, Jean thought. Oh, look, he's shivering—she didn't think he could be more than five or six weeks old. Where was his mother? Where were all the other puglets? And then it was so clear. Whatever Scully said, she'd go directly to New York, returning by the most powerful instinct to her original territory. She was homing.

New York

Lurching into the city from Kennedy Airport, Jean didn't want to distract the driver—a stressed Sikh shouting into his cell phone—by asking him to slow down. Was he plotting a murder, or putting in one very exacting dinner order? Forget him and his girlish nape with its long black hairs, and look at your own hometown—right there on the horizon, glowing in smoggy, timeless monochrome. The grimy heat extended a wobbly carpet to the great mirage that was Gotham, and Jean was excited to be back and happy, her life recently returned to her. Scully had given her the all clear ("though we'll want to have another look in six months"), and she received the stay of execution, the papal waiver, with elation and, very soon, with oblivious entitlement. She'd picked over this (hoping as ever for column yield), the physics of fear: how mortal fright could take you and hold you in its Kong-like grip and then, *phttt*, it was just over, like falling out of love, and you were frowning with incomprehension at all the medical notes you'd scribbled only the week before. Could it really be as if it never happened? Wasn't there some residue or stain—the fear itself taking years off your life, even if for now the cancer had been run out of town?

The taxi toiled along the Van Wyck Expressway, then onto

Queens Boulevard with its soot-caked clusters of nursing homes so unutterably grim that only the most despised old people could be remanded here. From this approach you hardly noticed the loss—less than two years before—of the Twin Towers, she thought, noticing all the same. It seemed to her that she alone remembered how hated they once were. But her early views were the voice of a mob, acquired when she went as a kid on a march protesting against their construction, with Auntie Eunice, Bill Warner's charismatic, conservation-minded law partner.

A pack of implacable New Yorkers plus Jean, they'd walked down the Avenue of the Americas from the West Village to city hall, chanting, "Too ugly! Too tall!" Her mother had thought marching not only ineffectual but tacky. Dad was proud: the making of a citizen. For Jean now, it was sobering to remember the simple rectitude of that protest, the passionate certainty. She'd come to recognize this day as the birth of her lawyer's heart, but the image that seized on her developing mind then was not the World Trade Center—it was the women's prison on Greenwich Avenue, and the thin arms waving through slit windows to the marchers below; a dozen Rapunzels trapped in another ugly tower.

After that march, like a tourist in her own city, Jean had gotten into the habit of looking up instead of down, and she went to the Village whenever she could—to the secondhand shops where she acquired a first style, composed from men's shirts and suits, and to Washington Square, grayer but more intimate than any corner of Central Park, the drug dealers more forthright. "Sense, sense, sense," they'd say, for sensemilla, and "Pass me by, won't get high. . . ." Among the dealers, she had a "friend," Wayne something, who come to think of it was not unlike Christian in St. Jacques—gap toothed, flirtatious, and black. "Need something for your head?" he'd ask; Jean always said no but was thrilled by such adult consideration. (At the time she was still coating her face each night with Phyllis's cold cream and then, on top of that, talcum powder, in the mysterious belief that this combination would blanch her freckles.) One afternoon, worried Wayne lose interest in her, she bought a nickel bag. When he invited her back to his place to smoke it, she said no and never returned to Washington Square.

The prison was torn down, Jean didn't know when, and now the Twin Towers were also gone; so improbably from the view of thirty years ago, they were greatly mourned: they were too ugly, too tall—but they were ours. Billy died only six months after that protest; his lift from the party plowed into a lamppost; his rib poked a hole in his heart. In the cab speeding to her ailing father, Jean was glad the masterful Sikh didn't permit air-conditioning. She wanted to feel everything. Today was Friday: she'd timed her trip to land her in town the moment Dad arrived back home and was ready for visitors. Or so she thought. But the day before, Phyllis had told her, "The doctors are keeping him in intensive care for observation."

"What does that mean?" Two days had passed since the surgery.

"Well, what it sounds like, I guess. They just want to keep an eye on him."

"In intensive care? That's a lot of eyes."

"I know. Thank goodness his insurance covers it. For a hundred days. Heaven forfend. The doctor told me his anatomy is *unusual.* Things are not where they're supposed to be. So it took them twelve hours to finish what should've been more or less routine. Now what I want to tell you, honey, is that the *operation* has been a great success, but of course anything like this is a trauma to the body."

Prescription phrases—Phyllis sounded like she was reading from notes—although Jean noticed she no longer said "procedure."

"He was more or less *frozen* for all that time. Shut down. And then they actually lifted his organs over to one side."

Jean could hear the fascination in her mother's voice, and she could understand that, but she wanted to get past it. "Isn't the hospital the most dangerous place? All those sick people and supergerms."

"There are plenty of people worse off than your father. That I can vouch for. And some of them are in the waiting room. Oh my God, Jean, you have no idea. The *asses* on these people. You don't know what America is. . . ."

Her mother was having trouble concentrating. Jean couldn't tell if this was a bad sign or a good sign. Good, she decided. How serious could things be if she was talking about American asses?

"They're all Dominicans up there, *packed* into clothes two, three sizes too small. Physically impossible, in fact."

"Mom, you must be wrecked. Is there anyone with him now?"

"Well, nobody. Nobody except a dozen or so nurses. You can't believe the hours they put in, nurses from around the globe—darling Irish girls, Africans, Filipinos . . . or should that be Filipin*as*? There's even a male nurse—fag, of course. With not one but two earrings, like a Gypsy. A girl Gypsy. They need male nurses to move the patients around, though you wouldn't want to meet some of the *fe*male nurses in a dark alley. Good people, though, Jean. Saints, really."

"Mom! I'm going to get an early flight tomorrow," she'd said—and here she finally was, once again unable to connect with her mother. Phyllis must be in intensive care, where they surely banned the use of cell phones.

Slowing down in Washington Heights, Jean got a blast of city sounds and smells: sizzling meat and fried dough from a quilted-silver vendor's cart on the island of the wide avenue; samba blaring, New Yorkers honking any chance they got—and today the sound struck Jean as convivial. And then, suddenly before the wide steps of Columbia-Presbyterian, it hardly looked anymore like New York City—instead a steeply pitched, leafy suburb. Along the steps, a pale wall—a great slope glittering with mica dust—was adorned by a frieze of white-and-blue-uniformed hospital workers, sitting, stretching, smoking, and chatting. Through the glass doors and into the chilled lobby, where Jean's suitcase, a discreet wheelie, attracted the unsmiling attention of security: check that in, then to the sign-in queue, show ID, get a large color-coded pass like a flash card for the sight-impaired.

It was in this final line that fatigue hit Jean with a powerful command to get horizontal. At least she was in a hospital, she thought, gripping the cool handrail in the elevator and silently watching the numbers climb until she was at last disgorged onto the fifth floor. Past the young doctors in the hall confiding to their cell phones, past the crowded waiting room, through the swinging double doors to the reception island, Jean was grateful all over again for her clean bill of health. But she didn't see her father.

The unsmiling nurse didn't even look up—sullen posing as efficient, too busy, no, too senior—when she asked for him. This isn't a hotel, you know. Steeling herself, Jean began her own rounds, reading the paper name card in the aluminum slot beside each curtained-off cubicle. Expecting to discover shellac-yellow patients choking on vomit, she started to peek behind the curtains.

Major surgery was the kind of surgery they did here: the clotted hearts of old men. But it was the sight of an old woman asleep with her head flung back, displaying her narrow rodent-like teeth, that made Jean want to leave. And then she spotted his feet—those high arches and extra-long toes—at the bottom of a pair of inflated gray tubes fitted like wine-bottle coolers around his calves against deep-vein thrombosis.

The bed was full. Dad, of course, though he didn't look like himself in that ancient-mariner beard, but also Phyllis, slotted along the edge beside him, the metal side bar especially lowered to make room. He was asleep, and she looked like she was, too, her small hand resting on Bill's naked oatmeal chest. A modern rendition of the Arundel Tomb, Jean thought. *What will survive of us is love.*

Her mother knew she'd be arriving around now, which only increased Jean's displeasure at finding her in bed with him. Wasn't it insanely proprietary, even dangerous, given his delicate condition? Or was it just unseemly? The sight offended, she would later realize, not because of where they were or because he was apparently comatose, not because they were long divorced and everyone had gotten used to that; it was because they were her parents.

But what had she expected to find? A young dark-haired Dad sitting behind his big brown desk in weekend corduroy, smiling at her over his folded *New York Times* as she came in, back home from Saturday-morning gymnastics? And then she noticed, across the cubicle on the window ledge, the bowl of green apples—Granny Smith, the kind they used to share on those mornings, cut into wedges with the skin left on and smeared with peanut butter.

Jean stood hesitating at the curtain, looking in, glad now for the staff's indifference. Everywhere she saw evidence of Phyllis's ministrations, her sandbagging against helplessness: the stack of CDs, classical compilations and Peggy Lee; skin lotion and a comb; a brief skyline of Tupperware containers with their shadowy sealed treats. Other items, Jean grasped, had been specially selected for their settled civility, their reassuringly expensive cheer, such as the engraved silver vase, a wedding present filled with pink ranunculus. But it was his aftershave that got Jean, the ornate bottle of 4711; she'd certainly cry if she smelled it. Her throat constricted again, her toes pressed onto the floor through thin soles.

There was nothing to do but wait. She moved to the window, careful not to knock into any of the equipment crowding the space: mechanical bed, respirator, heart monitor, the tangled rack of tubes and bags. . . . She looked down to the shiny river Bill wouldn't be able to see from his bed, a silver snake soundlessly wending its way to the sea.

Jean remembered a trip around the island with Larry Mond on the Circle Line the summer she worked for Dad's firm. It had been unbearably hot and humid—their bid for the river began in torpor. On the boat, just past the Statue of Liberty, it began to drizzle and then to pound and bounce on the slippery painted surface, a great clattering New York summer downpour; and, instead of following her inside the small cabin packed with tourists, Larry had held her back and smuggled her hand into his pocket, those joined hands soon the only dry part of their combined body, alone on the open deck. It had just been the right thing to do.

The right thing. Jean, reflexively fingering the biopsy spot, turned to look again at the slumbering parents, their bodies alternately rising and falling like carousel horses in the final lap. Standing there, helplessly watching, it was unbearable even to think of losing either one of them. Instead, she thought about the night she got Scully's good news.

An elated Mark had arrived back from Germany just in time to take his girls out for a festive dinner at Chez Julien, a large, noisy French brasserie in Soho. For the first time in months she'd actively wanted his company. He excelled at celebration—a talent she lacked, which was perhaps why, she suddenly thought, she'd been quite so pleased she'd been *able* to gambol and frolic unfretfully that night with Dan, never mind any special daring. She had a glimmer here, midreminiscence about their family dinner, that she might possibly consider her crawl around Dan's grotto, that swinging orange lantern in Hoxton, as a kind of Saturnalia, with Dan as the Lord of Misrule. Hadn't she played the master serving the slave, just as in the Roman feast?

Over champagne at Chez Julien, Victoria had at first been upset not to have been told about the biopsy. But she accepted her mother's familiar mystical reasoning, that she hadn't wanted to make it real by saying the words: breast cancer. Jean allowed herself to be teased—the superstitious, hex-attuned health columnist—and then she changed the subject. "Do you think the paparazzi outside are waiting for someone in particular or just hanging around on the off-chance?" Jean asked.

"Paparazz-*o*," Victoria corrected, "and an obvious employee of the restaurant. Lends an air of glamour. At Chez Julien's everyone's a star."

"Actually," Mark said, draining his glass, "the snapper was waiting for me—the man with the two loveliest women in London. Garçon!" He called after a passing waiter, holding up his empty flute. He'd positively enjoyed being ribbed about the contraceptive cream—How had he put it? "What if I'd used your friend's depilatory cream instead." There were toasts, and Jean's mistaken order of foie gras. She'd stared at the organ floating in broth as if expecting it to twitch, a tumor, obviously malignant, a spongy cyst extracted entire—imagine a thing like *that* in your breast and then getting it for dinner; and Jean had expected a slab of paste, the nursery color of dried calamine lotion. She managed to unload the unprocessed liver on Mark with a joke: he couldn't refuse with *bonne foi*.

That night, they'd made love for the first time in months. Energy and ease drawn from champagne and from relief. She was so grateful to be alive, to be given all these extra chances. To these they'd added another relief: everything still worked. Jean badly wanted to tell Vic, and sometime she would tell her: Mark was so proud of you he didn't stop grinning all evening. In bed the next morning, she thought with amused tenderness how he hadn't realized the approving nods from nearby tables were a response not so much to Victoria herself, but to his ruddy pleasure in her.

Mark had gone out for the papers and Jean contemplated getting up. She stretched, and felt, as a great luxury, relief also from complication. Somehow Giovana, as if she herself was the cancer, had been banned from attendance even among Jean's thoughts throughout the evening and night. And this morning as well: Jean, still not dead, was too happy to care. Amazing how self-fulfilling a pleasure this was, playing happy families. Of course she knew she couldn't shut out her troubles indefinitely, but neither was she just playing: she was cancer free and full of love—nothing had ever seemed realer. When she did at last get up, she found her hangover was mysteriously mild. Vic, in her old room at last, slept in.

Still hovering by the window in this hospital cubicle, it was with near incredulity that Jean remembered her conviction, in the coffee-scented kitchen, with the bacon spattering and popping like an old jazz recording and Elizabeth rubbing against her ankles, that strangeness had its points, but true love, or old love, was better. It was more satisfying, it was more intimate, and it knew so much more about her.

And then old love stirred right in front of her: *our lingering parents.* When her elfin mother sat up, looking just as rumpled and disoriented as Victoria had every morning of her childhood, Jean fought her tears. Poor Phyllis. Poor Bill.

But staying with Phyllis on an inflatable mattress in her cluttered, white-carpeted TV den fed her mood of suppressed agitation. Four days quickly passed in this routine of waiting, mother and daughter sharing the unspoken thought that if Bill wasn't getting better, he must be getting worse.

Jean was too restless and distracted to follow the news, too emotionally unreliable for phone chat, so she communicated electronically with Victoria and Mark—both, thankfully, very busy. When Mark wrote that he was going to the Continent for a week of work away from the office, she relaxed—it seemed her fear of Dan's confession even outweighed her misery over this latest assignation with Giovana. A sad, indeed sordid, state of affairs. In preparation for her series on sin, she'd been reading Dante. *Purgatorio,* where she felt very much at home.

And shoring up her strength, sharpening her moral wits— she finally began Larry's book, *A Theory of Equality.* She found his ideas both stimulating and strangely soothing. For example, the proposition that natural endowments of talent and intelligence are morally arbitrary and ought not to affect the distribution of resources in society. How Mark disagreed, Jean thought: for him, it was all a great dogfight, hard work, vim, vigor, and, yes, luck—*these* won the day, rightly so, every man for himself and sod the rest. But Larry was also tough, and his theory had a component beyond fairness. It was this, even if she'd known it before, that struck her in Phyllis's feminine aerie: human beings are responsible for the choices they make.

Bill was mostly asleep but not comatose, and he regularly awoke. All three Warners expended the great part of their energies working the nurses and doctors. The patient was gallant as he would be toward any woman, perhaps (it dawned on his newly attuned daughter) toward any woman who fussed over him in bed—never mind how much he must hate being handled, or manhandled, naked. In response to his recurrent pneumonia and a partially collapsed lung, Jean found herself eagerly offering a letter of recommendation for the pulmonologist's would-be journalist son, whom she'd never met. And she invested in Joe, the hoop-earringed nurse with a standout candor: a real find in this world of technical talk, shift change, and buck-passing specialization. Phyllis flattered all the nurses and resisted showing them what a hospital corner looked like in Salt Lake City: something as sharp and crisply ingenious as an origami swan.

In the evenings, mother and daughter were gentle with each other; Jean read Larry's book and Phyllis did intricate needlepoint; they oopsed and whoopsed as they do-si-doed in the galley kitchen. And most of the day, they sat for dead hours scanning magazines in the waiting room. Jean was stunned by the profusion of health columns, so many dieting tips, while all around them, just as Phyllis had said, were the obese families of the infirm, fat men and fat women, fat children and fat adolescents: the boys in rustling fat tracksuits and the girls with oiled tresses plastered to the skull and then unleashed below the neck over fat backs and great cartoon asses. It amazed Jean to think that, through Dan's comprehensive attentions, she'd only just discovered her own ass, and how quickly all that had again seemed alien.

She'd start her sin series with gluttony, she thought, riveted by the families in the waiting room. She counted back on her

fingers through the sins: Gluttony. Greed. Sloth. Lust, obviously,
envy, and pride. That was six. What was the seventh? *Anger.*
That didn't seem right. Pride and anger had crossed the road—
they were all virtue now. Lust had been liberated, at least for
some. Sloth was laid-back, low-key, and, at least since the abo-
lition of slavery, defiantly fashionable on St. Jacques, where
people lived to a Methuselan age. But for Jean, sloth had a special resonance. Dante described it as the sin of insufficiency—
not bothering to love—and he twinned it with sadness.

Sometimes they wandered to the cafeteria on four where the
soups weren't bad and the overfilled muffin trays reminded
Jean of the families in the waiting room. To escape AC and IC,
they occasionally walked around the block. If ever they strayed
farther, they were repelled, spooled back, as if they'd reached
the limit of an extendable leash or touched an invisible electric
fence. Mostly they sat or stood behind his drawn curtain, holding his hand, massaging lotion into his papery skin, reading
silently and aloud. Soon Phyllis would have to recover her
part-time job at the public library; she was overdue and her agitation was mounting daily like a late-book fine. Finally Jean
persuaded her mother to take a break, waving her off down-
town to the Upper East Side.

Bill slept a great deal, and Jean waited. Walking out one afternoon she spotted an Internet place on Broadway and stopped
to check her e-mail: There wasn't much that was new or interesting, but as she scrolled down, tidying and deleting, there,
apparently untouched, was that old message from France, *À
l'attention de* M. Hubbard, and Jean clicked it open.

Dear Mark,

I am so sorry I missed you in Londres. I will try to make new my
plan so I can see you. How is Victoria? She gave me this

address. You were right. I can never forget her. Thank you. Thank you for everything. You are giving me so much always. You say it is a gift and not a lend, but I will repay, je te promesse.

Sophie

Ps, I passed by the abbaye today it is jus the same. The top window at the last, it was opened. When I pass I think to become une soeur—a nunn?

Jean had in fact been thinking about Sophie de Vilmorin. Ever since her chat in the kitchen with Vic, she'd wanted to write and put herself in the frame, to interpose herself. Now she saw that it was not *Vic* Sophie had wanted. It was money—cupidity, not cupid. Not love, not friendship, not extended family: money. Jean had been right—there was something deeply suspect about Sophie. Still, money was the least complicated of motivations, and for that alone she should be grateful. Never mind if the e-mail was for Mark, the address alone—hubbardsabroad@hotmail.com—should've told Sophie it was a family account. Any renewed sense of breaking and entering was unfortunate: Jean had to dispatch a reply without delay, friendly but brisk, an acknowledgment, not an expansion.

My dear Sophie:

Forgive my replying in Mark's stead—he is horribly busy. We were both sorry to miss you in London.

She deleted this. Perhaps Mark had seen her since—it seemed from her e-mail she was trying to arrange a meeting.

Sophie,

I was sorry to have missed you in London—Victoria was thrilled to have discovered her old babysitter. Hope for better timing next time.

All the best
Jean(ne!)

Jean was about to send and then she hesitated. She wondered about Mark's helping Sophie. *Jean* thought she was creepy, but maybe Mark was touched by her. "Vulnerable" was his type—he loved a project. Or maybe he was merely intrigued by Sandrine's daughter, her modern replacement. A young *citoyenne* of the European Community not bound by too-early motherhood; a postcard from the unlived past. Or the insufficiently lived past—with its inexpungible allure. She'd listened countless times to his reminiscences over the years, summer of '67, definitely *his* summer of love, lying on the bottom of a moored and wind-rocked boat with sodden life preservers for a bed, madly kissing.

The scene had expanded, whether in fact or just in her mind she no longer knew, to encompass a mist of desperate daily couplings on the beach after dark, protected from the violent wind by the great stone wall, the mighty ramparts of St. Malo. A month or two of blissed-out first love, which of course meant first sex, before the *fête* that would turn up the solid Breton who would win Sandrine away from him—a much more promising mate (a man and not a boy)—before the wind grew too strong and blew skinny seventeen-year-old Mark back across the Channel.

Perhaps, who knew, he saw in Sophie the woman Sandrine might have become if he'd stayed—rowed the boat out with his slender French bride, fishing net for a veil. Who didn't have such fantasies? Their French children, in striped sweaters and ribboned berets, playing on a beach in winter. Helping Sophie was possibly no more than his way of thanking the mother for that first love; Jean understood exactly how its glow only increased with time—no different, say, from her own recent thought for Larry on the Circle Line. Experimental nostalgia, not a game plan. It was part of being their age now, picking over the past like a shoreline, searching out the good shells and the green glass and (always ambitious, ever curious) the bottled message. The future was kids' stuff: lost in space.

Jean canceled her reply. Instead, in the message box she wrote: *Something for you,* and forwarded it to Mark's office address. Three months after her initial, and useless, reply to Giovana's letter, Jean was done mediating.

When Jean and Bill were alone for the first time, he waved her over: come close. It took her a while to understand what it was he wanted, his speech smudged by drugs and, she suspected (but no doctor would confirm), another stroke. Dad patted his beard stiffly, and he kept on patting it, swatting at it, his round eyes staring at her intensely, Father Time. His expression suggested this might be an involuntary spasm of the hand, and one that was scaring him.

Jean's difficulty in understanding him was increased by her own fear—this sudden leap into great age and no way of knowing if it would go quiet again or accelerate. Like a speeded-up film, she thought, tracking the decay of some soft fruit, peach or plum, time burrowing toward the irreducible stone. She was also hampered by inexperience; they had always understood each other effortlessly. So who was he, this old man with the fearful darting eyes? Maybe an ancestor, blue-eyed Confederate general, but not Dad.

Finally she got it. She held up his razor and gestured like she was shaving her own neck—without realizing, she had adopted his muteness. That was it. He wanted her to shave him. He nodded vigorously, humorlessly, head bobbing in accord or active senescence.

As she cranked his bed, then pulled and pushed the pillows at his back, she caught the flash of impatience in his eyes, as different in Dad as the beard: Bill, who had never shown anything other than infinite and witty tolerance. She hurried. A hot towel to loosen his pores; soap not cream. She steadied her right hand with her left and began, drawing down from cheekbone to jaw, desperate to live up to this honor—he might after all have asked Phyllis. Maybe he only *had* the beard because he was waiting for her to shave it off. And this turned out to be more difficult than she imagined. Like changing a diaper, it was a simple task that nevertheless could not be intuited.

Bill's skin had no spring and, afraid of scraping too hard, she pulled the razor gently, ineffectually, and repeatedly until he called her off, flapping his big hands in distress and irritation. Jean only managed to clear a single strip, like snow shoveled from a narrow walkway. She wiped the remaining soap, but the nurse who came in to give her a message looked doubtful—was this a rash, or an outbreak of alopecia? The note said Larry Mond had called, and he'd left a number. Jean had no idea how he knew she was there, but the mystery was soon explained, for after the nurse came Marianne.

It was the first she'd seen of her sister since her arrival, and Marianne's indifference had hardened whatever soft pockets remained between them. So Jean was surprised, when the dark head with a new boyish haircut appeared, by how pleased she was to see her. She could only attribute the shift in her feelings to their old man's humbling state, and to the memory—inescapable in this hospital setting—of Billy's death.

They sat with Dad—Marianne didn't comment on his patchy beard, presumably because she thought it his own handiwork—until he visibly tired, his lower lids drooping, wet and red rimmed as a hound's. They kissed him and went outside the building so Marianne could smoke. Another pleasant surprise—

for once she wasn't hiding it from Jean in a bid to seem more perfect.

Her sister had lost weight, and not all of it from her head. She asked if Larry had gotten through to her. Sitting on the steps, Jean was reminded that Larry knew Doug Micklethwaite, Marianne's lawyer husband, and all this seemed so promising she didn't notice that everything was promising compared with intensive care.

"What do you say we have dinner, tonight, *à quatre*?" Jean said impulsively. The phrase itself conferred an air of festivity, she thought. "Or maybe we should include Mom—if she can be persuaded to come out." Jean was high with restless inactivity and the discovery of a possible friendship with her sister, hardly daring to think about the chance to see Larry, and in the safety of a family gathering.

They called Doug, who'd get hold of Larry: the dinner was arranged. And then Marianne, looking in no way motherly in her tight prefaded flares, started to giggle. Jean knew it was partly the nervous tension from worry over Dad, but still she wondered if her usually downbeat sister could possibly be having an affair—how to account for this change of mood and shape and style, the pixie hair, the plausible hipsters?

"What *is* it?"

"I don't know why I'm thinking of it," Marianne protested, waiting to be begged some more.

"Come *on*—what's so funny?"

"Well, remember that vibrator you made me steal?"

"Yeah?" She hadn't *made* her steal anything, although it was true she'd encouraged her. And for admission into one of Jean's clubs, she'd also required that Marianne "get" a *Playboy* magazine and then plant it in the raincoat pocket of Desmond, the doorman. And yes, once, in a mad rush of power, she'd also stipulated a vibrator. When Marianne miraculously produced the thing, ivory plastic and about a foot long, Jean evinced a step-motherly annoyance. She wouldn't accept it—clearly labeled on the package, as she pointed out, a "massage wand"—and that had been their last club.

"You know—that time you refused to acknowledge my most fabulous feat? Well, you were right. In a way."

"How do you mean, I was right?" This was information Jean wanted to have.

"I didn't steal it."

"*What?* But I remember it. Vividly. It was about this long." Jean held her hands up, rigid, a yard apart. And soon they were convulsing—with tension and dread and nostalgia, inter-mittently gasping for breath, rocking, Marianne releasing the occasional honk through a new high-pitched laugh. She *must* be having an affair, Jean thought, recovering herself. And this new trill has met the approval of her lover—it was probably an echo of his own laugh. Other smokers looked at them and smiled; this wasn't the usual mood on the hospital steps.

"No, I didn't steal it. Didn't you ever notice they were kept on the wall behind the counter, along with the rainbow-swirl, corrugated, and chocolate-flavored condoms—you don't see *those* anymore."

"Hey, you're right. Weird they didn't catch on, huh?"

Marianne was fighting to go on with her story. "I bought it!" she said triumphantly.

"Really?"

"Yeah—I told the guy, do you remember the old guy at Drake's, the one with the walrus mustache?"

"Course. Mr. Drake."

"Well, I told him it was for my *father*." Both girls shrieked. "I told Mr. Drake that Dad had a sore back from tennis and needed a massager."

"I can't believe you had the nerve," Jean said, calmed by

admiration, thinking of the sober, grandfatherly figure of Mr. Drake. "What did he *say?*"

"He stared at me for a while like he didn't know what to do and then finally he turned around and got it off the wall and handed it over. He said . . . it was *nonrefundable.*"

Both girls burst out again, jammed snorts escaping as they tried to get themselves under control. "What did you do with that thing anyway?"

"Well, I tried it out, of course. Or *tried* to try it out, then I was so scared Gladys or Mom would find it I tossed it. In the laundry room—I stuffed it into someone's basket. And get this. . . ." She had to pause again, her eyes tearful slits. "Turned out it was Mrs. Wiedermann's laundry basket!" They were actually slapping their knees at the thought of this widowed neighbor with her antimacassared slipper chairs (the girls sometimes went over there for Mrs. Wiedermann's poppy-seed cake) uncovering such a thing among her fresh-laundered doilies.

Jean thought for a moment of confiding in Marianne about Dan—a ludicrous impulse. Should she not tell her about Bill's affair? No, indecorous here on his hospital steps, and anyway she didn't need to know. Jean thought that even as an adult her sister would be devastated by such news. But in the urge to draw her close, to somehow commemorate the drama they were all struggling through, she ventured an intimacy. "Can you imagine having an affair?"

"*God* no" came the automatic reply. Marianne was a person blessed by absolute certainty and a plan for everything, and for once Jean didn't sneer. Marianne was admirable—and she was right. "Imagine pawning your family for some lousy roll in the hay—yet you hear about people doing it all the time. Pathetic. Low-IQ behavior. Not to mention totally wrong and gross and lame. No, I think Mrs. Wiedermann's wand is the only solution." Jean, who was tiring of all this, saw Phyllis, one step up. Neither sister had seen her coming.

"I thought I'd find you two out here—what's so funny? What's this about Mrs. Wiedermann?" Phyllis asked, cautiously delighted by this new and public ease between her daughters. "Died last year, you know. Eighty-two years old. She had quite a sizable obituary in the *Times*. It said she was a survivor of the camps, I can't remember which. Lost her entire family. Arrived alone on a boat at sixteen without a word of English and not a soul in the world and got a job at Saks. . . . Mr. Wiedermann was a big store executive. And to think all those years we had no idea. Your father's asleep," Phyllis said, just the smallest touch reproachfully. "And what may I ask is so darn funny?"

"Listen, Mom, we've got a plan," Jean said.

"Yeah," Marianne chimed in, "and you're coming. Dinner with Larry Mond."

"Oh my goodness, is he in town?" Phyllis asked. "I can't think when I last saw Larry. In the flesh, that is. It would be fun, but really I don't think I can," she said.

"You *need* to get out," Jean appealed.

"Dad would want you to," Marianne said. "The three of us and Larry, and Dougie is going to join us later. When will we have another chance?"

"They don't let you in here at night anyway," Jean added.

"Well," their mother said, still puckered with worry but clearly basking in this consideration from her girls, "all right." She glanced up at the hospital as if Dad could overhear.

.   .   .

Attachment

That evening, the sisters marched Phyllis down Third Avenue, arms hooked as if in custody, the three of them chirruping all the way to the small French bistro on East Sixty-ninth. As they approached, Jean spotted Larry across the street: sage-green summer suit blown open, blue shirt flattened against his lean shape, a triangle of tan skin below the neck. First he embraced Phyllis, whose arthritic bejeweled hand tightly clasped his neck, then Marianne, and then, briefly, Jean, looking directly at her as he stepped back and just said, "So." He pushed aside a bit of hair at the front—longer now, Jean noted, more like the old days.

It was only seven-thirty and fully light outside, but the restaurant, semiunderground like Jean's kitchen, gave a feeling of the night unfolding—the waiters in their formal black and white, the vellum glow of a dozen low-watt sconces, the red banquettes and many mirrors; a French chanteuse piping a wartime memory through hidden speakers. *Bien sûr, ce n'est pas la Seine . . . mais c'est jolie tout dé même, à Göttingen. . . .*

When Doug arrived, straight from court, there was renewed champagne, though there was nothing to celebrate, and the mood remained vaguely hysterical. Nobody talked about Bill's predicament. Any anecdote that brought in at least three people at the table was told and retold like a famous joke, producing grateful guffaws and a revelation for Jean: she'd been wrong all these years, hiding away. Her sister looked glamorous in a shiny green dress, and happy, Jean noted, once again impressed by Marianne. She seemed to be having an affair with her *husband*.

In fact, it was all going so well that when Jean heard her mother hoot and slam down her glass, she thought Phyllis was launching a raucous toast.

"I really don't give a *shit* anymore." She was practically shouting. "But don't, if you please, tell me it's not about tits and ass—I mean, honestly, Bill Warner is not going to *say* it's about tits and ass, now is he? Mainly tits, I can tell you. I don't care what he *said*. He said she was his *intellectual equal*. He said she's a person who can *understand what you're saying*. A person who listens, a person who hears. Well, *I* say, hear this, William Walton Warner, and understand: I'm—still—here."

Jean felt all her mother's humiliation—a sexual jealousy intact, and raw, after twenty years—is that how she herself would sound about Giovana when she was sixty-six? But her empathy was challenged by the cruelty of her mother's timing: unburdening herself with Dad hooked up on the fifth floor of the hospital, unable not only to reply but to speak at all. Was that why Phyllis had climbed in beside him in the mechanical bed? Now that he was helpless, she could reclaim him.

Doug looked at his plate and slipped an arm around Marianne's shoulder—which she didn't appear to notice, her brown eyes glassy with unshed tears. To think Jean had nearly told her, only this afternoon. Larry put his arm around Phyllis— brave man. And suddenly Jean knew exactly who her father's lover had been. The woman she'd called Auntie Eunice, her conservation-minded marching partner. It was true—once such a feature in their lives, she had disappeared completely, as if banished. The silence was so heavy, even the waiters were waxworks, an improvement on their ostentatious background tinkling throughout the evening.

Larry signaled for the check and Jean walked around the table. "Come on, Mom," she said. "Let's go home."

Outside, Doug and Marianne, picking her way in spike heels, walked west arm in arm—rare night alone in the city, and he'd booked a hotel on the park. Watching them go, Jean hoped they'd recover their date.

Phyllis, steadied by the night air, claimed she wanted to walk but was easily persuaded to accept a lift. Larry had driven—a green Land-Rover Defender, totally unsuited to civilian urban use. After he helped Phyllis into the front passenger seat—she may as well have been mounting a horse—he opened the back-seat door for Jean, and before she could hoist herself in, awkward with her unyielding sateen pencil skirt, he touched her wrist and spoke quietly.

"Have lunch with me tomorrow. I'd like to see Bill, if he's receiving—I could pick you up."

Jean could only nod in reply—no energy for confidences. She felt palpably weak. Things losing their force, Jean thought; this time the thing was ourselves.

"Call me in the morning and tell me how he is. How you all are."

"Yes," Jean said, pulling herself in. "Mom is in the library tomorrow morning," she added, hatching a whole plan without secrets. "Maybe you could bring her up when you come to visit Dad." She wasn't going to leave Phyllis alone.

They settled on one-thirty, giving Larry time to dispatch what he called his morning load, which made Jean think of laundry, and therefore of the two of them encumbered, last December in the Paradise. Larry hadn't once mentioned his wife, presumably in Princeton while he toiled through his summer, alone in the city.

Outside Phyllis's building they said a quick good night, and Jean shepherded her mother, smaller than ever, into the polished lobby. He waited until they were inside before pulling away, and the groan of his army engine, even this reminded her of Dad. The moment Larry was gone she returned to worrying. Bill's difficulty breathing today, how long could it possibly go on? Instead of getting better he seemed to be breaking down, in sections. Phyllis slumped on the elevator bench and Jean closed her eyes and leaned against the mirrored wall, thinking about the morning and the drive up to the hospital, wondering if she should call Marianne when she got in. She buried a crazy impulse to find Auntie Eunice, as if she alone could make Dad better. If she was even still alive.

The next morning Jean got up to the hospital a little later than usual, her head pounding. She was intercepted in the hall by Joe, their ally among the nurses in the ICU. He explained that Bill had been taken downstairs to have a breathing tube inserted into his throat: intubation.

"Why couldn't they do it here?" she said, fearing a surreptitious tracheotomy. "Is there some *more* intensive care somewhere else, like a breathing department?"

The nurse, who admitted he didn't know why, got no credit for his straight talk, and Jean's blood pressure rose sharply when she saw her father, feet first, being wheeled back into his cubicle. He was unconscious—sedated—and ashen, with his flaccid mouth open and drooling around a blue plastic pipe, looking as if he'd swallowed a snorkel. But eventually Jean was persuaded that, although it was violent, at least they were finally acting like they were trying to help him. How much of this he was aware of, no one could tell them. She left the hospital early, desperate for air herself and convinced that he was out cold for the day. She'd perch in the sun on the gleaming mica-dusted wall and wait, to warn Phyllis about Dad's tube before she went up to him, and to head Larry off.

Despite all the worry, Jean was looking forward to lunch. But where were they? At two o'clock the lunchers on the steps began to thin out, drifting back into the chilled tower. At two-fifteen people came and went, but nobody sat—just Jean, staring at the street with its steaming manhole, that quintessential New York item.

Attachment

She thought, People routinely say of a crisis, any crisis, you find out who your real friends are. So who were hers? This was the question the whole nation had been asking for the past twenty-two months, not just Jean. And as she sat transfixed by the slow ascent and dispersal of the city's ghostly vapors, she remembered the smoke surrounding the collapsed Twin Towers, still rising nearly a month after the attack—and how she'd felt then the same helpless urgency of this visit to Dad in the hospital, that she absolutely had to get home to New York, and what she'd seen three weeks after the event was like this: a vast, steaming, theatrically lit manhole, so evocative of that whole swath of the population—vaporized.

"Please let him live." Jean, not sure with whom she was pleading, could explain: she wasn't ready for a greater loneliness.

"I haven't figured out who my friends are yet!" Now she was appealing directly to her father. He would understand; he would intercede. "I know I've been stupid." She thought of Bill's marriage-ending affair. Was it really Auntie Eu—certainly a person who could understand what he was saying. Did that make any difference? She felt sorry for Phyllis, already a mother at eighteen, her entire young womanhood turned over to her husband and children. At the same time, Jean could now understand what Bill had done, and the important information it could deliver: that you weren't dead. Maybe it didn't matter so much who it was. Stripper, stewardess, or an infinitely subtle legal mind, what you wanted to know was: am I truly alive, and am I truly loved? Of course, in addition to yes, what everyone also wanted was one name, the same name, signing up to answer both questions.

Jean felt hot and miserable out on these sparkly steps. Greater loneliness was exactly what she was feeling already— and, she realized, what she'd been feeling for some time. First

brotherless, then husbandless, and now almost fatherless—
what happened to all the men? She was stunned she'd been
quite so stupid. Just when she needed to prepare herself for her
effective orphanhood (*sorry*, Phyllis) she'd distanced herself
from Mark with his idiotic infidelity and even, however briefly,
allied herself with his enemy; wouldn't Mark, if he knew, call
Dan that—his enemy?

She wondered if Mark could be a comfort now, or ever
again. Recently, in his great alarm, he'd been eager, palpably
concerned, as when they were waiting for the news from
Scully, though of course he hadn't actually been with her when
it came. When he *was* there, he was distracted, or drunk.
Including the time they made love after Chez Julien gassed on
champagne—like last night at the bistro: champagne to celebrate not being dead. And what about his rush to be off that
morning; when did Mark last *linger*? Never apologize, never
explain; he pecked his wife good-bye and then took his giant
steps to the front door and got the hell out.

Of course he'd been meeting Giovana in Germany—why
else would he have gone to such legendary trouble over his
hair? Jean could laugh to think of that baby pompadour. But
Giovana—now there was one hell of a man-size running joke.
She thought of a sentence from Larry's book, a quote from
Nietzsche: *A joke is an epigram on the death of a feeling.* As she
waited on the hospital steps (thinking this was why both her
parents pushed their credo and their call, Be Busy! Be Useful!),
it was *Mark* she saw in the jimmied metal bed, the side bar lowered not to let her in but to let his feet hang over—it was much
less clear who sat beside him, massaging his calves: Aminata or
Gladys? Giovana or Jean? Jean or Mrs. H.? Mrs. H. or Phyllis?
Noleen or Dan? Victoria or Sophie? Mark definitely didn't
know who his real friends were.

When the Defender finally rolled up, Jean began to tell

Phyllis about the tube before she was all the way down out of the car, and for a moment her mother, in a crisp white shirt, the collar upturned, paused on the high galvanized-steel step. She was leaning precariously forward like a bistro mirror. Jean told her carefully, wanting to preempt any feelings of guilt following her uncharacteristic outburst the night before, now that Bill had undergone a traumatic intervention—but there was no stopping the regret that flooded her mother's face, her lightness left behind in the Defender like an empty paper cup as she rushed up the stairs without saying good-bye.

"I'll see you at home later," she called, looking over her shoulder, remembering them. "I'll leave when they kick me out at six. Larry, you're a darling!"

He held up his loosely open hand—something between a wave and a fist of solidarity. He didn't need to be told this was not the day for visiting his old boss. "Let's get out of here," he said, helping her up. "Can you be at all hungry?"

"I'm ashamed to say I'm absolutely ravenous—where were you guys?" She didn't quite realize how much she'd been minding until the words came out, carrying with them knotted feelings, like ropes of seaweed on an anchor.

"Well, we were on our way and then had to go back to the library. Your mother forgot her bag. She's a little distracted, isn't she? Understandably."

"That's one way of putting it," Jean said, glad he didn't seem to expect a replay of last night's revelation. But he'd worked in the firm at that time, and she wondered. "Was it general knowledge in the office—it was Auntie Eu, wasn't it?"

"Nobody else knew," he said, "or so I thought." At least he was able to confirm her hunch—and to keep a secret. Jean saw that Phyllis had forgotten her tortoiseshell sunglasses, and she immediately put them on. They were cool in the bright sun, the brown tint ice tea for the eyes, but soon she took them off again——she did not want to look like her mother.

"How about the River Café——if you can hang on all the way to Brooklyn. Should be quick at this hour, straight down the West Side Highway."

"Perfect. This must be what Friday afternoon feels like to people with real jobs."

Larry smiled, his heavy engine straining into gear.

The hot wind along the highway, the bright green slivers of park, the sun on the Hudson—by the time they got to the bridge Jean was feeling light and free and weirdly alert. She'd forgotten that about Larry; his natural athlete's ease masked a lethal sharpness. Just being near him made you feel smarter, his expectation of it maybe, his confidence in her, or was it just him spilling over? Of course it helped that the conversation never waded into the dull waters of *design* and *marketing*, but Bill always said he had it; he called him a diabolical debater.

Despite last night's dinner and, with Phyllis's moment, the inevitable deepening of their intimacy, they were slightly nervous, alone and facing each other across a restaurant table. Jean heard everything she said played back, like an echo on a long-distance phone call. They drank bitter lemon *pressé,* and Jean swore this was the lightest omelette that was still buttery enough to be worth eating: unreproducible at home.

"It's like air," she said, "*buttered air.* This simple thing that is in fact incredibly hard to do. Like shaving Dad."

She told Larry about her failed attempt, making it more comical than it was, and he listened quietly, his expression amused but also apprehensive as if his pleasure came not from

her little story but her proximity. A woman shaving a man—
maybe that was a pretty intimate thing to do. Larry mentioned
Milton, as a blind old man, being read to by his daughters, and
this led to the etymology of "amanuensis": "A handwriting
slave," Larry said, "like a law clerk." From the way he moved
his whole head to take his eyes off her, she judged that he too
was experiencing seesaw impulses: spontaneous contact up
against an adult dread of consequence. What *was* this, her continuing will to flirt—just the flip side of intensive care, or the
backwash of her Olympic dive into the porno pool? Whatever
it was, she'd never let him see it.

Larry told her Princeton was trying to lure him back. "A
great course and timely—Civil Liberties and Foreign Relations, at the Woodrow Wilson School of International and
Public Affairs. Mercifully," he said, "known as Woody Woo."

"Do you think you'll take the job?" Wouldn't that say something about where he intended to live?

"Well, there are other possibilities," he said vaguely, "perhaps something in the philosophy department at NYU. More
and more, my interests lie in pure philosophy. Not even juris-
prudence. First causes—epistemology. My version of a midlife
crisis, you might say. Maybe so—but one thing's for certain.
After this case, I'm going to give up private practice."

Behind him on the terrace the magnificent bridge sprawled
over its heavy foundations, webbed rays of spangled cables, the
solid and the soaring. Beyond Larry and the bridge, in rich
afternoon sun, lay Manhattan.

"I was right here when it happened," Larry said as inevitably the talk turned to September 11. Usually unnervingly
direct in his gaze, he was focused on the middle distance. "I was
staying in Brooklyn Heights—this was before I got use of the
firm's apartment—at a friend's, right over there, a penthouse

on Montague Terrace. I'd just stepped out onto the deck with my coffee when I saw the first plane go in, and then the second plane."

"God. What did it feel like?"

"For a couple of days I kept going to the bridge, or walking along the promenade. I'd just watch the papers fly—office papers, spiraling and fluttering and falling through the air like ash from a chimney, brilliant against the blue. Well, you've seen it. A part of me became loosened as well. Unhinged. *Unfixed*. Though anything but light. Like half the city, I suppose. Some weird chemical change took place. . . . I could have sworn my feet actually weighed more. But I kept going back. And going back. And I'd watch the fluttering office papers some more. You know, it felt insanely *personal*. Like all the papers of my life thrown up in the air." He paused, but Jean remained silent.

"The thing is," he went on, "and I think this has been a part of my difficulty with that day and all that it's come to mean. I've always believed in justice—given my life to it, you might say, with"—and here he laughed—"the regrettable exception of our amigos in the field of shipbuilding."

"Ah yes, the Dirtbags."

"But what, by this act that I after all witnessed . . . was made of our tools for the administration of justice? The question has of course gained terrifying point in the past few months. With the preemptive strike. Entirely illegal—a grotesque evolution, this new kind of warfare. All we have is the law. It's all I have. It's all you have, too—all society has. We live in and by the law. Of course, I'm quoting here. The law makes us what we are. Citizens, husbands, people who own things. It's both sword and shield. And yet it's abstract—our ethereal sovereign. We *argue*, endlessly, about what the law has decreed—I argue, I'm a lawyer, that's what I do. But if even we don't know—if our commitment is instead to *interpretation*—how can we per-suade others? Especially *this* other. The moronic certainty. And what might reasonably be called a commitment to death. How, then, can we persuade ourselves? And for how long? Suasion—my talent and my belief—was in one single morning, a glori-ous, blue morning . . . eviscerated."

Larry told her that, for a while after September 11, he couldn't speak to his children—he'd reassured them immediately, and for the first time ever he felt his words were hollow. "What in honesty was there to reassure them about? What is to be their future? And how on earth are we supposed to protect them, our *job*. Nearly two years later, this may sound extraordinary, but at the time all I could do was walk the bridge, walk the prome-nade, look up at the sky. No more planes, only paper. Then no more paper. Only sky."

It made her uneasy to hear Larry talking in abstractions—using his hands and a wide-eyed blankness of face to convey what he couldn't clearly describe. Not so different from Dad just now. Larry's too-blue eyes took on an evangelical sheen when he was talking, the spirograph irises of the lately con-verted. But he was a precise man, precise as a surgeon—and this helpless comparison made Jean more uneasy, and more frightened. How precise was a surgeon?

Instinctively, to lighten the mood, she reminded him of their undercover mission in New Jersey. "And your shirt—it got ripped on that fence."

"Did it?" he said, smiling. Was it possible he didn't remem-ber? Well, naturally the sudden sight of his own brown torso wouldn't make the same impression on him, but she kept this thought to herself.

"Ripped halfway up your back, your shirttails glowing in the sun. . . . And I want to tell you—no one who was that guy can be depressed for long." She hoped he wouldn't think her flirtatious, or dense, because she believed it. Not for his body but, once again, for his clarity of purpose. And as on that distant day, Jean felt remarkably content and not in need of anything. She was staring across at the big, light-catching city of her youth while Larry pried a credit card out of his thin black wallet.

The waiter returned and said he was sorry, he couldn't process the card because the power was out. "Should come back on in a minute. Sorry for the delay, Mr. Mond. These are on the house." He set down two flutes of champagne. As they sat and sipped and talked—the need to create diversion for Phyllis in the coming days, the chances of Bill being released before too long, Larry's case looking like it would drag on through the summer, the usual plans to spend late August with his children falling through because suddenly they all had plans of their own—they heard a voice from inside the restaurant saying the power was off everywhere. What was going on? A Brooklyn blackout?

"What happens if the power failure reaches the hospital? Could it?" She was asking Larry because Larry would know about grids, how they worked, how they were organized.

"Doubtful. But even if it did, a big hospital has big backup. They have enormous generators. Hospital like that, they could probably supply the city."

It was nearly four-thirty, and Larry gave the waiter a check.

In the cave of the indoor parking lot it was going to take some time to find the car—in fact the attendant looked convincingly occupied, standing on the sidewalk with his hands on his hips, frowning at a small transistor on the ground as if it was a disgraced dog (broken antenna tail jauntily angled, playing cute for forgiveness). The attendant was shaking his head.

"I doan know. They saying the power's out all the way from Canada on down to Florida and over west to Detroit." He gave Larry a significant look. "You do the math."

"What does that mean?" Jean asked, squinting at him and then at Larry. Neither answered her. Larry tried his cell phone: dead. Eventually the attendant was persuaded to leave the radio and get the car.

"Come on. Let's get up to the hospital," Larry said, over-tipping the man and clapping him on the shoulder. "You take care of yourself!" He steered his heavy rig out onto the street, heading round the corner for the bridge access. For now Jean felt safe only in the Defender, biting her lip so as not to ask him again about the grids and generators, about Dad, about Phyllis, about everyone in the city, peering up through the broad glass windshield into the deep blue air.

The clock over at city hall said four-eleven, and so did the next one they saw, at Greenwich Avenue and Sixth, Jean's old haunt where the women's prison used to be. Four-eleven, the hour and the minute the plug was pulled. Buildings were lined with people. A tentative atmosphere filtered through the crowd: the abruptly unmanned feeling reminded the entire city of only one other day in its history. Wary store owners pulled down their metal grilles; still, this universal knowledge also ushered in a new friendliness—one aided by the suspension of cell phone service in addition to the suspension of light, chilled air, and jammed underground travel.

A third clock confirmed the time at Fourteenth Street, on the corner bank. The tide swelled with greater purpose, people and cars, office workers heading home. Volunteers were directing traffic: at Sixteenth Street, a beefy redhead with rolled shirt-sleeves and a batter's swagger; at Twenty-third, another doing what he did most days, only this time more people seemed to be listening. *Let my people come,* the black man beckoned, his hair like a hook rug and both arms raised, looking above them to the vanishing point where the towers should have been, Moses before a Red Sea of gleaming lancing cars, his shopping cart full of unreturned cans and bottles, smack in the middle of the honking avenue.

"Will Mom be allowed to stay in the hospital?" Jean said, punching Marianne's number into her cell phone, hoping somehow to press it into life. "Oh, look," she said, twisting to see through the window. "Let's stop." A heavily pregnant black woman in heels and a red dress was staggering wide legged down the street, leaning back, not seeming to notice or care that the sweater in her hand was trailing behind her on the sidewalk. Larry pulled over as Jean rolled down the window and yelled.

"Excuse me! Miss—ma'am! Can we give you a lift?" The woman looked over and nodded gratefully, too stunned or too hot to speak. She waddled over with no increase in pace and climbed up into the car whose back door Jean contorted herself to open. Four other people pushed in after her and Jean reached out an arm to protect the bursting woman.

"Thanks," she said. "I'm Melba."

"Hi, Melba," Larry said, nodding to Jean to shut the door. The heft and elevation of the Defender was a boon. Jean looked outside for evidence of plunder and pandemonium. "Everyone all right back there?" In addition to Melba, they were carrying two very small middle-aged Hispanic women; a young seersucker-suited man hugging his briefcase; and, in the very back, a Latino boy of about nineteen.

"Yo, man, thanks for the ride," called the kid from the way back. "Where you from?"

Jean turned to look at him, the smudge of fluff on his upper lip, and downgraded his age to fifteen. As for his question—this was complicated enough on a normal day, so she was relieved when Larry said, "We're turning onto the West Side Highway at Forty-fourth Street. Where are you headed?" His question was for Melba.

"Forty-fourth is fine; I'm on Fifty-first and Eighth—I can walk the rest of the way."

"We'll take you home—and the rest of you will have to get out there, too, I'm afraid, unless I have anyone for Washington Heights."

The small, possibly related Hispanic women murmured assent, saying "Fifty-first okay, Fifty-first good," but seersucker piped up.

"Look, I'll give you a hundred bucks to take me to Eighty-ninth and Park."

"Sorry, pal. We've got to get up to the hospital."

"Fine. I'll give you *two* hundred."

Larry looked in his rearview mirror to assess the face of this man sitting, uninvited, in his backseat. "I said, we're going to the hospital."

"Five hundred bucks!" He was screaming. "Come *on*, man."

Jean didn't dare look around. Larry pulled over—not a simple maneuver in this swollen river of hot metal—and he turned around and considered the sweat-streaked face, and the briefcase he was still clutching as if it was lined with gold bricks.

"Do you want to get out here? Or at Fifty-first Street?"

"Fuck you, man. What do you want? I am not fucking paying more than five hundred."

Larry got down and, calm but clench jawed, opened the passenger door. "Get out," he commanded, not raising his voice.

The sweaty man stepped down, taking his time. "Asshole,"

he said, knocking Larry on the arm as he pressed by, vanishing into the crowd.

Larry smiled at Jean as he climbed back in, and looked over his remaining crew. "Onward, citizens!" His amused tone let everyone know they were safe, though Jean felt only she and Larry—the grown-ups in the front seat—had anything like real apprehension about what was being done, and not just to their day. If it was the worst case, what exactly would that mean—the entire Eastern Seaboard a mass hostage? And how soon in this heat before things got ugly?

She'd focus on immediate need—Dad, Phyllis, and, oh my God, Melba. Melba was panting, practically hyperventilating. Her head hung down as if she was looking for something she dropped. Was she working on some learned breathing?—although, as far as Jean could remember, her breaths should have been longer, deeper. Jean touched her arm and asked her if she was all right. She nodded that she was and swigged from the bottle of mineral water Jean pressed into her hand.

"Maybe you should come with us to the hospital," Jean said, briefly touching Melba's wrist, trying to tell if she was a good judge of her own condition.

She vigorously shook her head. "Better just get home."

The tiny women kept quiet; the boy twiddled the dimmer lights on the passenger ceiling, absorbed like a kid in a cockpit. "Keep your eyes peeled for a gas station," Larry said to no one in particular. They'd passed two, but one was closed, and one had a line around the block. Most had electric pumps, electric registers; self-fill, self-pay, only credit, no cash. In Times Square crowds gathered outside the big hotels, in front of the theaters. Larry glanced over. "They're kicking them out because of the smoke alarms. Those people probably have rooms and they can't use them because it's against the law if the smoke alarms are down."

She saw people lying in doorways, using water bottles for pillows. It wasn't late but it was broiling, and the shady spots were being staked. They looked like people queuing for prized concert tickets, hunkering down for a long night—many of them in pastel outfits and tracksuits, as if by some tourist voodoo they'd all gone out that morning in their pajamas. The gas tank was less than a quarter full. They pulled up at Fifty-first and Eighth.

Jean tried one last time. "Melba, are you *sure* you won't come with us to the hospital?"

The woman shook her head again and set about stepping down from the car, gripping a headrest as she felt her way with a foot she couldn't see. It was five-forty when Larry and Jean turned west toward the highway. The two little women smiled and said, "Thank you—thank you," making Jean think for a flash of Mark and his double-strength good-byes. He'd be worrying about her—how could she contact home? If he was home. As they trundled on, Jean thought of the Latino kid with his jeans belted so low they cleared the buttocks altogether, and wished she'd asked his name. Unbidden, he'd lifted the little women down out of the Defender, one at a time, before reaching back in again for his jacket and to say thanks, giving Larry a high five.

"That boy was sweet, wasn't he," she said.

"Not very, no. He stole my tennis racket," Larry said, shaking his head, laughing. "Right out of the back."

"*What?* Why didn't you say anything?"

"I didn't see till he was already gone. Didn't even try to hide it once he was out of the car. Son of a bitch, high-fiving me like that, too. Pulling together in a crisis, you see. Welcome to New York."

It was only when they arrived at the hospital, to find it barricaded shut and no sign of Phyllis among the dozens of people milling around outside, that Jean started to panic. In the crowd, faces came close to hers, worried eyes mirroring her own, scanning for help. How could she have lost track of both her parents? No one in the hospital would speak to her, though finally she got a mouthed no in response to her written question, *Are there any visitors still in the building?* The guard moved away from the glass door before she could ask anything else. She had to assume Dad in intensive care was among the city's coolest, and safest.

"We've *got* to find Phyllis," she said to Larry, insistent, as if he was disagreeing. "She must have gotten a lift. My mother is not going to walk a hundred blocks home." She tried to remember Phyllis's footwear that day: rope-soled apple-green mules, high.

"No point staying here," Larry said, guiding her from the small of her back, interposing his body between hers and the crowd. Once he'd installed her, he helped five others into the car. Crammed as they were, Jean barely noticed. Larry decided to go through the city streets and not along the highway in case they ran out of gas. There was more honking than earlier, and more wild driving, many people sitting on the sidewalk, still a river of moving people, walking, walking, walking.

It was past seven-thirty when they arrived at Seventy-fourth Street and, right outside, they found Phyllis, chatting with the doorman, Manuel (whose name Phyllis pronounced *manual*, as in labor). Jean didn't think she'd ever been so happy to see her mother—apple-green feet in a wide, first-position V—or so irritated.

"Mom! How'd you get here? Wish you'd left us a note or something."

"A note? Honey, you have no idea of the scene. Where have you *been*? My God, you look dreadful. Thank goodness you were with her, Larry. Let's get her inside."

Upstairs, recovering from the seven dark unventilated flights, they drank lukewarm ice tea in the twilit living room, and Phyllis told of her miracle lift in a taxi. There was still no news of the outage's cause.

"I felt rather guilty. I mean, why me, all alone in this taxi, while people are shouting and slamming on the roof to get in? I didn't even run when this cab appeared out of nowhere—how am I going to compete with all those eager beavers? Fabulously pushy, a lot of them. Frightening, really, and quite a few in hospital uniform, I'm sorry to say. But the driver singled me out, he pointed and called me over: he chose me."

"Why do you think he did?" Larry asked her.

"Well, once we were on our way I asked him just that. And you won't believe what he said. He said, 'You remind me of my mother.' And—did I tell you?—his name was Mustafa Sherif."

They all laughed, but no one dared ask: Who *is* responsible? Jean said, "Any news about Dad?"

"There's no getting through. Nothing to do but wait."

Larry stood up. "I think I'd better go out and try and find some gas—or how are you going to get up to the hospital tomorrow? If I get lucky, I may buzz out to Connecticut and see my folks tonight. Knowing Pop, they'll have been well prepared, a basement full of baked beans, but they'll be worrying about all of us trapped here in the city."

Jean noticed he didn't mention his wife. "I'll go with you," she said. "To find gas, I mean."

"Maybe you'd better rest, Jean. You do look tired."

"Well, you'll just have to live with that because I'm going with you."

"Well, okay," he said, looking pleased. "What about food, Phyllis? Can we bring you back something? They'll be giving it away, all those restaurants with no fridges."

"I am not budging from this apartment until I get through to the hospital. See that fruit bowl? That's my dinner you're looking at. Don't you worry about me."

"Okay, we'll have a gander and see what we can find."

The sky was an unremitting pewter: cloud cover like a lid over the city, shutting out the starlight, sealing in the heat. How easily Larry had slipped into Phyllis's dated way of speaking. It wasn't conscious mimicry, she thought, or remotely patronizing, just Larry making things easier for the next person, finding the right idiom. He had that gift, like St. Francis talking to the animals.

"God," she said, "it hasn't cooled off at all. It's going to be a very dark night." But back in the car, she felt invigorated: they were resuming their mission. Judicious circling led them to the West Side and one hour waiting in line; by ten-thirty they had their gas. Both tried their cell phones. "Look at us," she said. "If you add us together we're almost a hundred years old and here we are, calling our mothers. Or trying to—it's the thought that counts. What do you say we park and take a stroll? See what it's like on the streets."

Finally on foot, they turned down Seventy-seventh Street toward Columbus, Jean clutching Larry's arm. The night was a solid, velvety dark; the only perceptible figures were glowing in torchlight—faces from Flemish paintings dotting the steep stoops of brownstones.

"They look like worshippers at an altar, on their special saint's day," Jean said, "each stoop's a peculiar shrine." Assemblages of candles, paper bags with candles hidden inside, a blue-glow camping lantern, the smell of kerosene and paraffin. People walking in the dark appeared suddenly; Jean was not aware of them until they were no more than a foot away, often announced by a pungent urban reek.

"Great night for crime," Larry said, and Jean expected the sound of shattering storefront glass. Her fear was irrational. It was dark, but the mood had never been more friendly, a block party on every street.

"Do people on the Upper West Side sit on their steps *every* night singing folk songs?" Jean asked. "Look what we were missing in our tiled high-rise on the East Side. I knew it. Actually, it reminds me of St. Jacques. Just sitting on the porch steps at night, that's what people do for entertainment, strumming and singing or just smoking and talking."

"Sounds incredibly civilized," Larry said. "I could use a lot more strumming and singing." He sighed. "And talking."

"They sing to keep away the darkness. So they say."

A radio broadcast technical talk of grids. Down the block, on another radio, the nasal promise of a tired-sounding city official; from still another, a tally of the intifada groups who were already jockeying to claim credit, promising more and worse.

"Imagine taking credit for a massacre you *didn't* commit,"

Jean said, unambiguously frightened now, glad when he took her hand in his and squeezed it there, no chance of her slipping away. "It's like the death of people you love. Terror, I mean. Each fresh affront stirs up the previous one, amplifying the earlier fear, the older grief. . . ."

"I'm sure you're right—nothing is ever lost," Larry said. "People can be brutalized, but, maybe surprisingly, they're never really inured."

On Columbus, the scene brightened. "Apparently safer to stay open than to go home," Jean said as a small Japanese man outside his wood-faced sushi bar tried to stop them, put his hand on Larry's forearm.

"Thanks, pal, we're just walking." When they'd moved on a bit, he said, "You wonder how much a person can charge for a piece of rotting tuna tonight of all nights. Though even if it were free . . . somehow I just don't feel like raw fish."

"How about cooked cow?"

They stopped outside an Argentinean steakhouse. Through the open windows, a collapsed bonfire gave off light and heat—over the flames on a pulley, a grill the size of a twin bed, angled just like Dad's. The fire was nursed by a sweating man in white, his jumpsuit smeared with blood. Half a cow, sausages, coiled innards, a whole pig's head—all across the great rack they sizzled and spat.

"I can't believe these places are open—what about your smoke-alarm theory? Or is this just too much carnage for a doggie bag?"

"Counting on the cops having better things to do—and we'd better hope they have. In fact, there isn't the police presence you might expect on such a night."

Then they noticed the two policemen leaning against the building, gnawing on some ribs in the dark.

"Zgots to eat," she whispered to Larry as they approached, gripping his elbow.

"Evening, gentlemen. Any news?" he asked.

"Great ribs," one of them joked, wiping his mouth with the back of his hand.

"They're sounding pretty confident we're going to have power tonight," said the other.

"Hey! So what are they saying?"

"It's the grid. Three hundred fifty-five thousand volts of power were downed east of Cleveland, on the Lake Erie loop—that's the series of transmission lines that run around the lake."

"Fantastic news—what a relief. Come on," she said, her stomach remembering the heaps of tarred ribs. "Let's get some grub. Before they run out."

An injection of red meat and strong red wine from the Andes, and they walked back uptown toward Larry's car, draped in darkness and again locking arms. The world for the moment was holding steady—dark, but steady—and they felt as if they'd just escaped a disaster on a biblical scale. But until the light returned, how could they be sure? She thought if she didn't hold on to Larry she might fall down or bump into something or lose him. On the corner a man was selling T-shirts, laid out on top of a duffel bag, illuminated with a flashlight.

I SURVIVED THE BLACKOUT, the shirts said, white stenciled on black, and black stenciled on white.

"That great entrepreneurial spirit, undimmed even in darkness—it is wonderful, isn't it," Larry said. "Wish I had more of it."

"We haven't survived it *yet*," she pointed out.

He squeezed her hand, and they strolled on in silence, slowly, in no rush now to get back in that car.

Which, anyway, they couldn't find. Unworried (it must be here somewhere), they walked the block up and back twice before they finally found it. She leaned against the door, waiting for Larry to work the keys, sad too that this strange evening was nearly at an end, unable to believe quite how long ago the day began. The door was unlocked, but neither one of them moved to get in. Then Larry leaned over and kissed her— emphatically, briefly, fully, and unreturned, so sudden and spontaneous was his landing. Time to go home—that's what that was, she thought: punctuation and nothing more. She could hardly ask him, speechless as she was, settling on the high seat as he started the engine. The streets were lit only by headlights, and Jean—eager now to be unstirred by that no doubt meaningless blackout kiss—worked up her feeling, as they made their way cautiously across town through the park, of being on a country road.

"Wouldn't it be great," she said, shutting her eyes, letting the rocking of the high car lull her for a while, "if we really were heading out, on a great trip across the country—manifest destiny."

Larry was approaching Phyllis's building. He pulled in at the curb just beyond the entrance and, with deliberation that Jean thought might be taken for regret, or at least ceremony, he turned the key. They sat not talking, safe in the car from the darkness, quiet cast over the city like a net.

He lifted her hand; it seemed that he was going to kiss it but instead turned it over as if he could read her palm in the dark; he smoothed it, patted it, and gave it back to her. Again he looked out the front window, and she thought she could make out that blunt profile.

"We made a really good team today," he said at last. He leaned over to kiss her on the cheek. Jean turned her head to meet him, so that he kissed her on the very corner of her mouth.

"Good night, partner," she managed to reply.

Human beings are responsible for the choices they make. Typical of Jean to think of something like this, from his book, while actively not kissing him. She knew she should just get out of the car, but instead she turned her whole body toward him, which meant sitting on her feet, a position like an egg spinning on its end, or a dithering kite in the moment before being carried upwind: provisional. Active or not, that kiss hovered between them and she wanted to explain. But she couldn't possibly recount how she'd already used up the line of credit even married people might be extended in extraordinary circumstances—though she thought she could make out the blue of his eyes, or maybe like a lake or a pool it was refreshing just to know it was there.

She didn't want to say anything—disclosure, apology, promise, a single word. Surely he knew what she was feeling. *Can I trust you? Can we really be thinking we can go back in time? We both know we cannot—we're grown-ups; we've made our choices.* But Larry in his still intensity seemed to choose only the darkness. He didn't have to get the message. Not tonight. But she did have to insist. She turned away. *There is still time to get out, to avert a crisis.* Jean thought he must understand. *You've brought the wrecked plane in and we're safe; we've done this, so let's not crash now.* But he didn't move. He just waited, or waited some more, for her to look back—bravely indifferent in this precipitous drop to the earth rushing up to meet them.

She leaned, in fact, fell on him, awkward in that army rig, her face in his neck, as if only by becoming a single, solid form could they avoid making out in the parked car—the natural enactment of their American essence in a time of fragility, on this one very dark night. His being American did seem so important now; she could never have predicted that. He stroked her back with his left hand, the only part of him he was able to move at all in the lock of her embrace, and the touch of his skimming fingertips reverberated through her, like a series of pins dropped in the famous acoustic tabernacle where some of her ancestors had mysteriously prayed. And then the lights came on.

"Congratulations," he said. "You fixed the blackout." Larry and Jean pulled apart as if it was morning, the alien electricity hauling them from this dream of intimacy and ease. Jean knew it was over and that this night was no kind of blueprint—it was just a blackout, a freak occurrence they'd not so much survived as inhabited. But she let it go with all the resistance she'd felt as a child at the end of a car journey, secure in her father's arms and only pretending to be asleep, deliberately flopsy so he wouldn't put her down. When she climbed out, practically falling from the car, Larry reached to steady her, but she found she couldn't look at him. Not merely disoriented but grief stricken, she saw that, once again, their time was up.

Back in 1980 there had been such a different landscape, and desire had been framed by the possibility of other offerings: an orchard of children—and, yes, why not?—the harvest of years. What might they have in front of them now? An afternoon. A snack, a chaste stroll through a gallery followed by what? Frenzied coupling? Frenzied it would have to be, and not because they were married to other people, but because a lifetime was a lot to compress. His being there with her when someone was born. Summer after summer in the same house, campanula creeping up the shingles, drunken bees in the honeysuckle. Bike paths, dog tracks, poison ivy hidden in the grass, sandy lanes banked with rosehip and beach plum; dirt roads in her mind so narrow no one can pass; they're all alone, last sun warming the backs of their legs, walking home.

She had imagined another life, in detail: only in detail—usually no more than a single moment from this other life, an incomplete act, evanescent, but while it lasted vivid enough to stand in for the rest. She *knew* the lineaments of this life as if she'd had to draw it, sketching as she traversed overhead, flying in a small aircraft (her good pilot at the controls), the scene unfolding in miniature, miles below. Seemed Larry planned to make it for one thing, however: being there with her when someone died. Not someone—Dad. That's what really brought them together after all this time, wasn't it? And that towering car of his, with its deafening engine and dimmer lights, was just another waiting room.

Larry lifted her face to look at his and said, "You want to know something?"

Jean nodded yes, unable to speak.

"You were a truly *terrible* paralegal," he said, and pulled her close. Then he reached in his pocket and fished out the car keys. "Here. You'll need to get up to the hospital tomorrow morning. This morning. I'm going to walk down to the apartment. And I can walk to work."

Jean hesitated for a couple of seconds before snatching the key chain, and closing her hand around them, she whispered, "Thanks." The stars were switched off, no longer visible. With a last hug and a glance around the Defender, Larry walked west toward Lexington Avenue, hands deep in pockets, looking skyward. As she ducked into the building, having roused the plumply dozing Manuel, Jean thought there was something different about Larry's walk. He was bouncing on the balls of his feet, ever so slightly, a spring in him as new as her sister's new laugh.

Quietly, Jean called the hospital as soon as she came in. The nurse in ICU who finally answered would only say that the doctors had made no new rounds and that Mr. Warner was doing "as well as can be expected." When pressed, she said he was asleep. But Jean was not ready for sleep. She tiptoed into the bathroom and stood in front of the mirror and had a good look at herself: this was her face for the next thing, she thought, not quite wanting to articulate that it was fatherlessness that she was staring at. And she thought she looked all right— better now than before, even with the all-weather frown line— better than when she was younger and fuller and less defined.

Opening her mouth only a couple of inches from the mirror and instantly losing track of time, she saw that a couple of her lower teeth were quite drastically worn down by grinding. It's taken *years* to get that dip, she thought, fingering the dippiest. Like generations of pilgrims piously smoothing the steps of St. Peter's—or thousands of cows' tongues licking out a crescent from a pillar of salt. And her *hair*. She pulled out a few more wisps from the remains of a French twist. There. Better a little messier still, a little more lived-in, like the hollows in her lower canines, more used up. And it *was* better.

Jean finally understood, might even have said, if there was anyone to hear, that twenty years ago she'd been too young for pleasure. So there was this good news from her night with Dan: she was now in her prime. But what she'd thought about Larry all those years ago (when her *body* was in its prime) was, No point going on with this because he isn't the kind of man I want to marry, though she hadn't troubled herself to find out what kind of man he was, apart from the kind who was American and a lawyer, like Dad. How in the world had she mistaken their complete mutual ease and understanding for a soft option, something *too* easy?

Yet here she was, on the brink of forty-six, an acknowledged brain, a syndicated brain, and it seemed she wanted to be taken for a fox—because yes, she wanted *Shroud of Dew* all over again only different, better—that is, with someone she loved—and she hated very much to think she might never have it. Jerking back from her reflection, then moving closer, she saw one thing she didn't like: that darting expression of doubt and self-defense—its sharpness reminded her of Bud the kestrel, beady eye aglitter. When had that started?

If she had to pick a moment, Jean thought, the eye in question just inches from the glass, it might be the day Wayne the Washington Square pot dealer sold her that nickel bag and invited her back to his place to smoke it; how he'd touched her cheek, making it clear he wasn't entirely focused on which bong they might use. Skinny, freckled, twelve-year-old Jeannie Warner dressed as a small man, suspenders ranged over her panel-flat chest—she knew even then you had to be a runaway from Pennsylvania, or farther, from Minnesota, to agree to a thing like that. But a part of her was immensely flattered. She'd also been devastated. That was, just possibly, the very beginning of her not wanting to be taken for a body, Jean thought. She'd wanted to be taken for a *mind*—of course she did, she was Bill Warner's daughter—though almost any kind would do, a wit, a brain, even a clown or a freak in a dead man's suit, but please, let it be something for my head: sense, sense, sense.

She turned on the water to wash her face. Had something like that happened with Larry in the Whipple conference room? He was teaching her the *vallenato* when most people were queuing for their hot dogs. And she was catching on, beginning to dance and feel the lightness and exhilaration of an unmoored unity, even though all the while she was fighting her idiotic fight, fighting as if Larry was Phyllis's idea—which he kind of was. It was such a shame, but you couldn't help how old you were any more than you could dodge the freight of each age. Did he have any idea how hard it was to get a First in Law at Oxford? A lawyer with multiple degrees and honors, yes, of course he knew. How *hard* she'd tried. Any secretary could learn the *vallenato,* was that what she'd thought? Little fool.

What she wished now, Jean thought, settling down at last on the squeaky blow-up bed, was that she at least had more memories in her cupboard—more to work with in the decades of solitary reminiscence that yawned before her; that she had, just a little more often, said yes instead of no. A dainty regret, perhaps, but it was hers: not for what she had done, but for what she hadn't dared try.

Bill Warner was not asleep at ten the next morning. He was unconscious. The generators had indeed worked all during the blackout, running respirators and monitors and scanners and defibrillators. But there was no air-conditioning, and his temperature had climbed to one hundred and four. He was comatose. Panic occupied her skull like tinnitus, a fire drill only she could hear. She was sure he had entered his own blackout, never mind if the nurse called it sleep; never mind if they didn't *call* it death. And she thought that, much as they wanted to get him out on day one hundred, they might want to keep him in until day ninety-nine, while his insurance lasted.

Jean had her people on the ground, and they all helped a little. She saw less of Larry, but continued to use his car, and he kept in touch about Bill. Mark offered to come over, but she discouraged him. She had no energy for feeding him the case history; he'd be restless—there wasn't even a clear stretch of Phyllis's floor long enough for him to sleep on. Furthermore, she thought heavily, so long as he was linked with Giovana, he wasn't allowed in her hometown. Her calls to London and St. Jacques were limited to telegrammatic assurances, skeletal debriefings; she avoided all extraneous persons.

One friend, however, was insistent—Ellie Antonucci. At a

Starbucks on Lexington, Ellie appeared with a newer new look than her newly blond hair: Oscar. He was enormous, and firmly latched at the breast, mother and son indifferent to the zero-tolerance glances of less demonstrably fulfilled women. She'd waited a long time for Oscar, and she wasn't about to hide him now. The first thing Ellie said, when Jean mentioned she'd run into Iona Mackenzie at Hatchards, was "Could you tell?"

"Tell what?" Jean asked, lowering her foot-high paper cup of milky coffee, seeing in her mind Iona's injection-smoothed face.

"Double mastectomy," Ellie said. "You didn't know? You didn't notice?"

"I did *not* notice, and no, I didn't know."

"About six months ago. It was all very sudden. Something like five weeks between the diagnosis and the operation. But she was very lucky."

"Oh yeah?"

"Yeah, really. Lucky they ever spotted it at all. There was no lump. No, seriously: no lump. *Slight* dryness on one nipple and the occasional drop of discharge. She has, or had, something called Paget's disease. Rare form of cancer for much older women, hugely aggressive if it takes off. Iona *would* get the high-octane kind, right?"

Ellie was feeling her way to their old joke about how Iona had to have the maximal version of everything. "And typically butch of Iona to have both off, the second a kind of citizen's preemptive strike, and then just leaving it like that, no reconstructive surgery. *Cool,* don't you think?"

"I think it's dignified," Jean said firmly, and she thought, I'm a hopeless friend. An increasingly rich field for regret. She could not say a word, and so Ellie went on uninterrupted.

"They take skin and muscle from your back and piece it

in. . . ." Ellie's fascination had a professional feel to it. "You can have it with or without the implant," she said, as if she was talking about shoulder pads for a costume. "The tricky bit is the nipple—a lot of cutting and scrunching and tattooing—though apparently there's a new technique they're using in South America, where they cadge a bit of skin from the inside of the cheek. . . ."

Jean got up, muttering about getting back to the hospital, and headed for the door as Ellie waved but didn't stand, pinned to her seat by a sleeping Oscar.

When Jean got to the fifth floor she found Phyllis at the ICU desk, barely able to see over it, trying to get someone's attention—anyone's attention. She was convinced the green squiggle on the heart monitor was too weak, almost flat; she was "just wondering" shouldn't someone take a look?

And to think that Phyllis had asked the same question, in a different hospital, thirty-three years ago, before some of these nurses and doctors were even born.

They seemed to plan their rounds for the ten minutes the women were barred from the ward, to let Bill be washed and turned. And Phyllis had seen this too: they avoided the families because it was in these faces, in her face, that their failure was most clearly drawn. Though Bill alone presented a vivid reflection—heavy, helpless, mute, like a wounded elephant seal stranded on the beach, one who was done thrashing.

That evening, as Jean was about to head down and out of the hospital, she bumped into Joe the nurse, coming out of the elevator. Even he had been elusive these anxious last days. Jean, holding a stack of Tupperware empties to bring home, let the elevator go.

"Please, Joe. Talk to me. I can't get anyone to talk to me. We're losing him, aren't we?"

The nurse toyed with one of his earrings. With the paper head cover tied over his forehead he looked like a pirate. Or like a gay man dressed up as a pirate. He was searching for words, and Jean was not moving till he found them.

"It's a long time," he finally said. Joe looked poised to clarify—backpedal, Jean felt—when another elevator opened and they were forced to part, to make way for people to pass. In lieu of a wave, she lifted her tower of plastic tubs and stepped into that elevator, going down. She would call Marianne soon as she got outside. And Larry. From Mom's she'd call London. And after that, she had no idea.

The twelfth day of Bill's coma, like the previous eleven, was marked by the contorted face of the anguished dreamer. "ARDS—acute respiratory distress syndrome," the doctor told them, unable to do anything but name it. And then, just at the end of visiting hours, both his girls and their mother still sitting beside him and watching the heart monitor, listening to the whir of the respirator, he opened his eyes and asked for ice. Everyone laughed to hear that voice, barely audible for the damage to his cords. Because of the water on his lungs the nurses wouldn't let him have any. When they left the room, Jean moistened a towel and gave it to Dad to suck on. The next day, sitting mostly upright for the first time in two weeks, he couldn't talk anymore, but he drew a picture of a house with a steep roof.

"Not a bad little drawing," Jean said, though the lines were shaky.

He got out a word. He said "two" (or maybe "do"), stabbing at the front of the house. Jean, who was sitting alone with him, thought of a summerhouse they used to rent on Fire Island—it had just such a steep roof and a wide covered porch. He wanted to sit on that porch for a couple of hours. He wanted to sit on the porch—just us two. "You too." "Let's do." Who could say? He was very weak, diminished. And he had drifted off again. But he was still here.

As Bill improved, as his color came back and he could breathe for spells on his own, Marianne returned to her children, and Jean and Phyllis began again to relay their time. Every afternoon, Jean went out walking. Once, in a Madison Avenue window, she caught a glimpse of a squashy chocolate-brown handbag and stopped to inspect it, thinking of Iona, taking in the cruel joke of the dark-haired mannequin with solidly permanent breasts. She hurried on. She missed Victoria. She even missed Mark, though every flash of him was marred by one of Giovana, popping in—instant messaging Jean's most private thoughts.

After a particularly discouraging morning in the hospital—Bill was unconscious for the duration—Jean went alone to the Brooklyn Botanic Gardens and then to the Brooklyn Museum. How was it possible she'd never been there before? Just growing up on the Upper East Side—or maybe it was Phyllis's fear of the "outer" boroughs, even if she had managed to find home on East Seventy-ninth Street all the way from Utah. When Jean got back to the apartment she changed into a loose gauze dress she'd bought on the beach in Grand Baie. (All these details she'd never forget.) She was hot and very tired. Phyllis must be on her way home by now. Jean put an ice cube into a tumbler of coffee from the morning's pot. She phoned the ICU. The nurse, not one she recognized, couldn't find him. Jean repeated his name. *William Warner*—William Walton Warner. The nurse couldn't even find his name.

He was gone.

Attachment

Before Jean could say a word, she was put on hold, listening to a loop of digitized "Greensleeves."

"*No!*" she cried, sinking against the kitchen cabinet to the floor, knocking her coffee off the counter with the cord, clutching the phone with both hands, and ignoring the expanding continent of brown at her feet. The nurse had gone to find an accredited messenger of death, a certified bringer of bad news, to tell her—she knew this: she'd signed the form; she was on the list. But Jean, convulsing and sobbing on the spattered linoleum, had misunderstood. Bill had been moved upstairs, out of intensive care.

St. Jacques

POSSESSION OF DRUGS WILL BE PUNISHED WITH DEATH. There it was again, the hand-painted warning—*de la peine de mort*—over the dinky luggage carousel of St. Jacques' tiny airport. Waiting for her luggage, Jean wondered how the local powers would punish adultery. She could imagine mutts trained to sniff out envy and lust, or a bleeping wand that detected sloth or anger. She'd thought a lot about the series she'd promised for *Mrs.* This week, in addition to observing Bud's flight, she'd start writing up the sins.

Jean squinted through the glass partition beyond the conveyor belt to where Mark would be standing—or maybe Victoria, who had recently, on the third try, passed her driving test. She and Vikram had been here for over a week, waiting for Jean to return before setting off to Indonesia. She'd heard the eager restlessness in her daughter's voice and remembered that feeling, just about. Vic wouldn't be able to see that the present moment was perhaps the best part: poised on the brink, and ready. Jean thought of that tiny jewel of suspended flight, Emerald the hummingbird, and wondered if she was still in residence in the garden.

Briskly wheeling her stack of suitcases toward the dozens of boys hustling by the exit, she scanned the crowd for Hubbards.

She'd left a message, clearly unreceived, saying she'd make the early flight. All around her there were scenes of joyful family reunion. Never mind; she'd get a taxi and sleep on the way.

Outside, the heat cloaked her like a wet poncho. And there was Mark at the far end of the parking lot, hunched over the driver's door, fussing with the key. By now she was looking forward to the transition period of the cab ride. . . . Jean waved but he didn't notice, tucking in his shirt and blindly striding toward the low terminal.

"Yoo-hoo!" she called as he drew near, not overjoyed but affectionate; there *was* something very dear in that long-bodied lope. His smile when he saw her made her feel better at once; and for perhaps the thousandth time during their life together, she wondered if he was late primarily to witness her visible relief upon his eventual appearance. Mark assumed charge of her luggage, and Jean settled in the passenger seat with her canvas tote and, sticking out the top, Larry's book. As the planting of yellow Post-its indicated, she was three-quarters of the way through, and it was thrilling. The arguments, but also Jean using her mind—she was out of shape here too. She wondered if she could be bothered to go back to the gym, and those toned women, still climbing the stairway to nowhere. She couldn't wait to discuss *A Theory of Equality* with Victoria.

She was too tired to read more now. Instead, Jean reviewed the Larry gossip she'd had from Marianne before leaving for the airport. According to Doug, the Monds were splitting up. Certainly, Melanie never seemed to be around, not even in conversation. It had made Jean uneasy to hear this from anyone but Larry—still, if it was true, she was impressed. All that time in New York he must have been churning with it; yet he'd said nothing and instead he'd comforted *her*.

As she waited what seemed an age for Mark to stow her suitcases—through the back window she saw him unfurl a tarp like a sail, then a series of flying cables—Jean watched a convoy of gussied-up well-wishers pull over at departures. Many of the leavers, she knew, weren't going on holiday. They were emigrating, with their jumbo waist-high suitcases banded in duct tape and rope. Life's most stirring dramas unfolded here at the little airport—soon the Hubbards would be back themselves, waving Victoria off on her grand tour. Jean bottled her childish wish that Vic had come to meet her. Of course she should stay home at the hottest hour of the day.

"How was your flight?" Mark asked, wiping his brow, settling at last into the driver's seat.

This, from him, was never a perfunctory question. Intolerant of so many ostensibly more interesting topics, he nevertheless always wanted the details of weather and travel—what the food was like, which film, the offenses of the worst fellow passenger. Life as usual: after six weeks of strained hospital vigilance, she'd almost forgotten how it was done. He then filled her in on the local news, such as the transfer entire, this past week, of Christian's affections to Victoria. Jean delighted in the thought, and in the knowledge that Mark would find satisfaction in this disloyalty.

The familiar savagery of the landscape, where nothing was quartered, tilled, or fenced in, was restful on her eyes, despite the tropical brightness, and on her spirit. But she was startled afresh by the poverty—the scrap and cardboard shacks, the collage yards, the three-legged dogs and bony horses, the distended bellies on the children along the road—that she knew she'd stop noticing in a few weeks.

As they turned onto the coastal road, Mark gave her the bad news. Victoria and Vikram had left two days before. Not allowing her even a moment to be understanding, he rushed to defend the decision. It was leave then or wait another week for connections to Indonesia; besides, all their flights were fixed and prepaid, on top of which their classes began again in the third week of September. Jean felt harassed. She wasn't interested in painstaking consideration. She was desolate, choking. It was like falling down in a crowd—you didn't want people rushing in with their concern and commitment to seeing you upright. A month and a half had passed since their family weekend in London, and now, through no fault of her own, she'd missed Victoria by *two days*. And tomorrow was Jean's birthday.

"We didn't know when you'd be coming back. It might well have been another week, and of course no one wanted to rush you. It was *right* that you took the time you needed."

Jean struggled to suppress her misery, her irritation at Mark's giving her permission. She felt utterly punished—and more so for her expectation of praise and celebration, her great return from care. "What a shame" was all she could manage. She turned to look out the window, for the rest of the trip offering Mark the back of her head.

Inside the office-house she was sad all over again. She wandered through the rooms, on the trail of her absent daughter. Vic had stacked the big pillows for sitting on the living room floor. In the guest room, her wildflowers wilted in wine bottles and tumblers; a fat candle was welded to the edge of the bathtub. On the covered veranda, twin hammocks hung side by side like a droopy double bed.

Mark was in the kitchen, practically bustling. He'd made her a good omelette, finished with sprigs of coriander and a drizzle of some juniper elixir from his well-stocked bar, and now he'd done the dishes. Everything except the skillet; he always left the pots and pans: for the unseen cleaner-upper—his mother, Jean—the someone *behind*. Still, he was trying, and she knew she also had to try harder, even if the mere thought filled her with fatigue.

"I think I'll have a little nap," she said. "Early start tomorrow. I feel all emotional, as if I'm going to Bud's graduation ceremony—which I guess I am." Inside the bedroom, glancing across at the open closet door, she could tell at once that her clothes had been used by Victoria. She pulled out a sarong and sniffed an alien coconut suntan lotion. Jean had planned to give her these for her trip, pass them on—these and so much else, the silver beads. She'd wanted to give Vic everything, but she hadn't gotten here in time. She fell asleep facedown on the bed.

appy birthday!" Mark was almost singing. It was late afternoon, and the sun was still blazing.

"It's not till tomorrow," Jean said, stepping into the garden, sleepy. She was wearing a small pink T-shirt, Victoria's, and a coconut-scented sarong.

"What's to stop us celebrating now—no time like the present."

"Not sure there's anything to celebrate," Jean said, taking in the festivities already advanced. She'd wanted to collect her thoughts about the kestrel project, not work on a hangover for the launch.

"Well then, how about your glorious return? I'm *so* pleased you're back. Come on, darling. Have a glass."

"Actually, what I'd really like is a cup of tea."

Mark was holding up a half-empty bottle of French champagne—an even greater luxury on this island than at home, almost inconceivably expensive. Jean had read that, before it became lust, the sin was known as *luxuria:* extravagance. Mark's sudden slump told her he felt her different track as a kind of rebuke, and he was right about that. He should have waited.

"All right then, tea *and* champagne. As I'm pouring. Though

I intend to go *on* pouring throughout this and the great day itself and on into the great beyond, Mrs. H. So long as supplies last."

Ass, Jean thought. She hated the way he pushed when he wanted someone to drink with; hated even more his already being high without needing her high alongside him. He was a bully when he was drinking, a bully cloaked in amiability, a bully and a bore. She wondered if Mark had been drinking this much without the excuse of her birthday, when Victoria was here. Maybe not. He tended to let himself go when he was alone, more drinking and less bathing, and this *she* felt as a rebuke. As he expected and wanted her to—his sloppy dramatization of her neglect.

Most of the expats they'd met here were drunks. "Escaping the rat race" was the way people generally described their year-round binge. Like the old guy from Wisconsin who ran the Bamboo Bar. He'd told his captive audience, as they downed first an Old Pal and then a Sundowner (both his own secret recipe), "One day, out on the freeway, the cars, the rain, the *snow,* and I said to myself, Who *needs* this shit?" And he'd been buzzing on St. Jacques ever since.

Jean accepted the flute of champagne from Mark, not ready to make any great point of her own. And anyway, what the hell. It was always easier to join Mark. This was another thing that made her angry—with herself, with him.

Mark emptied his glass and stood with his hands on his hips squinting at the view. Trying, Jean could easily imagine, to remember who he was. She knew it would take time to reestablish a rhythm after the long separation, but she still didn't particularly want to be alone with him. When she mentioned once again the bad luck of Victoria having left only two days before, he snapped.

"Honestly, Jean—the world cannot, and dare I say *should* not, stand still because you are called away."

"Called away, huh? Actually, it was Dad who was nearly 'called away'—the rest of us were just standing by—the hardest job I know. *Called away.* You know I really don't get you. Thanks, anyway, for the support."

Mark looked momentarily abashed. "I offered to come out. You declined. Clearly not needed."

"Ah, back to you then. No—not needed when you call completely bombed at three-thirty in the morning."

"Silly me. And I thought I was staying up to ring you at a civilized hour, when I'd find you back from hospital—what time was it there when I rang? Seven-thirty p.m., no? I'm very sorry if my tone was insufficiently solemn."

"It's not about you. And Victoria? She hardly called at all. You might have reminded her. He is her grandfather, you know—her only grandfather, and perhaps not for very much longer."

"I don't honestly see any great gain in blaming Victoria for your father's angina."

"*Aneurysm,*" she barked, furious he hadn't troubled himself to absorb this basic fact, the origin of the entire calamity, that he acted as Victoria's defender, when it was him she was mad at.

"Of course I don't *blame* her. I just wanted to see her. I don't know why I rushed back here. I'm the one who's clearly not needed. And *you* clearly have no real concept of the hell we've been through. He's not out of the woods yet, you know. And here you are, exactly as if nothing's happened."

Jean, circling the terrace with her arms crossed, was beginning to think how to get out of this conversation, recover some common ground, scratch for peace. She was not so far gone she couldn't see regret on the horizon. Birthdays, she reminded herself, were always a bit of a downer—the mortality bulletin. But it was Mark who spoke, in an unexpectedly sober tone.

"Then perhaps you'd like to tell me exactly what did happen in New York."

"Can you possibly be serious?"

Mark fingercombed his hair. "Oh, yes—never more so."

Dirty hair, Jean noted. In fact, he was looking downright seedy, after a mere two days on his own. For no good reason she felt that, since she had never confronted him about Giovana, he, in return, should be impeccable: gracious, generous, grateful, and, at the very least, clean.

"What *are* you talking about? You know perfectly well what happened—and what's *still* happening in New York. If you're going to persist in this tedious vein I'm going to have to lie down." Instead, she collapsed into a director's chair. Now Jean was annoyed there wasn't more champagne. What was the point of offering someone half a glass of champagne? Seedy *and* greedy. "Any more of this stuff?" She twirled her glass in the air by the stem, smiling like a clown, with her eyebrows raised, the kind of expression she knew he hated.

He went to get another bottle from the fridge and, tugging at the cork, he said right on the pop, "Larry called."

"Any news on Dad?" Her neck and back burned with renewed heat.

"No, nothing about your father, or nothing he cared to share with me, at any rate. Just wanted you to know he called. Who is this Larry, Jean?" Mark was standing before her, pouring. He paused to look at her.

"What are you trying to say? You know very well who Larry is—Larry Mond. My old teacher. My old boss."

"What I mean is, who is he to you? Are you seeing this Larry, Larry 'Mond'?"

"I *saw* Larry, yes. And? Never mind the outrageous suggestion, but how can I be *seeing* Larry? You weren't *there*. Is that what the problem is? Feeling left out? Neglected? Did I spend too much time in intensive care?"

"Sounds like you spent rather a lot of time with 'Larry' in New York."

"No need to wiggle your imaginary fingers. Save your quote marks for someone who finds a perfectly ordinary name funny—the soul of wit, aren't you? Yes, I saw Larry. We all did." She put her glass down on the marble tabletop a touch too firmly. "He was very helpful, in fact." It was clear enough Jean meant *unlike you,* but she enumerated all the same. "He lent us his car—you don't realize, the hospital was a hundred blocks away, hardly in New York at all. Larry saved our lives in the blackout—you do remember there was a massive outage in New York?"

"*Saved our lives,* now, is it?"

Mark was standing with his hands on his hips, pompous, Jean thought, and foolish, too, with his big bleach-white feet pointing outward.

"*Listen* to me. In our time of need, Larry was a friend—to Mom, and Dad in particular. A sober, serious, grown-up friend—what they call a *rock*. How else can I put it? He was *there*."

"Yes, I should say he was. Rock around the clock."

"Where is your sense of decency? Your *trust*? Or has your long vacation from reality—and from this marriage—made these concepts hazy? A basic duty of trust has been trampled. And over so vast a period of *time*. That, I think for me, is the hardest thing." The moment had come, and Jean found she felt calm, even energized, as if from great lungfuls of mountain air. Why had she waited so long? "We can talk about Larry, sure. What else—or who else—should we talk about? Maybe you'd like to begin."

"Well, yes, if you'll not insist on changing the subject. I shall begin, or begin *again,* because, you see, *Larry*—is that even short for Lawrence, or was he actually christened 'Larry'? Larry P. Mond. You see, I think it's rather *odd,* Dr. Mond at the ready with his miracle car in New York—how marvelously handy in a blackout. How exactly did Larry Mond *save your life,* Jean, do you want to tell me that? I see you're studying his latest tome."

Jean's voice was low and controlled. "It's a great book. Not that you'd be remotely interested. What *are* you interested in, Mark? Do you even realize you haven't asked a single thing about Dad? Or Phyllis, for that matter—your great chum. I think that's mighty odd. You want odd? How about your fun-loving gal pal, with one *n* and at least two of everything else—"

In the kitchen, the phone rang. Mark, no doubt suppressing cartwheels of joy at this interruption, answered with such hysterical ferocity that Jean could hear every word through the window.

"*Yes,* Dan? . . . No, I'm afraid I cannot oblige. Not in front of me at the minute, you see. . . . No, Daniel, I cannot at this precise moment give you the fine print, the skinny, the *mode d'emploi* on the coolant apparati, are you with me? And would you dispense *instantly* with the 'Brunhilda,' you fucking *yob,* it's driving me up the wall. Is there some purpose to this call other than my telling you how to *do your job* or are we merely rallying for the gaiety of nations? . . . Correctly surmised, my dear Watson, this is *not* the ideal moment for a 'natter.' " She heard Mark toss the phone onto the kitchen table as he strode out of the house, the screen door banging shut behind him. "I'm going to get a fish for dinner," he yelled back from the truck, apparently not wanting to appear entirely buffoonish, childlike, *and* guilty, as he scuttled off, she'd wager, to the Bamboo Bar.

Jean worried about Mark's driving on all that champagne—

a worry mixed with rage, because he knew her terror of drunk driving. Her head throbbing, she went into the kitchen. She picked the phone up from the table to put it back in its cradle and was alarmed to hear a familiar laugh—Dan's. Mark hadn't switched the phone off. "Mark, Mark—keep your hair on, mate. We do really need that copy. Today, in fact. Helloooo—Boss?"

"He's gone out now," Jean said, stepping back outside, trying to keep all emotion out of her voice. "He'll call you back later."

"Jean!" Dan said. "Are you all right? The boss man's a bit of a dark cloud this afternoon. Trouble in paradise?"

"Everything's fine. Sorry about that."

"Not to worry. In fact, Jean, I'm really glad you picked up because I've been wanting to speak to you. You see, I'll be off very soon and . . . are you sure you're all right there?"

"I'm sure, thanks. Listen, don't let me keep you." His familiarity made her cringe; she really couldn't be bothered to ask him where he was going for his vacation. "I'll be sure Mark gets back to you this afternoon."

"That's grand, but wait just a second. Can you talk? I just wanted to say, well, a big thanks."

"For what? Oh, God. Well, look, I'll let you run. . . ."

"Don't go. I know I must've disappointed you—but it's just that you were so *good*. I didn't realize for ages that they were from you all along, that—"

"That what were from me?"

"Come on, you don't have to pretend. Please. I don't myself feel that it's anything to be ashamed of—quite the reverse. You are talent, Thing. Better than Mark. So good, in fact, that I didn't twig it was you until we spent the—"

"Thing?"

"Actually, her name is Magdalena, but yeah, Thing, Ginger . . . Come on, Munyeroo! And of course Cruella, but that's another—"

"Stop!" Jean's stomach was a burning hole.

"Don't *worry*. Mark knows nothing about it. He may have seen one or two pix of Magdalena, but in her incarnation as Brunhilda. I can't even remember if you've seen those. All very confusing. Once I realized it wasn't Mark who was writing, I realized—yeah, it's true, he was never very keen. Doesn't have your talent, if you want to know, Mrs. H. And Gio? I'm sure he only ever saw one or two of Giovana. She's our little slice of shared-history pie, our own private duologue—"

"Good-*bye*." She hung up and slumped back into her chair. She felt weightless, panic-stricken, nauseous. The earth could open at her feet and she would gladly lean forward, tumble right in. Dan as Giovana: How could that have happened? How could she be so stupid?

The phone rang again almost immediately. Jean looked at it, summoning the nerve to answer—maybe it was him again, calling back to say this too was all a joke. And not one she'd sickeningly played on herself. And on her husband.

It was Victoria. "Mum? Your phone has been engaged for *ages*. And I'm getting a terrible echo, so I'm just going to be quick. . . . Happy birthday! There's something else I want to tell you. Vikram and I were at Borobodur early this morning. It gets to be thirty-eight or even forty degrees so you really have to do as much at dawn as possible. . . . It was amazing, hundreds of Buddhas and all these great latticed bells of stone . . . but I'll show you pictures when I get back. Listen, I have wonderful news."

"Good. Where are you now, darling?"

"I'm in Yogyakarta. *Guess*, Mum. I'm sure you can guess." There was a silence and Jean thought the line had gone dead. "Mum?"

"Hm? You know, darling, I really don't think I can." Her
own recent "news" had left Jean in doubt about whatever she
might say, think, feel; her head was swirling with the implica-
tions of Dan's emergence as Giovana's keeper and perpetrator
and voice. Of *course*. That night in his loft—they'd rehearsed it
by e-mail for months. No wonder he'd thought her so "playful" and "daring." No wonder he'd showed her those films.
"Isn't that what you asked for?" Yes, she'd asked for it, all
right. Or at least she'd asked Giovana for it, up against the
kitchen counter.

"Mum? Are you there? Please, try."

"Try what? What is it, sweetheart?" Jean was thinking—
despite her passionate credulity, none of this actually happened
to Mark; but it had still happened to her. She couldn't unthink
those violent thoughts, or reverse the profound incremental
shift in her deepest feelings. Could she? Just run the new information through her brain and sit back as life gradually returned
to normal, let the color flood black into this black-and-white
world?

"No, *you* guess. Wonderful, wonderful news. Mum? Are you
all right?"

"I'm fine. I don't know. You're engaged," Jean said—the
last thing she really believed.

"I knew you'd guess." Victoria sounded not amazed but
gratified: here was the confirmation of the ineluctable. "It was
very romantic, at the top of the temple just as the sun appeared.
We just spontaneously decided, not really like a question and
an answer. It was all very natural, only one element of a wonderful day."

Jean tried to hold back tears. She took a deep breath. "I'm
going to cry. I'm so happy. And I am, I'm going to cry."

"Mum!" Vic was laughing; she turned to speak to Vikram;
Jean couldn't hear what she said but knew she was telling him

that her mother was about to cry. Not, perhaps, for the exact reasons she imagined, but certainly for some of them.

"Dad's not here, sweetheart. He went out to get a fish. He'll be desolate to miss you. Can we call you back? Wait a second, I hear the truck now—"

"*Mark!*" Jean ran out toward the car, calling him. "It's Vic!" Panting, she gave him the phone and stood there for a moment, arms crossed. Mark was just listening and not talking while she looked at him, this man she'd known so long and so well and then somehow betrayed, and she felt spongy kneed, leaky, pierced through with sorrow and also panic. Clearly she'd wanted to go to bed with Dan so much that she'd persuaded herself not only that this was "the culture" but that it was one imposed on her by Mark—professional foister of the new-fangled.

One piece of wild luck—thanks, improbably, to Dan's calling—she hadn't uttered Giovana's name. And her pious words about *trust,* he might think, were those of a careworn wife—not the residue of her smoldering hexes, honed over months and capped by vindictive God knows what with his *employee.* Like Bill's illness coming on the heels of that lunatic foray into Dan's lair, undeniable reality rained down on her again, pelting shame.

After a minute, she took the plastic bag hanging from his finger, the fish. So he hadn't gone to the bar. He'd gone, just as he told her, to the fishermen. Was there anything she didn't get wrong? She'd let him speak to Vic alone. This, between father and daughter, was a long-anticipated moment—an "iconic" moment, Mark might've said if he was writing the copy. And even though she had no wish to deny any impulse of his ever again, she dreaded his inevitable moping and whining. Victoria was very young, but an engagement could go on forever. To Jean the real news was that her daughter was truly happy.

Back in the kitchen, she turned to the fish, which seemed to be staring up at her as she prepared it for the oven like a corpse for entombment. Perhaps Mark's trip to the fishermen contained a gesture: making dinner was a ritual and, like most any other ritual, this one offered salvation by minutiae, deliverance for a time from ruin. She thought for a moment of what Larry had said—all we have is the law. Well, a recipe was a local ordinance, and this kitchen was her fiefdom, her command-and-control station. Jean wasn't going to fall apart. She wasn't going to drink dinner from a jar. She'd serve the fish à la Grecque—roasted whole with rosemary and lemon—as in the tavernas on that first trip they'd made together to Mykonos, before Vic was born. And now Victoria—who, it seemed to Jean, only a few fish dinners ago didn't even *exist*—was engaged to be married. Her gratitude to the newly affianced was inestimable: they alone could restore this family.

She leaned to look out the door. Mark was walking, all hunched, the phone in his neck. He'd stay outside, she knew, and wait to watch the sun as it slipped behind the hills. She didn't go out to join him; instead, she returned to the kitchen sink. Through the window she caught sight of Emerald, hovering in the bougainvillea in the last gleam of light. Her wings were beating so fast you could hardly see them, and this added to the impression she gave of being more fish than bird—swimming on air.

Mark had said no more Brunhilda. He was in his way a participant, she thought, willing some kind of balance. She cut the potatoes into wedges, scattered thick salt and oil over them, and shook them out of the bowl into the pan. And for the first time, she stopped to think about the real "Giovana"—Magdalena, Brunhilda, one and the same, Dan's bird. How many people had drooled over this young Brazilian? Jean felt weak, as fragile as the sand dollar balanced on the window ledge. With one or two exceptions mostly relating to advice on hairdos, she'd distanced herself from Giovana, made no true acknowledgment of her, after all a real girl somewhere, and so ill used. There was your betrayal of trust, Mrs. H. Jean opened the oven door and shoved in the tray. It was too dark now to see if Emerald was still outside, though she never lingered. Jean wondered where she went. In all her searches through the garden, she'd never found a nest.

She was going to skip dinner—and the dinner conversation. She scribbled a note about not feeling well, which was true, and put herself to bed in the guest room.

Jean was on the road at seven and headed for the Domaine du Pêcheur, a dense reserve with a roaring river and the closest thing left on St. Jacques to a wilderness: the Beausoleil project's field headquarters.

She was glad to have work today, and this job in particular. In the drive of the Domaine, a couple of old jeeps converged: hardly the media event she'd imagined when she dressed in her airport-and-interviewing skirt. There were only three journalists—Jean, a Mauritian in absurdly oversize sunglasses, and a reporter from *Le Quotidien* who wandered around the log cabin that belonged to the center.

The project assistants reminded Jean of a group of prop mistresses before curtain time—they consulted one another in low voices, checked and then rechecked their monitoring equipment and, occasionally, Bud, their ward. Zeb, a zoologist from London, listened to the Mauritian journalist talk about the wildlife program on the Big Island: "complete rescue of the near-extinct pink pigeon and the echo parakeet." Zeb was nodding so enthusiastically he was practically pecking. But Jean found herself unmoved by the fates of these other birds, despite their equally dramatic dips and resurgences and their more obvious charms, the bright wing coloration. The kestrels were more like *her:* relatively sedentary and solitary creatures, even their chest feathers were spotted like freckles. No, all her feeling was for the runt, as if he was her family; unpromising though he might seem, he was the one.

Jean remembered that today was her birthday. Looking over at Bud, the caged prince, she wondered for the first time if all this worked-up survival was the good thing everyone assumed it to be. They were beautiful, the little falcons, and of course she knew the arguments for restocking. But maybe, if they couldn't rally on their own, the kestrels should be allowed to die out, like the flightless dodo over on Mauritius. Others had survived DDT and habitat loss—for instance, humans. Jockeying made you strong. Or was it going to be prekilled mice forever? Along with egg pulling and egg clutching, artificial incubation and hacking, hand rearing and fostering and predator control?

She thought of Vic and Vikram beginning their life together, and how unquestioningly happy they must be, with everything falling into place and no end in sight.

> *. . . I know this is paradise*
>
> *Everyone old has dreamed of all their lives—*
> *Bonds and gestures pushed to one side*
> *Like an outdated combine harvester,*
> *And everyone young going down the long slide*
>
> *To happiness, endlessly. . . .*

Larkin again—he saw them going down the long slide "Like free bloody birds." Would Bud pair up with the right mate when he went down the long slide? They went for the most promising breeder, she knew, but with little or no discernible difference, with nothing like a hip-waist ratio to guide them, how could they tell who that might be? Bud was such a little player, a mold breaker—who was out there waiting for him? Maybe another kestrel, or maybe one very endangered pink pigeon. And she wondered how she'd ever make up for all that she'd done. Her column and even a more in-depth article about species survival seemed ever more abstract.

Finally the great man appeared: Bruce McGhee, the project's creator, looking more Old Testament than ever, with his bushy sideburns and ear hair like unblown dandelion fluff. How fitting for a species rescuer, Jean thought, that he resembled God as you first imagine him: the long white beard and look of stern regret, signaling that this pestilence and that drought and those floods hurt him more than they hurt you.

"Hello, Bruce," she said in her creamiest, serious-newspaper voice, holding out a hand.

"Good to see you again," he said, pumping her hand. He was grayer and more grizzled than when they'd first met. Maybe, Jean thought, it was time Bruce was released back into civilization.

"We all here?" he said, glancing around as he tucked in his shirttail, obviously disappointed by the small turnout. "Any questions before we get under way?"

"How do you reckon old Bud here will feed himself in the future?" Jean asked.

"Good question, Jean. The truth is, this has been a more gradual weaning than it might appear." He explained that Bud had been let out on occasion and attracted back each time with a pan of mice. Now that daily meal was at an end. She thought Bud was definitely stockier. He looked like he was wearing his own small yoga pants, baggy, then tapering sharply at the twin twigs of his ankles. The littlest kestrel as well as the last, he hopped and dipped his head to both sides and shook out like an Olympic athlete about to begin the event he'd trained for all his

life. Which was about right, Jean thought, feeling in her bag
for a pen. Bruce, man of few words, lifted his arms.

It was on her way home that she was overcome, alone in the
truck and finally crying: her own foolishness, her busy wrongdoing, but also, just now, the image of Bud. Jean, privileged
witness at the moment of freedom not conferred but *seized:* his
initial uncertainty, and then, looking over at his trusted captors,
tasting it, soaring. "Just like when you were born," she said
as if her daughter could hear, "your skin hot and slick with
that waxy roux of vernix, and I watched as your tiny chest
sank, and then rose, and then sank—expelling air, breathing,
all by yourself."

Jean took a great spluttery gulp and cried a bit more, spas-
modically, quieting down. She started along the last big stretch
of coast, the heroic landscape. Only a mile to go before their
turning, then inland through the hills and beyond, to the red
track and, finally, home. She loved this road—for the silver
view but also for the promise of arrival, to the zinc-roofed mining office on the steep coconut-littered slope. But was it still,
could it possibly remain, the good place?

"*Why* are you crying?" she asked herself out loud and not
quite rhetorically, rejecting self-pity. Somehow the question
demanded a real answer. And then she knew. She'd never
released Victoria.

Instead, Jean had released herself. And, incredibly, it hadn't
struck her all this year. She was away, but Victoria was gone.

Without any very clear intention, she and Mark had side-
stepped the historic moment of their daughter's flight, the beating of maiden wings, nurtured by good example and bad,

perspicacity and neglect, whole food and half food and slow food and fast food, and no home team to cheer her on. This hurts me more than it hurts you. And the feeling that spread through her now was like a kind of pesticide poisoning, Jean thought—its lethal effects might not even show for a generation, grief by then curdled into regret—a vast decrepitude of missed chances. As Victoria, aged five, had asked her parents: What kind of people *are* you? (She'd just discovered the frozen half lamb, laid out on newspaper in the cool pantry, sawed by the butcher right down the middle.) The kind, Victoria, who chuck the emptying of the nest.

Just as she parked, it started to rain—an almighty downpour, the kind that couldn't last. Now great explosions of thunder, and Jean rested her head and closed her eyes, singing a song Gladys used to belt out on stormy nights to beat back Jean's fear.

> *My Lord, he calls me by the thunder,*
> *The trumpet sounds within-a my soul . . .*
> *I ain't got long to stay here.*
> *Green trees a-bending, poor sinner stands a-trembling,*
> *The trumpet sounds within-a my soul . . .*
> *I ain't got long to stay here. . . .*

Trapped in the truck, she wondered how Gladys was. How could she not know—*Gladys,* the center of her universe for so many years? She sat in the humid cab waiting out the worst of the rain. Before long the windshield was steamed over, and then drops of water started falling *inside,* faster and faster, watering Jean from a chorus line of dancing droplets all along the edge of the glass, the whole truck threatening to come apart in the wet, like something Victoria used to make in school, from painted egg cartons.

Rain, rain, rain. Jean thought of that miserable wet afternoon in London just before they came to live here, when she'd seen Sophie de Vilmorin, so utterly bedraggled in the dry cleaner. And the obvious now struck her: the person Sophie reminded her of was *Vic*. Even if SdV was scrawnier, untended, frightened, and unlikely ever to become engaged to a handsome cosmologist. She wasn't nefarious; she was just a runt, a trapped Rapunzel—Jean's specialty. Then, with equally sudden clarity she saw what she wanted to do next. Not her column, which could only offer inadequate solutions to women she'd never meet. And not only a better class of journalism. No, it would be something more direct; she'd go back to the law, and finally use her degree—could you volunteer as a legal adviser at Women's Aid? But she'd start with Sophie, take her in hand. Why hadn't she seen it before, this chance to be truly useful?

Jean made a dash for the house, disappointed to find Mark not there. She wanted to tell him her new plan—before she could think of all the reasons not to carry it out. There was a note. *Gone for a walk on the beach.* For once, she didn't read this as code for a jaunt to the Bamboo Bar; she believed him. She dried herself and sat right down at the kitchen table with a new yellow legal pad and Bud's picture propped against the honey jar. Without moving from her hardback chair she sketched out her piece in twelve paragraphs, and just as she was finishing he came through the kitchen door. Jean didn't let him catch his breath.

"Mark, I've been thinking. About Sophie de Vilmorin. You know how she's been on my mind, and how I worried about her hanging around Vic. Well, I got it all wrong. *Wait*—just hear me out. I know, you're going to say this is a crazy scheme, but we've *got* to invite her to St. Jacques. Please, hang on a minute before you jump in. . . ." Mark, sitting down, looked decidedly unenthusiastic, even alarmed. "I'm totally serious—and I want to ask you, just give it a little thought before commenting. Vic is growing up; she's finding her way, and brilliantly. Our job is done—well, for now. Of course she'll be back, and nothing is ever *done*. But, don't you see? It all dovetails. She needs us. Sophie, I mean. And she needs us *now*. I don't suppose she has any useful skills, but maybe, when the article is published, I can ask Bruce McGhee if he might take her on at the project. It would restore her completely, you have to see what those kids are doing down there. . . ."

Jean stood up; she was exhausted but too excited for sitting. Then Mark spoke.

"Are you done? Shall we sit outside for a moment? The sun's come out. I'll get us a cool drink."

She was suddenly exploding with heat. "Okay. It's baking in here."

Mark took the ice-tea pitcher from the fridge. She sat in a director's chair outside and watched as he poured and then paced, and then sipped, apparently preparing himself, gearing up. "How to start? I'm very relieved to see you're taking a different tack—I think we can agree that we got off on the wrong foot yesterday—but yes, we need to talk. . . ."

It seemed he was going to remain standing. In case he needed to run away in a hurry, Jean thought.

"Of course I've been waiting for this to come up," he continued, still hesitant, "ever since you saw that e-mail."

So that's it, she thought. Giovana. It's never going to go away. He knows—he knows everything. Her vain hope of a swift and painless reprieve vanished. She tried not to think, instead she drew her legs under her, gluing herself to the seat. In the distance, she heard the whine of a drill or a mower, the revving of a motorcycle down the road.

Mark took a deep breath. "You know who she is, of course. What you don't know is that . . . incredible though it may sound, Sophie has got the idea . . . Sophie has for many years *clung* to the idea . . . that I am her father."

"What *are* you talking about?" She was making a visor with her hand, peering up at him.

"If you would let me speak. I met her around the time Victoria was born, and she made a connection. Since then . . . let me try to explain, what I understand of it anyway. As you know, her father was killed before, possibly even as, she was born." Jean was puzzled, borderline annoyed. This old story again? Mark was running both his hands through his hair, squinting at the tiled patio floor as if his unlearned lines were written out there in chalk. "Well, seemingly because of that tragic and central event surrounding her own birth, she somehow attached herself to the birth of Victoria, *our* central event if you will, and she, I don't know, I suppose she wanted to *be* that new person, with a fresh start—as much as that much-wanted, much-loved daughter—our Victoria."

She held her breath. What was coming here? She distrusted Mark's invoking "our Victoria," in what seemed to her a general bid for connection and forgiveness. She didn't move and she didn't interrupt.

"I swear to you, the woman is mad. It's a nightmare—it has been a nightmare. She has *plagued* me. She would just appear in the office. Ask Noleen—ask Dan. The one living female even Dan has the sense to avoid. She'd be waiting outside the house when I'd leave for work and there she'd still be when I got home. Why do you think I never wanted to go out? Why do you think I was so keen to come here? I became convinced, not without reason, I assure you, that Sophie would be waiting on every corner. I tell you she is a *terrorist*."

Jean was finding it hard to take in—not just the amplification of Sophie, but the diminution of Mark as she'd always understood him. Was it really possible that she'd misunderstood their glorious self-sufficiency, her *definition* of marriage, one restored to her only the day before by Dan? Mark, her twin in reluctance, her retiring reflection, her secret sharer—where was her husband now? By her side, or merely in hiding? It was as if her own dear man was, after all, aligned with Giovana: unreliable and unreal, other. As if the whole Giovana excursion had been grotesque prep for this bigger, bolder disillusionment . . . and all just because he'd *maybe* fathered a child before she even met him? *Look,* she wanted to shout, I'm already adapting—that was before my time. But why believe Sophie? He said himself she was crazy. And she was—she was a fantasist, a stalker; for this Jean had seen evidence. One thing was clear: he didn't believe Jean could be trusted to know anything at all. Had he ever really belonged to her? Well, it seemed she was going to find out.

Mark was too busy unpacking his long-rehearsed story to register his wife's dismay. "You remember that time in the south of France at Les Oiseaux, where we went that Easter with baby Vic. That's when it started. She just *appeared,* do you remember? I tried to be nice to her. We were all nice to her. You were a darling. Obviously a mistake—mine, I mean, but I thought, After all she did lose her father, and her mother in a way. Sandrine was by then off in Canada, rebuilding her life. Sophie did go out there and I don't know what happened. It didn't work out. She didn't get on with Sandrine's new bloke; the school was a disaster, apparently she took a lot of drugs, LSD, I don't know what. Needless to say, my communication with Sandrine such as it is, or *was,* has not been much use in all of this. Nothing worked out for Sophie. Nothing ever has. I tried to be kind, supportive—quite honestly I thought if I *wasn't* kind she'd be even more trouble. I tell you she's a nutter.

In and out of institutions her entire life." Mark was circling the terrace, pacing.

Jean couldn't help feeling that, for all she didn't know, she'd have heard if Sophie de Vilmorin had been committed. And LSD? The young girl Jean remembered was not the druggy type. She was innocent—unusually innocent, Jean always thought, and lovely, her lost-waif qualities having not yet reached clinical dimensions. And Sophie now? That wilting vegan in the dry cleaner's? Hardly an enfant terrible. It suddenly struck her that Mark wasn't telling her the truth, or that he was at least deflecting her from the main point. She could feel her skin searing in the late sun and she didn't move to cover herself.

"I thought she'd been in a convent for a while," she said. "Is that what you mean by institutionalized?"

"Well yes, far as I understood. In France the convent does for the loony bin."

Jean, half listening, thought about that Easter in Provence. She could see the place perfectly—up in the hills near St. Paul de Vence, a small inn with richly decorated rooms, the ancient walled garden, the famous food. Vic had taken her first steps on the paved patio of Les Oiseaux; in fact Sophie had cheered her on right along with Mark and Jean. This young woman, no more than seventeen, had appeared unexplained and alone. She could see the moment they realized who she was, the hugs and the toasts, the *patronne* herself setting Sophie a place at their table. They got on well, and even wary baby Vic loved her. The last night she'd offered to babysit, giving them their first evening off in a year—brilliant! Naturally they'd invited her to come and stay.

Maybe it wasn't a chance meeting—how incredible that this had never occurred to her.

"When you say you first met Sophie around the time of Victoria's birth . . ."

"Yes."

"Well, then it wasn't at Les Oiseaux, was it? Vic was a year old when we went there."

"That's right." Mark sat down. He looked exhausted, resigned.

"So where'd you meet her?"

"In Paris."

Mark had gone to Paris so often throughout their marriage, he could've met her at any time.

"Paris when?" But even as she said this, Jean knew exactly when. That strike, when he'd missed his flight. "When Victoria was born you were with Sophie, weren't you?"

"Yes, yes I was."

"You were in Paris with Sophie de Vilmorin." Mark hung his head, waiting for whatever came next. Finally Jean understood. Sophie wasn't his daughter. She was his lover. Rage ripped through her like a brush fire slow to catch but now consuming. "Wait—so first you fuck her and then you slander her? Was that before or after the convent slash loony bin? Or maybe you just borrowed her for the weekend and sent her back to the sisters when you were done. Or perhaps you *weren't* done, not so fast. Just taking a break to meet your brand-*new* baby girl. Was there even an air controllers' strike or baggage handlers' or whatever the hell it was that supposedly kept you in Paris?"

"Yes of *course* there was a strike." Mark stood up, protesting. "That's how I found myself hanging around the hotel bar in the first place, waiting to get out. I ran into her in the street."

"That's a lie."

"It is *not* a lie."

"The hotel bar—or the street? Which is it?"

"I ran into her coming out of the metro in St. Germain and she walked with me back to the hotel where I'd gone to collect my bags, basically. I was told about the strike, and so we talked in the bar. . . ."

"And?"

"And yes, I was with her that night, that one night and only that one night, and believe me, you *must* believe me, she is insane. Not that it makes any difference, I realize. Not that it makes any difference that she completely threw herself at me, insisted I take her to bed, and then stalked me—still does stalk me twenty years on—she didn't think I was her father *then*— no, that was a later addition, a subsequent horrific nutter's 'revelation.' *Yes,* I made a mistake," Mark said, slapping the back of one hand into the palm of the other and squeezing it there. "And Jean, I assure you, I have paid for it. I have paid and paid and paid."

She could hardly believe what he was saying. How old was Sophie then? Sixteen? *Fifteen?* When she "insisted" he take her to bed—and what, dragged him into the elevator? "Just how much *have* you paid? No, please don't answer. In fact, it would be great if you just shut up. Please." Mark walked over to the garden hose and doused his entire head.

His favorite place to stay in Paris had always been the Hôtel de l'Abbaye in St. Germain. Now she understood Sophie's e-mail, how she walked by the Abbaye, how it made her want to be a sister, a "nunn." Oh, that was sweet. And over twenty years he couldn't find a different favorite hotel—no, l'Abbaye was where he and Jean always went on their romantic weekends in Paris.

But once, long before, he'd gone there by himself. Jean, forty-one weeks pregnant, stayed home, her overnight bag packed and ready by the front door. It was very early on a Sunday morning—hard, she remembered, to get a cab. So when she'd checked into the Lindo Wing at St. Mary's Paddington, he'd checked into a *chambre de bonne* at the Hôtel de l'Abbaye, Sophie's "top window at the last." When she'd ridden up alone in the hospital elevator clutching her bursting belly, he'd gone up in the hotel elevator, his hands around Sophie's tiny teen waist. As she'd paced with her contractions, frantically inhaling from the tank of gas and air, he'd devoured this girl. And as Jean entered second-stage labor he'd entered Sophie, both women crying out in pain. And after seven hours of laboring, when she finally pushed Victoria out, and began the *second* birthing no one had told her about—that giant steak of a placenta—what was Mark doing then? He'd birthed himself, in a pool of virgin's blood, is that what he'd be telling her next? An event so mesmerizing, so shaping, that he'd spent the next twenty years in preoccupation and repetition, trying to get back to that first time, trying ever after to *get back inside*, oh Mrs. H., Mrs. H., Mrs. H. She'd heard of men who couldn't bear the arrival of the competition; she'd had letters from her readers on this particularly noxious form of envy, but she'd never fingered Mark for one. Had Sophie been where he'd gone all those times he went "ashore"? Perhaps she *was* the shore.

Girls and men and their pregnant wives—cornier, if possible, than sultry blooming Giovana, though she supposed the one paved the way for the other, first the soul and then the flesh, never mind if Giovana wasn't "real"; she'd still infiltrated their marriage. She couldn't think anymore. How she'd soiled herself in reply, in echo, in revenge. It was no comfort to realize that, deep down, she'd always known: why else had his missing the birth always weighed on her quite so unaccountably? Mark was back and he was talking to her—his tone was pleading, operatic—and she could hardly take in the words.

"I couldn't tell you. Should I have, really? To relieve myself of the burden? I knew it would hurt you. I didn't *want* to hurt you, can you not see that? You are my life. You and Victoria are my life. If I am to be punished for this one wrongdoing, by *God* I have been punished, Jean. I have lived with it every day. I have been sorry every day. I didn't know at the time about her madness; not, I do see, that it makes a jot of a difference. How I have *hated* Sophie. Hated myself. Just as I have loved you and Victoria, how I have hated that woman."

Jean didn't want to speak and it seemed he'd never stop. "The only thing I've never been able to work out is how her real father can have known she was a bitch—a *witch*—before she was even born. His 'accident' was an act of incomparable brilliance and foresight. Yes, Jean, I've thought more than once of just ending it all. Because I have tried everything. I've tried to pay her off. To send her away. I've arranged places for her to live, to work. I've reasoned with her, begged her, sent her to innumerable psychiatrists, *threatened* her."

"Yes, I see you've been very busy," Jean said quietly, thinking Mark was the least suicidal person she knew. Was there nothing he wouldn't say now? "Except you never told me. Don't imagine I don't know how hard that is to do. But you didn't just fail to mention it. You invited her into our lives. She looked after our baby. You let her in. First you go to bed with this . . . *child,* and then you invite her into our world—where she's clearly made herself at home. In our *bed,* Mark. And where is she now? Here on St. Jacques, just as I proposed? Stashed in a hotel down by the port? Or in one of those pastel bungalows in Grand Baie?"

"Don't be ridiculous. What an obscene thought. I honestly *believed*—at the time I thought it was the best way to manage her—I didn't realize at first she was so unstable. High-strung, emotional, nervous, yes, but not mad. She was at her best when she was with me, with *us*. You have no idea. It was weak of me, I grant you that, but it worked, at least for a time. Calmed her down, rooted her. She thought Victoria was her *sister*, for God's sake. She still thinks that."

Jean leapt up. "*Don't* you bring Victoria into this! You let that woman approach Victoria. Then and now, *this summer*."

"How could I stop her? Do you not see I have spent the past twenty years trying to stop Sophie? Trying to shield you and Victoria from her?" His face was crumpled, and he was practically crying. Jean thought of his anxious love for Victoria, his protectiveness. Victoria, so sane, so lovably sane.

"I have tried every way I know how to convince her, but she will always insist that I am her father."

"Well, *are* you?"

"Jean! *Jean*." He looked stung, hurt, radically aged. "Why would you even *want* to say that? I don't deny she was young enough to be a daughter—does that in itself make any real difference between you and I?"

"You and me."

"Yes, Jean, you and me. That's exactly right. I never imagined this would be the thing that bothered you so much. I'm telling you what happened, a very long time ago, and—"

"Of course, it bothers me, Mark—though I wouldn't call it a 'thing.' How can I explain, since you obviously don't get it. I have done some very stupid things. Fantastically stupid. Who hasn't? I guess I can't help thinking of myself at fifteen." Or Billy at fifteen, she thought for a moment, his life already over. "But let's stick with what we can both understand. *Victoria* at fifteen—a child. You do see when it's Victoria at fifteen, don't you? Is that why you freaked over that guy Rick—you saw your own reflection, didn't you? And Victoria was a good bit older than that too, at least seventeen, maybe more."

"Oh, for fuck's sake. I don't know why I told you. You will never let it go. The permutations are endless, I can see that now. You will never forgive me."

So no point in asking then, Jean thought. "What do you think this is? Because I'm American, you imagine you're talking to some self-help group where everyone applauds you at the end, whatever you have to say? Thanks for sharing, Mark, good job? Not to mention that it's illegal to have sex with a fifteen-year-old—did you ever think of that?"

"Jean! A mistake—I made a terrible mistake. I slept with her. Once. And obviously I've thought of that, though it hardly seems the worst of it. I slept with her and I slept with her mother, as much as possible, along with half of St. Malo, Jean, over *thirty-five years ago*. Though in fact my innings with Sandrine only lasted a couple of weeks before she moved on. Naturally."

She could not fathom why he was going over this old ground, except maybe to change the subject. But she said nothing—she was almost curious to see just how far he could go.

"I tell you Sandrine was already with Sophie's father before I left the family, and I was relegated to the role of family friend. You've seen the pictures of their wedding, on that beach at dawn. Typically demanding of Sandrine, I might add, a *dawn* wedding." He took a long pull of his drink. She hadn't noticed when the ice tea became a bottle of beer.

"Why are you going on about that summer a hundred fucking years ago?"

"What I'm trying to say, Jean, is that Sophie is a victim. An orphan, basically. I was *nothing* to Sandrine. No one was. Not even her own daughter."

Jean could not take this. "So what? You improve her lot by raping her? Skinny know-nothing little virgin?"

"Oh, for fuck's sake—I did no such thing. And she wasn't a virgin anyway."

"As if that makes any difference! And how would you *know* if she was or wasn't a virgin?"

Mark sat down, infinitely weary. "Jean, I am really trying to tell you what happened, a great many years ago, and you want to go after every alternative version, follow every irrelevant thread. You want to win some kind of feminist argument? Fine! You win! I *agree*. But what I'm telling you is it's knowledge she's wanted, that's all. Sophie is hungry for any connection to that time of her beginning, before everything went wrong forever, starting with that dreadful accident. Then, much later, I thought—completely wrongly, I know better than anyone— I thought, after what I did, and I don't deny it, I could at least try to give her that. Connection, solace—some idea that there had been beauty and truth in her tiniest beginnings."

Jean thought she might throw up—before now she thought that was just an expression, something Maya Stayanovich might say.

"I am so sorry, Jean."

The parrots were warring in the trees, and inside the phone was ringing.

"Do you want me to get it?" Mark asked, beginning anywhere he could, to inch his way back.

"No, I will. It might be about Dad." Jean went into the kitchen. "*Mom*, hi."

Outside, Mark tidied up the terrace table, straightened chairs, carried in the glasses, ducking to clear the kitchen door frame. "Everything all right?" he asked, very tired.

"Yes. No more fluid on the lungs. The pneumonia is completely cleared. He's breathing independently for twelve hours at a time. Mom says when he can breathe on his own for twenty-four hours they're going to release him. He'll still be bedridden, of course, and very very weak, but at least he can be at home. Mark, I'm going to have to go back."

He looked like he'd been hit.

"Nothing to do with all this, obviously. There just *is* no one else. Marianne's swamped with her boys and Mom's apartment—well, you know. No room. And he's going to have all this hospital equipment—the bed, the respirator. Anyway, he wants to go home, to his own place, and I'll need to be there. I *want* to be there. I have to go. It's not going to be immediately. Not for a week or so. Maybe more."

"I'm going down to the beach for a walk. Do you want to come along?" Mark asked.

"No. No I don't."

And she didn't want him to drive, but he was never more likely to insist than when he was drunk. He bumped his way down the track and she walked around to the little garden behind the house. If the pots on the terrace were any indication, everything in it would be dead.

Narcissism, vanity—pride: surprisingly, until recently, this was considered the absolute worst of sins. It was, in fact, a form of sloth—not bothering to love. Was she able to listen to Mark—to listen and *hear*?

As she approached the fenced-in patch with its lean-to frame, she could see that the black mesh which shaded the beds was ripped and hanging down like a black flag. It was hard to tell, when she unlatched the low bamboo gate, what was left amid the weeds. She walked through, squeezing rubbery string beans, most of them yellow and as long as rulers, and saw a scatter of rotten tomatoes on the ground, most of them pecked by birds, along with all the strawberries. In the corner, marrows the size of dachshunds, and overgrown lettuces like vast, green Ascot hats.

Jean gathered every usable tomato into her upheld sarong, and she thought it was at least possible it had been just the once with Sophie, as he insisted. Though he hadn't been able to talk to her about it for twenty years—and he still couldn't, not very credibly. But as she looked around her trashed, unloved garden she wondered what, exactly, there was to forgive. He'd tried to protect her—she believed that. Why had she seemed to *need* the full security detail, a buffering emotional bodyguard for a husband? Because she didn't need it anymore—not, perhaps, since Bill's crisis. She thought of her father and *his* earlier crisis, the one that cost him his marriage. It was a fact that Mark had seized on a young body—a very young body—while his wife labored in another country. But she could hardly be pious about succumbing to a stock temptation. Jean was so tired. Blame, even forgiveness: these subjects, though barely explored, seemed, just for the moment, in the category of last year's columns: filed.

Under the more urgent strain of Dad there was no room for more instability in her life. She would listen to Mark, and if he asked her to, she'd try to help him. This seemed freshly possible because she knew this was, finally, his problem. When she read Larry she thought his proposition about personal responsibility was excellent and only seemingly obvious—but still it was a proposition, abstract enough for Jean, like most people, in practice to ignore. Had it really taken all this grinding in the dust to grasp that the rule applied to her, that she must, and even enjoyably would, from here on in, be responsible for her own happiness?

When she stood up from the engaging detail of her grubby little beds and looked out to where the horizon should be, beyond the blue hills, she couldn't see the ocean, but she knew it was there. Preserving, down in the cold dark deep, Billy's remains. A walk along the shore was a really good idea—though even on a beach she tended to look down, scouring for interesting shells, ignoring the vast blue. So maybe "things," including Jean, would start to look up, she thought, now stretching her neck, her back, looking at the sky. Certainly there would be change. And she could sense, remarkably free from guilt, that her most generous impulses derived from the promise of a clear horizon.

Back in the kitchen, Jean dumped her garden catch and washed her hands. She wanted to call Larry back while Mark was out. She punched in the thirteen numbers, and even before she heard his voice she could hear cars honking. He was walking down the street, and she covered her free ear, straining to catch what he said, and asked about Bill.

"As a matter of fact I'm heading up to the hospital right now. He's a changed man, Jean. You wouldn't believe it— sitting up, cracking jokes, reading. And threatening to leave, or escape. Apparently he keeps wandering off down the hall, which they don't like at all. He's desperate to be gone— pushing for early release. For good behavior. Or maybe for *bad* behavior."

In her mind, Jean glimpsed court documents releasing Larry from his long marriage. What would be the stated reason and who was the plaintiff? "How are *you*?" she asked.

"*Well.*" He sounded thoughtful. "A certain amount of strain hereabouts, but nothing like what you've all just been through. . . . I'm hopeful I'll bring the case in by the start of classes. Did I tell you I did agree to teach? NYU."

"So—the philosophy department at last. You took the plunge—congratulations."

"Yes, I'm pleased about that. And I think I might persuade the firm to let me go on using the apartment a while longer. Partner emeritus—how does that strike you?"

"Christ, what do they call *Dad*? But now that we're all becoming parents emeritus, I'd say it sounds very respectable. And tenant worthy, more to the point. Listen, I'm going back over soon. To settle Dad in, at least."

"That's great. We were all hoping you would. He needs you. And I don't have to tell you that I—" The background noise suddenly blared, a mass honking, an indignant *group* honk. "But you knew that."

"What? I couldn't hear. What did I know?"

"Oh, nothing. Listen, give me a little warning and I'll pick you up."

"Out of the question. But thanks . . . for everything. I couldn't be here if I didn't know you were there. I'll call you when I get in, soon as."

Feeling much calmer, she separated out the few good leaves: they'd make a salad for one—or for two very unhungry people, and the image struck Jean as utterly dismal, as circumscribed and impoverished as her future. Was that what lay ahead, not a vast horizon but salad-for-one? Wasn't this more or less what Melanie Mond was feeling right now? Her first wave of empathy: maybe she could learn friendship, though possibly not with Mrs. Mond. She added in some chopped *ciboulettes*—for a moment unable to think of the English name. *Chives*, not so nice. That had been a good thing about this island, not only the garden but the names of the things in it.

Like that fish she'd prepared but hadn't eaten. Tilapia, it looked like, though they called it something else here. When they first moved to St. Jacques, Jean had started a list of ridiculously difficult French words just as, in her student days, she'd made a list of impossible British words, of which she remembered only snog, spondulicks, rawlplug, shambolic, and road drill for jackhammer—the rest had been absorbed and forgotten. Add these lists to the pyre of abandoned projects, if a list of names could be a project (Giovana, Brunhilda, Magdalena?). All her efforts at do-it-yourself—*bricolage!*—had been variously hampered by the long list of the unlearnable and, Jean thought, please don't say that if children can speak the language, it must be learnable. Of course *children* can. And children do. This weirdly light diversion—as she fended off a grief as big as a house—was spoiled by its unhappy reminder of the child Sophie, a child who learned to fuck.

Back in the kitchen, she opened the bottom drawer, home to duct tape, string, and her yellow legal pad, which she tugged free. She pulled a wine bottle from the fridge. She heard Mark coming in, and quickly, quietly, she stepped outside. The phone was ringing: his turn to pick up. Jean was glad to be alone on the terrace. The sky was streaked red and white like a steak marbled with fat.

In the dying light, she made a new list: *April, Mar, Feb, Jan, Dec, Nov, Oct, Sept, Aug, July*. Nine months between Mark's summer idyll with Sandrine and Sophie's Easter birth. She could've worked it out in her head, but she wanted to see it on paper. Then Mark came out, and she put the pad facedown on the table.

He looked very pale. "So Dan Manning has betrayed me."

Jean didn't say a word, but her face felt scorched. She leaned back, literally bracing herself.

"He's leaving the firm. Taking with him not only his entire harem from Copy but the fridge campaign as well. *My* fridge campaign. We'll see about that. Flattering, eh? The *nerve*. He offered to stay on, for the 'transitional period,' which we of course can't manage without him. I told him to clear out. I'll have to go back straightaway. Morale check, if nothing else. J. Walter Thompson! 'Offer of a lifetime,' " Mark imitated Dan's accent. "He *adored* telling me he's being made a senior partner—Worldwide Creative Director."

"Mark."

"Two hundred K starting salary. Which I seriously doubt."

"Mark."

"Hm?"

"It *could* have been you."

"Gosh, well yes, thanks very much. Speaking of 'thanks for the support.' Yes, I suppose it could have been. Twenty years ago. If I'd wanted to be an employee, that is. Bite the hand that feeds you, kill the father, or wot? Quite a theme here today, that. I mean isn't the boyfriend supposed to *ask* the father for his daughter's hand? Well the answer is fuck off out of here and back to Bombay—oh, sorry, Mumbai. And that son of a bitch, even more intolerably pleased with himself now, he's playing *way* out of his league. J. Walter Fucking Thompson, so imaginative! *Goddamn* it if that isn't the limit."

He slumped in his chair, rapidly tapping his fingertips on his thighs, and this time it was Jean who leaned to refill his empty glass, wine over beer traces, confident he wouldn't mind. She wasn't going to point out that they'd been talking at cross-purposes—not only because it would be hard to say when, exactly, that started. The sky was fully dark, and a vast yellow moon hovered—rounded and low and weighted as a belly at full term.

Jean slapped her ankle as Mark slapped his neck. She struck a match and lit a citronella candle on the terrace table, illuminating their two faces. Tilting the second candle to meet the flame, she said, "Why do we think for even a second these things will protect us from *anything*?"

"Hm?" Mark wasn't listening. Agitated, he sprang up. "I'd better get on the horn to Connie and Theo, see that the rot doesn't spread."

He disappeared inside the house, and Jean sat there, staring at the candles. She remembered the shrines arranged over the stoops of New York on that long black night she'd spent with Larry, searching for her mother and ferrying strangers. The pregnant woman they'd given a lift to—Melba—she'd have had her baby by now; Jean wondered what she got. She worried for a moment about Bud on his first night alone in the woods. Kestrels didn't make nests: on which crag, in what crevice or damp tree cavity, would he find respite? And she thought of Marianne and her haircut, and their new friendship, and the mysterious life span of passionate unease: this, too, had lost its force. As Phyllis liked to say, "You can't push a string."

Jean stood and leaned against a porch pillar, actually basking in a moonbeam, she thought, probably getting a moontan. When she saw Vikram next, she would ask him about the gravitational pull that controlled not only the tides and the female cycle but the complex eddies of their human moods, among them lunacy. She had so much to learn; she had to get to grips with a force that could reach right through the earth.

She stepped out into the cold blue of the garden and, looking down, saw that Mark, strangely, had left the gate open. She thought of his private war with the homemade loop—a simple wire fastened there by an undesigning local—that Mark was convinced twanged open by itself, just to thwart him. And though she'd always considered his obsession with keeping it shut in the first place the ultimate fool's errand, she ached to remember it now. She didn't hesitate to fill in for him, making her way down to the gate in the moonlight, one more time, to secure the shifting catch.

Acknowledgments

All of Ronald Dworkin's writings are inspiring; in this novel, I owe a debt to his books *Law's Empire* (1986) and his discussion there of the law as our "ethereal sovereign," and *Sovereign Virtue: The Theory and Practice of Equality* (2000).

The open *moleh* comes from Caroline Moorehead's invaluable book about refugees, *Human Cargo* (2005); she learned of this concept from Liberian refugees in Guinea.

I have been inspired by the work of Carl Jones and the Gerald Durrell Endemic Wildlife Sanctuary on Mauritius, which I visited in 1996. Jones—a Welsh biologist and talented crusader for the endangered—is the man responsible for the rescue of *Falco punctatus*, the Mauritian kestrel, beginning in 1974, when he went out there and found only four remaining kestrels: the rarest bird in the world. None of my characters, or the captive breeding project in which I involve them, represent an accurate portrait of the real conservationists or their methods, any more than my made-up island, St. Jacques, is Mauritius.

For all kinds of help, from readings (and rereadings) to specialist fact-checking and borrowed desks, I am very grateful to Elizabeth Fonseca and Dick Cornuelle, to Katherine Bucknell,

Acknowledgments

Jim Krusoe and Annalena McAfee; to Vera Graaf, Michael Glazebrook and Sarah Lyall, to Nancy Southam and Amanda Moffat; to John Ryle, John Holmes, and Rich Baum; to Elena Fonseca and Caio Fonseca.

I could not be luckier in my editors—Rebecca Carter and Gary Fisketjon. Thanks to Alison Samuel, Publishing Director of Chatto & Windus. Thanks to Andrew Wylie and everyone at the Wylie Agency. Thanks to Liz van Hoose, and to Susan Bradanini Betz, painstaking copyeditor.

London 2008

A NOTE ON THE TYPE

Pierre Simon Fournier le jeune, who designed the type used in this book, was both an originator and a collector of types. His services to the art of printing were his design of letters, his creation of ornaments and initials, and his standardization of type sizes. His types are old style in character and sharply cut. In 1764 and 1766 he published his *Manuel typographique,* a treatise on the history of French types and printing, on typefounding in all its details, and on what many consider his most important contribution to typography—the measurement of type by the point system.